D0501945

A City
Dreaming

A City Dreaming

Daniel Polansky

Regan Arts.

New York

Regan Arts.

65 Bleecker Street
New York, NY 10012

First Regan Arts hardcover edition, October 2016

Library of Congress Control Number: 2016939704

ISBN 978-1-68245-038-3

Interior design by Nancy Singer
Cover design by Richard Ljoenes

Printed in the United States of America

10 9 8 7 6 5 4 3 2 1

For Lisa Stockdale, Myke Cole,
and Andy Keogh.

And, for the city of New York, of course.
May you last a little while longer yet.

1
—

A Night in Paris

It would help if you did not think of it as magic. M certainly had long since ceased to do so. He thought of it as being in good with the Management, like a regular at a neighborhood bar. You come to a place long enough, talk up the chick behind the counter, after a while she'll look the other way if you have a smoke inside, let you run up your tab, maybe even send over some free nuts on occasion. Magic was like that, except the bar was existence and the laws being bent regarded thermodynamics and weak nuclear force.

So when Idle walked into the Talleyrand, throwing off intangibles like an arc welder, what M thought was—*Man, this guy must have naked pictures of the owner or something.*

The Talleyrand was a small tavern on a Parisian side street a few minutes' walk from the Seine. It was one of the places around town where people like M occasionally gathered, which most days was reason enough for M to avoid it. But the Talleyrand had a stash of prewar absinthe, from back when you could still taste the wormwood, and M liked to get drunk on it when he was feeling nostalgic.

Idle was tall, with ash blond hair and surfer-boy good looks, as if to spite which he'd pounded about a half kilogram of metal through each orifice and any fold of skin that would allow it. He was dressed like an extra from a Clash video, and he sneered at everything and everyone that came across his path.

He spoke no French and was the sort of person who saw no reason such ignorance should be an impediment to living in Paris.

Idle stood in the door a while, scanning the bar with a dazed expression, the bystanders growing nervous without quite knowing why. M hunched low in his chair, though it soon became clear his vague attempt at concealment was futile. Idle picked up two pints of Belgian stout at the bar, then made his way over. He set one in front of M, and he sat down behind the other.

"Idle."

"M."

"What's going on?"

"I'm here to kill a man."

"Oh."

"Not you."

"Happy to hear it."

"Have a drink."

M thought it imprudent to argue. The tattoo on his left forearm was of an umbrella holding off rain.

On the jukebox Johnny Cash was doing a version of "A Boy Named Sue" with lines that M had never heard before, which no one had ever heard before, some pocket reality version of the Man in Black called up from all the energy coursing about the room. Idle stared at M with bloodshot eyes and a scowl more unpleasant than the one he normally wore. "No one likes you, you know."

"No?"

"You're always laughing behind your hand at everyone."

"Am I? Behind my hand, you say?"

"Like that," Idle said, tugging at the copper hoop that ran through his left nostril. "Like that exactly."

"What are you up to, slick?"

"I told you—I'm here to kill a man."

M thought hard on what he would have to do if Idle really lost it. A slim handful of possibilities came to mind, and he was rejecting them each in turn when the door opened and the object of Idle's antagonism became blindingly clear.

St. Loup was tall and dark as charred hardwood and very handsome. His suit was straight from La Belle Epoque, the sort of sartorial affectation which M didn't suppose was any handicap to picking up American girls on the Champs-Élysées. M knew St. Loup somewhat, in the sense that they had been running into each other for half a human lifetime. They had never had any problem, at least none that M could remember, but then again St. Loup was not on that list of people for whom M was willing to die. This was, in fairness, a very small list—this was a list that would fit on the back of a movie ticket, or the torn corner of a cocktail napkin.

Another thing about St. Loup was he had some weight to him, a lot more than Idle. M wasn't great with time, most of the people in his line weren't—you see enough of it and it stops meaning much—but St. Loup was pretty old, not ancient but venerable. Under normal circumstances, M would have picked St. Loup to put Idle down easy, like a bitch does with a pup.

But these were not normal circumstances. Energy rolled off Idle like stink waves in a Sunday comic. It was too much pull to be carrying around up here in reality; it made the Management antsy, got them focusing on you in an inauspicious fashion.

If M had been St. Loup, he would have turned around and walked straight back the way he had come, maybe even sprinted. That was what M told himself he would have done, at least, though M had on occasion been known to live above himself, or below. Regardless, St. Loup didn't run, not even after Idle ripped himself upright with enough force to send his chair spinning to the ground.

"Bonsoir, monsieur," St. Loup said, folding his gloves beneath his arm and doffing his top hat. "Is there something that I might do for you this evening?"

M had it on good authority that St. Loup had gotten his training as a gris-gris man in what was now the Dominican Republic, reading the future in chicken entrails and cooking up love potions. Why he had chosen to remodel himself after a member of a decayed aristocracy that had fallen out of fashion some several world wars previous M could not say. He had seen other adepts with far more eccentric and unpleasant tastes. M would, for instance, take St. Loup's impersonation of a character from À la recherche du temps perdu over Idle's deliberate deformation of his body.

"It's not because you're black," Idle began. M wasn't sure if it was the sheer amount of draw that was making Idle talk like a crazy person or if Idle had just gone crazy.

"I'd hope not," St. Loup said. "This is the twenty-first century, after all."

"It's because of Katherine."

"Who?"

To judge by the sudden shuddering that overtook Idle just then, this was the wrong question to ask. "Katherine, my girlfriend. Was my girlfriend. Now she's your nothing, I guess."

St. Loup made a sound in the back of his throat that conveyed some vague sense of regret. "Kat, you mean. I daresay that she played things out the way she wanted it."

"And what about what I want?"

"Well, my friend," St. Loup continued, with an impressive degree of sangfroid, given that he was staring at a primed cannon, "we don't always get what we want."

"Not always," Idle agreed, "but tonight."

Johnny's voice hammered through the speakers, angry and dissonant, like something running you down in the dark. M was widely considered the coolest thing on the continent, and his heart was beating so hard in his chest he thought he might scream. Idle crackled, and reality stretched to accommodate him. The walls pulsed and warped, existence going hallucinogenic. The lights went strobe and the crystalline ornament on top of St. Loup's cane shattered, sending fragments through his hand. He screamed. The bystanders screamed also. Idle laughed in a rather maniacal fashion. M stayed quiet.

St. Loup stumbled back toward the bar, half tripped over a stool, then righted himself, calling up whatever he could, trying to spark some burst of energy through the agony of his pulped fist and the virtual certainty of his demise. A swirling copper carapace tightened up from his ankles, over his pressed pants and the clean white cream of his shirt, coiled and contorted around his wounded arm, sealing off the flow of blood and protecting him— in theory at least—from further injury. It was the sort of patently impossible thing at which the Management tended to look askance, a work of wonder that could only be accomplished by an adept of great talent.

It also was no help whatsoever. Idle was all but glowing, he was so thick with the pulse. He wiggled his index finger, and the air around it coalesced into slender crimson tendrils, and then the tendrils shifted into flat-headed vipers, a surging mass of them, and then the mass flowed through the air, snakes atop snakes swimming through the firmament, and then they had surrounded St. Loup and his copper shielding, and then they had penetrated it. And then there was no more St. Loup to be seen, the spectral serpents swelling over and obscuring him.

And then they were gone as well, and what was left was something closer to a slab of meat than a human being, and it collapsed and leaked blood out onto the floor.

Idle seemed as happy in that moment as anyone M had ever seen, happy as a child on Christmas morning, happy as a virgin bride, happy as a junkie who just topped off. He did not have long to enjoy it.

Because here's the other thing, to return to our earlier analogy: No one is such a good customer that they can, say, start throwing glasses at other patrons or take a dump behind the bar. You push the boundaries far enough, and at some point the Management will have to call in the bouncer.

And reality has a hell of a bouncer.

There was a sound of something screaming. No, there was the sound of everything screaming: M and the rest of the patrons in the bar, and the bar itself, the heavy oak counter, the seats and the leather booths, the taps and the kegs they led to, the bottles of whiskey and vodka, the floor, the ceiling, the air between them, the cobblestones on the street outside, the night and the city and the world beyond that.

Everything but Idle, who turned then to look at M for a single moment, smiling, apparently pleased with the choices that he had made.

And then Idle was not standing next to the counter, victorious in single combat. And then he was not sitting at the table with M, and then he was not walking into the bar, and then he was not opening the door. And then he was not on the sidewalk outside, and then he was not in Paris at all, and then he had not been in London either, and then he had never been born.

St. Loup was still dead, of course. Not even the Management could bring a man back to life—this was something M had learned long ago, to his not-insignificant despair. But as for the remainder, or at least the majority of Idle's other works, these had been rendered null by the Management's alteration. The surgery was imperfect, leaving bumps and tears in the record, particularly for those who had known the man well or been around to witness his demise. There was a scar in M's mind that would never go away, and if he worked very hard at it, he could get a sense of what had happened in a fuzzy sort of way, at the price of a headache that was more agonizing than painful.

It was while M was sitting in the Talleyrand, wondering how he had ended up with two half-drunk pints of beer in front of him, that he decided he had seen enough of Paris in autumn, and it might be time to toddle off back to the States.

2

The Pocket

The greatest advantage to being in good with the Management was that things went well for you so long as you moved out of the way and let them. M thought of this as being in the pocket. Being in the pocket meant doors open just before you walk into them, taxis stop when you toss your hand up, and bank errors always turn out in your favor. It meant throwing a hard eight after you'd just put your last bill down, meant that the cop who busts you for possession turns out to be an old drinking buddy. It meant walking down the street in perfect synchronous rhythm with the music on your iPod and the traffic lights and the pulsing beat of existence itself. It was why M didn't worry about little things like money or travel visas or having a permanent residence or much by way of possessions.

And what did the Management demand, in exchange for all the kindnesses it saw fit to bestow on M? M wasn't altogether sure, and he'd learned from experience thinking too hard about being in the pocket was the surest way of falling out of it. Just do what came natural and let the chips fall where they may. Not being big on forethought anyway, this suited M just fine.

M met Jessie a half hour after landing at JFK, in one of the bars in Terminal A. She was a stewardess for Singapore Airlines—the Occident had long since switched over to flight attendants, but in the East they still had stewardesses, and Jessie was clearly the latter: burnt sienna skin and walnut brown eyes, an ass like a ripe peach. After finding out M had no place to stay, she decided to give him one—her apartment in Queens, or the bed in her apartment in Queens, to be precise. And since, being a stewardess, Jessie wasn't in Queens that much, she said she didn't mind if M hung around a while, just until he could get back on his feet.

They spent two days cocooned in love, then M walked Jessie to the subway so she could catch her next flight. On the way back to her place he stepped into a bar for a quick drink, brushing past a furious, goateed gentleman who was on his way out. It turned out that the angry hipster was the bartender, or had been the bartender but wasn't any longer, and the manager liked M's look and also was desperate, so he asked if M knew how to mix a drink. M didn't, really, but he said he did, figuring he could pick it up as he went along. The first night some of the patrons were less than pleased with their Negronis, but after that M pulled it together.

The tips weren't bad and it was a good way to meet girls, but M got pretty sick of it after about three days, so he was happy when on the fourth a tall, thin man with wild hair came in and ordered a Belgian ale. After three of these and an hour listening to M's travel stories, the man broke down in despair, said he was sick to hell of the city and had just broke up with his girlfriend, and here he was about to hit thirty and he hadn't been out of the country in almost a year, only once to Toronto, and that, they both agreed, didn't really count. And so M told him, Hell, if that's the way he felt about it, he should just go, split right on out, M would look after his apartment while he was gone. M was the sort of person who could explain things to people in a certain sort of light, and after an hour, the man returned with a packed bag and an extra set of keys for M to use.

Which was just as well because by then Jessie was back, and either the idea of having a scruffy-faced wanderer eating her Fruit Loops had become less attractive or she somehow had sniffed out the fact that M had not been entirely faithful while she was away. M's new place was in Crown Heights, and he didn't think it made sense to commute all the way from central Brooklyn to Queens for a job that he didn't want anyway. It was fortunate for him that while drinking away his last twenty at a bar near his new digs he ran into an old friend—well, not quite a friend, but an acquaintance at least, a small-time wonder worker M had met years ago and not thought much about since. It turned out that this half chum needed someone to go on a ride with him and perhaps say some strong words to some people they would meet at the end of it. M was a person known to use such words on occasion, though in this particular instance it was unnecessary, and his presence alone proved sufficient for him to come back to his apartment sometime later that evening with eight thousand six hundred dollars, everything he could chisel out of his sort-of friend.

Thus it was that within three weeks of repatriating, M had found an apartment, spending money, a wardrobe, and a slate of electronics that the previous generation could not have imagined but which their children considered a critical requirement, all without putting any deliberate effort into it. That was the one problem about being in the pocket—sometimes you got the sense that you weren't the one in the driver's seat exactly, that the Management, or the universe or whatever, had marked out the route already, and you were just going through the motions.

But it was hard to worry about that sort of thing now that M was back in New York, and have you heard of New York, and do you know that it is the center of the universe? Its inhabitants will be happy to educate you, tossing back cigarettes and shots of liquor, bustling between job interviews and blind dates and Ponzi schemes, so confident it's hard not to believe them. It had been a long time since M had left the city, and returning to it with virgin eyes, he was bowed by the glut of options, activities, opportunities, adventures. Do you want to eat Mexican-Korean fusion at four in the morning? Have cocaine delivered directly to your door, swifter and more reliable than your local pizza parlor? Go see an experimental play inside of a prewar meat locker?

M did all of those things the first few weeks, spilled himself into the city's recondite enormity. October is a good time to be in New York. Evening comes quickly, but the weather is warm enough to get by in a long-sleeve T-shirt and a leather jacket, and M looked good in a long-sleeve T-shirt and a leather jacket, as a happy few of the city's females came to learn. M wandered back streets and side alleyways, smiled at children, frowned at beggars, scowled at corner boys, leered at the preening flock of beauties that made up the larger portion of Manhattan Island. He did nothing to draw the Management's attention, beyond generally finding himself luckier than most of the rest of the population. He made a point of not letting any of his old acquaintances—friends and enemies and that far larger category somewhere in the middle—know of his return. Word would spread soon enough, and with word, trouble.

But for a while it was enough to slip through the city like vapor, to remember and rediscover, to take pleasure in the surfeit of human possibility which is New York's defining quality.

3
—

Gowanus Canal Pirates

M was shame-walking his way back to his apartment in the hours just before dawn one Sunday morning. Her name was Melanie, he was pretty sure, but it had been loud in the bar and he knew better than to ask once they'd gone back to her loft. M hadn't wanted to stay the night, but he had hoped to cuddle for maybe half an hour, just to get back within stumbling distance of sobriety. But Melanie (?) was having none of it. Maybe there was a rival coming home at some point, or maybe, outside of the flattering half light of the bar, she had decided M was not someone worth knowing any longer. Regardless, around three in the morning, M stepped out of the door of an apartment building in Tribeca, and who in this day and age lived in Tribeca, apart from pop stars and the heirs to oil fortunes? It took him twenty minutes to acknowledge no cab would pick him up and another twenty-five waiting at Chambers Street for the night train and a half hour atop that before he was back in Crown Heights. When he reached the street he was scowling, making sure none of the late-evening denizens mistook him for someone worth hassling, and he did his best not to stumble on the way back to his apartment.

He had just taken off his coat when his phone started to buzz. Normally M ignored his phone late at night—what good could possibly come of a text at this hour—but he unsoberly supposed it might be Melanie (or whomever) dropping him a postcoital compliment.

It was not. "KDNAPD GWNS CNL PRATS —BOY," the text read.

M sighed and spent a few seconds wondering how Boy had figured out that M was back in town, but Boy knew lots of things people weren't supposed to know, and there was no time to dwell on it, not with Boy's text-speak still to decipher. The first word was easy enough, and he could only assume that PRATS was "pirates." Boy was not British, and anyway, if she had been captured by a pack of prats, she wouldn't have had any trouble dealing with the situation herself. That left "GWNS CNL," a linguistic construction that M's drink-addled brain struggled to unravel.

"Gowanus Canal!" M erupted cheerily some moments later, happy to have found the right fit. But the smile fell off his face near as swift as it had gotten there, and when he again spoke the words aloud, they sounded more curse than exclamation.

In the end, M figured there was one of two ways this situation would play out. The first was that the pirates would flog Boy with a cat-o'-nine-tails or keelhaul her or make her walk the plank or some other sort of nonsense. M didn't think this was very probable, but he wasn't mad about the possibility. It seemed far more likely that, despite her rather desperate text, Boy would find some way to break free of her captors, murder them all in a fashion at once brutal and novel, and then come knocking on M's door, prepared to do the same thing to him.

M liked this possibility even less.

Gowanus was a forty-minute walk from his apartment, which at least gave M time to clear his head. It was not as clear as he would have liked it to be, given that the situation seemed certain to get nasty, but it was better than it had been at least. Gowanus was all but deserted at night; even the bums and thugs had better things to do than stroll around the abandoned factories and industrial warehouses and shuttered artist colonies, smelling the ripe raw sludge of the canal.

M had not known that there were pirates on the Gowanus Canal, but it didn't exactly surprise him, either. He stared for a while into the canal itself, the slow-moving water so dark it failed to reflect the moon, which was now edging toward the horizon. Indeed, the lateness of the hour was a source of some concern. M didn't know anything about canal pirates, but he did know

that things that did not entirely exist often ceased to exist entirely after sunrise, and no one could say with any certainty what exactly would happen to
any souls unfortunate enough to get caught among their number after that.
Nothing good, M supposed.

M's understanding was that the last time anyone had bothered to analyze
the water in the Gowanus Canal, they discovered it was mostly herpes simplex
2 and heavy metals, mixed with a smattering of human feces for garnish. So
wading upriver was straight out. Boy was just about M's oldest friend in the
world, but there were limits to everything. Scowling, he pulled out his key chain
and the small clasp knife attached to it, then drew a not particularly shallow
cut along his hand and let a few drops of blood leak into the water below. One
would hardly think, given the fetid morass that was the Gowanus Canal, that
two or three centiliters of fresh blood would have been enough to draw any
particular attention—but M had long ago discovered that in these sorts of situations, the old traditions worked best. Anyway, he didn't have any other ideas.

M was midway through his second rollie when he noticed the stink of
rum and gunpowder and heard a faint sea shanty chanted off-key. Everything
that M knew about sailing could be distilled into a shot glass and thrown
back without wincing, but all the same he couldn't help feeling that whoever crewed the boat was skirting the lines of coherency, likely to draw the
Management's ire. It was as if you had taken a clipper and compressed it into
something the size of a large rowboat, each individual feature miniaturized
into absurdity. The prow was an anime mermaid—big eyes and bigger tits
and no nose to speak of—and hanging over it was a fat man wearing a pair of
bright purple trousers and a curved dagger in his teeth. The crow's nest was
barely larger than a custodial bucket, and it swayed back and forth, as did the
pendulous, ill-protected breasts of the woman who rode in it. Rounding out
the trio was a too-thin man standing on the quarter deck, scowling and shaking a cutlass in M's direction. "Avast there, ye scurvy landlubber!" he yelled,
right hand on the hilt of his blade, left on the beard that hung down toward
his ankles. "For what do you call the Pirates of Brown Water! Speak true or
meet with swift retort!"

"This is how this is going to go?" M asked, disappointed but not really surprised. "You picked up a friend of mine. I'd like to get her back. Or at least I'm going to try to get her back."

"A friend of yours? A fair lass, perhaps?" asked the one hanging on the prow. "Might be we have her. Might be we haven't. You'll have to talk to the captain about that."

"I'm guessing he's somewhere back up that river of shit?" M mumbled, but he knew the saying about pennies and pounds, or in this case, shillings and doubloons. Throwing aside any concerns that his added weight would capsize the craft and leave them all with mercury poisoning and super-AIDS, he leapt gingerly aboard.

"I'm Rum," said the one still hanging on the prow.

"I'm Sodomy," said the girl on top of the crow's nest,

"I'm La—"

"I get it, I get it," M said, waving them along. "It's very clever. Can we get a move on? I've got an appointment with a bed that I'm late for."

"Tack windward!" Lash yelled up at the mast.

Sodomy scrambled down from her perch and then did something with the sails that resulted in the ship making a graceful three-point turn and heading back in the direction it had come from.

"Fucking Christ," M said.

Rum hopped down from his place at the prow, and despite the thick rolls of fat on his arms and his waist and his neck and various other places, he gave the impression of being capable enough with the knife that suddenly appeared in his hand.

M sighed. "By Poseidon's beard," he said unhappily.

"By Poseidon's bloody beard, indeed!" Rum exclaimed.

From the back of the boat—it had a special nautical name, but M didn't know what it was—Lash began to belt a sea shanty that sounded remarkably like an early Smiths tune. Sodomy and Rum also took it up, singing zestfully. It was not at all the sort of sound that M would have chosen to hear, what with his drunk rapidly turning into a hangover and also hating sea shanties and not particularly liking Morrissey.

They should not have been able to sail upriver, as the Gowanus Canal is surrounded on both sides by buildings large enough to block out the wind.

But they were well past the point where things functioned logically, and M was not surprised to find their little ship, despite running low in the water with his added weight, made good time. The longer they sailed, the louder the three chanted; and the louder they chanted, the wider the Gowanus Canal seemed to get, until one began to feel that it ought really to be called the Gowanus River, and at some point the Gowanus Bay, and then, finally, the Sea of Gowanus, though M crossed his arms and resolutely refused to offer it that title.

After what seemed a longer period of time than the evening had remaining, they came to a version of the Union Street Bridge, which was mostly wooden and somehow extended over the infinitely expanded body of water atop which they floated. M could just make out the barrel of cannon by the dimming moonlight and the flickering torches set beside them.

"Who goes there?" a voice bellowed down from the bridge. "Say the password or face my musket!"

Lash looked at M warily, unhappy about risking security in front of an outsider. Then he turned back around and shouted out toward the overhang. "Arggggghhhhhhhh!"

"Arggghhhhhhh!" the sentinel shouted back at them.

"Argggggghhhh!" Sodomy and Rum added.

Having nothing to add to the conversation, M kept silent.

They floated beneath the bridge and then into some sort of subterranean chamber, which distantly resembled a sewer, the real city merging with the strange, piratical existence that Lash and the rest of his crew had collectively willed into being. They tied up at the quay a hundred or so yards into the cavern, sharing space with two-man rowboats and jury-rigged catamarans and Arabian dhows, as improbable and anachronistic a fleet as had ever been gathered in one place. The waiting mob of pirates offered M a distinctly unpleasant greeting, punctuated by the occasional buffet or elbow, as well as a running speculation as to the sanctity of his anus and how long he might be expected to maintain it.

If M felt nervous, you would have been hard-pressed to tell. They moved him past surplus East German army tents with barrels of grog sticking out of them, and piles of what looked like costume jewelry scattered about the ground; past drunken wenches and severely inebriated catamites; past three monkeys and a one-eyed parrot reciting what M thought was a passage from Rimbaud. They came finally to a chair made of bone, atop which sat a man the size of several men, drinking from a goblet also made of bone. His beard was black as night, and slow-burning fuses had been set inside the braids. His eyes were brutal. His nose was hooked. He was not, by any stretch of the imagination, unarmed.

"Captain Grimdark welcomes you to the abode of the Pirates of Brown Water," he said, leaning forward on the point of his cutlass. "Seems we're getting awful popular with you bright-siders."

M found himself distracted by the tawny roots in the captain's beard—brunet leading into ebony—but he shook himself out of it. "Thanks," he said. "Yeah, it's quite a place you've got down here. It's . . . real subtle."

The captain rose up from his chair with a grace notable in such a big man, flung his arms wide, and went into easy oration: "For year upon year, we've lived beneath you, growing strong in the dark, learning the secrets of the city's waterways. From the coasts of Staten Island to Montauk, women weep when they see our colors above the mast, and mothers quiet their children by mentioning Grimdark's name! Our swords are sharp, our cannons primed, our . . ."

M's phone beeped, and he fished it surreptitiously from his pocket while the captain was involved in his melodrama, thinking it might be from Boy. But it wasn't.

Unknown Number: Did you see my earrings on the way out?
   M: Who is this?

"—meaner than Black Bart, prettier than Anne Bonny, Frencher than Francois l'Olonnais—"

Unknown Number: Madison.
   M: You think I stole your earrings?
  Madison: I'm just asking if you saw them.

"—taken more plunder in one day than Kidd did in his whole career—"

M: Did you check your nightstand?
Madison: Of course I checked my nightstand.

M's looked up to discover the tip of Captain Grimdark's cutlass a few inches from his throat. "We boring you, boy?"

"Sorry, sorry," M said. "It's this girl I went home with last night. Tonight. Whatever. She thinks I stole her earrings."

Apparently this bit of theoretical villainy was small potatoes for the captain. "What did you come here for? Answer fast or feel the tickle of my blade!"

"Oh." M put his phone away. "Nothing, as it turns out. I was checking on a friend, but she'll be fine. This is a great setup, though. Looks just like a LEGO play set I once bought a girlfriend's nephew. Maybe you could just take me back to where you picked me up? Or, actually, is there a 3 train around here?"

"If ye think," the captain began, swelling up like a snake bite, "you can stroll into the nest of the Pirates of Brown Water and stroll right out again, then you're madder than a drink-crazed Scotsman!" There was much affirmative hooting and hollering from the assembled crowd. "Mayhap there's someone up above who'd pay to have you ransomed? Or should we just make you a cabin boy? You can fetch me grog when you aren't taking your time in the barrel!" More laughter followed, as well as the firing of muskets.

"So no 3 train?" M said, taking a seat on one of the nearby crates. "Fair enough. She probably won't be very long."

Rum scratched at his neck fat. The embers on the captain's beard burned down a tick. Water lapped against the beach. The one-eyed parrot began the first line of "Man From Nantucket," but there was a thud and a squawk and it went quiet.

"What do you mean," the captain asked finally, giving voice to the mob's nerves, "she probably won't be very long?"

"At some point Boy's going to work whatever party drug she's on out of her system, and then she's gonna wake up with a hangover and a keen instinct for mass murder. You ever see someone pick their teeth with a spinal cord?

It's . . ." M struggled to find the words, then gave up. "I wouldn't want to ruin the surprise."

"Pig's guts!" the captain remarked after an awkward silence. The crowd mimicked his merry disregard. "You'll need more than a bluff and a prayer if you hope to win free of the Pirates of Brown Water!"

"I don't pray that much," M admitted. "Honestly, when I got her text, I figured you guys were some sort of interspatial privateers, freebooters floating through space-time, not a bunch of extras from a Jerry Bruckheimer movie. Boy will be cleaning viscera from beneath her fingernails before dawn, and I'll be wondering how to explain to my cleaner why there's brain on my sweater. Again." M shook his head back and forth unhappily. "I knew I should have ignored that text."

He got another one then.

> Madison: Maybe they fell into your pocket somehow?
> M: I told you I didn't steal them.
> Madison: I didn't say you stole them. I'm just wondering if maybe you accidentally scooped them into your pockets on your way out.
> M: That's a clear euphemism for theft.

"Who is your friend, exactly?" Lash asked.

Actually Lash had asked several times, but M had been busy with his phone and also wanted to build some anticipation. "Are you telling me you kidnapped the most dangerous human being within six or seven realities, and you don't even have any idea who she is? Boy the Infernal? Astarte's nemesis? The Doom of Atlantis? I suppose I can't entirely blame you. People who meet her have an unfortunate habit of not living all that long afterward. Actually . . ." M checked the time on his phone. Below his wrist was a tattoo of a choirboy kneeling. "You guys made it about what, three hours? That's not bad. You're beating par."

"We caught her stumbling near a porthole," said a scruffy man with an E-Street Band headscarf. "She said rude things about my parentage!"

"That sounds like Boy, all right. Sharp tongue, but you can get away with it if you've got ichor in your veins, instead of blood. Can any of you claim divine heritage? No? Likely go quick then. Say, you didn't leave anyone to guard her, did you?"

The captain looked at Lash. "Just Tibault and Callahan."

"Well, I hope no one liked Tibault or Callahan that much." M's phone rang, and he answered it casually. "Hello? Yeah. Yeah? Great. The nightstand? Yeah. All right then, be well." He put the phone back in his pocket. "Girls, man. What can you do?"

But the rest of the assemblage seemed not to suppose M's romantic difficulties the foremost issue at the moment.

"If your friend's so terrible," the captain asked, "then how did we snatch her so easy?"

"I dunno. Maybe she was in a K-hole. Probably she didn't think there was anyone stupid enough to make trouble with her. You know, actually," M said, again standing, "now that I think about it, she might decide to do all of you indiscriminately, with fire or acid or some sort of giant worm monster, and all things considered I'd rather not be around for that. When she gets death on her mind . . ." M sucked his teeth. "Not pretty. But you guys will be fine. Sure, I once saw her make a Great Old One weep, but you have, like, antiquated firearms and whatnot."

"A Great Old One?"

"All those tentacled eyes bawling—let's just say there are some things humanity was never meant to see."

"This whole thing was an accident!" the captain protested. "We meant no offense!"

"That's really how you're going to play it? You accidentally snatched her up and shoved her into a dungeon?" M shrugged. "Good luck. I ought to warn you, Boy's not really the forgiving sort."

"There must be something we can do!"

"Suicide? Though she might decide to track you down in hell, so I can't guarantee it would do any good. Look, guys, this has been great and everything, but the longer I'm here, the more likely it is something gets done to me like what's inevitably going to get done to you, and I'd really rather not have that." He waved at the crowd, and they parted obediently, like the waters before Moses or preschoolers before a gym teacher. "I'm sure I can find my own way out. You'll probably be busy praying, or weeping quietly in corners."

"Wait!" the captain said.

M stopped short. "Yeah?"

"Couldn't you talk to her?"

"Me?" M asked incredulously. "What could I do about it?"

"Explain the situation! No harm, no foul!"

"I don't know, guys. It's late, I'm tired. I'm already deeper into this whole thing than I had intended. Also, I took those cracks about my anal virginity a bit on the chin. I can't say I'm really in a favor-doing mood. But . . . maybe if you sweetened the pot?"

Captain Grimdark looked at Lash, who seemed to be his second-in-command. Lash looked at the rest of the mob. The mob looked generally elsewhere. Heavy is the head that wears the pirate hat.

Negotiations took some time because M didn't want to be paid in bales of silk or doubloons, the first being heavy and the second being difficult to exchange on the modern market. They settled on a small bag of loose diamonds, which to M's untrained eyes looked like about a year's rent. At the last moment, M, feeling that old instinct for trouble, demanded Grimdark's tricorne and watched angel-eyed as he took it, slowly and ignominiously, off his head.

"I'll do what I can, but if I were you, I'd make for the hills, or the nautical equivalent. When Boy gets hungover, she gets a little bit jittery." M finished rolling a cigarette, then leaned over and lit it from one of the burning brands set into the captain's beard. "Your dye job is starting to run," he added as a parting shot.

M followed the direction he had been given, down a long stone hallway indifferently lit by guttering torches, till he came to two men standing in front of a wooden door.

"Tibault," M said. "Callahan. Good seeing the both of you."

"Who the hell are you?" the taller one asked.

"I'm the new captain," M said. "Can't you see the hat?"

"What happened to Grimdark?"

"We had a sword fight on a wooden plank suspended above a pool of hammerhead sharks. It was super exciting. I'm sorry you missed it. The long and short is, I went Errol Flynn on his Basil Rathbone."

"What?"

"Johnny Depp on his Geoffrey Rush."

"Oh," the shorter one said. "Shit."

"Yeah, shit's right. Now open the door or I'll have to . . . wear your guts for suspenders. A fedora. Something old-fashioned sounding. It's very late," he explained apologetically, though the guards didn't seem to mind, impressed with his hat and his general air of carelessness.

Inside the store room were rusted cannon and boarding pikes, empty bottles of Brooklyn Lager, crates of stockings, jars of parrot food, hard tack, salt pork, and a hundred and twenty pounds of punk rock devilry, long legs and no breasts and a pixie cut. M had not seen Boy for a long time, years and years, and she looked exactly the same—cruel and wild and nearly beautiful.

"The fuck took you so long? I texted like an hour ago."

M put the pirate hat on her head. "You're welcome."

"You sneak in here?"

"No, no, they were happy to let me take you off their hands once I explained to them the sort of person you are. I may have exaggerated one or two minor details."

Boy looked at him a while. "Where you been?"

"I was out, it took me a little while to get down here."

"I meant the past five years."

"Ah."

"You missed my birthday."

"Five of them, apparently."

"How long you been in town?"

"Not very long."

"Didn't think to call me?"

"I figured you'd hear I was around. And I figured at some point you'd get in trouble and drop me a line. I didn't figure it would be this humiliating, though. How exactly did you manage to get captured by a Gilbert and Sullivan cast?"

"In a word: acid."

"You have any left?"

"No."

Which was just as well, as this was hardly the right time to drop acid. M would have done it anyway, of course, but still he had to admit this was objectively not the time.

"It's good to see you," Boy said finally.

"It's good to see you too."

Boy wobbled some as she stood up, but not badly, given that she was apparently on enough hallucinogens to get ejected from a Phish concert. "Come on," she said. "I'll buy you breakfast."

"Least you could do," M said, making sure the purse of diamonds was still firmly in his pocket.

4

The White Queen

M had been back about two weeks when he started to get the urge to look in on Celise, but since it wasn't really his urge at all, he managed to avoid obeying it. Still, it had the tendency to pop up unexpectedly, and sometimes it would be a few minutes of thinking, *Gosh, that Celise, what a sweetheart, I ought to go over and see how she's doing*, before he would remember, *Wait, I don't even like Celise*, and he would scowl and go back to chopping carrots or record shopping, or once, in what he freely admitted was not his best outing, performing cunnilingus.

After a month back in the city, however, Celise had begun to slip into his existence in aggressive and unsubtle ways. Stray tangles of overlapping graffiti arranged themselves into the letters of her name. He kept running into random mutual acquaintances who would, without any prompting, bring her up in conversation. There were also troublesome bouts of surprising ill luck: keys lost in the trunks of cars, taxis failing to appear, subway cards being cleared suddenly of value, even though M put a fresh twenty on it last night, goddamn it. Goddamn it.

Still, most of November passed without M giving in, though he knew he was only delaying the inevitable. Initially he had hoped that Celise might just lose interest in him, a passing fancy to be forgotten as soon as the next shiny thing caught her attention, but this appeared not to be the case. And when M began to have recurring dreams in which Celise chased him naked through an old growth forest, saddled on a black charger and leading a pack of hounds, and when he got popped three times in one week for jaywalking—a transgression that one would not expect to be a law-enforcement priority in so fractious a metropolis as New York—he decided it was better just to get it over with.

So on a foggy Thursday evening, M put on a pair of pressed jeans and a dress shirt and went to pay homage to the Queen of New York. One of them, anyway. She had the top two floors of a turn-of-the-century building some ways up Fifth Avenue. M had not been inside for years, but he had memories of brass and glass and art that M either did not like at all or liked desperately, as well as a view of the park, which was, by any standard short of avian, spectacular.

The doorman was doing a poor imitation of humanity—with a moment's glance you could see the real him peek through the facade. But of course the superwealthy do not look at doormen, any more than they do waiters or valets, so the deception went generally unnoticed. M had to give his name twice, and even then the thing that was not a doorman scowled and called up, and between all that, it was almost ten minutes before he found himself in the elevator.

Celise's apartment reminded him of the inside of a Fabergé egg, three of which were in fact on display atop one of the mantels. The partygoers were too pretty to converse with; it was like trying to trade pleasantries with the Venus de Milo, if the Venus de Milo were a twenty-year-old Eastern European girl who couldn't quite speak English and wouldn't have much to say even if she could. Waiter-actor-models carried silver trays of food, the appearance of which gave no indication of the taste: little puff pastries dotted with cream that looked like caramel but turned out to be liver, faintly fried slivers of something that M was disappointed to discover were not beef. The bar only served champagne. M found it impossible to get drunk on champagne, but he made a manly effort at it, fortifying himself for the conversation ahead.

Of course he had noticed her as soon as he'd walked in. Celise—it had to be said—was quite possibly the greatest hostess in the history of hospitality, made Madame de Staël seem like Procrustes. She was standing near the windows, the center of a crowd of perfect-looking humans, each captivated, entranced, positively enthralled by whatever it was she was saying, or at least doing their very best to look like it. Celise was a very good person to know, which was why there were so many people trying to get to know her. Having already had the pleasure, M spent most of the next half hour examining the various objets d'art and shuffling his feet awkwardly.

Finally, in a rare convergence of happenstance, there was a brief interlude when Celise found herself alone, and M moved swiftly to take advantage of it. "Celise," he began, bending down to give her an air kiss, "what a pleasure."

M had come to recognize that Celise was beautiful inverse to the length of time that you spent with her; so that, if you were for instance to catch a glimpse of her just before getting on a bus (in the instant before *you* got on a bus, of course, Celise would no more ride a bus than she would shop at Walmart or put her hand in the garbage disposal), you would have carried that image to the end of your life, imagined her in every whore you ever bought, in the face of your wife in the morning. During a brief conversation you would have been astonished by her physiognomy but capable of maintaining a reasonable grip on the normative. But as the clock hand rolled round, she seemed to run like grease paint, and her eyes became savage little dots in her head. After forty-five uninterrupted minutes—and you would never get forty-five uninterrupted minutes with Celise, not even if you were lovers, since she was far too busy and important a person to give forty-five uninterrupted minutes to anyone not a Rothschild—but if you were to have gotten forty-five uninterrupted minutes with her, you'd begin to feel a growing sense of nausea as the mask went completely.

Not having seen her for something between five and ten years, M struggled not to become enthralled entirely by her otherworldly beauty. "Darling," Celise answered, "how wonderful it is that you've returned." Celise spoke with a sterling patrician drawl, and wore a dress that seemed to be formed of spider silk. She smelled of something ineffable but pleasant. She was, in short, more than the epitome, she was the very author, of taste, manners and etiquette.

This was not why M disliked her, though it did not help. "Celise," he said, smiling falsely. "A lovely party," and it was, so long as you went by the decor and ignored the attendees completely.

"Oh, I don't know, I don't know." Though M thought she very much did. "New York is so terribly dull this time of year. Everyone who is anyone is in Milan."

M had to admit that Celise knew everyone who is anyone, and thus could make this statement with a high degree of confidence. But then Celise said everything with a high degree of confidence. In moments of kindness, M wished she might one day turn out to be wrong about something, just as a happy novelty.

"And where have your wanderings taken you?" she asked, continuing on before M could answer. "When you left, had people already started going to Williamsburg? Or had they already stopped?"

"The former, I think."

"Regardless, they've started going back, there's an underground cocktail bar that does the most *amazing* things with mescal. Promenade Theater has replaced urban art, and no one likes NoMad anymore."

"I'll remember that."

"Of course, if you want to eat there, I could give the maître d' a call . . ."

"No, no, you've convinced me."

"Of course I have," she said, grabbing a flute off a tray and handing him another. "Quite the time to be back in the city, quite the time. The real estate market, you just wouldn't believe. You didn't happen to think of holding on to a bit of property the last time you were here, did you?"

"I own Baltic Avenue," he said. "If I get my mitts on Mediterranean, I can start putting up some houses."

Celise had this way of laughing at things that made it impossible to tell if she had gotten the joke. "Planning to set down roots finally?"

"Like kudzu," M said, "so I'm sure we'll be doing lots of this. Bridge parties, evenings in your box at the theater. Though as it happens I have a terribly early morning tomorrow, so perhaps I'd best just . . ."

"Oh, M, you can't leave until you've met Cassandra," Celise said, pointing seemingly at random toward one of the sea-foamed Aphrodites who graced her gathering. "She's just inked a deal to be the face of Chanel's new line."

"Make no trouble on my account. Cassandra seems quite busy with her bulimia, virtually a full-time occupation—"

"But I've already made so much trouble on your account," Celise interrupted. "An account, I might add, that's been accruing interest in the long years since last you graced the city with your presence."

"Why am I here, Celise?"

Five minutes in and her face was not so lovely as it had been, a feigned expression of injury that would have gotten her laughed off the boards of a community playhouse. "Because I've missed you, of course. Because it's been too long, far, far too long since I've gotten to have a look at you. Because I wanted to hear all about what you've been doing, your adventures and experiences."

"You're too kind."

"And also because I wanted to remind myself of why I've liked you enough to warrant doing you so many favors in the past. And for you to be able to remind me that these kindnesses have not yet been forgotten."

"Have we done that yet?"

Celise set aside her drink. "I don't know, M, have we?"

M looked down at his shoes. "We have."

5

Bad Decisions

It began with an argument as to what was the quickest way to get from Greenpoint to SoHo. Stockdale maintained that if you grabbed the Z train from Nassau Street, you could be sipping a gin and tonic on Houston within ten minutes. D8mon, who had never had much luck with the Z, spoke rather passionately for the % train—true, sometimes it did not come for hours, and sometimes it came twice within two minutes, but once you got on, it was a straight shot across the Abandando Bridge, twenty minutes at the very most, and there was a dining car that sold the loveliest little bits of finger food. Admittedly, they only accepted payment in guineas, but one never knew what was in one's pockets, and sometimes you could trade with one of the other passengers.

It will come as no surprise to anyone who has ever ridden the New York subway system, that vast esophageal labyrinth, that there is more to it than the MTA will admit. Indeed, there are few places in which the world that M inhabited and the world known to the rest of us parallel each other so closely. Who, standing on a trash-strewn platform in a far corner of Brooklyn after midnight, has not had the sensation that if they let the 3 pass them by, the next train would offer passage to some strange and foreign existence? Who hasn't waited until right before the door closed, only to see their conviction dissipate in the face of reality's cold waters, and the certainty that the next train won't roll past for another half hour?

Well, I tell you—if you had held to your fantasy for five minutes longer, if you had let that 3 slip by, you might have been privileged to watch while the Ø train rolls into the station, plopped down on a crushed velvet seat, put your boots up on the sterling silver railings, and let it whisk you home in style. Or perhaps that evening the Alkally Special would deign to make its appearance, universally regarded as having the most comfortable private rooms since the decommissioning of the Orient Express.

On the other hand, you might also have been unlucky enough to take the last spot on the Kafka Limited, which takes a whopping two and a half hours to go from Union Square to Van Cortland Park, is always packed, and smells worse than the urinals at a professional football game. Or stepped unthinkingly onto a southbound Herbert Express, which is said to lead into the maw of the sort of creature large enough to swallow a subway train, though of course no one has ever ridden it and come back to say for certain. So maybe you did all right, sticking with your reality.

"My watch stops working any time I get on the %," Stockdale said. "And by the time I get off, I can't remember where I was going or when I was supposed to get there."

Stockdale and M had been friends for longer than he could remember. This was a literal fact, not an exaggerated piece of sentimentality. He was a decent enough chap, apart from being ramrod straight, rather bigoted, long-winded, overly enamored of his own person, and, above all, utterly, determinedly, deliberately British. He dressed like a country squire and carried himself like the hero of a Kipling story, an affectation made all the more curious by his being an ethnic Pakistani and thus on the wrong side of the White Man's Burden.

"My kind of trip," M said.

"Oh, it's a pleasant enough interval, no doubt about it—but try telling some bird that you're two days late for drinks because you got caught up playing whist in the dining car of a train that—so far as she's concerned—never existed."

D8mon laughed. D8mon had the best pompadour that M had ever seen on a man of East Asian descent—one of the best pompadours he had ever seen period. D8mon sometimes seemed very clever and other times only seemed sort of clever, which to M's mind was a very dangerous medium. D8mon was rather new to the game, and M had heard that he could do some things with technology that other people did not seem able to do.

D8mon pulled a package of clove cigarettes from inside the pocket of his jeans, no easy task as they seemed to be painted over his legs. "Zenegal of Bombast would be the person to ask about this," he said. Zenegal of Bombast, the Graffiti Prince and High Priest of the Cult of Funk, had been the acknowledged expert on the intricacies of the subway system since it had been opened—and, rather curiously, for some time before that as well. "But I've heard he's in Sao Paulo."

"I heard an invisible wind picked him up from the ground one day, carried him screaming off into the clouds," Stockdale corrected.

"So either way, he's not here to break the tie," M said.

The conversation turned to Zenegal of Bombast. Where he was, if he was dead, what he had done before he had been made so.

"Did Zenegal ever tell you about the time he got to the Nexus?" Stockdale asked.

It is axiomatic that all roads, if you follow them long enough, connect to all other roads. The Nexus was the concrete realization of this hypothesis. Previous incarnations had seen it as a dusty crossroads, a hostelry, and a coaling port, but these days, in keeping with the zeitgeist, it was a subway station.

"Yes," M said. "Many, many times."

"You believed him?"

"I didn't entirely not believe him," M said, taking a sip of his gin and tonic. There was a tattoo of a steam engine below his left wrist. "He said it was a long ways, but if you made it, you could hop a train anywhere you wanted, a straight shot, no connections."

No one said anything for a while, mulling over that possibility in silence.

"I've always had some hankering to get a good look at Shimla, back when it was the second city in the empire," said Stockdale.

"I've never actually been to Tokyo," D8mon admitted, rather ashamedly. "I keep meaning to go, and something keeps coming up."

Where it was that M wanted to go, he didn't say. Regardless, when

Stockdale stood up wordlessly, leaving enough cash on the table to cover the three of them—in short, when it was clear that the challenge had been offered—he was not slow in taking it.

It was a bad decision. They had no real motivation in heading toward the Nexus, no plans and no provisions, nothing but a few words from an absent friend with which to begin their quest. And one thing about Zenegal was that, in spite of, or at least in addition to, being the Graffiti Prince and High Priest of the Cult of Funk, he had a rather loose relationship with the truth. But the thing about good decisions is that making them exclusively turns out, curiously, to be the worst decision a person can make; it leads to ruination, to a business-casual existence, to eating takeout and watching network sitcoms.

In short, a bad decision is required to even things out every so often, and M was feeling up for making one that afternoon. Perhaps Stockdale and D8mon felt the same, or perhaps they were both foolish enough to mistake their bad idea for a good one. M was never entirely clear on the point, and afterward, what with how the whole thing ended, he never really felt like discussing it.

• • •

The Q from Seventh Avenue started normally enough, hipsters crawling their way into Manhattan for an evening's entertainment, no odder or more sur-real than your average ride on a New York City subway system, so fairly sur-real. They got off at Kings Highway, six or seven stops down the line. M rarely rode the Q and so was not sure if Kings Highway was a real place or not, real in the sense of existing in the reality that M had been born in, rather than some other to which they were playing tourist. If it wasn't his world, it was another similar enough not to stand out particularly, and they slipped onto the B without experiencing anything unusual. But fifteen minutes later, at Grand Flatroad Station, the train was suddenly packed with bipedal insects, not quite man-size, dressed in gilded-age hand-me-downs. One of them touched a spindle-haired tendril to his bowler hat and chittered something.

"No," M answered, realizing with a shock that he had understood the question without difficulty, "I'm not sure if this train goes to Moss Bottom Road. I'm not exactly from around here, you see."

The insectoid clicked its mandibles together. M found himself staring into the thing's multifaceted eyes and had to remind himself to answer.

"Thanks for the suggestion—I'm not sure we'll be staying long enough to see the sights."

It bobbed its antennae back and forth in understanding, then turned to the paper it held in one of its . . . hands? feelers? claws? The headline read PRIME MINISTER AGREES TO TROUT NEGOTIATION—WAR WITH PRUSSIA AVERTED.

"Peace in our time!" Stockdale said, rather too loudly.

The mass of surrounding creatures edged away uncomfortably.

"Don't be an ass," M muttered

At Idlewyld Station they snagged the back table in the dining car of a Victorian-era steam-engine train. It looked like a Victorian-era steam-engine train, and the people occupying it looked very much like Victorian-era citizens, but the meat that D8mon was picking looked distinctly greenish, and M was fairly certain the waiter had asked if they wanted "fish, chicken, or wyvern." M stuck with gin, sipped it while staring out the window at a rural version of Brooklyn, quaint villages and bucolic forest scenery.

Suddenly the car door opened and a pale-faced woman burst in. "Come quick! For the love of God, come quick! It's the Admiral! He's been murdered!"

"Well, this is me," M said, dabbing his lips with his napkin and standing. "I absolutely refuse to get involved in another locked-room mystery."

"I should say not," Stockdale affirmed, grabbing his cigarette case off the table and following M out.

D8mon forked a last streak of green meat into his mouth before joining them.

• • •

They were sitting on the Four Humours Express, surrounded by men in buckskin shouldering tarnished blunderbusses and dour-faced women in homespun cotton. On the seat across from M, a bony child held a fat pig. Whether the Four Humours Express was the vehicle that would take them all west—assuming that was where they were going—or if it would only leave them in front of a waiting fleet of Conestoga wagons, M could not possibly say.

"What time is it?" asked a loud voice from the other end of the train, followed by some introductory music playing from a tinny boom box.

"Showtime!" answered his hype man.

"Christ damn it," M said.

The skinny child across from M gaped in horror.

"I hate showtime," D8mon said.

"Everyone hates showtime," Stockdale said.

"I haven't enjoyed watching anyone break-dance since Kool Herc was on the decks," M added.

"Maybe they'll just do some juggling."

"Or recite a poem."

"Even worse."

But when they got off the train five minutes later, M was smiling. "Credit due," he said, "that was amazing."

"I didn't think it was possible to fit a squirrel up there, let alone a badger," Stockdale responded, lighter by twenty dollars.

Our three adventurers were taking dinner at a bar in the vastness of St. Alban's Station, which did not exist on any of the subway lines that M was aware of, though M very much thought it should have. A small establishment but bustling with folk of literally all sorts—day traders and MTA workers and Soviet cosmonauts and slumming international royalty, Brazilian vaqueros in leather chaps and bullwhips, spindly punk kids with safety pins stuck through their lips and eyebrows, white-clad Buddhist monks ordering red ale via hand signals so as not to violate their vows of silence. There was sawdust on the ground and a giant blackboard hanging over the bar read:

Beer 5¢

12 Oysters 10¢

Fancy women, gnomes, and cyborgs not welcome

"An admirable entrance policy," Stockdale observed to the barman as he brought over three more pulls of stout.

"These are the best goddamn oysters I've ever tasted," D8mon said, slurping one out from its shell.

"Your first time in here?" asked the man sitting next to them, bullet-headed, the chain of a watch coming out of one pocket and the butt of a revolver sticking out the other.

"Our very first time," Stockdale said, "though, Lord willing, not the last."

"Where you from?"

"Crown Heights," M said.

"Crown Heights? You aren't from one of those New Yorks where the Brits won in '76?"

"If you call disentangling yourself from a bunch of ungrateful provincials losing . . ." Stockdale began. It was Stockdale's considered belief that the British Empire did right in leaving the subcontinent and wrong in leaving everywhere else.

M cut over him. "Our New York is part of the United States, by the grace of God."

But this wasn't quite enough for their new companion, who was staring over at Stockdale in the way that a person might stare at someone before hitting them. He was barely more than five feet, but every inch seemed made of hard oak and scrap metal. M was wondering if maybe he could convince D8mon to fight him and then eat all of D8mon's oysters while he was so engaged.

Though it didn't come to that, because all of a sudden Stockdale raised his half-empty glass of beer toward the sky and said in his speaker's corner voice, "To the Apple herself, the beating center of the human race, mad and fierce and lovely. There was never in all the worlds a woman more beautiful or more heartless."

"To New York," M said.

"To New York," D8mon said.

"To New York," the stranger added.

Everyone drank what was left of their beer. In a fit of civic pride, everyone ordered another glass and drank that as well.

"When did you say you were from, exactly?"

"2014," Stockdale said.

"2016," D8mon inserted.

"Yes, right—2016."

"Hell's bells, that's a few years past expiration. I suppose you don't see many of these, when you're from?" he asked, pulling at the ends of his handlebar mustache.

"Actually, a lot more frequently than you'd think," M said.

The stranger didn't quite know what that meant, but he was in a good enough humor to overlook it. "What are you boys here for, then?"

"We're heading to the Nexus." D8mon was drunk enough for his voice to carry a few stools down.

"That's a ways."

"You ever been there?"

He shook his head. "The ¿ train should take you as far as Fourth Via Station. You want to get any farther, though, you're going to need to find yourself a berth on the Alighieri Special."

"That's an ominous title."

"It's aptly named. If you're set on going, I can tell you this much: The line goes through some of the . . . infernal regions. The train itself is safe—nothing can touch you while you're on it. But the things that live round those parts are a tricky bunch—if you step out, you're theirs. And that"—he shuddered—"doesn't bear thinking about."

But they did think about it then, for a while, the three companions and probably the stranger as well, who added, "You sure you aren't better off having a couple more oysters and then heading home?"

Actually at that point M wasn't at all sure of this fact, but there was no way at this point to bow out gracefully, and after a moment, Stockdale—who never missed an opportunity to utter an epigraph—answered for him: "Death or victory!"

"I wish you the latter," the man said, toasting their fortune.

. . .

They had been waiting on the platform of Fourth Via Station for about half an hour when a strange rattle could be heard moving toward them. Fourth Via Station looked like it was located in one of the realities that never got over having knights and so forth—the floor was cobblestone rather than concrete, the only illumination came from the flickering torchlight, and the name of the station was hung on an elaborately embroidered tapestry, complete with heraldry. Below it a filigreed hourglass hung from a wall arm, falling sand indicating the arrival of the next train.

The platform was empty, except for M and his two companions. It seemed to be late in the evening. It was very dark, at least, but then torches don't shed as much light as neon bulbs.

It was these torches that revealed the source of the rattling. They looked at first like children, an impression aided by the fact that they coasted forward on old-fashioned roller skates, orange wheels sewed into burlap. But even by the dim light that conjecture faltered almost immediately. Their bodies were too thick, their skin a strange mixture of white and green, like a corpse that had been left in water. They wore heavy leather jackets and bright red ski caps, and their teeth were narrow, nasty little points.

One had a length of chain in his hand that he swung back and forth in a fashion unsuggestive of amity. He called out in a language that seemed to have a lot of C's and W's stuck together. M didn't speak it, but he understood a taunt regardless of the idiom.

"What do we have here?" D8mon asked, though it was obvious enough in the broad strokes.

"We call them redcaps," Stockdale informed him. Actually, Stockdale's people would have called them Rakshasas or something to that effect, but M did not think this was the time to deal with his friend's false consciousness.

"I'd call them trouble," M muttered.

They circled the three travelers like a pack of wolves that had recently seen the film *Xanadu*, to torture a metaphor rather cruelly. One of the bogies took Stockdale's lapel between two of his clawed fingers, rubbed at the fabric, and smiled rapaciously.

"What ho, chap," Stockdale began, stiff-arming the goblin back a step. "You've got some cheek, all right, to place hands on a gentleman."

Stockdale's new admirer chattered fiercely in his unseemly tongue. One of his confederates stopped in front of M, staring like a hawk at a coney. He had a string of bone fingers on a chain around his neck, and the coat he wore was emblazoned with scenes of slaughter and cruelty. M was wearing only his street clothes, faded jeans and a leather jacket, and he didn't have any weapons on him that you could see. But after a moment, the goblin faltered, looked down at his roller skates, and backpedaled into the dark.

There was a brief moment when M thought maybe they'd be able to bluff their way past, but then there was the sound of loosed steel and one of the goblins was angling a rusted dagger at Stockdale.

Hari Kumar Stockdale was many things: He was a lover of nineteenth-century adventure stories. He was a frequent wearer of hats. He had once seen service on a whaling ship. He could not use chopsticks.

He was a very hard man to kill. Inside of his jacket pocket was a gravity knife, a four-inch handle with a blade much larger, and then it was outside his pocket, and then it was open. If M knew Stockdale at all, and M did, this was one of the happiest moments of his life, playing Aragorn in the dim outskirts of reality. Worth the trip, you had best believe. And he proved himself up to the challenge, neatly dodging the goblin's attack, pivoting and responding in a fashion that left the green-skinned creature bled white and tumbling, gracelessly, into the train tracks.

The remaining hobs shrieked and faded back the way they had come.

"You don't really carry that everywhere, do you?" M asked.

"Only when I leave the house," Stockdale said.

"Where are they going?" D8mon asked, sounding a bit worried. It belatedly occurred to M that he didn't really know D8mon all that well, knew him to get a drink with maybe, but not to stand back-to-back against the rising tide.

"To fetch us some tea and scones, I would think," M said. But just in case he was wrong, they overturned a couple of the nearby benches, barricading themselves along the platform.

There was a horn blast that made M think of a hanged man shitting himself, and then they rolled out of the darkness four deep, carrying knives and chains and planks of wood with nails sticking out of them. They hooted and they hollered and they screamed madness in their gutter speech. Stockdale held his blade aloft, looked ecstatic to be doing so. One of the goblins came closer than it ought, and Stockdale's counterfeit Caliburn struck a second time, and the thing screamed and fled backward, missing an ear and much of its face.

"The blood of Edward the Black runs in my veins!" Stockdale bellowed. "William the Marshal and John Churchill! Chandragupta and Zahir-ud-din Muhammad Babur! I am Hari Kumar Stockdale, and I will die with my boots on!"

M was happy that someone was having a good time. The pack, the scrum, perhaps even the mob of goblins, were now wary of the barricade and of the flashing blade that hid beyond it, contented themselves by skating back and forth just out of reach of melee weapons and shouting.

D8mon pulled an iPod out of his pocket and held it up in his right hand, pointed skyward. It crackled and sparked for a quarter of a second, and then there was a sound like a MIDI thunderclap and a streak of light seared the chest of the foremost redcap, before dovetailing and hitting two more behind him. The rest scattered back into the darkness.

"Not bad," Stockdale said.

"Thank you," D8mon said. "I wish I'd brought my laptop, then you'd really have seen something."

"What's the hourglass read?" M asked.

D8mon looked over his shoulder for a minute. "There's less sand in the top half than previously."

"Lovely."

"They seem to have slacked off, at least."

But then the platform began to, if not shake, at least resound loudly enough that one could be forgiven for thinking it was shaking. The thing that lumbered into the torchlight did so on its own two feet, rather than gliding along on a set of wheels. The thing did not seem graceful enough to remain upright, had it been roller-skating, though it made up for its lack of agility by being huge and muscled and mean-looking. It was twice the height of M at his shoulders, its skin was the black-green of a bad bruise, its tusks, somewhere between walrus and elephant-size, jutted out from its jowls. In one hand it carried a club fully the size of a normal man, knotted and warped as the thing's skin, thick metal apples on chains hanging from the business end.

"If you were thinking of saving the day in some heroic and unexpected fashion," Stockdale said to M, "now would be the time to do so."

M took a deep breath, smiled, and hopped up over the barricade. "Bill!"

he said, strutting forward toward the monstrosity. "I haven't seen you since the ten-year reunion, back in '08!"

The ogre cocked his head at M, a task made somewhat difficult by the fact that its skull seemed to be attached directly to its overbroad shoulders. Its club hung forgotten in his off hand. After a moment it croaked an unintelligible response.

"And how the hell have you been? You were planning to set up a distillery in Inkinshire, if I remember correctly—double malt, you'd promised me. How'd that end up going?"

Bill made the sort of sound which, were it coming from your car, would suggest you needed to have your brake pads replaced.

"And Madge? How is Madge these days? I hope you held on to her, she's a good egg if ever there was one!"

Another shrill squeal of a similar type.

"I hate to make a break for it, Bill, what with us not having seen each other in so long—but my train's just a moment or two out, and it would be a damn shame if I missed it."

Bill grunted something that sounded rather regretful.

"Don't suppose you could do me a solid and keep this riffraff off our backs? Bad element, you know. Not to be trusted and so forth."

Bill nodded and smiled, exposing crooked green teeth the size of M's hands. Then it turned and let out a bellow that flickered dark the nearby torches, and began to wade back the way it came, its club swinging lustily.

Things screamed in the dark.

M returned to the other end of the barricades and the astonished looks of his comrades. "Confidence is nine-tenths of everything," he explained.

The screams grew louder, so loud that they nearly drowned out the arrival of the train, which had the facade of a Gothic church, and no windows.

"Where's it going?"

"Gotta be better than here," Stockdale said, holding the door until his companions could enter.

But as M took a seat and looked back the way he had come, he saw that above the door was a stained glass panel reading, "Abandon all hope . . ." and he thought to himself, *Fuck.*

. . .

The Alighieri Special was in a state of furious decay. The standing bars were bent, most of the seating had been torn out, and there was trash everywhere. The lights flickered on and off. The scent of urine was almost overpowering. It was somewhat worse than your average L train.

"Happy Valley Station, next stop," a voice said.

"Rapists' Corner, next station," it said again a few minutes later.

"Your Mother Never Loved You, change for the 4 train, the B train, and the Long Island Railroad."

"That's a bit much, don't you think," D8mon asked, licking his lips.

"Isn't it just?" Stockdale commented.

The doors closed, the train began to pull away.

D8mon lit his last cigarette and tucked it into his smirk. "They'll have to do better than that."

But of course, they did.

A few stops later M's cell phone began to emit a loud, bleating shriek, as if transmitting from an abattoir. Stockdale's began to do the same a moment later. For some strange reason D8mon's iPhone began to play a remix of a Katy Perry song. D8mon swore that he didn't have any Katy Perry on his iPhone, but no one believed him. By the next stop, all of their electronic devices were behaving in ways contrary or at least unrelated to their normal functions. M's phone showing something that seemed like a pornographic snuff film involving humanoid bunny rabbits, though M did not look at it long enough to be sure. When the door opened next, they tossed their mobiles onto the platform. M half expected something to rise up and catch them—severed hands of the hell-caught dead— but nothing did. M did not suppose he'd be so lucky if he stepped outside himself.

The urine smell was replaced with rotting flesh, and then cotton candy, and then rotting flesh again. The voice coming over the loud speaker began to tell the story of a child being tortured and eaten, a few sentences each stop ("and then they sharpened their knives against her sternum, and then they nibbled at the corners of her clavicle"). M ignored it, and eventually it stopped. For a very long time afterward the names of the station were the only thing that could be heard, and mostly they seemed straight from an unpublished H.P. Lovecraft story, consonants crammed inconsiderately against one another.

"Grand Army Plaza, next stop."

D8mon perked his head up all of a sudden. "Did you hear that?"

"Yes," M said.

"The conductor said Grand Army Plaza."

"I heard him."

There was no need to observe that this was the first stop in however long they had been on the train that existed in the reality they came from. Grand Army Plaza Station was deserted but looked like it always did, like it had a thousand other times that M had seen it. Part of his soul died when the door closed.

"Next station will be Franklin," the speakers announced.

"I'm going to take it," D8mon said, standing up swiftly. "It could be our last shot."

M didn't move. "It's a trick," he said.

"What?"

"Franklin doesn't come after Grand Army Plaza."

"Of course it does," D8mon said, wanting it to be true enough to speak with certainty.

"It does not."

"You're out of your mind."

"If you're heading downtown, then it goes Franklin, Eastern Parkway, Grand Army, Bergen. If you're heading uptown, it's the reverse. But either way, Franklin does not come after Grand Army Plaza."

"They're trying to fuck with you," Stockdale said.

"They already have," D8mon insisted. "Don't you get it? This is hell, right here, the three of us stuck smelling piss for the rest of eternity." And after he said it, he stood up, took a few steps toward the door, and wrapped his hands around one of the poles.

"Hell is not an existentialist play," M said, "it involves knives and hot poker sodomy. Do not get off this train."

"D8mon," Stockdale repeated, "do not get off this train."

The train started to slow down. D8mon was still standing at the doorway, wide-eyed. "How long have we been here?"

"I don't know."

"Could it be years?" D8mon asked. His eyes were blinkered. His pompadour, however, was still immaculate.

"It could be centuries," M said, and if you didn't know any better he seemed very much to be losing his temper. "And it doesn't matter—because hell is eternity, my friend, and it's an eternity with needles in your eyes, and I assure you what we have at the moment is preferable."

D8mon reached into his pocket and came out with a small caliber handgun, the kind of thing that might be used to rob a convenience store. The way he held it, M got the sense D8mon hadn't had a lot of practice. Then again, you don't need a lot of practice to shoot two friends at close range. "If you don't have the balls to make a move, that's your business," he said. "But I'm not going to spend the remainder of forever stuck in a subway car."

"You'd rather be blowing razor-blade chewing gum?" M asked, but he put his hands up, to show that he had no intention of obstructing the man.

Stockdale looked like he was going to say something, but then he too shrugged and leaned back against the wall. D8mon was a big boy. He could make his own mistakes.

The train opened, and D8mon took a few steps closer to it, till he was skirting the exit. Then he whooped loudly and leaped onto the platform.

The doors shut sooner than they should have, or at least sooner than M thought they did on normal trains, like a trap closing, or a coffin. D8mon was quickly lost from sight.

M sat back down. Stockdale did also. M began to silently rethink his policy on bad decisions.

"Eastern Parkway, Grand Army, then Bergen?" Stockdale asked.

M didn't answer. The names of the stations went back to being incomprehensible or horrifying and often both.

• • •

The door opened. "Last stop," said a voice from the speaker.

They sat there a while, a long while, still half fearing it was a trick. Finally an attendant came on and asked them politely to leave, and they allowed themselves to be ushered off.

The Nexus was bright and very clean and seemed to be built mostly of crystal. It was vast beyond comprehension, but somehow its vastness was not intimidating. Smiling travelers moved by swiftly but without any sense of hurry, commuters on their way somewhere, youthful travelers with bright eyes and heavy backpacks on their way anywhere. On a board stretching upward to the sun every conceivable destination flickered past, the letters rattling over one another loudly. They found their way to an information kiosk, where a pretty young woman in a sky-blue outfit smiled at them. "Can I help you get somewhere?" she asked pleasantly.

M looked at Stockdale. Stockdale looked very tired. M thought he probably looked the same.

"Crown Heights," M said.

The attendant smiled and nodded and gave them directions. It was a straight shot, she said, thirty minutes to Nostrand.

They found their platform, the train arriving not long thereafter. They found a seat. Half an hour later the doors opened on reality, for whatever that was worth. It was morning. M and Stockdale found their way to a nearby breakfast joint, had a bite to eat, smoked three cigarettes each, and then went home to sleep.

No one ever saw D8mon again. No one has seen him yet, at least.

6

A Moral Obligation

M found himself on Washington Avenue late one rainy afternoon toward the beginning of December. He often found himself on Washington Avenue in the late afternoon and often afterward found himself inside a dimly lit little cave called The Lady, and then up at the counter, and then down on a stool. And why not? An establishment where a person will serve you alcohol in exchange for money? That was a good idea, to M's way of thinking. M could see how it had caught on.

And The Lady was most definitely a place where you would be served alcohol in exchange for money. The beer selection rotated weekly but was always very solid. The cocktail menu was cute but not too cute; the finger food was edible; the happy hour specials reasonable and perhaps even a bit more than that. The jukebox was all Britpop and alt-country. M would slip in with a paperback that he could read if things were slow but otherwise operated as an effective opening line for women who were doing the same thing: "You're reading a book, I'm literate," etc.

And of course there was Dino, thick and pasty and eternally good humored, a walking advertisement that being handsome was no great shake, at least not all the shakes worth shaking.

"Hey, Dino," M said.

"How you doing?" Dino asked, passing over a water.

M ordered a drink with rum and honey and beaten egg whites and warm water. It brought up his core temperature by about three degrees. Celsius, that is, not Fahrenheit.

"You look down," M said.

Dino shrugged. It is a bartender's job to receive troubles, not pass them on, and Dino was a very good bartender. But M was a very good customer, and it seemed Dino felt comfortable opening up on the matter. "I think we're going to have to close the bar."

This would have made a lesser man spit up his cocktail, but M was made of somewhat sterner stuff. "Fucking yuppies."

"Not the rent," Dino said. "At least, not exactly."

"What's the problem?"

"There's this thing in the back."

M thought that no thing described as a thing in the back had ever done him any good and didn't anticipate that this one would break the streak. "OK."

"It's kind of special."

"Like, how you mean, special?"

"Like how the bar is kind of special, you know? Think about it."

While doing so, M realized that the first time he had come to The Lady he had taken a trolley car, a conveyance the city had, for no reason M could appreciate, long ago gotten rid of. And now that he took a moment to consider the matter, hadn't The Lady been in the Village then? But M could also distinctly remember dipping in one evening with a charming androgynous creature when he had been very, very high on uppers, and he was quite certain that it had been after coming out of a club in Alphabet City.

"I see," M said. It was not so very surprising. There were holes everywhere, if you cared to look.

"So this thing in the back," Dino said, "it's the reason . . . well, it's why we're the only bar outside of Belgium that can get Westvleteren on tap, and that the health inspector is always in a good mood when he stops by."

M thought about the many oysters he had enjoyed inside The Lady. "But if he wasn't in a good mood when he came in, you'd still pass, right?"

"Anyway, the last few weeks, it's been getting kind of hinky on me."

"Hinky, you say?"

"Hinky."

"Hinky like how?"

"Hinky like maybe it would be easier if you just took a look at it."

"Why me?"

Dino looked at M in a way that suggested M's reputation had preceded him.

This was not what M had been anticipating when he had walked into The Lady fifteen minutes earlier. But he righted himself from his stool all the same. Behind the counter was a trap door leading to the basement below, a steel gate just big enough for an unwary busboy to fall in and break his neck. Dino undid the bar, which was to M's mind awfully thick, and lifted it vertical. Standing next to it was a dinged-up Louisville Slugger, which Dino shouldered. "Things come out of it, sometimes," he explained.

The one other person in the bar looked like he never left it, and when he did it was only to go to another one very close by. "You're on till we get back," Dino said.

The drunk burped but didn't look up.

Going downstairs seemed to take a lot longer than M thought it should, though Dino didn't seem to pay it any mind. It was strange how quickly a person grew used to this sort of thing, falling into a comfortable armistice with the impossible. But it was an armed truce, and as they finally reached the basement, M was reminded why.

Things were going sideways pretty fast. The walls couldn't make up which type of wall they wanted to be, going from redbrick to cobblestone to a hideous shade of chartreuse paint. The stock likewise rotated through the preferred beverages of a dozen generations, oak caskets of grog mixing with crates of Old Milwaukee.

"How long have you had this place?"

"I bought it after I came back from the war."

"Which war was that, exactly?"

"I rode a horse, and we were mostly still using swords." At the back of the room was an access door, and Dino opened it and walked inside.

M could smell it before he saw it, burnt ozone and fresh gasoline and movie-theater popcorn. The thing inside was throwing off electricity, but the electricity was neon pink and hung weblike in the air for some seconds before bleeding away into the ether. It gave M the impression of a womb and an old-fashioned toaster and a dish of lukewarm blood pudding and also of a whole host of things that ought not be layered together flatly onto one point in existence.

"I don't know what this is supposed to be," M said, "but I don't think it's supposed to be doing this."

"No."

M looked at Dino. Dino looked at M.

"Free drinks for a year," Dino said.

Nation, ethnicity, language, regional sports affiliation, the vast slate of peculiarities with which most people define themselves, these are more or less marked out for you by birth, and to M's way of thinking, there was no particular point in getting worked up over whatever arbitrary whim of fate had made you German instead of French. But a man chose his bar, and that placed upon him a more serious moral obligation than country, race, or creed. M didn't really need free drinks for a year, but a man who wouldn't fight to save his own bar, the bar he's chosen as his own bar, or perhaps which had chosen him—well, these were not ranks of which M wished to become a member.

M sighed. M scratched his head. M wished he had taken a shot of vodka before coming downstairs. "Top shelf?" he asked. "Not just rail?"

"Anything you want," Dino promised.

The thing to remember about going into a place that *isn't*, or that *is* in an incomprehensible fashion, is to make sure to hold on very clearly to who you are, or at least who you want to be. "I am a bad-ass motherfucker," M said, reaching out to touch the glowing womb or the old-fashioned toaster or whatever.

"All right," Dino allowed, though by that point M couldn't hear him.

"I am an A-list, blue-label, two-fisted champion of all that is noble, upright, and sweet-smelling," M told himself as he made his way down a road of golden cobblestones, surrounded on all sides by a lush green forest, a forest that seemed more like painted on backdrop than actual foliage. Jumping back and forth just off the edge of the pathway were anthropomorphic swarms of characters, bright maroon 4's hopping on top of indigo capital D's. M noted their googly eyes and sharpened teeth.

"A is for atrocity," said the first letter of the alphabet. "And also abortion, apartheid, and anarchy!"

"Me times ten thousand is the number of children who died of sudden infant death syndrome in 2015!" a smiling number 7 informed M.

"When I bebop down the street," M retorted, "the ladies stare and moan, and the boys piddle themselves and wonder where I bought my shoes. I taught Hemingway to box and Casanova to fuck."

M walked against the current on a moving track, the kind you see in an airport but stretching off infinitely into the horizon. Running alongside the conveyor belt were a swarm of harried passengers, businessmen trying to catch the 6:15 to Houston and nuclear families that had missed their connection to Orlando, stuck in limbo wearing Mickey Mouse hats and swelled fanny packs.

"Airline travel is a leading cause of global warming," said a towheaded girl of about five, though with her thick lisp it sounded more like "Aiwine twavew is a weading cause of gwobaw warming."

"On your trip to Cuba you released ten thousand metric tons of carbon dioxide!" her elder brother exclaimed. "It resulted directly in the death of two subspecies of Tibetan grasshopper!"

"My penis is moderately longer than most men of my age and ethnic group," M observed, "and I am reasonably confident no one ever faked an orgasm in my presence."

M was standing in the doorway of the kitchen of his childhood home. His mother had a fetus cooking in a cast-iron pot on the stove, and her eyes were open wounds. "I never loved you," she said. "You were a disappointment in every way you could be."

His father echoed this sentiment from his spot at the head of the table. "I wanted to kill you before you was born," he said, "chisel you right out of her twat." Over the checkered tablecloth a copy of *The Telegraph* read NAZIS OCCUPY LONDON, KILL EVERYONE.

"I wish I'd listened," his mother responded, ladling the horror she had cooked into two bowls and setting them on the table. "Oh God, how I wish I had listened."

"I don't ever raise my voice except when I need to," M said, raising his voice, "and when I do, motherfuckers sprint off and hide behind whatever they can find to hide behind. If I look scared it's because I'm trying to trick you, and if you've noticed, then it's already worked."

He was standing on black pavement in an endless night, the only illumination provided by rickety lampposts at uneven intervals, dimming and glowing as if of their own volition. "There's no point to anything," a voice said.

"You're going to die, one way or the other," added a second. "Probably you'll die here and soon, but either way it's just delaying the inevitable."

"And it won't have meant nothing," a third added sadly. "Not to anyone. And you know that, even if you won't admit it."

M found he wasn't wearing shoes any longer, and each footfall echoed into his bones, up his legs and all the way to his spine. "I've been to every populated continent," M said, plunging onward, though he could feel his breath getting short and his mind starting to rupture, "and who would want to go to the unpopulated ones? I once hitchhiked from Vilnius to Donostia in two days, and I never paid a fare or resorted to magic."

The road swayed beneath him, narrowed, became a plank of wood running over an abyss. Distant drifting spheres streaked through the darkness, though as they came closer M could make out that they were attached to stalks, the little bubbles of light bait from the creatures gliding through the firmament.

"We will chew on you forever," said one of them, the sound like the movement of tectonic plates, the rumbling of a hatred outside the scope of human ken. "And every second for us will be a pleasure."

"We exist only to dream up torments," the voice of an early morning DJ added, "and we've been brainstorming since before the beginning of time."

"I once ate an entire ham in a single sitting," M said, struggling now. "I have the high score on Ms. Pac-Man machines in twelve different countries, and one of those countries is Japan!"

This seemed to be distinctly unimpressive to the vast and cumbersome forces that existed just outside of his vision, waiting impatiently for him to stumble. But now M could see what he was looking for, a glowing switch set eye level into the nothingness. Of course it was not this at all, only what his limited perceptions conceived of it as, but this is how M saw it and so this is how we will refer to it. To break into a run was to show weakness and thus court disaster; also, since he was not really running but passing a mental projection through an infinite nexus of alien possibilities, it would probably not bring him to his destination any more quickly. But M did up his pace a bit, as much as he dared.

And the things that did not want him to reach it began to gnash their endless rows of teeth and to moan and to howl, the sounds drowning out the echo of his feet against the bridge and the beating of his heart—but not, interestingly, his voice, which sounded weak and tinny but had not yet gone silent. "My vinyl collection is extremely solid, especially in terms of deep soul! I have several times made love to a woman on a beach! I am competent at the game of chess!"

And clearly now we were at the end of M's stock of ego, which, even to the most prideful of us, is not inexhaustible. But in the instant before being eaten by an infinite, tentacled vagina, M reached out and grabbed the lever and pulled it sharply down, and reality winked back into view.

He spent the next few minutes vomiting up unbirthed chunks of existence, formless blobs that came out as liquid and landed on the ground as parti-colored tarantulas with bejeweled wings and snotty slicks of gasoline and three issues of *Teen Beat* from the summer of 1986.

Dino ran dutifully about the room, bopping the more mobile of the creations with his baseball bat. M did not bother to help even after he had finished retching, just sat in the corner, trying to reestablish those blocks on his perception and understanding that allow a human being to maintain a semblance of sanity.

"Bar snacks too, Dino," M said, after a few moments had passed. "As many as I fucking want."

"Fair enough," Dino said, splattering the brains of an anthropomorphic slinky with razored teeth. "Fair enough."

7

Undead Labor Restrictions

M got a call from Andre late one Thursday afternoon. "Bonjour, my good friend! It has been far too long since last we spoke!"

"Too long," M echoed, though that might have been a question and not a statement.

"What are you doing tonight?"

"I hadn't quite narrowed it down yet."

"Fantastic! I'm heading to a charity gala, and I can sneak you as a plus one."

"What misfortune! Having just moved back to the city, I fear my wardrobe is not up to the task."

"Not any sort of a problem—I'd be more than happy to lend you anything you need."

"I don't have a suit jacket."

"Easily remedied."

"Or pants, for that matter."

"I have a pair that will go perfect on you. They match the jacket, incidentally."

"It would not be possible for me to provide a dress shirt."

"I have a cream one that I think would go best with the suit, which is black-striped, though perhaps blue would suit you better. We can try both on when you arrive."

"The black-striped suit you describe sounds marvelous, though, alas, it would demand a black belt as well, which I'm afraid is also beyond my resources."

"I always keep an extra belt around, in case anyone wants to asphyxiate themselves autoerotically."

"Forward thinking, indisputably, and while I'm sure your belt is a very fine one, it would hardly be appropriate for me to show up at this event dressed to the nines above the ankles, and wearing flip-flops below. And as the only footwear I own at this point are sandals and work boots, I fear that we have reached a firm and impassable impediment to my attendance."

"What size shoes do you wear?"

"Eleven and a half."

"Truly, we are in the midst of a rare collusion of good fortune—for eleven and a half are the exact number of inches of my own feet, for which I own many shoes, every pair at your service."

"A tie? Cumberbund? Cuff links?"

"Awaiting your arrival—which if you could make as rapidly as possible would be much appreciated."

M wasn't happy, but he could tell when he was fairly beaten. Andre gave him an address, and M smoked a joint and took a taxi on over.

The last time M had seen him, Andre had been living in a penthouse apartment on the Upper East Side that Andre had described with practiced indifference as "cozy"—but that was before the Fall, or was it the Crash?—and now he was living in a large but decrepit efficiency above an Italian restaurant in Nolita. He opened the door by saying that he was just "watching it while Bill is in Hong Kong." M wondered if Bill was aware of this fact.

Andre was not quite dressed, which was usually the case. He was as punctual as a very attractive woman. His apartment was full of things that were not furniture: crates of art and East Asian heirlooms, boxes of boutique vodka, a rack of fur coats, ermine and arctic fox and direwolf, the remnants and seeds of rooks, cons, and get-rich schemes. There was an IKEA sofa and a plasma-screen television. On a bar in the kitchen were three empty pizza boxes and an antique gold mirror with a few lines of coke laid out.

"Have a bump if you like," Andre said, "but do not look inside or you will see the face of your heart's true love." Andre reappeared from the bedroom. "You do not want to see the face of your heart's true love, do you?"

"No."

"No, of course not. Why ruin the surprise."

Andre had laid M's suit out on the bed. Looking at himself in the mirror afterward (not the magic mirror, a regular mirror) he wasn't certain that he was pulling it off, but Andre was complimentary and also rather rushed, and so there was little time for self-doubt, which, anyway, had disappeared with the rest of Andre's cocaine.

Andre paid for the taxi, which was only right, proper, and fair. M spent most of the way over talking about Gram Parsons in overheated fashion, the blow proving the ideal conduit between brain and mouth. Somehow Andre had never heard of the man, which was a situation that M felt begged to be rectified.

When they got out they were high up on the West Side, and M was starting to think maybe this whole thing wouldn't turn out to be a disaster after all. That was the worst thing about cocaine: It was not the aftertaste or the cost or its long-term health effects; it was that it made an optimist out of a thinking man.

The building was steel and mirrored glass, and it extended up to the top of the world. Andre said a few words to the two men guarding the entrance, who were square-shouldered and square-jawed and velvet-glove polite, and then they were through the double doors and into the elevator, a vast, square, iron thing with a meter in the transom. It ran, M noticed after a moment with curiosity though not shock, from –1 to 300. Amid the slate of buttons Andre found, then pushed, the one that read PH. The box lurched upward. The seconds ticked by, and then the minutes with them. Andre was cheery and composed, checking his hair in the polished sheen of the doors.

M was still talking about Gram Parsons: ". . . but then they didn't do a decent job of building the fire, so he just kind of charred a little bit, until his friends realized it wasn't going to happen, and then they left him there."

"That is quite a story," Andre said, settling back the single twist of hair that had come askew.

"Ain't it though?"

"By the by, M, there is one aspect of tonight's evening that occurs to me I have not yet had occasion to mention."

"Is it closed bar? Because I swear to God, Andre, if you made me put on this suit and come up here to pay twenty dollars for a gin and tonic—"

"The bar is open, of course—give me a little credit. No, the point I've thus far neglected is the possibility that there will be a man in attendance tonight who wants to see me dead."

"You mean it's possible that he'll be here, or it's possible that he wants to see you dead?"

"It is possible that he'll be here. It is certain that he wants to see me dead."

The hand on the altimeter had gone as right as it could go.

"Who is this man, apart from having good taste in enemies?"

"Alatar of the Upper West Side."

The doors opened. Waves of merriment rolled off the waiting party.

"Fuck me," M said.

"Quite possibly. The women at these things tend to drink heavily."

They entered a spherical chamber slightly smaller than St. Peter's, composed of white marble and lovingly accented indigo. In the back of the room was a large stage that no one was looking at. In the center of the room was a vast ebony bar, and this was getting far more attention.

"You know that guy hates me," M said.

"Does he?"

"For, like, decades."

"Excellent!" Andre said, walking them toward the bar. "Then there should be no need to play soft with him."

Curved tables running against the exterior wall held the merchandise that had been prepared for the silent auction, mint editions of *Action Comics* No. 1 and the last remaining copy of Nick Drake's undiscovered LP and the gun used to kill Franz Ferdinand and also the bullets used to kill him and also (though where would you put it?) the body of Franz Ferdinand. M caught a glimpse of something that might have been the head of John the Baptist, but he was not in a position to make sure, because before he could take a longer look, Andre grabbed him by the arm and hustled him off to the bar. As a rule, M disliked being manhandled, particularly as it was becoming clear that the reason he had been asked to this little soiree was to act as muscle in case things got rough. But he realized he could use a gimlet, and so he didn't protest.

The bartender was a handsome, silent Latino man who looked at M but didn't say anything. M ordered his drink and watched Andre watch the crowd nervously.

"You ever notice that you only call me when you need something?" M asked.

"You don't call me at all!" Andre said cheerily, handing M a glass.

"That's because you're the sort of person who only calls people when they need things."

"Bottoms up!"

They soon were.

"What did you do to piss him off?" M asked.

"Nothing. It is—how you say—a misunderstanding."

"That's how you say it. What does he think you did?"

"He thinks I slept with his girlfriend."

The crowd was the usual mix of people at this sort of thing—rich men and beautiful women. Onstage was a short, dark, sad-looking fellow. His microphone didn't seem to be working, and most of what he said was lost to the static. "*Kinshassa . . . blood diamonds . . .*"

"Why would Alatar think that?" M asked.

"Who can say why anyone thinks anything?" Andre said, saddened, even wounded by the errancy of mankind.

"But he might not be here?"

"*Hundreds of thousands of children a year . . .*"

"Who can be certain of anything in an uncertain world? Though on the other hand, he is throwing the thing, so his absence would be a rather severe breach of etiquette."

"What would possibly possess you to go to the party of a man trying to kill you?"

"Image is everything, M," Andre said, scowling and stretching his hand out toward his friends and acquaintances. "These people are hyenas, quick to spot weakness and take advantage of it. Can't have them thinking I'm afraid of a man like Alatar."

"But you are afraid of him—that's why you brought me along."

"Of course, but they don't know that."

The chubby African man finished his speech and walked offstage. At least he walked offstage.

"What is it with you superwealthy? You can't just rent out a ballroom and get drunk like everyone else, have to pretend there's some sort of moral purpose behind it, slap a few pictures of starving children on the walls? A party isn't a party unless it's got a garnish of human misery?"

"It's called noblesse oblige. Perhaps you've heard of it? A bit of giving back."

"A very tiny bit," M said. "An almost embarrassingly tiny bit. How much of the take do you think will make it to its destination, after you subtract for overhead?"

"I'm not entirely sure that these people are being paid," Andre observed of the waitstaff, beautiful men and women, dressed in stark black tuxedos, none speaking or making eye contact.

"I hope the irony is not lost on you."

Andre signaled for another drink. "Not entirely."

M wanted a cigarette, and of course he couldn't smoke inside, and so they made their way out onto the balcony. Stars twinkled above them, and the city did the same below.

"So, five years," Andre began.

"Something like it."

"The last time we saw each other, then, would have been at Talbot's Lammas party?"

"Sounds about right."

"I am sorry about that."

"Don't let your guilt overwhelm you," M said. "At least not while we're staring over the ledge."

"Did the burn scars fade?"

"Eventually."

"I'm happy to hear it!" Andre said. "And what have you been doing then, lo this half decade?"

"Wandering."

"I would think you'd have about wandered yourself out of places to wander, long as you've been doing it."

Which was the sort of thing that people who stayed in one place often think, though any traveler knows that seeing the world (and the worlds beyond) is a full-time job, because you can't see everything, and even if you could, by the time you got to the last place, the first place would have changed so much that you couldn't really say you'd seen it anymore. And also, what else is there to do?

"And what have you been up to?" M asked.

"Running in place."

"Sounds productive."

"Nice view at least," Andre said, putting his back against the railing and gesturing toward the party.

"I'm not sure I'd agree."

"Nothing to recommend it whatsoever?"

"The booze is free, I suppose," M said. "Speaking of which." He wiggled his glass, which was indeed empty or near so, then left Andre on the patio and went to fill it.

The new bartender was the same as the old except Asian, gorgeous, and ineffably quiet. The pockets of his tuxedo had been sewn shut, and his vest was buttonless.

"Thanks," M said, and handed out a dollar that the man ignored.

"Silent type, huh? Committed to your job? I can understand. Can you do me a favor and bring me a shot glass full of salt?"

Indeed the man could not do anything but, shuffling languid-eyed over to the other end of the bar and coming back with M's order. M took the glass, nodded thanks, and followed one of the other servers—an ebony goddess, long-limbed and mute—into the kitchens.

You will find servants' quarters rarely keep pace with the elegance of their masters'. The kitchen looked like any other kitchen you could find— fires beneath saucepans, sharp knives chopping, servers whirring about swiftly. However, it did not sound like any other kitchen you could find, the usual chatter replaced with silence, broken only by the scuff of shoes and the occasional rattle of silverware.

Another difference between this kitchen and other kitchens was that no one seemed to pay any attention to M walking around inside it, the waiters and the line cooks utterly engrossed in their respective tasks. There was no break room, but there was a sort of alcove with a tower of plastic cups standing next to a glass ewer. M took the top off and dropped the shot glass inside. No one noticed, or at least M did not notice anyone noticing. They were not the most fiercely observant group, the waitstaff.

M went back into the main room and drank his drink and sniffed around at the prizes for the silent auction and wondered if he should bother to try to steal one. That there was no visible security suggested he ought not, probably they were cursed, and touching them would rot off his hand or some such. On the other hand, M really wanted that Nick Drake LP.

After a while of weighing pro against con he remembered Andre, and his sort of nominal purpose in having been there, and he went back out on the balcony. But Andre had vacated the premises, left behind nothing but a half-empty glass on the balcony and a cigarette end stuffed into a planter. A further moment of observation and M noticed the security latch on the fire escape nearest to the balcony had been dismantled. He sighed, opened the door, and went to save the life of his sort-of, sometime friend.

The emergency exit led to a blank white corridor, faceless and institutional in comparison with the main room itself, and at the other end of it M could see Andre looking somewhat frightened. Standing in front of Andre, and presumably the reason for his concern, was Alatar of the Upper West Side. Of course M couldn't see his face, but he could see his back, which was covered in a long dark robe, and his hands, which were gripped around a shaft of elm with a crystal sphere atop it, and there were not so many people who dressed like that, not even among the sort of people M knew.

"You've got some nerve, sneaking into my party."

"Please, Alatar," Andre was saying, looking vaguely wounded, "I had an invitation. I even had a plus one!"

"That was before I knew of your betrayal!"

"There is a perfectly reasonable explanation, if you'd but allow me to get a word in edgewise . . ."

"No one steals from me and gets away with it!"

Andre grunted understanding after a long moment. "Yes, the bid on that tech company . . ."

"What did you think this was about?"

"Nothing, it doesn't matter," Andre said, just as cool as ice water having now caught a view of M. "In any case, it couldn't possibly have been more than a few hundred thousand dollars. Hardly worth bloodshed. I'm sure we can figure this out."

"It's not a question of the quarter million," Alatar said. "As a point of pride, I don't leave a thief alive to steal twice. As much a public service as anything else."

M decided at this point to make a clucking sound in the back of his throat, and Alatar turned swiftly to face him. He had a nose like a beak and eyes like glacial ice. His skin hung down in folds from his forehead and the nape of his neck. He had a ring on his index finger like the carapace of a beetle. He was, in short, a walking, talking genre cliché, though this did not make him any less dangerous.

"You," Alatar growled.

"I am me," M admitted, though it was unclear how he felt about it.

"I didn't know you were back."

"The sole blemish of ignorance on your sterling facade of wisdom."

"What?"

"Hmm?"

Alatar scowled harder. He had a face made for scowling, like a bush is made to flower or a knife to carve flesh. "You with him?"

"More like he's with me."

"You ought to choose your companions more wisely."

"I'll take that into consideration," M said.

"No doubt," Andre said.

"Did you know this fucking Gaul chiseled me out of a quarter million dollars?"

"I think it the twenty-first century's foremost tragedy," M said, "that your bank account is not quite so large as it once was. Truly a source of deep melancholy, though I'm succored by the certainty that it will swiftly regain its balance."

"I'm afraid I can't be so sanguine about the matter."

"It's a duel you're after? Fine, but as the challenged party I get my pick of weapons, field, and time. And I choose chopsticks, Xi'an Famous Foods, 4:00 a.m. yesterday. First one to drop a flat noodle loses their soul. Your man can call on mine."

"You aren't nearly as funny as you think you are."

"Come off it, Alatar, you know as well as I do that we're not going to have a pissing contest here in the middle of the hallway. This is Manhattan, in case you haven't noticed, and Celise doesn't like it when her pawns play without her."

"Don't presume too far on the White Queen's affections," Alatar said. "She's done without you for the past five years. I don't think she'll be beating through the bushes were you to disappear another time. And I'm not such a minor piece these days myself."

"A pale duke? A cream baron? An eggshell marquis?"

"I'm bigger than you are, anyway," Alatar said. His eyes were furiously stygian, flecked here and there with gold. There was a commotion coming from the main room, but he hadn't yet noticed it.

"That's possible. What are you willing to wager to find out?"

"I could ask you the same question—you actually like this one enough to throw down over him?"

"I've been wondering that all night, actually. Still haven't come to any conclusions, though in the event I think it's probably a moot point."

"I'm afraid I would have to disagree," Alatar said, crooked nails clicking against his staff. "I've allowed this frog to go on sharing my air for longer than I ought. For that matter I'm coming to feel the same way about you."

M cocked his head. "Hear that?"

And indeed Alatar did hear that, that being several hundred of the city's finest, or at least wealthiest, citizens, engaging in collective and full-throated shrieks of terror. It was unsubtle. It was the kind of thing you would have trouble missing.

"That's the sound of your waitstaff eating your guests," M said. "If I were you, I would get in there before the mayor finds his face gnawed off. Or I suppose you can stick around and we can have that fight you seemed so excited about."

But Alatar was already gone, back into the main room as fast as his steps could carry him. M noted that he did not use his staff.

"Thanks," Andre said.

"I'm keeping the suit," M said, following after Alatar.

Andre held the door open for him. "Seems only fair."

Back inside, the zombies had switched from *The Serpent and the Rainbow* to *Dawn of the Dead*, made furious by their necromantic servitude and looking to wreak bloody vengeance before falling fully into the grave. Of course, living or undead, human teeth aren't really made for, say, gnawing a hand off an arm, and the zombies seemed not to remember how to use weapons—but still it was a frightening period for the partygoers, most of whom were a good way to inebriated, none of whom had been expecting the evening would end with a mass melee against the undead. A man in a tuxedo barricaded himself behind an overturned table and was thrusting away at a gorgeous ginger woman with his umbrella. Two frat-boy finance types were trying to impale their ex-bartender with a wooden leg from one of the tables, apparently confused with the category of monster they were facing. Amidst the madness those waiters and servants who had not yet drank saline continued to go about their business, offering trays of grilled oysters and wagyu beef sliders to a group of partygoers now less interested in filling their stomachs than in avoiding filling something else's.

"It's a zombie rebellion!" Andre observed.

"Better than a zombie jamboree," M said, unable to resist the temptation. He lit a cigarette, which was technically speaking against the rules, but then again not so much against the rules as, for instance, cannibalism.

"What exactly did you do?"

"There are downsides to anchoring the flicker of a dead man's spirit to the flesh he previously inhabited," M said, "beyond the moral, I mean. It's an unnatural association, easily broken if you can put a bit of sodium into their drinks."

"Zombies don't drink!"

"That's a common misconception," M said, slipping aside to allow an aging blonde with fake tits and a floppy feathered hat to sprint screaming through the exit, and for her pursuer, by chance the same zombie who had been serving them drinks all evening, to follow her out. "But in fact zombies need to eat and drink, just like people. The only thing that separates zombies from people is that they can't eat salt. And that they're dead, of course."

"Salt?"

"Yeah. Shatters the bond. Drives them . . ." M made an encompassing motion with his hand at the violence in front of them.

"Crazy?"

"Actually this seems an altogether rational reaction to their situation. If I were them, I'd want to chew off someone's shoulder too."

Those members of the party who were in good with the Management were cashing chits left and right, blasts of light streaming across the air, curses and hexes whirring past each other. Alatar had taken up a position on the stage and was, so far as M could tell, engaging in a ritual to summon some sort of monster or spirit to deal with the consequences of his necromancy, a circular process that M found awfully shortsighted.

They fumbled their way toward an exit as the chaos turned to carnage. The zombies, of course, were unable to recognize M as the agent of their deliverance, but there was a lot of flesh to chase after, and Andre and M were not men entirely bereft of resources, and they managed their retreat without difficulty.

"This is why no one invites you anywhere," Andre said.

"People don't invite me places?"

"Never. Not anywhere."

M shrugged, grabbing the Nick Drake LP from where it sat forgotten on the prize table. "Try to remember that next time you think about asking me for help."

8

—

The Red Queen

M came out of a coffee shop with fifty cents that he had been meaning to give to the barista before she had rubbed him the wrong way, and so instead he dropped them in the cup of the homeless man leaning against the wall outside.

"Abilene would like to see you," said the vagrant.

"See if I give you anything again," M said, even though he knew it wasn't really the man's fault. "Well, where is she?"

"Who?" the homeless man asked, looking up confusedly.

M cursed a while and walked home. Two youths sat smoking a joint on his stoop, neighborhood kids he didn't know. Neither of them were tenants, but M's apartment building had the nicest stoop on the block, and so there were often people taking advantage of it. The younger looked up at M as he was getting his keys out. "She's having a party in Bushwick tonight," he said, rattling off an address. "You should drop by."

"Who the hell you know in Bushwick?" the older one asked.

"No one," the younger one asked, turning to face his brother, for only brothers are capable of such easy dislike. "Why the fuck you asking?"

In so far as Abilene was an unquestioned force for good in the world, at least in the most concrete give-food-to-the-hungry–shelter-to-the-sick–succor-to-the-weary kind of way, M could not bring himself to dislike her. But he could not really say he liked her either, or at least he never wanted to be around her, which is an awfully close cousin.

She'll probably try to foist a stray on me, M thought sadly. He began to wonder idly about how he might spend the evening if he did not go to the party, looked up movie times and checked if there were any concerts to attend, knowing as he did it that it was pointless; his evening was booked solid. And indeed, around 7:30 that evening, he put on a fresh shirt, bought a bottle of wine from a nearby liquor store, and started walking northeast.

Her block was run-down and less than lovely, but here and there you could see signs of resurgence: flowers crawling through the concrete, a health-food co-op on the corner. That was the way it was with Abilene. Her very presence was nourishment to the beclouded metropolis. The address M had been given led to a three-story brownstone, one of those architectural gems that dot the outer boroughs and can be found in even the most miserable and dilapidated areas. The door opened shortly after he pushed the buzzer. M wasn't sure if Abilene knew it was him by some extrasensory means or just didn't mind letting strangers into her party. Both, probably.

The stairwell was old and wooden and pretty and seemed to take forever to ascend, only partially because M did not want to be ascending it. M stood outside the door for a moment, with a bottle of cheap red and an RNC elephant tattooed below his wrist. After a moment's knock, the door opened, and a half goddess in an ugly dress opened it.

You wouldn't have made much of her, probably. Short, dowdy, muddy skin of indeterminate racial origin, frizzy hair, no makeup, fat thighs, and a pair of deep brown eyes that suggested a weight of lead or the dark infinity between the universes or the womb. Maybe you would have made something of her after all. She was smiling and held a calico kitten the size of a stick of butter. "My Mags just dropped yesterday! Here, hold her."

The kitten's eyes were large as silver dollars and plaintive as a redheaded orphan. M made sure not to look directly into them so as to avoid being hypnotized. "I'm really not in the position to foster a kitten right now, Abilene."

Abilene laughed and set the mewling little sack of flesh back on the floor. "A pet would do you wonders, M," she said. "Your problem is that you don't know what's good for you."

M thought he knew what was good for him just fine, considered himself something of an authority on the subject, and felt that undignified burr of pride that any professional experiences when their expertise is questioned. But it was Abilene's house party, and also she could break him in half with a wink of her crow's-footed eyes, and so M just handed Abilene the bottle of wine and let himself be ushered inside.

Abilene's place looked like it always did, whenever and wherever M had visited her, going back however many decades. Lots of growing things, flowers and vegetables and herbs, some of which could be purchased at a garden store, and some that could not—the rows of mandrake behind the couch, for instance, and the many-headed carnivorous plant that hung from the window and rustled though there was no breeze. The furniture was well-worn and comfortable, and there were tapestries on the walls and all sorts of not-exactly-attractive bits of artwork: Javanese puppets and South American soapstone and African sculptures that were either shamefully phallic or overwhelmingly vaginal. Some of these likely served as fetishes, but M suspected the better part were just crap that Abilene had collected. Power is no guarantee of taste.

Eight or nine people were milling about, and M did his best to give each a general impression of friendliness without having to actually converse with any one of them. They were peas in an organic pod, all afire for some personal passion and certain that his heart was dry kindling. M wanted to try to explain to them that his soul was damp wood, and they'd be better off trying to find someone in the treated briquette range, but they rarely seemed to hear him.

An hour disappeared, along with several bottles of wine and about a quarter ounce of hash. Then one of Abilene's associates, a slim Latina girl who looked like a lot of other slim Latina girls Abilene had collected over the years, announced dinner at the long wooden table in the other room.

You couldn't say that the meal was bad, exactly—it just wasn't really anything. Every ingredient seemed to have been substituted for something better, for you or for the environment or for the general spiritual health of the world—coconut oil margarine for butter and almond milk instead of heavy cream and bean curd instead of red meat. Seated to his right was Erin, early thirties, an editor for a young-adult imprint, bad tattoos and kind eyes. On his left was Ariel, who worked at three or maybe four different nonprofits, but what she really wanted to do was find some way to meld her love for interpretive dance with her passion for the rights of indigenous peoples. Had he met either one of them in a bar he might even have enjoyed the conversation, but their meet-cute being so obviously the product of Abilene's machinations, M found himself feeling distinctly monastic.

For a while it looked like they might have to play a board game, which would have been too much for M, regardless of his respect for or fear of Abilene, but Erin had to get back home to feed her cats and Ariel had an early morning meeting, and everyone else sort of faded into the background.

"That Ariel," Abilene said, when it was just the two of them. "Isn't she just the cleverest thing you've ever seen?"

"I think I'd rather take the kitten," M said, waving his hands quickly to indicate that this was a joke.

Abilene obliged him with a long, rich laugh. The joint she rolled didn't have a filter, and the tip was lip-wet when she handed it to him.

Of course, he smoked it anyway, and he waited quietly until Abilene felt like starting.

Because of course the other thing was that Abilene was a heavy hitter, a broom-riding witch from the old school, power settled into her like well-polished hardwood. It wasn't like there were official rankings, but you can spot the sun even through shades, and if Abilene wasn't quite the sun, you were still better off not looking directly at her for too long.

"So you're back," she said finally.

"I seem to be."

"And have you been to see *her* already?"

"You know I have."

"How could I know that? Do you think I pay any attention to what that . . . that . . . painted old hag says, does, or thinks?"

"Well, I didn't bring her up, now did I, Abilene?"

Abilene gave him a look that slightly shook the foundations of her home. "At times I forget why I like you."

"I'm clever!" M was quick to remind her. "You think it's cute."

"Not always," Abilene said, narrowing her eyes through the smoke.

For once in his life M recognized silence as the better portion of wisdom.

He drank the rest of his chamomile tea but steadfastly avoided looking into it. This close to the yippie goddess of east Brooklyn, the leaves were sure to reveal some hint to his future, and he preferred that every day be a fresh one.

"So what are you planning on doing, now that you're back in the city?" Abilene asked. She appeared pacified, but then people had said the same of Vesuvius.

M shrugged. He was pretty much already doing it, it being very little, as little as he could get away with. Running into old friends and trying to avoid getting into trouble he could not easily get himself out of. Inspecting the practically infinite corners of the city, seeing what had cropped up in his long absence. Drinking a lot. Checking out new restaurants. Trying to get laid. "The usual."

Abilene gave the sort of smile that prefaces advice. It was mostly the only smile that Abilene offered, and it was not one of M's favorites. "Aren't you getting a little old for that?"

"You're only as old as you feel."

"Don't you suppose it's time that you assumed the responsibilities appropriate to a man of your stature?"

"I already told you: I don't want a kitten."

"I'm not talking about little . . . Garcia? What do you think of that as a name?"

"It's a bit on the nose."

"I'm talking about your obligations to the community at large."

M did not like communities, which were usually filled with people, whom M liked even less. "Flattering, Abilene, but you overrate me. I'm barely more than an apprentice. Just bumbling about, not getting into anyone's way."

"Perhaps you're foolish enough to believe that. You know that I'm not. If you stuck around long enough to put down roots, you'd be elite soon enough."

M thought that this was a lot like saying if a bird decided to swim it would be a fish. "You're too kind."

"Of course, the thing about the major players is that they tend to tilt the balance."

"I almost feel like this is leading to something."

"Have you seen what she's been doing to the place? The Village is nothing but tourists! You can't find a crackhead from Five Points to the Guggenheim! And don't even get me started on north Brooklyn!" In her excitement Abilene had ashed the joint onto her rug.

"I won't. I promise."

"Don't pretend you like it. I know you're more mine than hers."

M liked to think he wasn't really anyone's, but again, one does not go disputing with the lion while resting in its den. "You know I'm on your team, Abilene. You can count on me if things ever go south. But I'm a gadfly, rowboating in a turbulent sea, and it's the most I can do not to get swamped." Some of this, chiefly the prepositions, weren't even lies.

"Won't you ever bother to live up to your potential?" Abilene asked.

"Maybe tomorrow," M said, taking what was left of the joint.

9

Love and the Modern Fae

"What are you doing after this?" Anais asked, turning from a shared glance at Ibis, which would have concerned M had he seen it.

M hadn't seen it. His attention was mostly occupied by their waitress, formed in the lovely-but-disinterested-brunette mold. "Nothing in particular."

"Feel up for an excursion? We were going to go visit that goblin market off Classon."

"I didn't know there was a goblin market off Classon."

"It's only in existence every seventeen years," Anais explained, "when the Earth Dragon mates with Cancer. I've heard they have some lovely holiday ornaments."

"Should be a good time," Ibis added, "if you've got the energy."

There is a school of thought that says that given the paucity of daylight hours in December, a man would do well to rise early and enjoy them. M did not hold with that view, but, disdainful of the sun's modest offering, chose rather as a rule to stay in bed until near evening. The point being that, so far as M's circadian rhythms were concerned, they had just finished eating brunch. "I think I can probably keep it up till midnight," he predicted boldly. "So long as you don't expect me to tap dance or anything."

Ibis was the sort of friend about whom M rarely found himself thinking. Actually all of M's friends pretty much fell into that category, though the rest tended to run into rooms demanding his assistance too often for M to forget them completely. That Ibis's life was comparably infrequently in such a state of disarray as to need saving was, M thought, largely attributable to Anais, whom Ibis had been dating for almost as long as M had known him, an amount of time the specifics of are not worth questioning. Ibis was handsome-ish and bearded and close with Abilene. Anais was sweet smiling and plump and far closer.

Stepping out into the frigid evening, the three of them were bundled in a loose ram's worth of wool, Anais and Ibis holding hands through three-inches of dyed fabric. On a temperate spring evening the walk to the goblin market would have been more than half a pleasure, but it wasn't a temperate spring evening, and the peregrination was appropriately less than joyful. "I think our friend Salome is going to come," Anais said offhandedly, her announcement half muffled by her handmade scarf.

Hearing the snick of the trap just too late, M looked around frantically for egress or escape, wondering if he would survive the ordeal or if it might prove safer to bite off his wrist in the interests of freedom. "Damn it, Ibis . . ."

"You'll like her," Ibis said after just too long of a second. "She's nice."

Which, to go by M's romantic history, was just exactly the opposite of what he liked.

"She works in fashion," Anais said.

"But she's not obsessed with it," Ibis added. "I mean, she's not a fashion person. She has other interests."

"She's very interesting."

"She does vinyasa yoga."

"It's not like the other sorts of yoga. It's different, somehow."

"It's faster."

"It's more active."

"Have we met before?" M asked, gesturing furiously, lamenting the cold and shoving his hands back into his pockets. "Are you suffering from collective amnesia?"

"Just give her a chance, M, for God's sake."

"Like you're so busy."

The goblin market was, this week, in this reality, contained within the basement of the Classon Avenue Episcopal Church just a few blocks from the G train. M remembered a time when the market's employees would not have come within a half mile of a church, even an Episcopal one, fearing the ring of church bells as they did cold iron. But it seemed in this part of the world the fae took religion no more seriously than their mortal counterparts. It was a pretty enough building, slate steeple towering over the surrounding brownstones. They passed a wrought iron gate, down a gravel path through etiolated shrubbery, stopping in front of a narrow set of stairs in the shadow of the belfry, waiting quietly for M's potential future wife.

She was twelve minutes late, which by New York standards was on time but was still twelve minutes longer than M wanted to be exposed to the frigid December elements. She hugged Anais and made an awkward attempt at kissing Ibis continental style. Anais looked at her brightly for a moment, then at M, then back at Salome.

"M."

"Salome."

"Nice to meet you."

"A distinct pleasure."

It was not going to work, M thought sadly, holding open the entrance and ushering them all downstairs. It was not that Salome was not pretty—she was quite pretty. She might have been, all things considered, a bit too pretty for M: modestly sized but voluptuous, apple-cheeked and melon-breasted, wearing an outfit that was too nice for a blind first date and altogether inappropriate for the season. M himself was sort of wishing he had known about the setup in time to have put on a fresh shirt or at least done something with his hair, though watching Salome's ass, he knew it would not make any difference. Only two people who had been together as long as Anais and Ibis, grown blind with love and contentment, couples cataracts in the corners of their eyes, would have supposed that Salome and M were people who needed to meet each other. She was not at all his sort, and he not hers.

The basement of the Classon Avenue Episcopalian Church was the size of a basement, but the goblin market taking place inside it was much larger. A packed mass of scenesters and slumming Manhattanites walked past slowly, perusing the offered wares, a mob of natives speckled with the occasional tourist, three-eyed or six-legged or otherwise inhuman. All matter of treasures were on offer, mixed up so only the most discerning or lucky

individual could determine which was which—matchless Babylonian artifacts sharing space with catchpenny handicrafts, tasteless woolen gloves, hats
and sweatshirts and sweatpants and many other articles of clothing all with
BROOKLYN written on them in block letters, just in case you needed remind-
ing of the borough's existence. It smelled of wet wool and mulling cinnamon
and wood smoke. It was warm and toasty. It was not at all the worst place a
person could be on a winter evening.

The liquor tent was a circle of wood surrounded by a square of colored
canvas, with a handful of wooden tables at the perimeters. Ibis stood at the
butt end of a line leading to an overworked bartender, four hands moving
in unison, decanting a bottle of wine with one pair and ladling punch with
the other. M grabbed some space for them at the distant end of a bench. Salome took the seat next to Anais and farthest from M, an arrangement which
boded ill for hopes of future progeny.

But Anais was a classic lost-causer, tramping forward against all odds.
"Salome's in a book club," she announced. "M isn't much of a joiner, but he's
always giving me things to read."

"Not anymore," M muttered quietly.

"I love to read," Salome admitted.

Though it was M's experience that this was the sort of thing that only
people who did not actually like to read were apt to say, and indeed when
pressed, Salome admitted that her favorite book (which M had not read) had
just been made into a movie (which M would not see), and the conversation
died unmourned.

Ibis arrived as salvation a moment later, having barely managed to carry
over their drinks. "Bottoms up."

"What is this, exactly?" Salome asked, sniffing at the steam rising from
her copper mug.

"Elixir of Cassonade," Ibis said. "Specialty of the house."

"It's like being kicked in the head by an anthropomorphic caramel
cream," M explained, his smile hidden by thick foam. "But in a good way."

"M, you've got something on your . . ."

"Thank you," M said, smearing it off.

Salome looked at the froth on M's forearm, then raised her cup gingerly.

"It's a bit creamy," she said after having a taste.

"I don't mind drinking the rest of yours, if you want something else."

"That seems clear."

Anais laughed awkwardly.

They wandered up from the table and back down the length of stalls, past an Acadian in a beaver-skin hat hawking the furs of long-extinct mammals, past an old woman selling glass beads, past a plastic table with plastic crates of plastic records, mostly Bulgarian field music and Nu Disco. Ibis spent a moment trying to persuade himself that he needed to spend eighty American dollars (or forty-seven Hanseatic Thaler) on a David Bowie 45 that had been released by an underground GDR label swiftly shut down by the Stasi but proved ultimately unsuccessful. They skirted the boutique of a Javanese puppeteer, rows of parti-colored humanoids hanging limply, hardwood faces just within the boundaries of the uncanny valley. Anais stopped at a large Dutch oven manned by a chubby hob with green skin and cherry cheeks, and bought a hot cross bun thick with sugar.

"Who wants a bite?"

Ibis obliged her, but as a rule M did not mix alcohol with desert, and Salome did not maintain her figure by indulging richly in sweets.

"I wouldn't have gotten it if I thought no one else would have any," Anais said, swallowing the last bite and licking a smudged finger.

A very tall, very black, very thin man who did not seem to be selling anything smiled brightly at M. "Feel free to give one a try," he suggested, waving at his nonexistent or at least invisible stock.

"Gorgeous," M said. "But it would never fit in my apartment."

The man smiled understandingly. Past a stall selling home-knit woolen beer cozies and antique steins, they came to a forest of larch and spruce and Siberian stone pine, thick trunks that had never known the bite of metal, boughs beneath which aurochs gamboled and rutted. A pebbled path led toward what looked like a brightly colored carriage, though it was hard to make out through the heavy snowfall.

"I've been just dying to pick up a new matryoshka." Anais took Ibis's hand, pulling him swiftly into the copse.

"That Anais," M remarked.

"She's certainly very . . ." Salome agreed.

Nothing else to do but continue past the fragment of an extinct arboretum and on to the next stand, the severed back half of a '73 bright magenta Caddy, an elf with a pompadour and a black leather coat presiding. The trunk was open to reveal stacks of browned newsprint, faded fashion periodicals, and outdated pamphlets, thick tomes with yellowed pages bound in skin that was not bovine. M flipped through a copy of *Life* magazine with a cover of JFK and his happy family on the day of their fourth inauguration. "The woman of 1972 prefers a rose tint to her spacesuit," he informed Salome.

"How interesting," Salome said, staring away disinterestedly.

M handed the magazine back to the proprietor regretfully.

"Where do you live?"

"Crown Heights."

"I don't get out there much."

"Where do you live?"

"The Upper West Side. Near the Museum of Natural History."

M did the subway math, came away with a commute long enough to make him happy that he and Salome had not hit it off with mad abandon. "That's a nice area."

"I like it," Salome said.

Anais and Ibis came back then, finally, and M could not help but note that, however much she had wanted a new matryoshka, she was not carrying one. Before he could comment on the lack, they were interrupted by six scuttling crab legs striking against stone, each the size of M's forearm, a living or at least ambulatory platform for a wooden pony keg that had been cinched into its flesh by a line of leather straps. A leash was attached to the thing's midpoint, where carapace met oak, and at the other end of it was a friendly-looking troll. "Fresh butter ale?" he asked.

"Absolutely," M said. The proprietor filled and distributed four shots into four hollowed-out, oversize, uncapped acorns. It tasted of strong cinnamon and spring.

"You know Celise and M are old friends," Anais announced.

"Really?" Salome asked, suddenly interested.

For a number of reasons M would have preferred this information, which he would have argued was essentially erroneous, to never have become public knowledge.

"Oh, yes," Anais agreed, smiling through M's evident discomfort. "Don't be fooled by M's excessive humbleness—he walks in the very highest circles of society, a figure beloved on both sides of the river."

"Tolerated, at best," M corrected.

"She never mentions you," Salome observed.

Which was just exactly what M wanted to hear. "There's that guy with the crab-keg again! You got anything bigger than that acorn?"

But the man did not, and so M had to settle for two of them. Salome did not seem enthused by M's enthusiasm, but at this point, M figured their union was a lost cause anyway. Barring some extraordinary change of circumstance, like, for instance, saving Salome from a roving gang of rapists, M did not think their first date would lead to a second. For his own part, M was having some trouble feeling his legs, which to M's mind was the zenith and limit of any good state of drunkenness.

They continued on through the market a while longer. Eventually Ibis and Salome split off to gather the next round, and Anais took M's arm warmly, nestling herself into the comfortable crook of his shoulder.

"I know that Salome isn't *exactly* the sort you go for—but I think if you gave her a shot you might grow to like her. She's got lots of good qualities,"

"I bet she's got an impressive collection of shoes."

"She does have an impressive selection of shoes," Anais said, "and you are a big prick."

"And what sort of friend would that make you, trying to set Salome up with me?"

Anais stopped at a modest flower cart, neat plantings in wooden bowls, bright white *simbelmynë*, bitter green *raskovniks*, a slender cutting of *yggrdrasil*. The vendor had a wide smile and muttonchops not dissimilar to the tops of the bonsai bushes that he was selling. Anais rested her hand for a moment on a mood tulip, satiny flesh flaring brightly in hot pink and happy white.

"How do you all know each other, again?" M drew the attention of a snapdragon and shifted back as one mouth tendril shot forward impotently.

Anais's flower had wilted gray. "Ibis met her at some party in Manhattan."

"And why did the two of you think the two of us would get along?"

"Couples love to create other couples." Anais's tulip looked like a storm gathering on the horizon, clashing blends of midnight and stark yellow.

"Shall I wrap it up for the madame?" the owner asked.

"No," Anais said. "Thank you."

Back in the thoroughfare, M took her arm again quickly, smiling like a lure, pulling her back into the general direction of happiness.

"You're such a good guy, M," Anais said. "You deserve to be with some-one who makes you happy."

"That's a lot of responsibility to put on Salome's slender shoulders."

"Not really. It's no more than I've taken on with Ibis, or Ibis with me."

"You're a lot stronger than I am, though."

"I'm not sure that's true. The thought of being single seems so utterly exhausting."

"Happy for both of us, then, that we've found ourselves in the conditions best suited to our inclinations."

The next stall had mirrors of all kinds: cheval glass and compacts and thin baking sheets filled with mercury, beaten lengths of shiny metal, little pools of unnaturally still water offering the full cruelty of reflection. Anais spent a while staring into one of those common sorts of artifacts that improved the viewer's form the longer they looked. "Don't you get tired of it after a while? All those nights waiting round for someone to text who you know will never text, and going out to bars that you don't want to go to, and drinking over-priced drinks? The endless tumult? The chaos and the uncertainty?"

"That's life you're describing. And yes, I do get tired of it, but the alterna-tive seems rather extreme."

"I just don't know what I would do without Ibis," Anais said, very much like she meant it.

The Anais in the mirror had hair that was just a shade more vibrant than her prototype had ever enjoyed. Her hips were narrower, her bust was wider and her smile bent sultry. "He makes me happy. Every day I wake up next to him I feel lucky. I know that whatever else happens, I can rely on him. We're a team, you know?"

"Sure," M said, turning away. "Of course." The collage of quicksilver distorted his slight frown, magnified and echoed it till it seemed to reflect back against him from every vantage point. Anais continued on a while longer, further paeans to the glories of monogamy. M remained unconvinced, but then again, M was not the target, and walking out she seemed happier than she had walking in.

"You get older, M, you start to like the idea of having someone around waiting for you."

"But I'm a lot older than you are, and I don't feel that way at all."

Ibis and Salome returned then, each carrying two fists of booze.

"And how are we doing here?"

"Lovely," Anais said brightly. "Everything all right?"

"Perfectly fine," Ibis answered, smiling broadly and handing his girlfriend her drink.

The next tent sold band posters from this and other realities, and while perusing the stock, Salome and M discovered they both loathed Jefferson Airplane. As a bonding agent, shared enthusiasm has nothing on mutual antipathy, and from such small seeds have mighty oaks grown. Further conversation revealed that Salome had been to Belarus once, which M thought was pretty interesting, M being who he was. He would not have expected it of Salome, and he was happily surprised as well to find that she not only knew every member of the Kinks, but could name them, and though neither saw any particular reason to purchase the black velvet painting that depicted them and had inspired this line of discussion, still it proved more kindling for the fire. In fact, with his blood now something like one and a half percent alcohol, M could admit that perhaps he had been too quick to judge Salome. In her favor remained the happy jiggle of her jiggly parts, as well as the new-found knowledge that he had been too quick to assume that said voluptuousness corresponded to a dullness of wit. This was another reason that M had trouble agreeing with Anais—because people, who were terrible and selfish and banal and just, I mean just horrible, just absolutely, you get the idea, were somehow also fascinating and occasionally quite lovely and, broadly speaking, worth meeting. M had simply never quite managed to figure the math by which one person was better than many people.

Though neither Ibis nor Anais seemed to be having any trouble sorting it out, occupied at a nearby prize booth, ensconced in their own love. She tittered and blushed. He mugged broadly. On his third try, Ibis managed to sneak a ball through a net, and Anais laughed and clapped her hands and rewarded her knight with a firm kiss, as was just, right, and proper. As spoils he received a sad-looking teddy bear, and when he passed it back to Anais, she blew up with joy like a tick with blood. They were the very picture of monogamous bliss. They were the sort of happy that might have made M, long accustomed to solitude, wonder if perhaps he was using his time to its absolute best effect.

"How long have you been sleeping with Salome?" M asked Ibis a few minutes later, before Salome and Anais had returned from the bathroom, but after they had purchased and mostly consumed a tray of yucca-fried chicken slices.

Ibis coughed up some hot honey sauce. "I'm not sleeping with Salome."

"I guess you'd best just find me a spot in bedlam, then, because I'm apparently going mad."

"If I was sleeping with Salome, why would I have invited you to go on a double date together?"

"You didn't, Anais did, and you couldn't think of a way to get out of it."

"And why would Salome agree?"

"To torment you, obviously. The same reason she's wearing that dress in this weather."

"She has a marvelous ass," Ibis agreed, rather sadly.

"You really aren't good enough for her."

"Who?"

"Both, but I meant Anais."

"No," Ibis agreed, "but she doesn't realize it."

"She really loves you, you know."

"I love her!" Ibis observed, indignant. "That's nothing to do with it."

"No, I suppose not."

"I just get . . . tense, you know? Anais is great and everything, but Salome is, Salome is—"

"Oh, I understand. It's not complicated. You'd prefer to have sex with more than one woman. There's no great mystery to it."

"No."

"I don't like you as much as I sometimes think."

"You know you can't say anything," Ibis added. "That's bro code."

"I was never signatory to that pact," M said. But he kept quiet after Salome and Anais had returned, offered them the rest of the food, which Anais munched happily.

"M just came back from traveling," Ibis said, though by this point it was clear his heart wasn't really in playing matchmaker.

"Really? Where?"

"All around. I was in Paris a little while."

"Did you ever go to that bar by Père Lachaise that serves housemade rum?"

"With the duck charcuterie?"

"Yes, and that voice in the bathroom that they say is the ghost of Jim Morrison."

"I don't think it is."

"No, me neither."

M laughed. Anais smiled broadly. Ibis drank the rest of his drink. They headed back out into the market.

The next booth was not a booth at all, only a space between them, and in the center of that space was a banked fire and two chairs. On one of the chairs sat a wizened old woman wearing a mottled assemblage of rags. On the other chair sat no one, and then M.

"You again," the woman said. Her accent was thickly Slavic—borscht and Basil the Bulgar-Slayer. "Didn't you learn your lesson the last time?"

"I'm too old to learn lessons."

"Suit yourself. Standard stakes?"

"I'm low on dragon scale this month. What would you put up against a child's first memory of snow?"

The old woman sucked at her few remaining teeth, yellowed calcite jutting arbitrarily through pinked gum. "Depends on how fresh."

"Daisy fresh."

"I could make you conversational in ancient Babylonian."

"Could I read it?"

The crone shrugged.

"So I could, like, order a meal in ancient Babylonian?"

"Something like."

"How often do you suppose that would come in handy?'

"Hmm."

"The recollection against the language, and I get to break."

"You're the visitor," the old woman agreed.

M spat on his hand. The old woman did the same. They shook over the graying embers of the fire.

"Thomas Edison," M began.

"Nikolai Tesla," the woman responded flatly.

"Karađorđe Petrović."

"Tito."

"Stalin."

"Ivan the Terrible."

"Catherine the Great."

"Jenna Jameson."

"Shit!" M said, then scowled unhappily and paid her.

"Any time you want a rematch," the woman said.

"You're cheating," M said, which was true but he knew he couldn't prove.

Salome looked on, half impressed, which was more than half the reason M had done it. "That wasn't bad."

"No, no," M said with perhaps a touch too much self-deprecation. "I never should have gotten involved in the Balkans."

"I suppose if she lost very often, she wouldn't be making a living at it."

M's reserves of false modesty depleted, he put two fingers on Salome's arm and pulled her slightly closer. "I suppose not."

It was getting late. The river of patrons had trickled to a stream. The vendors were starting to pack away their gear, cognizant of the remaining few hours before dawn. The greasepaint was beginning to run, the dream stuff to clot over. In a few hours it would be sawdust and taffy, and anyone foolish enough to wait round to see it might well discover that elves are not to be trusted, that their smiles hide sharp teeth. Also, Anais was tired and making no effort to hide it, yawning heavily, Ibis attending to her. A peculiarity of the goblin market meant that however long you walked you were never very far from where you came in, and by mutual agreement they headed back toward the exit.

Outside the wind had picked up, going from harsh to torturous. A cab was passing by, and with an instinct for gallantry that he rarely observed, M flagged it down and offered it to Anais and Ibis.

Anais hugged M tightly before she left and pulled him down to whisper something into his ear that was kind and reassuring and fundamentally misguided. Ibis shook his hand vigorously and stared too long into his eyes. "I'll text you tomorrow," he said, holding the door open for Anais and sending him strong psychic signals as to how he ought to best spend the remainder of the evening.

"No rush," M answered. The taxi sped its way back northeast, toward Park Slope and bourgeoisie normality.

"Well," Salome said, turning back to M before the car was out of sight.

"Yes," M said.

"This has been lovely."

"Entirely."

"Tired?"

"Not a bit of it."

"There's a bar nearby."

"There usually is."

Though in the event they gave it a pass and went straight on to M's.

10

Friends New and Old

It was about the size of one of those rubber balls that spoiled children get
from toy machines at the front of supermarkets, a reward for not shrieking
while Mommy is shopping, or at least not shrieking very much. It was the
color of a cherry-flavored fruit roll-up. It was the color of blood. Inside of it
a string of lights tumbled and swirled.

"I don't think I can swallow this," M said.

"You don't really need to swallow it," Talbot said. Talbot was wearing
tattoo-tight pants and a sleeveless T-shirt. His hair was mussed. M had
known him since the mid-'60s, when, for a while, he had been the only person on the East Coast who had a direct line to Owsley's top-secret, possibly
government-funded LSD laboratory somewhere outside of San Francisco.
And if that connection had dried up at some point over the last fifty years,
he could still usually be relied upon to provide narcotics at semi-reasonable
prices. M had always felt this to be a solid basis for friendship.

"What you see is only the physical manifestation of the creature on this
plane of existence," Talbot explained. "Once it comes into contact with your
aura, it'll dissipate entirely."

"But I have to put it in my mouth."

"I suppose it could be taken as a suppository."

"What's it called again?"

"Brain Rape," Talbot said. "It's all the rage in Berlin."

"Who ever knew the Germans to be wrong about anything?" M popped the thing in his mouth. There was a brief sensation of falling from a great height, and then of being caught and lifted back to his feet by hands both strong and kind. When he came back to, the capsule was gone. "What is this supposed to do again?"

"What's the farthest you've gotten backstage?"

"Pretty far."

"Ever get to where things that are start to run into things that aren't?"

"Once or twice."

"Brain Rape says hello to what lives there."

"How long does it take to work?"

"I'm not entirely sure. The guy who sold it to me sort of . . . disappeared."

"Oh."

Which sounded ominous, but after thirty seconds nothing had happened, and then someone began to bang loudly on the door, demanding they vacate the men's urinal, which they did.

"I want my twenty back if this doesn't kick," M said.

"Find me later," Talbot answered, before falling out into the crowd.

The start of a new year was not a source of any particular enthusiasm for M. He had seen too many of them. But still, any excuse for a good party, or *a* party at least. M had not yet made up his mind about this one in particular, but he was for frivolity in the abstract. The warehouse was far enough into the back end of Brooklyn as to have taken on some of the characteristics of fantasy—Brooklyn, being a slightly separate dimension so far as the Management was concerned—but other than a few sets of horns and the occasional pointed ear or third eye, there was surprisingly little to distinguish this particular gathering from your garden-variety warehouse party. Fey hipsters gamboled, bike messengers compared beard lengths, sweet young things tempted drunken passersby. There were three different DJs in the three different rooms, and M did not like what any of them were playing. The ground was unfinished, there were holes in the walls, everything smelled strongly of mildew, and yet a can of Pabst Blue Ribbon still cost you five dollars.

M found Andre where he had left him, overdressed and out of place. M was not entirely clear what Andre had done to get himself exiled from his usual crew of finance wizards and drug-addled debutantes, forced to half beg an invitation to accompany M to "whatever he happened to be doing for New Year's." No doubt he was strongly regretting it, Andre being that sort of Manhattanite for whom going to Brooklyn was a dishonor just this side of seppuku.

"Did everyone here come direct from their grandparents' closet?" Andre asked.

"I told you not to wear a suit."

"I always wear a suit."

"I can hardly be blamed for that."

"What took you so long at the bar?"

"I ran into Talbot on the way over there."

"Talbot? Surely you aren't mad enough to have taken something that Talbot gave you?"

"It's New Year's."

"Did you bring me any, at least?"

"Buying drugs is like playing dodge ball: Every man for himself."

"We don't play dodge ball in France."

"Something else for which I can't be held responsible."

"Why is one of your eyes a different color than the other?"

M could not see his left eye—that's not the way eyes work—but he did have the distinct sensation that something was off about it. To begin with, it seemed no longer willing to obey his commands, turning and twisting of its own volition; and to continue, the images it offered were hallucinatory yet infinitely precise. Closing his right eye and peeking down at his arm he could see through the skin and the veins, into sinew and bone and farther still through the cell and the molecule, and then deeper down into its constituent atoms and the things that were smaller than atoms and the things that were smaller than the things that were smaller than atoms.

"Hello," said the voice from M's left eye.

"Howdy."

"What are you, exactly?"

"A human."

"Same as the other one? Too bad."

"Why too bad?"

"He started to get very boring, I turned him off. I hope you won't be boring."

"Me? No, not at all. Quite the opposite. Fabulously interesting is how most of my friends would describe me."

"I've never described you that way," Andre said. "What exactly did you take?"

M ignored him. "Say, how long do you think this . . . association of ours will last?"

"Last?" asked the voice.

"How much time do you think we'll be spending with each other?"

"Time?"

"Time is the name humans use to describe the expansion of the universe. It's used to arrange events in sequence, and generally to avoid going mad."

"This is getting boring . . ."

"Look, there's Boy!" M exclaimed. "She's riveting. You're going to just love her. Thrill a minute, that one!"

"Yeah? You think?" Andre slicked back his hair. "Well, what are we waiting for?"

M would not have noticed Boy if she had come in by herself, dressed as she was like virtually the entirety of the rest of the assemblage—birth control glasses and carefully disheveled hair. But happily she'd come in with Bucephalus, and Bucephalus was the sort of person who stood out in a crowd, even if that crowd contained its fair share of not-quite humans. He was as big a man as M had ever seen and bigger than some things M had seen that were not men. He wore loose jeans without a belt and unlaced tennis shoes and a tight white T-shirt that barely reached above his nipples. He had biceps the size of M's head, and written in Gothic script across his bullock clavicle were the words EVIL QUEEN. He had a Union Jack do-rag tied around his enormous skull. His skin was black as ash, and he had painted his eyelids indigo. M did not like most of Boy's friends, but Bucephalus was the only one of whom he was somewhat afraid.

"He's fun-looking!" the voice from M's left eye said. "I like his hat!"

"Howdy," M said.

"Got any coke?" Bucephalus asked.

"Not on me."

Bucephalus shrugged and headed into the party.

"Charming as ever," M said.

"Better than yours," Boy said, running a long eye over Andre and seeming not to like what she saw.

"Andre," Andre introduced himself, reaching out to take her hand.

Boy scowled and ignored it. "I thought you told me you hated this guy?"

"I hate all of my friends."

"You said you hate me?" Andre asked.

"I've said worse things to you about her," M said. "Andre, why don't you go grab Boy a drink and tell her everything that's wrong with me. I'll pick you up again down the line."

Boy had a scowl that would peel paint, but she took Andre's arm all the same. M went outside to smoke a cigarette and try to get his head together.

"This is incredible!" the voice burbled happily. "This is so much fun! Everyone should do this all of the time."

"Tell that to the attorney general," M said.

"Smoke another one!"

"It's kind of cold."

"Smoke another one," the voice insisted.

So M did and managed only to get out of smoking a third by introducing his voice to the concept of alcohol, which M described as "using the same orifice for a somewhat different purpose," an explanation that was sufficient to generate enthusiasm on the part of his ethereal companion.

M was at one of the bars trying to decide if he ought to start the voice off on liquor or beer when Stockdale sidled over from the other end, a pretty Latin girl in tow. "Here's my man right now," Stockdale said, slapping M on the shoulder. "Good to see you. Got any coke?"

"Why do people keep asking me that?"

"It's not an unreasonable expectation. This is Adda," Stockdale said.

"Nice to meet you, Adda," M said. "I don't have any cocaine."

Adda shrugged unhappily.

"Having a nice night?" Stockdale asked.

"You know," M said, "I kind of am."

"Who's this?" the voice asked.

"Stockdale," M said. "We're friends."

"Damn right," Stockdale said, slapping him happily on the back before taking Adda off to a quieter corner of the party.

"What's a friend?" the voice asked.

"A friend is someone whose company you enjoy and whom you trust to get you out of trouble."

"Like Andre?"

"God, no. I wouldn't trust Andre to water my plant."

"Oh."

"But I kind of like him. I mean, he's good for a hoot or a holler." Two women of child-bearing age giggled at the other end of the counter. One of them had an ass like God's ass, if God were a twenty-one-year-old ingenue. M smiled at them both.

"What are we doing now?" the voice asked. "I'm getting bored again."

M spent a while trying to explain sex to his left eye, but it seemed that its species did not reproduce sexually or, for that matter, at all.

"So you make copies of yourself?"

"Not exact copies."

"Do the copies listen to you? Like, can you order them around?"

"Not really. At least that never worked on me."

"Why would there need to be any more of you? There seem quite enough of you as it is."

"More than enough, in fact. But that's not really why we do it. Not the only reason. I mean, it's not my reason for doing it at all, actually, more of a bug than a feature."

"Then what's the point?"

M spent a while explaining. The two girls at the other end of the counter moved away uncomfortably.

"So essentially it just boils down to friction?" the voice asked.

"I think that's simplifying the matter a bit."

"Well, you've convinced me. Let's go have sex with someone."

"And don't we wish it were that easy. Share a smoke?"

The voice was amenable, and so M was back outside when he saw Ginger and her crew walking through the crowd like Patton through Normandy. Ginger had red hair and piercing dark eyes and was dressed like a sexy vampire, which was the only sort of vampire that anyone ever dresses as. At her side an adolescent-looking androgyne in a Catholic-schoolgirl outfit smoked a cigar the size of a porn star's phallus. Taking the rear was a Pacific Islander wearing a charcoal suit and standing as tall as two regular-size people. There were a number of others, though M didn't bother to pay attention to them specifically—they were all equally hip, tattooed, fedora-ed, and mustachioed.

"Shit," M said.

The bouncer had squared shoulders and fat biceps and a swirling tattoo that ran up his face, and he was not mad enough to try to make them wait in line, let alone pay a cover. The long row of would-be partiers shot dagger eyes at their backs but didn't make a fuss either.

"If it isn't Boy's boy," Ginger said, sauntering past the velvet rope.

"That's cute, the way you put boy next to Boy like that," M said. "Where did you get your MFA? Sarah Lawrence?"

Ginger laughed and brushed her hand up against M's cheek. "I like your scruff," she said.

"Yes!" the voice exclaimed. "More of that!"

"Is your friend around?" Ginger asked.

"I have lots of friends," M said, pushing Ginger's hand away from his jaw gently. "And I'm friendly with all of them."

Ginger smiled that nasty smile of hers and tossed crimson ringlets off her pale forehead. "I hope not that close," she said, before leading her crew inside.

"Where did she go?" the voice asked angrily. "What the hell is wrong with you?"

"She was just flirting with us to try to get back at Boy," M explained.

"They do that?"

"All the time."

"I've got a lot to learn about women."

"You and me both."

"Let's get a drink!" the voice said happily, Ginger and her coterie forgotten in its enthusiasm to renew its acquaintance with alcohol. "And then
maybe take another crack at that sex thing."

"In a minute, in a minute," M said, stubbing out his cigarette and darting
inside.

But it took near twenty of these to find Boy, and the voice complained the
entire time: Why were they puttering around in the back rooms of this gathering when there was yet so much to taste, to swallow, to smoke, to desire, to
befoul, and to consume?

"It's called loyalty, damn it!" M explained. "There are more important
things in life than cigarettes, alcohol, and sex. Not by much, but still."

"Is this that friendship thing?"

"Yes, exactly."

When he finally found Boy, he found Andre as well, sitting close to each
other on a couch in one of the side rooms, and Andre was whispering something into her ear, and she had one hand on his knee and didn't seem to mind
their proximity.

"You know that scarlet-haired vixen whom you've been sort of perpetu-
ally feuding with?" M interrupted.

"Ginger? Sure, I put a half a bag of sugar in the tank of her Vespa when I
saw her on Halloween. And then last month I tricked her into visiting one of
those side dimensions with snakes and shadows that look like snakes."

"Well, she's here."

"Yeah?" Boy looked a little pleased, inspected her unpainted fingernails
elaborately. "I guess she got free then. What's it to me?"

"She's got the cast of *Glee* walking backup."

"Boy's got me," Andre said gallantly.

"I'll make sure to call you if I need a recommendation from the wine list,"
Boy said.

"Perhaps I'm being less clear than I ought to," M continued. "It's been a
confusing sort of night. I'm trying to warn you that there's someone in the
building who wants to kill you. More than one, probability would suggest,
but one for certain."

"I heard you," Boy said, tilting her neck in a fashion that let Andre look down her limited cleavage. "And what do you want me to do? Run? If Ginger wants to find me, she can find me. Or maybe I'll go find her. This party is boring as hell," she snapped her eyes back down on her quarry.

Andre smiled. "Perhaps we should try to find somewhere more interesting?"

They say opposites attract, but they were wrong, because Andre and Boy were exactly the same—ranging wolves with red-flecked grins.

"Boy did not seem to appreciate your loyalty," the voice from M's eye continued as M returned to the main room and the bar that occupied most of it.

"People don't always know what's good for them."

"Friends seem like a lot of trouble."

"You are not wrong."

Bucephalus was at the other end of the counter M ended up at, and he stared at M in his implacable, frightening sort of way.

"There's that man with the hat again," M's left eye observed.

"Fuck is the matter with you?" Bucephalus had a voice like concrete being rubbed against steel.

"I'm on drugs."

"What kind of drug is it that puts a god in the center of your brain?"

"He's on to us!" the voice yelled.

"The very strong sort," M said, but he said it rather warily, because in a room full of people who were not people, and people who could do things that regular people could not, Bucephalus had been the only one to notice M's change of circumstance. M had never been entirely clear whether Bucephalus was as good as he was frightening, but now he had his answer.

"Boy know the bitch is here?" Bucephalus asked.

"I mentioned it to her. She seemed unconcerned."

"You ever notice that Boy's a little bit reckless?"

"Yes, Bucephalus," M said, ordering shots for the three of them, "I had."

Bucephalus threw his shot back like it was water, then went to chat up a tow-headed queen popping gum at the corner of the bar. M knocked his two drinks down a bit more slowly, and after the second he was feeling the sort of happy that leads rapidly toward nausea. Also, his left eye was now distorting not only space but time as well, tracing through earlier transmutations of existence: what the warehouse had looked like before the party when everyone was setting up, and twenty years earlier when it had actually been used for storing things, and hundreds of years before that when it had been nothing but swamp and greenery, and also, simultaneously and more disturbingly, what it would look like at some point in the distant future, with the metal framework burnt and rusted.

"What's going on?" the voice asked.

"We've got the spins," M explained "You should lie down and put your foot on the ground."

"I don't have feet. Or a ground. This is part of this whole drinking thing?"

"Not the best part." M caught a glimpse of Stockdale's time trail, followed where he had been half an hour before to where he was currently, making the sort of conversation with Ginger that necessitated lots of touching.

"You again," M said.

Ginger smiled, winked, and turned back to Stockdale. "You had your shot, pretty boy."

"Can we help you with something?" Stockdale asked, in a tone that made M think Stockdale did not really want to help him with anything.

"I need to make wee-wee."

"I'm sure you can take care of that yourself."

"No," M said firmly, "I can't. Without assistance, I'm going to piss all over myself."

Stockdale swallowed the rest of his beer and nuzzled Ginger's neck, and then followed M in the direction of the toilets, though of course they stopped halfway.

"Is there a term for the opposite of a wingman?" Stockdale asked. "Footboy? Flippergirl?"

"What happened to Adda?"

"Adda and I had a difference of opinion over whether or not we should have sex in the bathroom," Stockdale explained gallantly, "and have parted ways. I've reason to believe that Ginger will feel differently."

"Have you seen the bathrooms here? Hardly copacetic to copulation."

"A coat room? The back of a friend's Cadillac? I'm not picky."

"You know that Ginger is at crossed swords with Boy."

"I'll make sure not to invite her to the threesome."

"And that she's only talking to you because you're friends with me, and I'm friends with Boy."

"Gift horses, teeth," Stockdale said. "You get my point."

"Ginger is a nasty piece of work."

"Actually, she and Boy are a lot alike."

"Of course they're a lot alike, that's why they hate each other. Have you ever met a woman before or did they just tonight let you out of your monastery?"

"Half-wit," said the voice.

"Good one!" M said.

Stockdale looked at M quizzically. "Boy's your friend. She and I are barely more than acquaintances. And weighing secondhand loyalty against that ass . . ." Stockdale shrugged and turned back toward Ginger's posterior, giving its owner a little wave. "You can see where this is going."

M threw his hands up and went to get another drink.

"I don't think Stockdale knows that you and he are friends."

"He knows, he's just letting his cock do his thinking at the moment."

"I think I'm starting to get this," the voice said while they stared at the flesh offered on the dance floor. "They cover up some parts so you pay more attention to the parts they haven't covered up?"

"Exactly."

"Clever sort of species, humanity."

"We do what we can."

M was using his newfound perception to identify those partygoers whose futures included him and a bed. There was a well-built brunette he had his eye on and who apparently, in a fair selection of the posterities M was looking through, found him charming enough to go home with even though he lived in Crown Heights and she in Greenpoint. Then he caught sight of Boy's future contorting its way through reality.

"Shit," he said.

"Yeah, doesn't look great, does it?" asked the voice.

"I think I'd somewhat underrated the degree of danger facing Boy."

"Well," the voice said, twisting his eye back toward the brunette. "We did our best."

"No, we didn't."

"Didn't we already decide that Boy was best left to her own decisions?"

"That was before I watched her get murdered in five minutes."

"Don't get too worked up about it," the voice cautioned. "Everything that is exists simultaneously with everything that ever was, will be, or might have been. Infinity overlaps to such a fine degree as to make the outcome of any event essentially a matter of perspective."

"I'm quite partial to my own particular time stream, in so far as I've yet to find a reliable way to break out of it." It took M a minute to realize that he was watching Andre and Boy head toward one of the back exits in the immediate present, and not in one of the countless infinity of futures through which he was flicking. Ginger and her pack, which now apparently included Stockdale, followed shortly thereafter.

"So Boy is your friend, and Stockdale is your friend, and they're going to fight each other?"

"I don't think so. Maybe. It's not impossible."

"This whole friendship thing makes not a bit of sense to me."

"Let's say you buy a new couch. Who do you think is going to help you take that couch up to your shitty walk-up apartment? Movers? They require a minimum of two hours, and that's like a hundred and fifty dollars for ten minutes' work. But more important, you don't want to be the sort of person who has to use a moving service. The sort of person who doesn't have anyone to help them carry a sofa up three flights of stairs is a sad person, a person with no hope at all."

"I don't have a sofa."

"That's not the point!" M yelled. People looked over at him, but he was too excited to care. "A friend is someone who, when they ask you to do something, you say yes, even if secretly you wish they hadn't asked you."

"Are we friends?"

"I'd say we're on our way."

"Yeah?"

"Yeah."

"All right, then," the voice said, sounding pleased. "Let's go do something awful to the enemy of my new friend's old friend."

On his way to the exit, M passed Bucephalus, who had just finished rolling a blunt on the bar and seemed to recognize what was going down despite not, to the best of M's knowledge at least, having an extradimensional entity lodged in his ocular cavity. "Been in a fight before?" M asked.

"One or two," Bucephalus answered, sealing his smoke and wedging it behind his ear.

"I don't think so," the voice said. "Are they fun?"

"They're fun if you win," M said.

"Damn right they are," Bucephalus responded, getting off from his stool and following Boy outside.

Some reasonable way down the alley were Boy and Andre, and to judge by their somewhat ruffled state and the shadow they were simultaneously occupying, violence was not foremost on their mind. Not quite so farther down was Ginger, who had Stockdale's hand on her ass and her crew of miscreants beside her. Not very far down at all stood Bucephalus and M and the creature living inside of M's eye.

"A standoff!" M muttered excitedly. "Damn it if you didn't pick a good night to visit New York!"

"If it ain't the bitch," Ginger said.

"That's queen bitch to you," Boy snarled, moving as seamlessly from sex to violence as an '80s action movie. "That's an interesting miniskirt. Did you go to Hot Topic and ask for something with which to catch a predator?"

"You're one to talk. You look like you've been trimming your hair with gardening sheers."

"What shade of dye are you using these days? Strumpet Scarlet? Whore's Red?"

"I'm afraid that concealer isn't living up to its name: Your pockmarks come through clear as crystal, or did someone throw battery acid into your face?"

"Reginald seemed to like it," Boy said, smiling nastily. "Carl, too, if memory serves."

"You steal this one also?" Ginger asked.

"Ladies, ladies," Andre began, putting both of his hands up as if to ward off criticism, "surely there's no need to resort to name calling."

Ginger pointed her index finger at Andre, brought her thumb hammer down against it. "Pop," she said, and Andre was flung backward against the wall of the alley hard enough for M to hear his skull smack brick. Boy snarled and darted forward, brushing off Ginger's second shot and diving at her enemy. They tumbled over one another, eschewing magic entirely, needing the visceral thrill of physical violence, bruised knuckles, bloodied lips. The hermaphrodite in stockings was breathing something into her hands that would no doubt have grown into a problem for Boy had Stockdale not hooked a foot around her ankle and sent her sprawling, true colors revealed in a moment of crisis, as M had known it would be. The Polynesian ogre returned the favor—cold-cocking Stockdale hard enough to leave a civilian drinking protein shakes through a straw. Bucephalus giggled and crossed between them, and then the two heavyweights were engaged in fisticuffs so swift and furious that M had trouble following them.

"This is great!" the voice said. "This is so much better than smoking! Is this what humans do all the time—fuck and fight?"

"That would be the larger part of it. You think you could help out a bit?" M asked his friend living inside of his left eye.

"How exactly?"

"Something big enough to make me look important, but not so big as to realign the axis of existence?"

"Like this, you mean?"

There was a sudden sunny flash, and an aria cut through the evening, and a sphere of bright, warm light came into existence in the air above the combatants. Then the illumination darted down in all directions, tentacles of moonshine striking Ginger and her coterie prone to the ground, nestling them in its heat, leaving each mewling like tummy-rubbed kittens, eyes staring blissfully up at the moon.

"Exactly," M said. "That was perfect!"

But the voice didn't answer, and after a moment M realized he was only seeing the present, and not very much of that either, and that the voice was gone.

M spent a moment in bittersweet reflection at the loss of his new friend. Not a very long one, however. "I am a mage both wondrous and terrible!" M insisted, stretching his arms up in the air. Below his left wrist was a pair of clasped hands in black ink. "My powers are ineffable and vast! Look upon me, mortals, and know fear!"

"Humble, too," Andre said, managing to lift himself up from the ground.

"I didn't know you had that in you," Boy said.

"I'm a very important sort of person," M said. "You don't give me enough respect."

"You spared me the indignity of sullying my hands," Stockdale said grandly, "and for that I thank you."

"A drink might square it," M said, "just so long as you remember what I'm capable of, and tread softly in the future."

Back inside, M discovered that they had just missed midnight, the crowd midway through the second verse of "Auld Lang Syne," the one that no one really knows, where you have to make up for ignorance with enthusiasm. Stockdale, punch drunk or just actually drunk, took up after them very loudly. Bucephalus was supporting him on his way to the bar, and once they got there Boy ordered a round of drinks for everyone.

"To M, and the year ahead."

"To friends new and old," M corrected.

11
—

The Spirit of the Age

When M woke one Tuesday a few weeks into the New Year to discover three more coffee shops had opened up in his neighborhood, he was perturbed.

"Harumph," he said.

Still, he did need a morning cup of coffee, and so he chose one of the new places more or less at random and walked inside. It claimed to serve Estonian espresso, which M, having spent some time in Estonia, did not remember being a thing. The barista was a pretty, short, dark-haired girl with dimples and a poorly chosen nose ring. She seemed disappointed M didn't want anything more complicated than drip coffee. January's favorite song played on the radio.

M sat at an unfinished wooden table in an unmatched chair and tried to remember how many coffee shops there had been in his neighborhood when he had moved in a few months back. He decided to count his neighborhood as ending at Washington Avenue, although some would have said Vanderbilt would have been more appropriate, but if he went by Vanderbilt he'd be sitting there all day. Park Perk and Eskimo's and Adieu's and the Brown Bomber and Solomon's Brew and Brokeland Coffee and Zummi's and the Happy Werewolf made eight. Nine with that joint the Hasidim ran on Prospect that he never went into. Also, any of the innumerable restaurants in the area would serve you a cup of coffee, and most of the bars as well. And also the bodegas, which generally had a pot going and ran about one to a block. And, of course, M had his own coffee maker.

"Does that seem strange to you, at all?" M asked a man sitting next to him. "Three coffee shops opening in one day?"

The guy laughed. "What can I tell you? It's Brooklyn."

Which was true as far as it went, but still.

Heading out the next afternoon, he grabbed a cup of coffee at the joint across from his house. A week earlier, it was vacant, a fit haven only for roaches and crack addicts, but in the interval, it had been refurbished in what was someone's idea of a Parisian salon circa 1920—though M had spent time in Parisian salons in the 1920s and didn't remember them being so hatefully twee. It had two tables that could have comfortably sat a family of gnomes. It had a full set of Flaubert's works, leather-bound, above the espresso machine.

The barista was a pretty, short, dark-haired girl with dimples and a badly chosen nose ring.

"Welcome to Marcel's!" she said, happily. "What can I get started for you?"

M gave her a nasty look. "You don't work here," he said.

The girl laughed. "Why, of course I do!"

"No, you don't. You work in that Estonian coffee shop. I saw you there yesterday."

The girl laughed again. M got the feeling that he would get the same response with anything short of physical assault. M glowered at her a while, but he still ordered a large coffee with cream. It was delicious, though M bitterly resented that the only available seating was a repurposed antique barber's chair.

When M walked outside of Marcel's, he called Boy and asked if she had time to meet up, but Boy was crawling out of her bed in Williamsburg, a short eternity from Crown Heights, and so M had an hour to kill at least. If it had been later, he would have gone to a bar, and if it hadn't been raining, he would have gone to the park. But it wasn't later and it was raining, so he ended up just going early to the coffee shop at which he was to meet Boy. It had a rather strong nautical theme, which didn't make sense on all sorts of levels. The internet connection was fast as lightning, the coffee as strong as a punch in the gut. The croissant he ate was flaky.

After Boy had been late thirty minutes, M decided to split, only to run into her outside, looking rather furious. Boy often looked rather furious, though in this case the target of her rage seemed to be M. "Where the fuck were you?"

"Where the fuck were you?" M asked. "The coffee shop at the corner of Washington and Park," M said, pointing back at the way he'd come. "I've been sitting there for half an hour."

Boy looked at M strangely for a moment, then pointed kitty-corner across the street to a cute little joint that hadn't been there when he'd walked past an hour earlier. It had wide bay windows and comfortable-looking couches.

They went to get a beer at The Lady, which seemed like the safest choice.

"I saw this happen in the late '70s," Boy said. "Broadway was an unbroken string of disco joints from the Financial District to the Bronx. There was a three-month period when I had to trek out to Jersey to buy a pair of pants. But this kinds of aberration doesn't last forever. It'll straighten itself out eventually."

"And if it doesn't?"

Boy shrugged. "It's not my neighborhood."

Crossing down Franklin the next morning, there were more new coffee shops than M could keep track of. Everyone he walked past seemed to be coming in or out of one of them—bodegas remained unvisited, boutique sandwiches uneaten, thrift stores unexplored. Walking past a black barbershop, M saw a line of empty swivel chairs, the proprietor looking out the window with big, dark, sad eyes. He held a razor in one hand and a cup of coffee in the other. It was almost enough to tempt M out of apathy. Not quite, though.

Then, on Friday, M went to buy some fruit at the only decent supermarket within twelve blocks in any direction only to discover it, too, with an incongruousness M felt was clearly pushing the boundaries of coherent reality, had turned into a coffee shop. "Are you fucking kidding me?" he asked. Since he was inside of a small warehouse, all of the shelving jettisoned to make one large, open space, vacant except for a distant section in the back with a counter and some chairs, his question echoed louder than he intended. The twenty-odd berets typing away at their MacBooks looked up at him unhappily.

M snarled, set his shoulders, and strode right up to the barista, head down, like a bull to a matador, like a soldier ready for war. "I need to see the manager," M said firmly. "Right now."

"Of course, sir," said the smiling ingenue working the register. "We'll get him in just a moment."

And sure enough a smiling man in a flannel shirt whisked his way out from the back and offered M his hand to pump. "I'm Nigel," he said. "Is there something the matter?"

"Not you," M said. "The *real* manager."

M was still not quite sure if Nigel and all the rest of his staff and all the rest of the Nigels and all the rest of their staffs had had a *Day of the Truffids* pulled on them or if they were just side manifestations of whatever was at the heart of this unpleasant change. That they had some capacity for independent thought (apart from the uniform at least) seemed to be confirmed by the look of pure terror that Nigel gave to the cashier. "Look, man," Nigel said, "I'm not sure that's the best idea. He's . . . awful busy."

"Look, buddy, if I need a recommendation on which flavor macchiato to go with, I'll drop you a line. Past that, I don't need advice. I need you to take me to the man you answer to."

Nigel shrugged and pointed at the door he just came through. "That way," he said. "Isn't a man, though."

But M wasn't listening. He unzipped his coat overdramatically and went to make trouble.

There was a moment after opening the door and walking through it wherein M wasn't doing either of these things, when he was suspended in some strange netherworld, an instant that would have been terrifying if he had been capable of processing it, but since he wasn't, it just seemed like a strange sort of blip in his mind, a scratch on an LP, snow flickering across an old television set.

"Come on in," said the thing sitting behind the desk. "Can I pour you a cup of coffee?" Before M could answer, it had already decanted half a pot into an oversize ceramic cup and thrust it across the table.

"Thanks," M said, taking a seat. He took a sip out of politeness. It was the best cup of coffee he had ever tasted.

"On the house!" the thing said. It was trying to look like a human and only partially succeeding. Its hair was hair until it got up close to its scalp, then became something that clearly wasn't hair. It had a flannel shirt and a badly rendered beard. The tattoos running up its arms were straight gibberish, random symbols and letters that did not add up to words, and M could swear that the hands at the end of those arms switched between possessing four digits and five, shifting whenever he looked away. It had big, brown eyes, dark as—well, as a cup of coffee, though it annoyed M to have to think that. "Always happy to speak with a satisfied customer—and if you aren't satisfied, then by golly, I'm going to satisfy you!"

The setting had the same not-quite-real feeling as the thing itself. There were bookshelves everywhere and books inside them, but if you looked closer you saw their spines were unlabeled, and M felt confident that if he had plucked one, it wouldn't have opened or would have opened on blank text. The landscape outside was windblown and barren, as if you had built an office park in the middle of Siberia.

"First, I'd just like to tell you how much I love the new shop." M had found that when it came to these strange deviations of reality, these ungainly manifestations of the zeitgeist that sprung up when the passions and prejudices and joys and miseries of the populace came in contact with whatever mystical current was required to give them some semblance of life, it was best to try to just explain the matter calmly, as to a child or a madman. Always being very conscious, of course, that children are cruel and madmen are mad, and that this particular tempestuous toddler or muttering transient could warp the foundations of existence in ways potent and incomprehensible.

"Thanks! It's about the community, really—setting up a space for people to come together and do their art or work on the great problems that are facing society. To live up to the full potential they have inside them, all with the aid of nature's most beneficent stimulant, the coffee bean."

M took a deep breath. This wasn't going to be easy. "And so many different franchises springing up . . ."

"How else to reflect the extraordinary diversity of the drink? From the common Ethiopian arabica, smooth-flavored and casual, to the precious kopi luwak, brewed from beans fermented by the digestive process of the noble Asian palm civet, truly, there's nothing like coffee."

M looked at his cup. "Digestive process?"

"We only use beans that are taken from *wild* civets. Some of our competitors use *tamed* civets, which," the thing shook his head back and forth, "well, you can imagine."

"Wild civets?"

"See, we believe that making good coffee is about more than just giving someone a smile while going about their day. Coffee can be a real source of positive change in this world. Did you know that every drop of our coffee comes from free-trade farmers in third-world countries? Or that, for each cup of espresso sold, we donate five cents toward a charity that provides support for organic Romanian goat herders?"

"So you're saying this coffee has been shat out by some sort of marmot?" M asked.

"Only the best!"

Something about having discovered he had just drank feces, or something that had been suspended in feces, gave M a little extra nerve. "I gotta say, there's been an awful lot of shops opening in the neighborhood these past few weeks."

"People love coffee."

"Believe me, man, you're preaching to the choir—I can't get through the day without having a cup. The thing is, I can't get through the day without other things too—food, for instance, and clothing—and lately those are harder and harder to find."

"People love coffee," it said again, and this time there was a weight on top of it.

"Look, I love coffee. Coffee is great. Coffee might be, literally, my favorite thing on earth. But even still, I don't think that I like it to a point where I would want to be exclusive. It might be nice if, in addition to drinking a great cup of coffee in the morning, I might buy soap or visit a bank."

"I don't think you know what you're asking," it said, hands up as if trying to stop M from sprinting off a cliff. "Sure, our expansion might have made it a bit more difficult for you to pick up some staple goods. But what is that when held against the joy of a freshly brewed pot?" Outside the windows in the room that was not a room, something crackled. It was not quite thunder, because thunder is caused by electrons flowing through clouds, and M was no longer in a place where the rules of physics, or at least his rules of physics, held much sway. "There are prices to pay for living in Brooklyn—one has to make certain sacrifices. If you want your box stores and your cheap groceries, you might as well move out to Jersey. You can buy your shoes at Walmart and get your morning coffee at a Starbucks." It snarled out the last word like a Serbian cursing.

"No one's suggesting that," M said, trying to mollify the minor god. "The one time I set foot in Starbucks I'd been forced at gunpoint, and even then the fumes were enough to make me vomit. If Adolf Hitler himself came in here right now, and he was about to bring a Starbucks espresso up to that little thumb-width mustache of his, I'd knock it right out of his hand. If you were to poison me and then mix the antidote in with a cup of their house blend I would die in agony on the floor rather than drink it."

The thing nodded again, happy that he and M were on the same page. "You had me worried there for a minute. I was thinking maybe you were one of these poor bastards who don't know a double-roasted espresso from a mug of Folger's instant!"

They both laughed at the absurdity. M decided to try a different tack.

"Really I just came by to congratulate you on all the good work you've been doing in the neighborhood. I have to say, the success you've been having, it's unprecedented."

"Thanks! Well, like I said, you make a good product, people will come, right? It's basic stuff."

"Absolutely, absolutely. And the product here is so tremendously good, I'm sure it won't be long until the whole country gets to appreciate it. It's amazing to think, in a few years, when you've got shops blanketing the nation, hell, the world, I'll be able to say I went to the original franchise."

"Excuse me? Every one of our coffee shops is independently owned and operated."

"Well, not really—if I'd walked into that Estonian joint you opened the other day and went through the stockroom, I'd end up here, right? So really it's just an elaborate franchise. You should be happy about it—pretty soon you'll be taking things national. Imagine it: One of your coffee shops in every strip mall in the land, sandwiched between the Cinnabon and Chipotle!

Hang out at Davos with all the other titans of industry, talking about synergy and . . . words like synergy!"

"No!" the thing croaked. "Never!"

"You can partner with Urban Outfitters and release a line of coffee-inspired clothing! You'll sell branded water, and prepackaged ham and cheese croissants!"

"Those things are disgusting!"

"It's unavoidable. It's the end result of any late-stage capitalist process. You know, Starbucks started as a couple of proto-hipsters and a dream, and look at them now! The way is paved for you, my friend. Bourgeois conformity within three years. No way around it, I'm afraid."

The thing about these—well, call them spirits or demons or *loas* or whatever you wanted—was that they had more power than any mortal adept, enough power to rework reality in any fashion they chose. But they couldn't choose much, the rules of their existence being adamantine and unbreakable.

"You could put out a line of instant brew!" M said, giving the thing one final shove over the cliff. "Just shake and drink!"

It blinked twice, horrified, and then reality blinked away also.

M found himself back in the coffee shop that had been a supermarket but was now just a big, empty room—an empty room partially filled with two dozen extremely confused hipsters, each trying to figure out why the internet had gone out, and the lights, and where the cute barista was, and, also, while they were on the subject, what in the name of God had happened to their coffee?

Outside the day was gray and rainy, and M discovered that whatever cosmic backlash he had caused had taken with it all of the coffee shops in the neighborhood, even the ones that had been around before this most recent wave of expansion, which was unfortunate, as he belatedly realized that he had not yet drunk his morning cup.

"Harumph," M said, not for the last time.

12

Sorcerer's Apprentice

A week into February and, for reasons that M could not quite put his finger on, he fell completely out of the pocket. Bad luck accrued around him. He arrived too late for things—buses and trains, ticket sales and happy hours and last calls. Or too early—for drink specials and to avoid meeting ex-girlfriends and their handsome, brutish boyfriends. He did not win a game of chess for ten straight days, not one, dropping match after match to half-wits and crack addicts and half-witted crack addicts, pushing himself up from chairs and away from computer screens while cursing his sudden stupidity. His brain felt slack, liked he'd laid himself out with sativa, which—fair enough—he had been doing, but this was a symptom or an attempt at a remedy, not the cause itself.

M was not sure what he had done to fall out of favor with the Management— why those cosmic forces, normally so inclined to look with favor upon his foolishness, had decided to avert their eyes from him. M did not understand a lot of things about his life. M thought that most of his peers were equally ignorant but less willing to admit it.

In practical terms, being out of pocket resulted in two serious difficulties: The first was that, against his desire and better judgment, he ended up taking on an apprentice. And the second was that a biker gang tried to kill him. But more on that in a moment.

M was at The Lady one late afternoon when the kid came in—and *kid* was the only word for him. He was stocky and short and blond and had the face of a newborn. He was wearing a polo shirt and red kicks. He took a stool one over from M, ordered a PBR, opened it, and sat drinking slowly for a while, building up his courage. "A candidate sits before you, awaiting initiation," he said, voice hushed and serious.

"Fuck you talking about?" M asked.

The kid had the sort of coloring that you could literally watch his blush spread across his face. "Sorry, is that not something you say? I read that in one of the hidden texts of the true Rosicrucians. It seemed like the real thing. Some of the exercises worked at least."

"Don't read books," M said. "Don't trust them. Not enough that everyone talks all the time, they have to go and start putting thoughts down all permanent like?"

M's wholehearted denunciation of literacy proved only a brief obstacle for the young man, who shrugged his shoulders and held out his hand. "My name is Flemel," he said.

"Bully for you, Flemel," M said, ignoring it.

"I know what you are."

"Tired of this conversation?"

Flemel laughed. M didn't like Flemel's laugh. It wasn't menacing or anything, quite the opposite. It was an amiable laugh, a natural laugh, a laugh between two friends. But M didn't want any more friends, and often felt he could do without most of the ones he already had.

"This has been great, but I'm sure you have something really important and exciting to get to, and I'd feel bad if I detained you any longer." M put a little bit of English on the end of it, enough to send his newfound admirer heading out the door and off to this nonexistent rendezvous.

The boy's eyes glazed over for a few seconds, but then he shook his head back and forth and smiled. "You'll have to do better than that."

There was no way that M was in so bad with the Management that he couldn't convince a civilian to look the other way. M had been convincing civilians to look the other way for—actually, M couldn't remember, but it had been a long time, M knew that much at least. And that meant that Flemel must be on his way toward being in good with the Management himself, even just a little, and that meant that M's life was about to get more complicated.

"Look, kid," M began, in his most reasonable tone of voice, "I'm pretty busy working on this day drunk. How about you tell me what it is I can do for you, and I'll tell you I can't do it, and then you can leave me alone."

M's beer was empty, and Flemel waved at Dino and pointed at it. "Another for my friend."

"Another for the total stranger was I think what you meant to say." But M ordered a stout anyway.

"You're an initiate."

"I told you already, that doesn't mean anything to me."

"One who walks the paths unseen?"

"Are you hitting on me? This isn't a gay bar, you know. Not that I have any problem if that's the way you swing, but just so we're all clear."

"A wizard?"

M just laughed and shook his head.

"You're someone who can do things that other people can't do," Flemel said finally, dangling from the end of his rope. "And I'd like to learn how to do the same."

"If I was what you think I am, would I be getting loaded in a dive bar in the middle of the afternoon?"

"Yes," Flemel said. "I think you would."

M scowled some more and downed his beer and headed out. Flemel stayed where he was and watched M walk out through The Lady's bay windows. M told himself on the walk back to his apartment that the hiccup was just that, and it would be gone by tomorrow. But it had been too shitty a month to really believe it, and so when he swung back around the next day and saw Flemel sitting next to his usual spot, smiling and waving, he was displeased but not surprised.

From then on, Flemel was waiting in The Lady most afternoons. He didn't say much, just sat near M, not quite staring but close enough. It threw off M's rhythm entirely, would have even if he wasn't already out of the pocket. He spent a while trying to convince Dino to throw him out, but Flemel hadn't done anything but sit quietly and drink, and you couldn't ban anyone from a bar for that.

It was Flemel who saw the guy first. A big man, huge really, closer to seven foot than six, ash blond dreadlocks falling down to his ass and a well-worn leather jacket with MOAB's MINIONS emblazoned on the back. He was moving past The Lady's front windows at a not-unimpressive clip, three long steps being enough to carry him out of sight, though at two and a half he stopped abruptly, went wide-eyed, and pressed his face up against the glass. Flemel could see where time had aged his features, crow's-feet stretching out from his eyes, his beard more white than blond. Flemel could also see where someone, presumably not time, had burned a stretch of flesh running diagonally across his face, from the right temple to the dimple in his chin. His eyes were fierce and furious and delighted. Flemel found himself afraid.

M was reading a paperback and did not look up when the man came in. Nor did he look up as the man walked over, though his footfalls seemed, to Flemel at least, as loud as bass drums. M did not look up until he could feel the man's warm breath on his face, smelling of onion and egg and liver, and even then it took a while.

"Can I help you with something?" he asked finally, sounding unhelpful.

The giant did a weird sort of thing with his face, the lower half expanding into a grin just this side of jubilant, the top half—his coal-black eyes, the functioning one at least—all but bursting with fury. "Bet you never thought you'd see me again." His voice was like a diesel engine pulling into gear.

"I hadn't really thought about it one way or the other."

"Twenty-five years and you still as pretty as the day we first met." The giant sneered, teeth like broken pieces of concrete. "Not for long, though."

M cocked his head up at the giant, looked over at Flemel, shrugged, and looked back at the giant. "Friend," he said, still pleasant, "you've got the wrong guy."

The giant laughed again. It was not a friendly laugh. It didn't really even sound like a laugh, so much as stones rumbling against one another or a round being chambered. "You aren't going to get out of this that easy."

M turned back to his novel. "I got no idea who you are. We've never met before."

The biker put two sausage-link fingers on the cover of M's book and closed it with some force. "Look again."

M sighed, tightened up his eyes, and sucked at his teeth. "Did you used to do my taxes?"

"Do I look like the sort of person that does other people's taxes?"

"Do I look like the sort of person who pays them?" M asked. "Did you sell me a scooter in SoHo?"

"No."

"Did you hit on me outside a gay bar in the Village?"

"No!" If the giant had been a rain cloud, he would have been pouring; if he had been a nuclear reactor, he would have been poisoning flora; if he had been a volcano, he would have been destroying the homes of the people foolish enough to have built their homes at his feet. Since he was just a man, albeit a very large one, his face got plum-tomato red, from the broken capillaries in his nose to the cartilage in his cauliflower ears. He ran one hand along his terrible scar. "You did this to me, and I've been waiting twenty-five years to do the same back. The same and worse."

"That's a nasty scar," M agreed. "I'm sure I would remember doing something like that to somebody. You got a name?"

"Aloysius."

"Well, that proves it. It couldn't have been me. How often do you meet a man named Aloysius, let alone burn out his eye? Even my memory can't be that bad."

"It was you."

M hemmed and M hawed. M drank the rest of his beer. "What were the circumstances, exactly?"

"Little Italy? 1988? You danced with my girlfriend? She had brown hair?"

"I lived in Little Italy in 1988. And I have on occasion danced with people's girlfriends. The brown hair isn't distinct enough to help us out one way or the other. But the rest . . ." M took another long look at the giant and shifted in his seat right to left to get a fuller picture. "No, I'm sorry. I can't remember any of this at all. Do you know what the bar was?"

"There a problem here?" Dino asked.

"Back away, fat man," the giant said, "this don't concern you."

But Dino seemed to disagree. Below the bar he had wrapped his fingers around the Louisville Slugger that he kept for chasing out vagrants and disposing of the occasional extradimensional entity. "This is my bar, and any-thing that happens in it concerns me."

"It's all right, Dino," M said, gesturing the shillelagh aside. "It's all right. How about you bring me and Aloysius a couple of shots. Let the man know I don't have no bad feelings."

Dino poured a few fingers of whiskey, but he kept his eyes on Aloysius and his hands near his weapon.

"Look," M said, handing one of the drinks to the giant. "You say I once did something that destroyed your face and ruined any chance of ever lead-ing a normal life. I say I didn't. This is a subject upon which reasonable men can differ. Let's drown our disagreement in liquor and call it even."

Aloysius smacked the glass out of M's hands. Dino had his cudgel out from underneath the counter, the end stained with red blood and purple ichor. Flemel tightened up his fists from a few spaces away, though he had no clear idea of doing anything.

M scratched at his ear. "No call to waste good booze."

"I'm going to kill you before the day is out," the giant said, backing out of the bar. "I'm going to kill you with my hands. I'm going to make your skull into an ashtray."

"I guess this is my shot?" M asked, then took it. "Each their own."

The giant left, but he didn't go far. He hung out on the sidewalk outside and spent a while watching M and making calls on his phone. M went back to his book.

"I can't follow you around everywhere," Dino said, putting the bat be-neath the counter.

"No, I don't suppose you can."

So far as Flemel was concerned, this was just about the most exciting thing that had ever happened to him. Two weeks he had been waiting around for M to do something that would justify Flemel having leeched onto him, something that would confirm his belief that M was a member of the confra-ternity the existence of which long study of esoterica had suggested and his own fumbling attempts at wizardry had confirmed. "What are you going to do?" Flemel finally asked M.

M licked his finger and flipped the page on his book. "About what?"

Outside the bar, two other men had arrived on Harleys, and if they weren't quite the size of the scarred giant, they were still not the sort of men with whom one would want to Jell-O wrestle. "About the guys trying to kill you."

"Oh, them," M said, turning to look at the trio of men standing outside glaring at him angrily. "I dunno. I'm sure they'll forget about me soon enough."

Flemel didn't think he was right, but then again he figured if having his life threatened by a man like Aloysius was insufficient to spur M into worry, there wasn't much he could do. After a while, Flemel went to the bathroom. While he was gone, M found a couple of paper clips from behind the bar, twisted them into a sort of stick figure. He grimaced while pulling out a few strands of his long, brown hair, then tied them neatly around the waist of his new effigy.

When Flemel came back from the bathroom, M had his coat on and was offering Flemel his own jacket. "Probably best if you were to split out before there's any trouble."

"You sure you don't need my help?"

"They won't do anything during rush hour on Washington Avenue." And indeed there seemed to be a few too many pedestrians milling about for the giant to deliver the torment he had promised M. "I'll give them a good shake on my way home and leave them tumbling aimlessly around Prospect Park. Anyway," M said patting him on the shoulder, "you have a lovely evening."

Flemel figured he would wait until M got around the block, and then follow the bikers who were going to follow M. He didn't know what he was going to do after that exactly; the few bits of chicanery he had gleaned from grimoires and frequent practice would be of no particular use in the situation. But what Flemel lacked in knowledge, strength, or planning he made up for in courage, or recklessness, which in a young man is virtually the same thing. Nor had it escaped Flemel that this might be just the opportunity he was looking for, a chance to demonstrate his utility, worm his way into M's good graces. But somehow M managed to give him the slip after barely a block: He took a left on Atlantic and Flemel took a left on Atlantic only to discover that M was no longer on Atlantic, at least not anywhere that Flemel

could see. And so after a few minutes of trying to catch M's scent and failing, he gave up and decided to head home. He was halfway back to the windowless room in the house he shared with a half dozen almost-artists in the
smellier portion of Gowanus when he felt a tap on his shoulder and then a
sudden, savage blow to the back of his head.

When Flemel came to his knees were scraping against concrete, then
wood, and then he realized that he was being carried into a vacant house,
dragged through a dilapidated corridor and into the nearest room, Aloysius
splintering the lock with his size-24 foot, an all-purpose skeleton key. The
two bikers spilled Flemel into a corner, though after a few slow seconds he
managed to right himself.

"Keep a lookout," Aloysius said. "Make sure the screams don't draw any
bystanders."

The chubbier of the two bikers reached into the back of his waistband
and came out with a .38. "You need to borrow my piece?"

Aloysius had a smile that would have swallowed a goose egg. He pulled
the handle of a butterfly knife from his jacket, extracted the blade with a
practiced motion. "No way in hell," he said. "I'm going to take my time."

The fat one put his gun back into his waistband, then followed the thin
one outside the room. The door shut.

"I don't know where he is," Flemel said. It was the honest truth, but he
didn't like giving it and felt disloyal, not that M had ever done anything to
deserve his fidelity.

"What?"

"M. I don't know where he is."

"This is a pathetic fucking attempt at humor."

"Hey, man, we're barely even friends. It's not like he keeps me abreast of
every move he makes. I don't even know where he lives."

"You think playing crazy is going to make me forget what you done to
me? Madmen scream just as loud," he said, aiming the tip of his butterfly
knife at Flemel. "Louder, even."

"What I done to you? What M done to you, you mean."

"What?"

"What?"

Two events occurred then simultaneously, or nearly so: Flemel realized he'd been played, and a little hiccup of sound wafted out from the corridor.

Flemel was too focused on the first of these to note the second. "I didn't do anything to you."

"You sang this tune already—I didn't like it any more the first time."

"No, I mean, M did something to you, obviously, but I'm not M. Actually at the moment I can sympathize with your feelings of vengeance toward the man."

"You want to die a lying little punk, you be my guest." Aloysius started toward Flemel with his knife.

And then the door opened and standing there was, so far as Aloysius was concerned, a duplicate M, and this alternate M had a tattoo of a smiley face below his left hand and the fat biker's revolver in his right. It was a confusing situation for Aloysius, one that this new M used to good effect, taking solid aim and firing off three shots. One went wide, but the rest lodged themselves in the knee and lower thigh of the leader of Moab's Minions, who screamed and dropped the knife and fell down on the ground and then screamed some more.

The M standing in the door lit a cigarette and watched Aloysius bleed. He emptied the rest of the bullets in his revolver onto the floor, then tossed it into a corner. He knelt down beside his enemy.

"So this is zero and two for you," M said, ashing his cigarette into the man's hair. "If you want to have a go at three, I'm down at The Lady most afternoons."

Then the one M snapped at the other, and both exited into the evening, leaving Aloysius to find his own way home.

Back outside, M reached into a side pocket of Flemel's coat, took out the fetish he had put there, and crushed it ruthlessly below his boot heel. "The first thing you gotta remember if you're going to be in this business," he said, offering Flemel a puff of his cigarette, "is don't trust anybody."

13

An Inevitable Coincidence

Introspection was not a strong suit of M's, nor of most of the adepts and practitioners he had known. He had faced dangers that would have made the hardiest gunslinger hang up his six-shooters, earned victories to satisfy a new Alexander, and suffered failures that would have driven a stoic mad with grief, though few of these found firm purchase in his mind. He wondered sometimes if a certain paramnesia was part of the payoff for being in good with the Management. But he didn't wonder that long, because, well, introspection was not his strong suit.

Still, there are things one does lose track of not so casually, like the heat of the sun or a pair of blue eyes.

It is an odd truth about New York, a city of millions of people, of five boroughs and hundreds of square miles: but one will inevitably stumble upon one's ex. M passed his coming out of the Strand one Tuesday afternoon, and before he could decide whether or not to pretend he hadn't seen her, she had already come up and given him a hug.

"It's you," she said.

"Seems to be."

Splitting with her had been his impetus to leave the city the last time, of course. Or had his leaving the city been the reason they had split? When he had thought of her—walking alone late at night on white sand beaches, and in the middle of the afternoon in busy cafés, and sometimes (and this had always made him feel deeply ashamed, but he had no control over it) while entangled in the limbs of another woman, breathing shallowly in that moment of almost-catatonia that comes after orgasm—he had hoped that maybe she would have grown less pretty. But she hadn't grown any less pretty. If anything, she'd done the reverse, which M felt to be poor manners altogether.

"When did you get back?"

M told her.

"Why didn't you call me?"

"Because then we would have missed finding ourselves in this uncomfortable situation."

She laughed.

There was a bar nearby. There usually is, that's one of the things about living in the city. They found it and sat down across from one another at a little table by the window. M ordered a beer, but she made do with seltzer. M tried to remember if he had anything to apologize for. He didn't think so. Or more accurately, there were many things he ought to apologize for—selfishness and pettiness and a lack of hygiene—but these were general failings, not germane to the conversation, not specific to their relationship.

The drinks came. They sat together a while, near enough that he could smell her flesh, but not so close as to touch it.

"How is Boy?" she asked.

"Masculine."

"And Stockdale?"

"English."

She smiled. "Give them my best when you see them."

"I will."

Of course, M had not missed the ring on the fourth finger of her left hand, counting from the thumb, but it was only then that M noticed the slight protuberance in her dress. Seeing the first had been like hearing your name called, turning to look for the source, and having someone strike you swiftly in the solar plexus. But the second washed over him smoothly, a pain so old and familiar that you couldn't even really call it that anymore.

"When are you due?" he asked.

"June."

"The father?"

She smiled and looked down at her belly. "He's a good 'un."

"I'm glad." Surprised to discover he wasn't lying, M decided to repeat it: "I'm glad."

"Thanks. It keeps me in a lot. I don't see much of the old crew these days."

"Don't you miss it?"

"Not so much. There's not really a point to it, you know? All those loud noises and bright colors but you never quite get anywhere. It's all a little," she shrugged, made a gesture with her hand like she didn't want to say anything to offend him, then went on and did it anyway, "childish."

Eventually the drink was over, and then a second drink was also over, and two drinks is the stopping point after which once lovers become lovers once again, and it was clear that was not going to happen. M insisted on paying, though he didn't really have any money that month, but still, better to skip a few lunches than sully your pride.

He walked her outside and caught her a cab, and she held his hand and stared into his eyes, and M wondered if maybe he should have pushed harder for that third drink, belly bump or no belly bump. She had very pretty eyes. The moment stretched. Beneath his turban the taxi driver scowled, annoyed to be wasting potential fare at the busiest time of the day.

She hugged M tight, and then she patted him on the back, and the moment was over. "You can't keep doing this forever," she said as she slid into the cab, M holding the door open to allow her passage. "We all have to grow up at some point."

M didn't answer. He watched her car retreat into the distance, thinking he would probably never see her again. Hoping, really, because this was as good an endpoint as you were going to find—a wise man notices when the credits start to roll.

Then he shook out a cigarette and lit it and observed an abandoned building in his peripheries, casting strange shadows on the asphalt. And he remembered this conversation about megapolisomancy he was having with Andre some days earlier: that certain buildings are nodes, nexuses of ley lines, pulsing centers of energy for the metropolis, which wasn't true as it turned out, or at least this building wasn't one of them. But in the basement, there was a creature that M had never seen before, and it was enough to keep him occupied until after dinner, and by the time he made it home that night, he mostly had stopped thinking about her altogether.

Mostly.

14

The Coming of the Four

They noticed walking out from the bar, though it might have happened earlier.

"Are those gas lamps?" Boy asked.

"Shit," M said.

"Who's been mucking about?" Stockdale asked.

"Wasn't me," Andre insisted. "Boy, did you sneak something into the drinks?"

Boy and Andre had started to see a lot of each other since M had introduced them, and this meant, by the inverse-square property of dating, that M saw a lot more of both of them. He had mixed feelings about this. He liked Boy and even sort of tolerated Andre, especially when he was kept on a leash, but being the mutual friend meant that he spent a lot of time watching them kiss and a fair bit of time stopping them from killing each other.

"Not yet," Boy answered, "though now that I think about it, the bar seemed a bit too authentic with its pre-Prohibition furniture, even by the standards."

"Nineteen twenty-five did not look like this," Stockdale said.

The snow had been there when they had walked into the bar, but not anything else: not the narrow alleyways, which curled below the steeples of castlelike brownstones; not the wood smoke hanging like an opaque shower curtain; not the cobblestones in the main street or the horseshit atop them; and certainly not the darkness, which alone would have made it clear they weren't where they had been, which lay thick as wool over a pre-electric or post-electric or at the very least un-electric city.

When M turned from inspecting their new reality, he discovered that Andre had somehow traded his ladies' jeans and button-down shirt for trousers, a waistcoat, and a set of aviator goggles. A short blade and a strange-looking flintlock with an oversize barrel rested on opposite hips.

"What the hell are you wearing?" Stockdale asked. Stockdale himself wore a black leather duster that ran down to his black leather boots. His rapier had a basket hilt and a jeweled pommel.

"Of course, you would have a sword," M muttered.

Boy was dressed in something between a corset and a wedding dress. One side of her head was shorn bald, and from the other a cascade of blond hair trailed down to her ankles. She carried a Gatling gun, which nearly equaled her in height and mass.

"You look like an extra in a pop-punk video," M said.

"You're one to talk."

M looked down to discover he also had on a rather striking Edwardian getup—though not for very long. Despite the cold he removed his coat and tossed it on the ground, adding an empty scabbard and a bejeweled spyglass, both of which had appeared as suddenly as his new clothes. "Not interested, thanks," M said, wrapping his arms tight and shivering.

"Suit yourself," Boy said, inspecting her new weapon.

They went into the bar and then out again, but it didn't do any good, as M had known it wouldn't. The entrance was never the egress in this sort of situation.

"If it's an illusion," Stockdale said, scaring some idling pigeons with a practice draw of his sword, "it's a remarkably good one."

"This goes on forever," Andre said, reaching his arm into a black leather purse that had appeared on his person. "That is not an exaggeration."

"We weren't near any of the main portals," Boy said.

"Impossible to be familiar with all of them," Stockdale said.

Boy's right shoulder, which coincidentally or not was the one her gun hung off of, was the mottled pink of an old burn. "A curse?"

"Forever, I tell you, that was not hyperbole." Andre was pulling out bottles from his pack, tiny vials like jewels and thick glass canteens that resembled grenades.

"Awfully elaborate," Stockdale said, running through a dance of thrusts, parries, ripostes, tripostes, coulés, derobements, and flèches.

"You learn those with your third from Oxbridge?" M asked.

"They sometimes are," Boy said. "I once spent three weeks as a child in Victorian-era Britain before I finally realized my boyfriend's ex-girlfriend was playing a nasty little trick on me."

"How'd you take that?" Stockdale asked.

"Badly."

"Wait, no, we've reached the end," Andre said, a row of philters, jars, ewers, jugs, and urns laid out on the ground before him, as well as the tools to make more of them, alembics and crucibles and pestles—a veritable alchemist's shelf. "Still, though, that's a hell of a satchel."

Boy and Stockdale spent a while longer trying to figure out why they were where they were, though M didn't really see the point. He had learned long ago that things are so much bigger than you could ever have any sense of that there was no point in supposing what was happening to you just now had any connection to anything that had happened to you before, or for that matter anything that had happened to anyone before.

And indeed, by the end of the discussion they had reached no conclusions, except that it was clear that this New York winter—for it was an ineffable but undeniable certainty that they were still somehow in New York—was far worse than theirs. Colder, at least. Despite her outfit, Boy displayed no care for the frost, laughing and dancing in the snow, which was white and soft as freshly sheared wool, though less itchy. Stockdale and Andre swaggered happily after Boy, hands tight on the pommels of their weapons. M alone seemed unhappy about the business, and not only because he had gotten rid of his coat. The city was lonely-beach quiet, back-of-the-moon quiet, locked-in-a-coffin-beneath-the-ground quiet. Occasionally the *clop-clop-clop* of hooves and the clamor of hansom cabs behind them broke the silence, and M was not slow to note that on every carriage, a man rode shotgun while carrying the same, and each stared hard at the companions as he passed.

"There has to be someone who can send us back," M said.

"Why do you think that?" Boy asked.

"There always is. Or a glowing door or something. It's the way these things work. The problem isn't getting out; the problem is not getting sucked in."

"What do you mean?"

"I mean don't get too attached to that gun."

"I love this gun," Boy said, hefting the barrel toward the sky. "I feel like Sarah Connor."

"Well, it isn't really yours and try not to get confused on that point. You're going to have to get rid of it eventually. Sooner rather than later, if I have anything to say about it."

They walked aimlessly. There was nothing else to do. Mostly they seemed to be enjoying themselves, their new toys and this fine adventure. Except for M, of course. After an hour they had passed hostelries and blacksmith shops, apothecaries and cobblers, towering cathedrals without any visible crosses and butcher shops with foreign cuts of meat in the windows. But they had not passed any magic portals or backlit doorways, nothing that suggested a passage back to their own existence. Down a narrow side street—and weren't they all narrow side streets in this faux-Dickensian hellhole—they saw a sign depicting a fat man eating a ham and stopped in front of it.

"A bite or two couldn't hurt," Boy said.

"Someone has clearly never read Washington Irving," M said, but he was too hungry to put up much of a fight. The fire inside was, if not roaring, at least mewling vigorously. There were long wooden tables and benches below those tables, all of which were empty.

"Good to see you, friends, good to see you," the publican greeted them, coming out from behind the bar. He had ears like cauliflower and skin like a potato. He was either a troll or an incredibly trollish-looking human. "Not so many come out to the Crown Inn now that the Pale King holds sway."

"That's enough, Mr. Tumnus, thank you so much," M said swiftly. "Just need a bite to eat, and then we'll be back on our way. No interest whatsoever in being dragged into any of this Pale King business."

"I wish you luck, my friends," the not-quite man said, leading them to a table. "But I'm afraid the Pale King's hand reaches everywhere and is not particular about what it snatches."

Dinner was roast turkey, or what looked like a turkey, skin crisped and crackled, served with stewed apples and thick brown bread and about half a keg of ale between the four of them.

"Who do you think this Pale King character is?" Stockdale said, forking a piece of meat.

"It's nothing to do with us," M insisted. In the candlelight one could see a portrait of a scowling child just above his left wrist.

"When evil roams without fear, is it not every righteous man's business? And woman's," Stockdale added quickly, hoping to avert trouble.

But Boy wasn't listening. "I'm going to be pissed if I can't fire this at someone," she said, buffing her gun with the fold of her dress. "Like borrowing Ron Jeremy's cock and going to mass."

"Any idea what would fit in my flintlock?" Andre asked. "The one thing that seems to have been forgotten in my bag is gunpowder."

"When did you start writing for *National Review*?" M asked Stockdale. "We have to start instituting regime change in fictional nations? Also, did any of your slick new outfits come with relevant money?"

Inside Stockdale's pockets were a handful of thick octagons made of some sort of blackish metal and featuring a glowering gentleman with a winter storm on the obverse. One proved more than enough to satisfy the innkeeper, so much so that he added another round of stout and even sat down to drink it with them.

"We're looking for a way out of here," M said, midway through his cup.

The innkeeper shrugged, his shoulders like knots in an oak. "We've a backdoor, but it just goes to an alley."

"No, I mean . . ." M thought for a while about what he did mean, and how he could explain it to the innkeeper. "Let's say we needed to get somewhere."

"Where?"

"I don't know. Oz. Lankhmar. Poughkeepsie. Not here. Who would we see about that?"

"Don't know if I can help you there. I'm just your average boggan, trying to keep his head down through the Pale King's winter, like all of the benighted people of the metropolis. If you're looking for a hymn of transport, the wisest of the witches and the highest of the magi can only be found within the walls of the island. But most of them have long since thrown in with the Pale King, and they'd be loathe to help you without payment, and probably not even then. The Spring Bride could have taken care of it in an instant, were she not frozen solid by the Pale King's curse, her dandy lions and legions of ivy kept sleeping long after their time."

"How long has she been frozen?" Stockdale asked, and to M's annoyance Boy had put aside her cannon and seemed to be listening eagerly. Andre was staring down at Boy's cleavage, rendered voluptuous in her new garments, but still, M could feel the thing slipping away.

"Who speaks of time, when each day brings with it the same blank snow, the same fierce winds? What is a year when there are no seasons? Besides, it is better not to remember the days of summer, nor even to mention them. The Pale King has many eyes watching, in the wind and in the night, for despite it all he still fears the Four to Come. The Four who will end his rule and bring harmony once again to the city."

"A bit on the nose, don't you think?" M asked, hurrying them upward and back into the evening.

Outside the gas lanterns were making a brave but futile stand against the falling dark. The moon, if there was a moon, was nowhere to be seen, obscured by the winter storm. Following them to say good-bye, the innkeeper's eye went wide as milk saucers, and he pointed one trembling finger into the night. "Winter men!" he shrieked, before darting back inside and slamming shut the door.

They must have been waiting in the snowdrifts, drawn by one of the Pale King's spies. Eight or ten of them, corpses made white from ice and black from frostbite, eyes empty, hands filled with frost-forged war scythes, shambling forward hatefully.

Ser Dale intercepted the first, parrying an awkward strike and following with a riposte that pierced the thing's skin, releasing an ichor that froze like maple syrup once it touched air. It collapsed backward into the snow, and then Ser Dale was over the corpse and in among his fellows. "What ho!" he yelled, as if he really meant it. "You'll find I'm made of sterner stuff than that!"

Lady cackled and spun the crank on her Gatling gun, razored rounds vomiting forth from the barrel, bringing a second death to the Pale King's

minions, bloodless flesh shreding like confetti. But more kept emerging from
the depths of the snow, finally awakening from their long sleep, rising upward to join the fray.

M watched the proceedings with antipathy bordering on contempt, even
as one of the creatures broke away from the pack and approached him. "I got
nothing to do with this," he said. "Can't you get killed by one of the others?"
But the thing seemed disinclined to parlay, slashing at M with his ice sickle,
glittering streaks of frost cutting through the air. M gave ground rapidly, trying to explain his position, until one of the cuts got a little too close. Then,
displaying rare nimbleness, he dodged forward, grabbed the thing by both
ears and said, "August twenty-first was the hottest day of the year in Tunisia,
which was where I was, the hubble-bubble pipes torturous to the touch, the
sunlight harsh off every reflective surface, even the most devoted of Mahom-
et's female servants worrying at their shrouds of modesty, sweat falling off
your nose and down into your tea, which never cooled, which came out of the
kettle boiling and went into your mouth boiling and boiled itself all the way
down into your gullet . . ." By then the thing was down on one knee, and a few
sentences of further description were enough to bring him all the way supine.

But despite M's grudging assistance, the contest still seemed in doubt.
Lady had gone through her clip with a rapidity that spoke more to amateur-
ish enthusiasm than the cool eye of a veteran, and she struggled to reload. Ser
Dale was being pushed back by a half-dozen winter men, unable to contend
with their numbers and the reach of their blades. It was at that moment that
Galahad, who had thus far been less valuable than M, albeit more engaged,
slapped shut the breach on his strangely fashioned blunderbuss and fired a
round that exploded in the sky above them.

For a brief few seconds it was summer: not only the warmth, but the sunlight as well, and the smell of fresh-cut grass and cooking asphalt, even that
dull lethargy that one gets after eating a few plates of barbecue in a suburban
backyard. The winter men stared up at August with growing smiles, then
slipped softly into the release the Pale King's cruelty had so long denied them.

Lady held her cannon aloft and hooted triumphantly. Ser Dale wiped the
winter men's ichor off his blade and returned it to its sheath. Galahad smiled
cheekily.

"A fine shot, Galahad!" Lady yelled.

M gave Boy a look that would have curdled milk. "Who the fuck you talking to?"

"What?"

"Who the fuck you talking to?"

"I was complimenting Andre on his aim," Boy said.

"No," M said, shivering and scowling, "you were not." But he didn't say anything further. The innkeeper refused to respond to even their most vigorous banging, and having nowhere in particular to go, they made west for the island. But soon it became too dark to continue, a heavy fog obscuring the gaslights and making farther travel impossible. It turned out that one of the things inside Andre's satchel was a tent large enough to fit all of them comfortably, as well as sleeping sacks, heavy blankets, and a brazier to keep them warm. They assembled them all in one of the small but not infrequent parks they came across, little wedges of old-growth forest sprouting up between the cobblestones. The Four went to bed that night exhausted but happy. Three of the four, anyway.

The next morning they discovered the ferry wasn't running, on account of a recent surge of attacks from the rat creatures that lived deep below the docks. They were forced on a quest to take the Rat King's pelt, and in the tunnels Lady's cannon did good work, and Ser Dale's blade did not remain long unbloodied. It took all of Galahad's cleverness to convince the half-feral children who manned the ferry that the pelt was authentic, however, conversing in their strange clipped cant, nonplussed by their catapults or their savage, beautiful eyes.

M alone did nothing to earn his keep. On the boat ride over to the inner city, when the turquoise giantess whose great torch illuminated the bay came to demand tribute, he looked up and shook his head and went back to vomiting over the side, leaving the rest of his companions to placate her. When they reached the platform and were forced into a running fight with the Blue Boys, the Pale King's corrupt and inefficient city guard, he could barely be convinced to keep up with the jog, let alone to extend himself so far as to attack their foes.

The Four survived, but only by fleeing into tightly packed tenements nearby, forced into the subterranean barrens where the larger portions of the city's population now lived, dug in deeply against the Pale King's icy fury. There they heard rumors that the last of the Spring Bride's thranes kept residence in the north of the city, secretly hidden at the very foot of the Pale King's lair. He was said to be as powerful a magi had ever lived and capable of crafting a verse that could bring a man to even the most distant realms, though, admittedly, it was only M who seemed interested in that particular point any longer. Regardless, they realized that they didn't have the money to continue north toward the village, nor begin to attempt crossing the gardens, which in the dead of winter would require sleds and dire wolves to pull them. They were forced to take a job from the First Portion, who had heard word of their accomplishments with the rat men and enlisted their aid in putting down a rebellion in nearby Zucodi Park. But it swiftly became clear that the First Portion was a thief and a liar and planned on betraying them anyways. So the companions found themselves allied with a group of earnest if somewhat exhausting tribals, leading them in rebellion and dethroning their erstwhile employer. With what they earned there, they managed to travel farther north, to the Morpheme City, where they mediated between the two rival sects of calligraphers who were near to open war over the possession of the sacred twenty-sixth, the letter that would give the reader absolute power over all the others. Having found it, the companions decided it was better lost forever, and with great regret, Galahad dropped the scroll containing it into the Well Unceasing, followed by a tear that mankind's enthusiasm for improvement was exceeded by its instinct for self-destruction.

Through it all M remained sullen, taking only what part in their adventures was necessary to ensure his own immediate safety, and even then grudgingly. In the evenings he would sit by himself and mumble long, discursive stories about places that did not exist and things that had never happened. Occasionally, though infrequently, he would fly into a rage and throw incomprehensible insults at his companions, saying that they "had the aesthetic sense of idiot children" and demanding to know of Galahad if "a dildo came complimentary with his aviator goggles." But the next morning he would arise unthreatening if not apologetic, and the rest seemed happy not to speak of it.

It was a source of measured concern among his companions. One night, in a hostelry some ways out from the Village, after M had retired early to his room with a scowl and a bottle of liquor to pour into it, they called an impromptu round table.

"What plagues him?" Ser Dale asked. "He has never been what one would call a team player, but I've never known him to give in to such constant loathing."

"He was always strange," Lady agreed. "Ever frowning when others smile, never satisfied with his hearth or the lot appointed to him, always searching, searching, searching. Also, he is very lazy and would rather mock or complain than apply himself to a situation."

"He dresses very shabbily," Galahad concurred, "and yet somehow seems prideful of the fact."

"It would not be a tragedy if he drank less frequently," Ser Dale agreed, "but this is not the purpose of the conversation."

"It is a mystery how he imagines himself a Lothario, the way his hair sticks up in the back." Galahad said.

"None would gainsay it," Ser Dale confirmed, "but again, we walk off topic."

"He worries me," Lady admitted. "He has worried me as long as I've known him. I think he is more miserable than he would like us to think."

"How did you meet?" Ser Dale asked.

Lady thought for a long time but found she could no longer remember.

• • •

And with one thing and another, some months passed, or seemed to pass. They had been forced to spend the Great Prismatic Snowstorm of '87 holed up in a vast, half-abandoned hotel, long days staring out the window as the parti-colored blizzard rose higher and higher up the tenements, only sprinting out to forage when the storm sent one of its less dangerous hues. Between freeing the Germingest Auberge from the rule of its inbred emperor and their work against the First Portion, they had long since marked themselves as enemies of the Pale King. Pursued across the city by his minions, they were forced to make common cause with the ragtag band of rebels who hoped to return the Spring Bride to her throne and finally free the city from winter's tyrannical grip. After long struggle, they met finally with the last thrane, who asked that the Four sneak into the Imperial Tower and steal the Pale King's eye, the source of his power and majesty.

And indeed that last night, they were trying to make their way to the top of the thousand floors of that legendary citadel, an escapade mad and supremely dangerous and certain to earn them a name eternal amongst the city's residents. Mad Myron's aerocraft had collapsed on landing, the steel burnt and twisted from the Corps of Wyverns that had contested their passage, the heroes lucky to have survived it. Things had not improved from there. The Custodians, the Pale King's last line of defense, faceless and insentient, pursued them relentlessly through the grim gray corridors of the hive building. Galahad's powders and flasks of morbid smoke, normally so effective, had proved useless, and they had only managed their way to the top by frequent aid of Lady's cannon; even the Custodians were not impervious to the *rat-tat-tat* and the sharpened splinters of metal that came an instant afterward.

"You'd best move swiftly," Ser Dale was saying, holding back a wave of Custodians with his rapier, hand moving at twice the speed of his tongue. "Reinforcements arrive."

Galahad knelt at the keyhole, and his lock pick held steady as he answered, "Yes, go faster. That's very helpful. Thank you. Lady, can you do something?"

"Not out of ammo, I can't." She had taken a shot from one of the Custodians glü guns and was cutting through the webbing with a hand knife.

A *snick* from the lock and Galahad pulled open the door and headed swiftly inside, Lady following him. Ser Dale pressed one of the jewels on the pommel of his sword, and the blade crackled a fabulous white, and then he threw himself into a series of passes, the traces lingering and hardening into a thickly woven wall of lightning. "Move fast!" he yelled. "My spectral shell will only hold them for a moment!"

M followed the recommendation, though with no great excess of enthusiasm. Last in, Ser Dale shut the door thunderously, and Galahad was quick to pour a sufficient quantity of his sealing wax into the gaps to buy them some time. Still, it would not hold for long against the more-than-human strength of the Custodians.

Then again, it did not need to. They had found the Pale King's eye, a sparkling glass sphere hanging motionless midair, each infinitesimally tiny facet displaying a strange and wondrous vision, portals and windows and apertures into foreign worlds, solar systems, universes, the effect of the entire thing a glittering ball of pure magic.

"Zwounds!" Galahad exhaled.

"By the Seventh Host of Atlan!" Ser Dale exclaimed.

"Baby Christ on a Cracker!" Lady added.

M threw away his cigarette.

"With that much energy we could free the Spring Bride from her stasis!" Ser Dale said. "We could regrow her armies and push the Pale King back to the North! We could return harmony to the seasons and justice to the land!"

"Sure," Lady asked, "but how the hell do we get out of here?"

"Fear not!" Galahad said, smiling and pointing toward the open window. "My alchemy might not be of use against the Custodians, but this philter of Soft Landing is proof against any fall!"

"For the love of God," M said, then put his hand up against the globe and breathed in deeply.

When they walked out of the bar the sunlight shone hard on the concrete and on the dull, gray, cold city. Someone had torn open a bag of trash, and the contents—rotted fruit and used hygiene products—lay scattered about the front.

"Spoilsport," Stockdale said.

"Killjoy," Andre added.

"Asshole," Boy muttered.

"You looked absurd in that corset," M answered.

15

A Boon for the Red Queen

M had hoped that his incapacity—not to say manifest disinterest—in having an apprentice or shepherding a youth into adulthood or really doing anything much beyond overseeing his own immediate pleasures would in time be enough to convince Flemel he might do better looking elsewhere for a tutor. Alas, an odd month after M had grudgingly acknowledged the boy's existence, he was still appearing with unbecoming regularity, stopping by The Lady several times a week and even, in a bout of almost unimaginable presumptuousness, showing up for impromptu tutoring sessions in M's parlor.

At least he generally had the good sense to bring an offering. M was devouring one of these—a bacon, egg, and cheese on an onion bagel from the Hasidic bagel shop near where Flemel laid his head—while Flemel was in the midst of attempting to perform some sort of cantrip, reciting words in a slippery, serpentine tongue and wiggling his fingers in a not altogether unsilly fashion.

A puff of smoke and M's couch, which heretofore had enjoyed existence as black leather, turned a pink paisley.

"That goes real well with the decor," M said, brushing poppy seeds out of his thin beard. "You got the rhythm wrong. It's broken beat, like a Tropicália tune. And your mental picture is off: You need to square the circle at the same time you land on the last syllable."

"I did that!"

"Obviously you didn't do that, or my couch wouldn't look like someone vomited Kool-Aid on the slip cover."

"How come I never see you do any of this? Is this just an elaborate effort to make me look foolish?"

"I wouldn't need to go through so much trouble."

M's buzzer buzzed, as buzzers sometimes do. M slipped up from his chair and answered it.

"M?"

Flemel had known M a few months, and in that time he had never seen M quiver, not when threatened with murder by a gang of oversize bikers, not when Stockdale was possessed by the ghost of a long-dead Five Point street tough, not even when they walked into The Lady and Dino told him all the beer taps were down. It was an impressive streak that ended just then, M's pallor growing ghastly and his eyes wide.

"¿Que?" he asked after too long a moment. "¡No habla Inglas! ¡Gracias! ¡Adios!"

"Hola, M. Tu acente es horrible, suenas como un gallo borracho. ¿Me deja ahora?"

"Sí," M said miserably.

"Who's that?" Flemel asked.

M didn't answer, taking his charge by the arm and walking him good-naturedly toward his bedroom window. "Say, Flemel, you ever climb down a fire escape?"

"No."

"No? Never? You just have to. It's a New York rite of passage," he insisted, opening the window.

"Why would I need to climb out the fire escape? Nothing's on fire."

"Is that the problem? 'Cause I can make a fire. I can make a fire anywhere I want. Actually, your pants look flammable as hell."

M was sure he locked the door after letting Flemel in, but all the same after two quick knocks it opened smoothly, and there was no longer any point in trying to get Flemel to climb out the window or in threatening to set him aflame.

"M," Abilene began, smiling that schoolmarm smile of hers. "How lovely to see you again!"

With his back to her, M was wincing, but when he turned around he had a grin to match her own. "Abilene!" he said, pulling Flemel forcefully across the same patch of ground they had just traversed. "What a pleasant surprise! I was just thinking how much I hoped you would show up unexpectedly and without contacting me first, and here you've done just that! Showing up unexpectedly without contacting me first, I mean. And what brings you here, exactly?"

"Oh, you know how it is. Just in the neighborhood. Thought I'd come in and check out your new digs." She appraised the aforementioned with a skeptical eye. "You really ought to get a rug."

"That's a good idea, I'll think about it."

"It would brighten up the place."

"I'll jump it to the front of the queue."

"That picture is hung crooked."

"The world is an imperfect place."

"And you should put bars on your windows."

"I'll call the super tomorrow."

"Do you have an alarm system?"

"When I moved in, I scratched some wards against unwanted visitors, but I'm not sure they're working."

"I see you have company."

"Oh, him?" M said. "He just came to fix the toilet."

"The toilet, you say?"

"Yeah, thing's been backed up for weeks. Feces all over the bathroom. Kitchen, too, though we've just managed to clean it. In fact, as much of a joy as it is to see you, given the high likelihood—I would say the virtual certainty—that the apartment is going to be knee-high in human waste in the immediate future, if I were you, I would beat a hasty retreat."

"M, if I didn't know any better I'd think you were trying to hide something from me. But the only reason you wouldn't want me to meet this charming young man is if you were lovers, and you're much too square for that, or—" Abilene's brown eyes went joyously wide, and she clapped a hand against her swelling bosom. "You took an apprentice!"

"The former," M jumped in quickly. "Not my usual bag, I admit, but he's so cute I can hardly keep my hands off the little bastard." And indeed he tightened his grip around Flemel's shoulder just then, though if you had been looking carefully you might have seen the youth wince.

"Oh, M, finally!"

"I told you, we're fucking," M said, starting to sound desperate. "Frequently. I just figured, you know, why fight it anymore? Actually, this isn't such a great time. I was just about to throw him against the bed and take him in a forceful fashion."

"What makes you think you'd pitch?" Flemel asked.

"Please, M," Abilene interrupted, "no one would ever buy you as a homosexual."

"Gender queer? Spectrum fluid?"

"In those jeans?"

"What's wrong with these jeans? They cover my legs. They've still got most of their original coloring."

"Nothing. They're lovely," Abilene said, dripping with insincerity. "Regardless, you've worn your heteronormative stripes far too long to be changing them." She looked pointedly at M, then back at Flemel.

M sighed loudly. "Flemel, this is Abilene the Red, High Queen of Greater Brooklyn. Abilene, this is Flemel, lately of butt-fuck Michigan, currently residing in the borough, not that we longtime citizens had any say in the matter."

After a brief moment, Flemel bowed low, coming back up with a little flourish.

"Aren't you the charmer," Abilene said, accepting his obeisance with a smile. "Clearly not something you learned from your tutor."

"Well," M interrupted, "it was really great seeing you, Abilene—a thorough joy all around. And thanks for giving Flemel something to tell his grandchildren, but if there's nothing in particular, I admit that—"

"Actually, M, it occurs to me all of a sudden that there *is* a little matter I could use your help with."

"Yeah? That just occurred to you?"

"We can bring your apprentice along—think of it like a field trip."

"He's not ready."

"You don't even know where we're going."

"Is it down to the corner bodega to get me a fresh six-pack? Because otherwise, he's not ready. That's not gel in his hair, it's afterbirth. He's a newborn. Let him fucking lie."

"Do you suppose you could go an entire paragraph without resorting to profanity?"

"Maybe," M supposed, "but why chance it?"

Abilene took a moment to center herself—among her many other esoteric accolades she had long ago reached the *shike* rank of Rinzai Buddhism, could reach tranquility in the midst of a wildfire or atop a wooden rollercoaster, an aegis that was generally sufficient to tolerate M for as much as two or even three hours at a time. "There's an old . . . acquaintance of mine whom I would very much like to pay a quick visit to."

"Don't let me stop you," M said, smiling brightly and waving to the still-open door.

"Far from being a hindrance, I see you as playing a positively critical role in my excursion."

"Oh? What would this friend's name be, exactly?"

"Qashi Corlo."

"I didn't know the two of you were so close," M said, not smiling anymore.

"Positively fraternal."

"Admittedly, it's been a while since I was peeking through my *Who's Who in Supernatural New York*, but I seem to recall that Corlo owes allegiance to the White Queen, rather than the Red."

"Who would be so gauche as to put political concerns over personal affection?"

"The White Queen probably would."

"She might," Abilene admitted. "Grasping little harpy. Which is why my visit needs to be of a rather . . . clandestine nature."

"That would be where I came in?"

"That would be exactly where you come in, M. I just need you to carry me onto the island, infiltrate Corlo's castle, and find the man himself."

"So I'm a courier, in essence?"

"Exactly! Nothing to it."

"You know, with the way the 4 train is running these days, it might take us all day to get over there, and no doubt this is a matter of some urgency." M snapped his fingers as in a moment of sudden revelation. "A bike messenger would be the best option! A quick shot over the bridge, don't need to worry about the vagaries of mass transit. And they look so cool in their cool pants and their fixed-gear bikes and vivid facial tattoos. Yup, a bike messenger would really be the way to go with this one. Me, personally, I've got this bathroom thing I've got to deal with—"

"We've already established Flemel is not a plumber."

"—I mean, this sodomy thing, this sodomy thing I was in the middle of and so—"

"M," Abilene began, in the voice of a fretful kindergarten teacher, or a wrathful Old Testament God, "I'm almost starting to get the impression that you're unwilling to do a small favor for an old friend whose own kindnesses toward you, were they to be stacked up in a corner of your apartment, would reach so high as to constitute positively a *health hazard*—"

"No, no," M insisted, "just . . . need to grab my shoes."

Flemel waited expectantly. M looked at him a while and considered the matter. On the one hand, what he had said to Abilene about Flemel being unready for even a casual escapade was essentially true. On the other hand, M didn't really want an apprentice, and maybe throwing him into the deep end would be sufficient to frighten him out of the whole wands-and-pointed-hats thing and into a more reasonable profession, like real estate or selling marijuana. Smiling at this unlikely but not impossible scenario, M gestured to his apprentice, and the two followed Abilene out the door and into the unfriendly February sun.

On the way to the subway, they passed a coffee shop, one of the new ones that had sprouted up since M's great act of exorcism. "Anyone want a drink?" Flemel asked with his customary friendliness, as grating to M as a horsehair shirt. "My treat!"

"Oh, aren't you just darling!" Abilene said. "I'll have a green tea. Thanks so much."

"I'll have a cup of coffee and a shot of espresso, and have the barista spit in the espresso, and then drink the espresso."

"A tea and two coffees, coming up," Flemel said, disappearing into the shop.

M lit a cigarette. "Stop smiling like that."

"Like what?" Abilene asked.

"Like your horse came in. Like your daughter just got married."

Two birds on a branch nearby, ignoring the cold and inspired by the goodwill of their sovereign, tweeted happily to each other. "I can't help myself, really I can't. To see you finally assume the promise that I've so long known was buried deep, deep inside you, that, I admit, I had sometimes supposed I might never live to see . . ."

"Look, Abilene, let's not read too much into this, OK? I felt sort of bad because I almost got him killed, and he kept coming round, and in the end it just seemed easier to teach him a few things rather than argue about it all the time."

"You say that now, but responsibility has a way of maturing us."

"Interesting that you'd say that, because despite your own weighty slate of concerns, I confess that this little errand that you've involved me in seems the very height of frivolity, not to say outright foolishness. I hardly need to mention that an unannounced visit to the city would be the sort of spark which might very well ignite a general conflagration?"

"Something so self-evident hardly required annunciation."

"And Corlo, to rely on the cheesecloth which is my memory, is one of those titans of finance who cling to Celise like cold sores on a truck-stop hooker. Any injury done toward him or, even worse, some attempt to subvert his current allegiance—"

"Do you suppose that I would think for one moment to blight my territory by inviting someone like Qashi Corlo to take shelter in it?" The happy tweeting birds had gone silent.

"Not really."

"I only offer that privilege to people I care for M, and in exchange for my goodwill and protection, I occasionally—very occasionally, almost never in fact—ask of them for some favor in return." Abilene was still smiling, though one of the birds squawked furiously, and the other fled in terror. "And in those rare circumstances when I determine the assistance of one of my many followers would be advantageous, I do not require that they *understand* every nuance and peculiarity of my thinking, a demand that would be unfair and entirely out of character with the generosity for which I am justly famed. All I ask is that they *perform* said act to the very best of their abilities—or be gracious enough to find themselves some other locale in which to reside."

Flemel came out just then, entirely oblivious to the moment of unpleasantness.

"You're a *darling* thing," Abilene said, taking the proffered tea. "He really doesn't deserve you."

M's MetroCard was cashed—it was that sort of day—and he had to give it a top-off before they could cross into the heart of Franklin Avenue Station. Of course, Abilene did not need a card—the turnstile, like everything else in Brooklyn, acquiescing neatly to her sheer force of personality. They made their way down to the Manhattan-bound platform and stopped there for a moment.

"What do you think, M?" Abilene began. "In what form shall I make my triumphant return to the city proper?"

"I've always wanted a pet gorilla," M opined. "Or a banana slug, maybe. Those things can get up to three feet in length."

"Perhaps something a bit more subtle."

"It's your show, Abilene."

"Indeed it is, M. I'm so glad that you've remembered. And your part in it, as I said, is a modest one—travel to the corner of Wall and Pearl Streets, sneak through some side exit, sniff around until you can find the owner, and then return me to my preferred shape."

"I got it."

"Don't try to get overclever with Corlo, either," Abilene said, narrowing her eyes. "He's out of your league altogether."

M grunted something that might have been agreement.

The screech of the approaching train stole the attention of the handful of awaiting passengers, and by the time it came to a stop, M and Flemel were standing above a short-haired tabby cat, more of the alley than the silk pillow variety. A quick bound and she entered the train while nestled in the crook of M's arm, her presence as clear a violation of the MTA's rules as her transformation was the broader laws of physics.

It was not until the doors shut that M recalled his long-standing cat allergy, a condition that had broken off nearly as many relationships as his poverty and general aimlessness. By Grand Army Plaza he was sniffling, by Bergen his nose was running like a gazelle with its tail lit on fire, and by the time they reached the Barclays Center and a horde of passengers flooded the train, he was sneezing all but uncontrollably.

It did not help his humor, which was ill to begin with. "M will not be free," he misquoted, "until the last queen is strangled with the intestine of the last cat."

"She seemed OK."

"Well, heck, you've known her for almost twenty-five minutes, your opinion on the matter must be just sound as sterling."

"But . . . she watches out for the borough, right?"

"She owns the damn thing! I put mice traps beneath my oven, but no one has any plans to award me the Medal of Honor."

"You've got a real streak of anarchy in you, M. I hadn't noticed."

"Not at all—the world is a terrible place filled with very nasty people. Wise government consists of finding the biggest one and giving them enough property so that they have a personal incentive to keep everyone else in line."

"What about her counterpart?"

"The Red Queen, the White Queen—it's the noun you need to be looking at here, not the adjective."

"If you hate her so much, why don't you leave her like that?"

"I don't hate her. I just prefer to appreciate her from afar. Besides, if she stayed a cat forever, there would be nothing to stop Celise from taking over all of the city. Believe me, the only thing worse than two queens would be one empress."

Across from them sat a family of tourists, milk-fed corn huskers of the classic model, fanny packs and oversize cameras and I ♥ NY shirts. "What an adorable kitty!" said the mother, thunder-thighed and wide-smiling. "What's her name?"

"Pudding Pop," M said after a moment. "Princess Pudding Pop the Third."

"What a lovely name."

"Thank you, yes. When I got her from the pound, I looked at her, and there it was, just leapt into my mind like a bolt of lightning or the living flame itself: Princess Pudding Pop the Third."

"Can I hold her?" asked the daughter shyly.

"Absolutely," M said without hesitation, shoving the cat into her hands, which he hoped were sticky with chocolate or gum resin. "She loves to be petted. Vigorously. She also really likes it when you pull on her ears."

"Cats don't like that," said the brother.

"Look, whose cat is this, exactly? It's mine, clearly, otherwise I wouldn't be carrying it on my lap all the way to goddamned Manhattan." This spurred off another unpleasant bout of sniffling. "I'm telling you, Princess Pudding Pop the Third loves nothing better than to have her ears vigorously stretched."

It was difficult to tell that from Princess Pudding Pop's reaction, which echoed unpleasantly through the train car. The family of tourists got off at the next station, looking back at M warily and wondering if they should drop a call to the ASPCA.

M and Flemel alighted at Wall Street and made their way topside. Flemel had to use his phone for directions, because everything in the Financial District looked the same to M—the buildings and the people, too for that matter, wading through a sea of faceless finance drones as if sprung from an off-brand dragon's tooth. The office building at the corner of Wall and Pearl Streets at least broke the mold slightly, the standard glass skyscraper buttressed by a strange profusion of esoteric symbols, pentagrams, ankhs, stars of David, mandalas, and rosy crosses. Guarding the front entrance were a handful of oddly serious-looking security guards, eyes hard and fast moving, shoulders stretching their suits. Seeing them, M sucked a tooth and continued on. Halfway down the office block was a chain coffee shop, and slipping through a door marked EMPLOYEES ONLY, they found themselves in the bowels of the adjoining building.

No doubt the lobby of Corlo's building was your classic monument to conspicuous consumption—a beautiful, ethnically ambiguous receptionist and a million dollars' worth of Damien Hirst on the walls. But the sublevel in which they entered was the usual catacomb. Princess Pudding Pop the Third jumped down from Flemel's hands and led them deeper into the labyrinth, possessed of some preternatural directional sense, scampering through the maze of passageways, stopping only when she came to a bright metal door, then turning and mewling expectantly.

"Shit," M said.

"What's the problem?" Flemel asked. "You can pick locks, right?"

"Not very well."

"You told that goth girl at The Lady the other night that all you needed was a hat pin and twenty minutes, and you could open any door in the world."

"A master thief packing a solid twelve inches," M said, shaking his head back and forth. "You are really an embarrassment to me, do you know that?"

"Is there a problem here?" asked a voice from behind them, one of distinct unfriendliness.

They turned to discover a very large man, bigger than M or Flemel, probably bigger than both of them set together, carrying an automatic pistol sized to fit his massive hands.

"Yeah, lots," M began. "First, you see, there's this cat, and I'm allergic to cats." M let out a violent sneeze as if in evidence. "I don't like them apart from that, to be honest. What's the point of taking care of a creature that would eat you if it was big enough? Just as soon have nothing to do with them, a feeling I share toward this apprentice whom I've got stuck with—not sure how that happened really. You use a guy as a scapegoat against a murderous crew of Nazi bikers *one time*, and he just keeps showing up, week after week, taking up space, changing the color of your couch, expecting you to teach him magic. Also, I'm starting to think I might have gotten finagled into tipping the balance of power between the two great potentates of New York City, whose continued stalemate is the only thing that keeps the place remotely tolerable. The ocean levels are rising at a rate unprecedented in history, I read a news story recently that said that *every single seabird in the world* has at some point digested plastic, they're making another *Transformers* movie, any objective observer would have to conclude that we are nearing the end state of a capitalist society that seems to exist for no grander purpose than to consume and consume and consume and consume, without meaning, point, or guiding philosophy, death is an inescapable and absolute foe against which no struggle will avail us, the Earth is only a few billions years away from being consumed by an exploding sun, the universe itself only a few billion years away from its own effective expiration from heat death, and I'm pretty sure there isn't a God."

"Oh," the guard said after a long moment, his eyes lost staring at the enormity of M's misfortune.

"Yeah, so . . ." M took a deep breath. "That's kind of weighing on my mind. Can you do anything about any of those?"

"I . . . don't think so."

"No?" M grimaced. "Then maybe just go ahead and open the door?"

Despondent, the guard took his hand off his weapon and filched out a ring of keys.

"Thanks," M said, rather brightly given the slate of concerns facing him, the race, and the planet.

"Don't mention it," the man said mournfully, then wandered off to find a bar or put the muzzle of his pistol to his temple.

Through the egress and Princess Pudding Pop the Third again took lead, down another hallway and then up a small flight of stairs and into the spring sunlight. In the center of Corlo's vast metal edifice, a facsimile wilderness had been created—some shrubbery and even a few stunted oak, a well-manicured wood-chipped path leading round it. The centerpiece of this cut-rate pleasure garden was an artificial stream that jutted up from some subterranean reservoir and trickled on its way about a hundred feet before disappearing back into the ground. On normal afternoons no doubt the patio was filled with financiers and PR potentates enjoying the twenty-five minutes of personal time they were allotted daily, swallowing office doughnuts and power bars while frantically checking their stock tickers, faintly cognizant of the greenery that surrounded them.

But today was not a normal day, and the only person to be found in the small swath of faux wilderness was the owner himself. Qashi Corlo belonged in a hand-tailored suit, charcoal or jet black, with a rhino-leather briefcase carrying inside it a hundred million in bearer bonds. He did not belong in waders and an oversize hat with colored lures hanging from the brim, holding on to a rod and a reel that seemed nearly the length of the river itself. This was what he was clad in at the moment of M's arrival, however, and, as co-incidence would have it, at this self-same moment Corlo laughed and reeled back his catch, a spot of silver pulling up from the artificial waters, wriggling bright in the afternoon sun.

M drew his attention, deliberately or unintentionally, with a loud sneeze.

There are limitations on how furious a person can manage to look while holding erect a fishing pole. Corlo bumped neatly against them. "You can't have it!" he yelled. "It's mine!"

"You can keep it!" M responded, seeming just as angry, indeed more so. "I wouldn't take it if you gave it to me! I wouldn't take it if you sent it to me on a silver platter carried by a beautiful naked woman! What is it?"

"The Salmon of Wisdom, of course!" Qashi yelled, then a moment later and under his breath, "Shit."

The Salmon of Wisdom begins life as a fry of modest intellectual ability, and over the course of its long centuries and even millennium of existence, swimming, feeding, spawning, observing the foibles of the various surrounding species, contemplating the categorical imperative, it eventually grows to full maturity as the living repository of all knowledge—animal, human, and divine. Until at some point, it slips up, as even the cleverest of creatures are apt to do, and gets snatched by some or other pisactor that absorbs its collected erudition by means of consumption, and the process begins all over again. In keeping with its inconceivable omniscience, the Salmon of Wisdom is capable not only of navigating the traditional routes of its kind, but also of finding itself in any other running body of water—oceans, estuaries, bathtubs, sewage systems, and, apparently, the small fake river that some Frank Lloyd Wright epigone had installed in the courtyard of Corlo's building.

"So that's what this is about," M said after a moment, to himself, or to the firmament, but in any case not really to any of the assembled—feline or human. "How'd you find it? Finnegas had to wait around for half a lifetime before it showed, and that was back when it confined itself to Eire."

"Old Finn did not have access to the latest in big-data technology. I've had a handful of supercomputers working on this problem for the better part of the twenty-first century, figuring out the exact moment when the salmon would make its arrival in my domain. And now I have him!" Corlo said, gesturing at his captured fish. "All the world's knowledge, a vast, nigh-infinite understanding, the secrets of the cosmos, the hidden names of all living things, celebrity gossip, incantations foul and pure—"

"How were you thinking of preparing him?"

"What?"

"Fry, baked, boiled—what's your plan?"

"I hadn't thought about it really." Corlo admitted after a moment.

"You hadn't thought about it?" M asked, incredulous. "All these years waiting around to capture him, you never spent a moment wondering how you were going to eat him? Here's what I'd do, personally: find one of those little hole-in-the-wall joints in Chinatown—Queens would be better, really—an authentic one, where you're the only English speaker and there are typos all over the menu, and have them fry it up for you."

Corlo shrugged, unenthused. "I'll probably just steam it on a bed of kale. Better for my diet."

"God, I hate you," M muttered to no one in particular.

"Be that as it may—I don't care how you found out about it, and I've no desire to debate culinary matters any longer. The salmon is mine, fairly caught, and if you imagine I'd allow you to come in here and steal it from me—"

"Me?" M asked, as if the suggestion had never occurred to him. "You misunderstand entirely. I'm just hear to bear witness. I'm not the one who you're going to need to go tête-à-tête with if you hope to ingest the condensed wisdom of the planet. I'm not the one against whose magical abilities you'll need to measure yourself." M sneezed again, rubbed his nose, and nodded at Flemel. "It's big man over here."

"Him?" Corlo asked.

"Me?" Flemel asked.

"Yeah, him! Flemel here is a two-fisted killer of the old school, a real bruiser, Pelé with a pentagram, the mystical Michael Jordan."

"He looks like raw meat at a NAMBLA convention," Corlo added.

"OK, that was pretty good," M conceded. "I'm going to probably steal that and use it later. But the fact remains that you're face-to-face with one of the deadliest duelists in this reality and three or four of the adjourning ones."

"He's barely a child!"

"I bet those were the last words of a bunch of people who met Billy H. Bonney."

Princess Pudding Pop the Third was showing marked evidence of feline fury, scratching at the cuff of M's jeans and hissing vigorously.

"If he's so deadly, then why haven't I ever heard of him?" Corlo asked.

That Flemel was as yet too terrified to utter more than a monosyllable of English served M in good stead just then. "He's European. I imported him special from Norway, just for this little get-together. A cool half million and an ounce of powdered unicorn horn, just so he could turn you into a newt or send you hurtling into some alien dimension. I mean, I'll leave it to him—he's the specialist, after all—but whatever it is, it won't be very good."

They say that to find the killer in any given room, you'd do well to search for the quiet one, the unassuming one, the one who looks like they aren't try-ing to prove anything. And certainly, there could be few individuals with any claim to supernatural accomplishment who looked less prepossessing than Flemel just then—a youthful hipster, slightly chubby, wearing a faded band T-shirt and scuffed trainers.

Corlo inspected him for a long time, trying to find the lion lurking be-neath the surface. "I don't buy it," he said finally, "or in any event, I'm willing to chance the matter. I've been waiting for the salmon to fall into my hands for nearly forty years, and if that means squaring off against your hired help . . ." Corlo set his rod in a waiting holder, the salmon wriggling at the end, then brushed brine off his waders and stood squarely to face Flemel. "So be it."

Flemel went from his usual pink to something resembling eggshell.

"You know something," M admitted, "you are very slightly smarter than I'd earlier credited you."

"Thank you."

"It was a low bar, however. Abilene, if you would be so kind . . ."

And then, where Princess Pudding Pop the Third had once been hissing unpleasantly there stood the Red Queen, Nineveh's second, an early draft of the mother goddess herself.

Flemel looked less worried. Corlo, rather more so. M maintained his usual composure.

"After this is over," she began as a quick aside to M, "we're going to have a long conversation about your sense of timing and, for that matter, the appropriate matter in which to treat a cat."

"What in the name of all the gods are you doing here?" Corlo asked, for the moment more shocked than anything else.

"Stealing the Salmon of Wisdom," M clarified. "That much I was being truthful on. Everything else, however . . ."

"This is an act of war, Abilene," Corlo interrupted. "Celise will be forced to marshal her forces and respond in kind."

"Undoubtedly, were she ever to learn of it. But then who's going to tell her? Are you so keen to reveal to your mistress that you took it upon yourself to absorb the full strength of the salmon, during its first visit to the city in a hundred years? Do you imagine she will find failure sufficient defense against disloyalty?" Abilene tut-tutted disapprovingly. "I'm afraid she would do something very unkind to you before attempting to do the same to me. Though once I take this little morsel home for sashimi, I doubt I'll have much to worry about from her end regardless. It will mean a violation of my strict veganism, but then, godhood requires certain sacrifices."

On the waiting rod, the Salmon of Wisdom jackknifed and buckled unpleasantly, straining for freedom with every bit of its fleshy strength. In front of it, Abilene and Corlo stared hard at each other, the first step in a process that would, if continued, almost certainly culminate in the destruction of the building and the surrounding neighborhood and much of the Lower East Side. In the midst of this interlude, the calm before the magical storm, M turned toward the fishing equipment and let out a tremendous, a prodigious, an absolutely Rabelaisian sternutation, sending green gobs of phlegm onto the stonework. No one seemed to notice, however.

And then, just as the afternoon was to climax in a contest of cataclysmic or near-cataclysmic proportions, Corlo sneered and turned toward M. "I will not soon forget today's intrusion—you've made more of an enemy today than you suppose."

"What about him?" M asked, pointing toward Flemel. "He's the one you really should be angry at."

Flemel gulped, and Corlo scowled and stalked off into the building, rubber boots trailing water onto marble. He left behind the tattered shreds of his dignity and the ingenious *Osteichthyes*, the ingestion of which was sure to end Abilene's status as coruler of greater New York, leaving her as sole claimant to the position.

Abilene basked in her moment of glory for a time before speaking. "An excellent job, M, all things considered. Of course, it took you rather longer than was absolutely necessary, but then, all's well that ends well. Don't think I'll be slow to forget your assistance, once the full and unfettered knowledge of existence courses through my tummy. Nor you, young apprentice—I hardly need omniscience to suppose your future a bright one."

Meaning to bow graciously, Flemel was taking a short backward step toward the fishing equipment when the black rubber treads of his kicks slid on an unseen tract of mucous and, arms windmilling wildly, stumbled and knocked the rod straight into the artificial river. Freed from its cruel torment, the Salmon of Wisdom was swift to make good its escape, a spurt of silver and it had dissapeared into the depths of the false stream and onward to some other body of water.

"Oh, no!" M yelled with all outward appearance of regret. "Oh, no, Flemel, what have you done! Oh, you stupid, stupid, stupid little child!" He grabbed his apprentice by the shoulder, pulling him up off the ground only to shake him vigorously. "You've ruined everything! Now Abilene will never get to eat the Salmon of Wisdom!"

This was more or less what Abilene was going to say, though perhaps accompanied by some form of punishment more severe than M was delivering. In any event, M's doing so meant her thunder was pretty well purloined. "I'm sure it was an accident," Abilene said through clenched teeth.

"No, no!" M insisted, shaking Flemel back and forth like a pit bull with a rag doll. "He doesn't get let off the hook that easy! That paisley thing is the last spell I ever teach you! For a while at least! Three, no, five weeks! And bring everything bagels in the future! Not whole wheat either!"

"I . . ." Flemel attempted, but his teeth rattled too hard to allow full answer.

"It's fine, M" Abilene said, though the scowl marring her usually cheerful countenance might have made you think otherwise. "The important thing is that Corlo didn't get it."

"Yes, that is indeed the most important thing," M agreed, though he shook Flemel a few seconds longer all the same, only stopping when Flemel's pale pallor had gone green. "It's nice to know I can count on you to offer perspective in these moments of seeming despair. Do you want to reassume your cat shape here, or shall we wait until we get to the lobby?"

It seemed the latter, though there was no clear answer, Abilene stepping swiftly out of the courtyard wearing a rare and unbecoming frown. Flemel followed behind her, trying to think of some apology or explanation that might satisfy the Red Queen's ire.

M kept an even pace behind them, humming a vague tune and very nearly smiling.

16

Tit for Tat

M took a flier from an East Asian adolescent near Canal Street one after-noon, discovered the reverse had an intricate insignia formed from a sweet-smelling ash, dropped it, and immediately started running. Halfway down the street he heard a child laughing and the crack of ice in a spring thaw, and then he was knocked off his feet and into a nearby wall, and then he bled for a little while.

M had figured that returning to the city meant that at some point Rjurik would come for him. Reliability is one of the upsides of a good nemesis, and Rjurik was most definitely that. For the first month or two, M had walked around uneasily, though he knew Rjurik was too smart to come at him right away and would wait until M had dropped his guard. Which is what had happened, obviously, otherwise M would never have been so foolish as to accept a curse from a stranger, one M felt working on him from the moment he touched it. It was clever. Rjurik didn't go in for that sort of thing; he was strictly occidental in his style, must have brought the kid in as backup. The body blow was Rjurik's own, though, and M did not think he would survive a second.

Grim moments call for rash deeds, and there was no point playing by the rules any longer. The Management could call in his tab if it had to, better than giving Rjurik the satisfaction. M caught a glimpse of him coming out from an alleyway across the street, wearing a Brooks Brothers suit and smiling like the happy sadist he was. And then M began to speak, softly but distinctly; it would not do to make an error and unspool existence. The ringing in M's ears was terribly loud, so loud that he couldn't hear what he was saying, but he could feel the words take hold in the firmament, in the nebulous connectors that prop up reality.

And then all the neon lights on Canal Street—there are many of them, if you haven't been there—erupted, a falling cascade of sparks, shuddering droplets of fire brighter than the winter sun. If M wasn't already deafened, he would have been then, as the mass of tourists—there are always tourists on Canal Street, even more tourists than there are neon lights—began to scream and run about frantically. The river of human flesh overflew its banks, and in the chaos M managed to pull himself up to his feet and start moving.

M sprinted until some combination of his injuries and his smoking habits brought him up short. Then he made himself sprint a little bit longer, down into a subway station, through the turnstiles, and onto the next train. He rode it to Forty-Second Street, by which point his hearing had mostly returned.

On principle, M did not like to ask for help, because he was incandescently arrogant and also because he did not like to return a favor. But misfortune has a way of laying bare the true bedrock of our characters, and once he was back at ground level M pulled his phone out of his pocket to call Boy.

Except that Boy wasn't in his phone anymore, and neither were Stockdale nor Andre nor either of the Queens nor anyone else. His contact list was as long as it had ever been, but the entries were all in Cyrillic and Kanji and Wingdings, and when he started calling these randomly, the lines just rang and rang. He finally found a working pay phone, though it took him another twenty minutes for his memory, corrupted by years of electronic assistance, to provide her number.

"Yo," Boy said.

"Fabulous falsehoods fall foul to the furious force of fact!" M shouted into the receiver. "Bulbous bowels bring bright bile to bitter boys!"

"Fuck off, perv."

Things went similarly once he finally got in touch with Stockdale: M's words contorted into gibberish, this time with an unsubtle flavor of racial bigotry. M gave up after that. He couldn't remember anyone else's phone number, and he knew that any other means of communication would get similarly jumbled, emails tortured, texts strangled and bent.

He sat down against an alley wall for a few moments, trying to ignore the swelling in his ankle as he teased apart the strands of his curse. It was a clever one. It was tightly wound and touchy, and since M had actually held the fetish, it had particular potency. If he'd had the time to spend on self-loathing, he would have spent it, because that was a moment of breathtaking stupidity, but the situation was clearly too dire to waste in angry reflection.

It had not been a particularly brutal March, but it was March all the same, and very nearly a March evening, and M was getting cold. Rjurik would have his apartment staked out, and he would find enough there to track M, nail clippings and pubic hair and the taint of old dreams. There were upsides to being wealthy and having lived in New York since before it was named that: You could put down roots into the ley lines and make friends with bad enemies. M was already in shit with the Management for that trick he had pulled getting out of Chinatown; he could feel himself grinding down against the pavement, reservoirs all but depleted. Rjurik's had been a good plan, if rather inelegant—isolate him from anyone who might be of assistance, then break him right in two.

M crossed the street to where a group of homeless men were playing chess, swapped coats with one of the less odoriferous, traded his cell phone for a ski cap. South a few blocks, he passed a busker singing pop-punk covers and gave him everything he had in his wallet, just north of a hundred dollars. The boy thanked him effusively and asked if he had any requests. "Burn your guitar," M said, then threw his wallet into a mailbox.

That first night was the worst. March is a false month, offering sun just long enough to convince you not to bring a coat, then hitting you with a row of sleet for your presumption. M walked until he could not stand, to try to keep warm and because he had nothing else to do. Night fell and the temperature dropped and M smoked his last cigarette, severing his final ties with his old life. Then he dropped the empty pack onto a subway gutter, and then he curled up in his new-old coat and went to sleep beside it. It had been years since he had slept rough, and he had forgotten how terrible it was, shuddering yourself awake every fifteen minutes, ceaselessly exhausted yet unable to attain release.

M had last seen Rjurik in Edinburgh, unexpectedly getting a whiff of him around the Royal Mile and luring him into a nearby bar, one of those classic Scottish joints that go back before the Union, filled with the ghosts of long-dead patrons. M had convinced one of the sadder and more powerful of them that Rjurik was her long-lost lover, back now finally from the wars. When M left they were waltzing together silently, the ghost wearing that ecstasy known only to the dead, Rjurik blank-eyed and senseless.

The cop who woke M the next morning wasn't as unfriendly as he might have been, not as unfriendly as the people M tried to ask for money. M did not have it in him, or at least he did not have it in him at first, to actively panhandle, walking mad-eyed through subway cars spinning stories of need and despair. He found an empty coffee cup, took a seat against a wall in the Garment District, and waited to see if anyone would fill it. By dusk he was lightheaded with hunger, and it was getting cold again, and he had ninety-four cents to show for twelve hours' supplication. The group of homeless men he approached as darkness fell treated him with professional courtesy, not as an interloper, and gave him directions to a nearby church where he could find something to eat. That something was tasteless verging on inedible, and the God botherer who served it to him unpleasant, but M slopped it down gratefully before heading out to find a place to sleep.

The time before Edinburgh, M was working on a post-breakup drunk in Alphabet City, and Rjurik had come in, fully charged and ready for a tussle. M fled through the backdoor and into a side existence, Rjurik on his heels, sprinting farther and farther into the firmament, past pocket universes and reflected realities, until they were so deep in the outskirts of eternity that the most basic of concepts—position and direction, substance and thought— become intertwined to the point of meaninglessness. There was a creature floating in the not-sky, something like a jellyfish and something like a premise, something like pure thought, and M had managed to get its attention, and the next thing he knew he was in Bangkok and thirty-six months had passed.

M was attacked the fourth night, in one of the big shelters, hundreds of bunk beds tucked together in a subbasement, the echoed snoring loud

enough to veil any untoward activity even if anyone had been around to listen. There were two of them and M's ankle had not yet healed, but he was
younger, or at least his body was, and he was protecting his anal virginity,
which he thought was a prize worth fighting for.

While kicking the teeth out of one of his would-be sodomites, watching
the little flecks of white spray across the concrete floor, screaming furiously
and in triumph, M was reminded of this one time he had taken over an abandoned house in the Bowery—this was back when the Bowery had abandoned
houses instead of boutique coffee houses—and spent three weeks ringing the
walls and the ceilings and the foundations with runes and wards and patterns meant to get the Management to ignore you, a sort of mystical blind
spot. Then he had tricked Rjurik into following him inside and beaten him
savagely with a length of piping, beaten him near to death though stopping,
for whatever reason, just short of it. If Rjurik had been a civilian he would
have spent the rest of his life on a feeding tube, but obviously Rjurik was not
a civilian, and when he had come back around to try to kill M five years afterward, he walked upright and was as pretty as ever.

By the second week M had gotten good enough at scrounging through
dumpsters that he mostly did not need to go to any of the shelters for food.
He went about his business methodically and without shame—indeed it
astonished him how quickly he got used to living as something not quite
human, the stares and the lack of them, the absence of attention. He did not
blame the passerby for ignoring him; one could not be expected to look at
the face of things all the time, one had to go about one's business. M smoked
crack for the first time in an abandoned subway tunnel. The MTA will tell
you that there isn't anyone living down there, but there are, little enclaves
distributed across the city. He didn't like it, but you never like a drug the first
time you try it, and he felt confident he could pick up a taste if he decided to
make the effort.

Many years before, alone in a mountain hut in Lesotho, M and Rjurik
had riddled for hours, the wind howling outside the walls, a summer storm
the likes of which neither had ever seen nor would see again, talking until
their voices gave out and the sun had returned. In the morning, they parted
ways without a word.

By the first days of April, the weather had changed, and M realized what mankind had lost by subduing his environment, by lying down in a heated apartment—that knowledge that you are a very small part of the world, that the grandest and the lowest of us alike are held in check by the rain. The curse was too tight to uncoil, but it could be sloughed off, like a starved man wriggling free of bounds attached when he was sleek. For three weeks M let his character melt off his frame. He forgot things about himself, music he had liked and books he had read and women he had held briefly. Foreign beaches and candlelit dinners and a song his mother had once taught him. He let poverty and despair grind down around the hard essential core of his hatred, like a stone smoothed flat by the ocean. He caressed and formed it, he nurtured and loved it, until it began to take on the characteristic of a bullet in his mind, an arrow shaft of awfulness, the distillation of a short lifetime spent among the miserable and the impoverished and the defeated.

Once in a Five Points brew house, Rjurik had walked up and shot him twice with a revolver, M only being saved by the intervention of a pack of Dead Rabbits and his own preternatural fortitude. Once at the funeral of a mutual acquaintance, they had each put away a bottle of scotch, sitting across from each other and observing the peace, waiting to see who would drop, knowing and expecting that neither would. Once they had been friends. Once there had been a woman.

On a busy afternoon in April, M recognized himself in the burnished metal of a hot dog stand, staring blindly while the Arab inside screamed at him. The reflection was sallow and gaunt and his beard had gone from hipster rugged to flat-out begrimed. His eyes were on the wrong side of madness. M figured it was time to go and take care of the thing, while he still had some loose idea of who he was.

...

Isaac was at the back of the pack, thrilled to have been asked along and just wanting to get through the meal without drawing too much attention to himself. It was a badge of honor, a junior associate like him keeping pace with the big dogs, even though it was only coincidence that he had been in the conference room while plans for lunch had been made, his presence allowed but not outright requested. Isaac had long since realized that an exaggerated commitment to modesty would do him no particular good in the world of high finance. These were proud men, arrogant men, you might even say, though didn't they have reason to be so? Starting salary for a trader at Edeilweiss and Grommer was two-hundred-plus bennies, and anyone still making that three years in was a borderline retard and ought to be sterilized in the evolutionary interest of the species. All you needed to do was keep putting in your hours, climbing up the greased slope to wealth and its inevitable by-products: happiness and satisfaction.

And at the apex was Rjurik, six-feet-three inches of Nordic muscle, top seller since, hell, forever, for so long that if you asked HR about it, they looked at you cross-eyed and told you that junior associates don't need to be bothering about that sort of thing. He was the platonic ideal of the investment banker, a Wall Street timber wolf, unapologetic in his greed and lust and strength.

It was not that Isaac did not see the homeless man sitting blank-eyed on the park bench as they passed; it was that one does not make an effort to notice every ephemeral bit of stimuli that filters in through the senses, every cloud and trail of dust, every passing tourist, every pigeon or rat. Maybe walking alone late at night he'd have given the man a twice-over, but noontime on a Tuesday, surrounded by a half-dozen millionaire alpha males, only taking time off from making money to hit the gym, Isaac did not suppose there was a vagrant within the city limits mad enough to target them for aggressive panhandling.

Rjurik wasn't paying attention either, not until he had almost run into the man, and not much even then, turning toward him with a snarl, biceps ready for violence. But then the transient took Rjurik by his arms and belched fiercely, and Isaac smelled something indescribably foul and had a sudden impression of the most extraordinary despair, irremediable and absolute, although when he told the story to the cops of course he didn't mention it, and when he went home that night, he drank enough whiskey to try to drive it from his memory—that night and many nights to come.

Isaac and the rest of the group—Masters of the World each of them, thousand-dollar suits and hundred-dollar haircuts, half still jacked up from the previous evening's coke binge—recoiled in horror. Rjurik dropped cross-legged on the ground, ruining his suit, and his eyes were blank and unresponsive. Standing above him triumphant, the vagrant reached down and pulled a pack of Camels from Rjurik's breast pocket, lit one somehow, then spent a slow moment enjoying it.

"Your move," he said, before flipping off Isaac and the rest and walking, casually and with no hurry, into the park and the city beyond.

Ten minutes elapsed while they tried to bring Rjurik out from his state of catatonia. When that didn't work, Isaac made the executive decision to call an EMT, which he felt displayed a level of composure that he hoped would not go unnoticed by the rest of the team. It was clear, after all, there was now an opening.

• • •

Back in his apartment M bundled his clothes and threw them into the incinerator. Then he took a long shower and shaved himself carefully. Then he took a longer bath, waking up in lukewarm water before managing, with great strength of will, to pull himself off to bed.

17

Little Else Happened in April

Some months are like that. M enjoyed the slow improvement of the weather, and he spent a lot of time exploring the neighborhood coffee shops, which is less worthy of discussion than, say, exploring the Pacific Northwest. He read a lot. There was a girl around for a while, but nothing came of it, and then at some point M didn't see her anymore. He enjoyed being within walking distance of a credible ramen restaurant. That was about it.

18

May, However . . .

. . . was just busy as hell, started busy and never wound down. M woke up one day and the city had shrugged off the last remnants of winter, a great brilliant lumbering beast recalling its strength of old, stamping its feet, roaring defiance at the heavens, threatening to scale Olympus and uproot what it found living there.

Or something like that. M kept running into people he hadn't seen in a long time, kept getting pulled into bars, parties, misadventures, tragedies. He would go out to grab a quick cup of coffee in the afternoon and wind up back in his apartment fourteen hours later, holding on to someone's hand likely as not, a bright-eyed beauty stumbling through the world at a breakneck pace, both of them wanting so hard that they almost believed it a need.

In one week, M made close to fifty thousand dollars, half taking care of a thing that needed to be taken care of for Abilene, half the next night at the World's Oldest Floating Craps Game, rolling against a short, shriveled grandfather with a beard white as bone and skin black as pitch. M's neck and the right side of his face were puckered with what looked like hickies given by a star-faced mole, courtesy of the thing Abilene needed doing, and he rolled seven times without direct assistance from the Management, statistically comparable to being struck by lightning while simultaneously bitten by a shark, and he would have rolled it again if the man hadn't gone bust, revealing empty pockets and exiting without remark, never to be seen again in

Manhattan proper, though M heard occasional rumor of him out Bronx way.

He blew most of it next weekend on Stockdale's birthday dinner, a seven-course meal of creatures that were extinct or had never existed: mastodon steaks and foie gras of phoenix and minotaur headcheese in a mandrake reduction. The wine parings were exquisite, and there was some drunken fumbling for the check afterward, but M ended up with the top hand, or the bottom, and walked out of the place smiling, having dropped in the course of three and a half hours the down payment on a small condo in Tribeca or a mansion in Long Island City.

But what was money anyway, in the city, in spring? And of course New York is *the* city. It has enjoyed that distinction at least since the collapse of the British Empire, Stockdale be damned. It is not the prettiest city in the world. It is not the safest. It is not the cleanest. It is miserable in the winter, and for large portions of the summer. Many people, visitors and short-term residents alike, find it absurdly expensive, stultifyingly pretentious, not worth the time or the trouble or the expense. And they aren't entirely wrong, but their opinion does not carry with it any weight of importance. Like the sun, like the Old Testament, like a beautiful woman, New York does not care what you think of it. History has rendered its judgment, and it is left to only us to uphold it.

Consider: Suppose an alien being, some unworldly creature with origins in a distant nebula—superintelligent lichen or a giant floating amoeba or even the ubiquitous gray—were to appear on Earth desirous of seeing what we here on terra firma call a city. Where would you take him? To smoky London? To once-divided Berlin? To Tokyo and its spires? Of course not. You would buy him a ticket to Penn Station and apologize for how ugly it is, and afterward you would step out into Midtown and you would tell him that this is what man *is*, for better or worse.

For that month, at least, it seemed to M the former.

19

A Sunday Sojourn

M's feet began to itch one Sunday morning around noon. He walked down-stairs, but they kept itching. He walked to the end of his neighborhood with-out finding a remedy. He walked to the museum, and then past the library. He walked to Prospect Park, and then he walked to the end of Prospect Park, and then he walked to the end of Green-Wood Cemetery, and then he kept walking, south into the hinterlands that led toward the bay. Still, his feet con-tinued to itch.

M was unsurprised to discover that, fifty or so blocks farther than he had ever been before, there started to appear things that were not on the map, at least not on any map M had seen. He had once known a girl who lived near Owl's Park, but he felt certain that he had never seen mention on the MTA displays of a Heartsbane Wood Station, nor of the neighborhood known as Bucali's Castle.

This was the way things were in the city, and indeed in the world, as you yourself will know if you have ever tried to get from point A to point B. What seems very certain at the outset of a journey becomes shakier farther into it, for maps are slippery things, false as a whore's embrace.

But M was a stouthearted sort and had little going on that Sunday, and, also, he did not like to start going somewhere and then turn around before arriving. M did not have this completionist fetish regarding other matters—

he would happily leave a meal uneaten and a book half read—but in matters of travel it was something of a matter of pride. In the distance the supple curves of the Verrazano Bridge stretched over the Narrows, and M swore he would rest beneath it before returning home.

He walked past apartment buildings that seemed to be mostly glass, and he walked past tenements like fortresses, like small cities, families and extended families and even little subnations packed within its walls. He walked past Apostle Island brownstones and Hummelestown brownstones and several types of brownstones, the construction of which he remained ignorant. He walked through a hipster neighborhood and a Spanish neighborhood and an Italian neighborhood and an Arab neighborhood and then another Spanish neighborhood.

He grabbed a late brunch at a small diner in a neighborhood called Fort Crain. The waitress had been scowling for so long that it had worn a groove in her face, and her legs were mostly varicose. He ordered the country breakfast, sunny-side up. The eggs came out on a platter like the rim of a truck tire, and they were bigger than any egg M had ever seen, bigger than an ostrich egg, which is a very big egg, certainly as large an egg as you would ever need to eat. M did not ask about their origin. Instead he sopped them up with a trencher of bread, spreading yolk onto the side of fried potatoes, enough spuds to shame an Irishman. The coffee was strong as the kick of a mule though far more pleasant, and two drops of the house-made hot sauce were as fierce as a bale of pepper. For perhaps the first time in his life, M did not manage to finish a side of bacon, pushed aside his feast with half a pig remaining. The bill came to sixty-five cents. M put a dollar on the table and split.

Having swallowed enough food to Mama Cass a hippo, M strode onward with a fury. He walked past St. Tobhein's Park and Billicker's Way Station. He strolled past Alp's Favor Square, a happy suburb of smiling parents and stumbling toddlers. He walked past a hundred bars and five hundred restaurants and two thousand liquor stores. He halted briefly in the Church of the Unwary Traveler, lit a quick candle, and then returned to the sunlight.

He found a seat on a bench at Tabby Skin Park overlooking a portion of the Hudson Bay that was bluer and cleaner than any length of it he had ever seen before. Serious-looking men with tawny skin tossed lines into the water and pulled out fat, flopping fish large enough to feed a family. M texted Boy and told her that he was going to have to take a rain check for dinner that night. Then he rolled a cigarette and rubbed his legs, which were starting to remind M that he was not a long-distance runner. There was a commotion from the fishermen, one of whose catch had responded badly to being caught, leeched a long, purple tendril around his tormentor, and struggled to pull him into the brine. A fellow piscator grabbed a knife the size of a cutlass and moved quickly to sever the stalk, while a group of others grabbed the angler turned quarry, trying to keep him from being reeled into the sea. M waited to see how the contest ended—victory for the bipeds, always to be celebrated—and then continued on.

M did not carry a watch anymore, in part because he was just too devil-may-care and in part because in situations like this they tended to become either inert or unreadable. M had spent a small fortune on timepieces before this had become clear to him, could remember an awkward conversation with one watchmaker in which he tried to explain why all of the components in his double hunter had turned into dark chocolate. Never again, he had promised himself afterward. Anyway, without a watch he could not be sure but still it seemed to him that this Sunday afternoon was lasting much longer than other Sunday afternoons he had known. He walked and he walked and he walked, and the sun beat down on him, long after it ought to have surrendered its stage to the moon, as it did so gracefully most evenings.

And still the city stretched onward, onward and forever. M had never realized the sheer ethnic diversity of this part of Brooklyn, Khazars going up to Barth Street, and from then on it was mostly Scythians until one came to Little Bactria, red-and-green flags fluttering from every window. M stopped at the sort of restaurant that served paper plates on plastic tables and ate a chunk of charcoaled lamb which could have been spitted on a Tartar's lance. It was the best thing he had eaten since brunch, the skin crispy, the flesh itself spilling over with juice. The owner, who was also the hostess and also the wife of the cook, brought him some complimentary tea afterward. "Where you from?" she asked in better English than M could have replied in whatever her own tongue was.

M told her.

"Where is?"

M told her.

"I have never heard," she said, dismissively. "Where you go?"

M shrugged, pointed south.

She looked at him a long time. She was that certain type of ex-Soviet woman who would have killed more than her share at Stalingrad. "Is not nice place," she said, but when it was clear he was not going to change his mind, she shrugged and let him pay his bill.

Hours later and the Verrazano Bridge remained immutable in the distance. There were no longer any street signs, or if there were, they had been removed by the inhabitants. M's legs ached, quietly but growing louder. He did not feel like ducking into a bar to rest any longer, especially as time, which he thought had clearly been on pause at some point, was back to functioning normally—which is to say that it was getting dark, and perhaps getting dark rather too quickly, although M's circadian rhythms were at this point so mangled that he could not say for certain. What he could say for certain was that the increasing numbers of youths he was walking past, who seemed of some no-longer-determinate race or nation, were staring at him with increasing hostility, and there seemed to be more of them. He had not seen anything written in any language with which he was familiar in a very long time. He wore blisters onto his feet and then those blisters burst and the leather in his sandals—which he would not have worn if he had known he was going to be doing this—were damp and sticky with blood.

And still M continued. He had the bit between his teeth now, when momentum becomes purpose, the sheer impetus of motion, forward, forward, forward. Below his left wrist was a tattoo of a wheel, and it seemed to spin as you looked at it. The hooligans on the corners, the dacoits and the bandits, the purse snatchers and the knockout artists, saw a man possessed with a sense of purpose that there was no point in shaking, any more than you would stand in front of the L train, and gave him a wide and respectful berth.

In time the unfortunate inhabitants degraded further, until they seemed so desperate and miserable that they were no longer even objects of fear, incapable of doing anything other than staring with wide, tragic, hateful eyes. M walked past them without returning the compliment, without a break in his stride, with the even rhythm of a session musician, as if he could walk forever, as indeed he was beginning to think he might need to.

Wealth decayed into poverty decayed into anarchy decayed farther into wilderness, and things seemed only to get softer, quieter. At first there were more vacant lots and the vacant lots were greener, but then at a certain point the vacant lots seemed to make up most of the horizon, with only the occasional empty building to blot out the verdant sea of weeds. These overgrew the stairwells of the R train that M continued to walk past, reality insisting on maintaining some tenuous grip even in the most distant corners of its domain, though the signposts had ceased to have any names, and the roads were pot-holed and crumbling. There were crickets. It had been a long time since M had heard so many crickets. The stars twinkled lustily in the night sky, their grandeur undiminished by streetlight. He could still see the Verrazano in the distance, and he no longer held any hate for it. It beamed down beneficently, so high above the world's foolishness that it could even afford a sense of sympathy.

M trekked onward. His legs no longer hurt. He could not really feel them. He could not really feel anything anymore, only the soothing rhythm of his steps, which were flagging but had not yet failed. M's iPod, which had been blinking sad messages at him for a very long time, went out finally. He wrapped the headphone cord around it and laid it respectfully into the green.

He saw the end of the road approaching with surprise at first, thought it was a mirage, or something like the bridge, which was not a mirage but which seemed impossible to reach. When a few blocks farther on it failed to recede into the distance, shock changed to elation, and then a quick mingled burst of regret, as at the end of every journey.

It was very late. The Verrazano arched above him, its anchor points lost in the infinite horizon, stretching eternally in both directions. The water went on forever, Staten Island lost in the soft darkness. M slipped beneath a chain link fence, climbed down onto the empty overpass, jumped the ledge. Beneath it the beach was wide and white and made whiter by the moon. The bay lapped against it, a soft black brilliance to contrast the sand. A girl sat on a rock near the waves, and she wore white as well, and M found he did not dare look at her directly.

"It was worth the walk, wasn't it?" she asked.

"Yes," M agreed. "Yes. By God, yes."

20

A Soporific for the World Turtle

Boy came running into The Lady one early afternoon in May. "We've got a problem."

M had been trying to teach Flemel to play chess for the better part of a month, but Flemel did not seem to have any head for it. M had said it would help with his studies, but this was a lie; he just thought it would be nice if he could get a decent game together without having to walk to the park.

M sighed. It was a sad commentary on humanity that no one ever came sprinting into a room to tell you good news. "Someone will solve it," M said. "Someone always does."

"He's waking up," Boy said.

"That's impossible," M answered, taking Flemel's rook with a fianchettoed bishop.

Flemel sighed.

"How many times do I have to warn you of that one?" M asked.

Flemel's mouth spread into an O, but before he could respond, Boy upended the board, spilling carved wooden pieces everywhere.

"Why did you do that?" M asked. "Now he has to pick them all up again." M turned to Flemel. "Well? What are you waiting for? Pick them all up again."

"Will you forget about beating the child at chess? We have bigger problems: He's waking up,"

"You just told me that," M said, "and I just told you that he isn't. He only wakes up once every half century, and I was around last time when we put him back to bed. I can't remember when that was, exactly, but it couldn't have been more than a decade or two."

"I was there last time also, you overconfident little shit," Boy hissed, "and I'm telling you that our old rules have gone invalid. He's waking up. Haven't you noticed anything off today?"

"I had Indian for dinner last night. Sometimes it plays with my digestion."

Boy looked very much like she wanted to hit M then, but she managed to set aside her rage, given the gravity of the situation. "The queen has called a meeting."

"Which one?" M asked.

"Both of them."

"Shit," M said, pushing aside the board that Flemel had just finished setting up.

"I told you," Boy said, "He's waking up."

"Who's waking up?" Flemel asked.

"Take the set and go back to your apartment," M said. Then, checking himself: "No—take the set and get on a train going west out of the city. West," he repeated rather stridently. "Under no fucking circumstances are you to go through Penn Station. Do you understand?"

"Why? What's going to happen in Penn Station?"

"It's an all-hands-on-deck sort of thing," Boy said. "We might as well bring him along."

"You understand in that saying that *hands* refers to 'sea hands,' meaning sailors, meaning people that can be of assistance in the situation, meaning the rookie is out."

"Positive reinforcement is not his strong suit," Flemel told Boy conspiratorially.

That he was impossible to offend was one of the things M did not like about Flemel. M kept trying anyway, though. M was not one to back down at the first sign of difficulty. "That was not a suggestion, that was an order. I'm the one wearing the conical hat and sweeping the wand around, dig it? It's your job to mop my fucking floors, but today I don't want my floors mopped. I want you to find a way out of the greater metropolitan area."

"You keep telling me I'm not your apprentice," Flemel said. "You told me that three times today. When I came in, you told me that I wasn't your apprentice and that you never wanted to see my baby face again. And then I think you called me 'Backstreet Boy,' which really just showed your age."

"He probably wouldn't be able to escape the flood," Boy said. "Not unless he can get off the Eastern Seaboard. But either way, we don't have time to argue about it—and your presence most assuredly will be missed, so let's get a move on."

M couldn't think of a clean way to leave Flemel behind, and anyway it sounded like he was going to need every drop of Managerial goodwill that he could hold on to, and so Flemel ended up following them to the nearest subway stop and onto the next train.

"The old meeting spot?" M asked.

"Yup," Boy said.

"You want to do the honors?"

"No need. The queens have sprung for a gate—anybody with a hint of talent will find themselves on an express train to Midtown."

"Shit on a shingle."

"I told you, it's crisis time."

"Is someone going to explain what this is all about?" Flemel asked.

M shrugged, stared out the window at the underground caverns below, and made a gesture toward Boy like she might as well satisfy Flemel's curiosity.

"You know Manhattan Island?" she asked.

"I think so."

"It's not really an island."

"What is it then?"

"It's a lot of things, depending on how you're looking at it. But for right now, it's a giant turtle who's been kind enough to hang around a while, so that we could build the greatest city since the fall of Rome on his back."

"Oh," Flemel said. "OK."

"He's a lethargic fellow, the World Turtle," Boy continued, "and when he gets fitful, every fifty years or so, all the practitioners in the city get together and give him an extra-strength shot of Xanax, and he dips back under."

"But?"

"But for some reason he hasn't slept as long as usual," M broke in, "and if he wakes up he's going to go wherever it is that he was before he was in the river, and that will be trouble for those several million people who live and work and fuck on top of his shell. In hopes of heading off this unfortunate event, the two most powerful magicians in the city, who have hated each other desperately and for the better part of forever, have put aside their differences and called a conclave in a magic clubhouse, and we're going there now, to meet up with everyone who can do anything that everyone else can't to try and figure out some way to put the old bastard back asleep for a few more decades."

The train slowed to a crawl. "What's below the turtle?" Flemel asked finally.

"It's turtles all the way down," M informed him, stepping out of the now-open doors.

The chamber had been built a century earlier, when the great lords and ladies of that age—the Childe Rothstein, Alastair "Bossman" Tweed, the being whom the uninitiated refer to as Mary Astor—had hoped that building a council house might serve to unify the city's wizards, to offer a neutral territory to hash out the problems of the day. It had been a stupid idea. M had told the Childe that once, in a bar in the Bowery, celebrating the beginning of Prohibition with Canadian liquor. Wizards were a factitious and untrustworthy lot, and there wasn't any point in spending untold millions (and back then, millions had been a lot of money) and no small amount of the Management's goodwill just to build a drawing room that wouldn't see use more than once or twice a century. As it turned out Rothstein hadn't gotten to see it at all: He was shot in the back over a gambling debt, if you believed the history, though everyone who knew anything about anything knew he had been carried down into Hell for trying to fix a papal election. But that had been the thing about the Childe—too smart for his own good, didn't like a scam unless he could watch it double back on itself a few times.

The parlor he had envisioned had never been very good for much, for all of the reasons M had outlined, but one had to admit that it was really very pretty—the platonic ideal of the early-twentieth-century drawing room, except bigger, as big as it needed to be, growing antechambers and bars and tables and stools and waiters and liquor and finger food and everything else that might be required at any given moment. And today, with the entirety of the city's wonder workers pressed inside it, the chamber needed to be plenty big—plenty big, indeed.

"Close your mouth, junior," Boy said, elbowing Flemel in the side hard enough to make him wheeze. "You'll catch fireflies."

"Fairies more like," M said. "Christ, what a sideshow." M forgot sometimes just how many of them there were, these wonder workers and necromancers and illusionists and diviners and cantrip makers and artificers and channelers and chronomancers and psychics and half-holy men and he could go on and on and on but he would rather not. So far as M was concerned being in good with the Management was a means—a means to a supernaturally long life, a life of ease and, if not plenty, at least sufficiency. A means for meeting pretty girls and getting into interesting sorts of trouble and getting out of that trouble with your skin and your skull and your soul intact. So he forgot sometimes that for the greater portion of his confederates, being in good with the Management—oh, hell, why not just say it at this point, everybody else was—being able to do magic was an end in and of itself. It was what made them special, what set them above the rest of the world, would-be Merlins spending their days sniffing around for a dark lord to fight, some grand quest to justify their own pointless existence. They could keep it, M thought. M did not suppose he was destined to do anything, but if he had a fate outlined for him since birth, it involved islands off the coast of Brazil and freshly made caipirinhas.

"They've called in all the freaks on this one," M said, making their way toward the bar and leaving Flemel to play catch-up.

"You won't have far to walk if you need your palm read," Boy said.

"I take back what I said earlier: The kid could outwork half these hacks." One of whom—pale, ponytailed, wearing a black trench coat—shook M's hand in passing and pressed a business card on him. Continuing on M discovered it read, RAVEN DARKFYRE, INITIATE OF THE THIRD CIRCLE, then dropped it with a swift shudder.

"He's kind of cute," Boy said.

"I suppose if you're in the mood for something emo. Wait, you mean my apprentice? You can have him," M grumbled, but then, seeing the predatory look in Boy's eyes, amended his statement. "For the love of God, woman, he's not enough meal to tide you over till dinner. And what about Andre?"

"What about Andre?" Boy asked.

It turned out M didn't really have an answer to that either. He saw Ibis and Anais through the crowd, was thinking of heading over when he noticed Salome standing beside them, laughing at something Ibis had said, and decided against it. Their liaison had ended the morning after they had met at the goblin market, never to be repeated, and by mutual, if unvoiced, consent, neither had bothered to contact the other. M was wondering vaguely how many other ex-paramours were in this audience when Alatar of the Upper West Side stepped out from the crowd and obstructed M's passage with the tip of his quarterstaff.

"Why, if it isn't Dumbledick himself," M said. "That's a lovely phallus you're carrying. Bigger than last time, or am I wrong?"

"Last time, last time, last time," Alatar repeated. "You mean when you ruined my party, set my servants to eating my guests?"

"You shouldn't brood so much over past injuries—bad for the digestion."

"You got lucky."

"And I'm feeling lucky today," M answered, "and anyway we're in the conclave right now, and I'd hardly think the queens would appreciate it if you violated their peace."

"The queens won't always be around."

"You know where to find me," M said, thinking as he said it that he should probably move apartments and change his number.

"How do you know the heavy?" Boy asked, eyes crossed. Boy did not like to be left out of the loop on anything.

"Ask Andre," M muttered, who by coincidence he happened to see then, taking up space at one of the many bars that dotted the chamber—little islands of alcohol set amidst the opulence, each manned by a pair of floating, oversize, white silk gloves. Bucephalus sat at the other end of the bar, looking frightening and earning himself a wide berth. Stockdale was standing next to him, though in fact M had always gotten the sense that Stockdale didn't like

Bucephalus, only tolerated him because he was friends with M. Of course M didn't really like Bucephalus either, only tolerated him because he was friends with Boy. God only knew why Boy tolerated him.

"Can you make a Gordon's Breakfast?" M asked.

The glove snapped its fingers and set to it.

"What's the news?" M asked after he had finished fortifying himself.

"Apart from the fact that the old man is looking to take another dip?" Stockdale shrugged. "We're all waiting around for Red and White to get the thing started."

Bucephalus began to curse then, lengthily and potently enough that M worried it might attract the attention of some malevolent deity. He paused to take a swig from what looked like a bottle of grain alcohol, and then he said, "You know how much pull this is going to take? Last time we put him down I didn't have enough mojo left to light a candle."

"I remember," M said.

"I don't," Flemel said, having found them again despite M's best efforts. "How did we manage it?"

"Brute force," Boy said. "Don't get too close to any of these seventh-rate chicanerists. Half of them will find themselves drained to the quick come evening."

"What do you mean?"

"Small fish tend not to fair so well in these sorts of things," Stockdale said. "Get pulled too deep into the ritual, exhaust themselves entirely."

"Speaking of which, anyone know what ritual we finally settled on?" Boy asked.

"It was lunar-based," Stockdale recalled. "The Chinese zodiac, if I'm not mistaken. So no help there."

"I remember it took the queens three days to agree on it," Boy said.

"It'll be worse this time." Stockdale finished his old-fashioned and was handed another by the floating left glove. "They hate each other more."

"They hated each other quite a bit back in the day."

"Sure, but back then they were just two women who didn't like each other. Now they're ideas, sides, team colors. It's not the same."

"How the hell are we going to put him to sleep?"

"That's not really the question, now is it?" M asked quietly.

"What is?"

"Why is he waking up?"

But before they could speculate there was a—well, it wasn't a sound exactly, but that was the easiest way to think of it, as if a small man inside your skull was ringing a cocktail spoon against a glass flute. And then the room did something that violated the laws of Newtonian physics and probably quantum physics as well, though M was not as familiar with the latter. And then they were all, every one of the several thousand individuals in attendance, circled closely around a small stone dais atop which the elite of New York magical society sat.

"Wow," Flemel said.

"Don't embarrass me," M hissed.

There is no position so critical, no office so important, that the occasional, and even the more than occasional, utter incompetent will not wind up filling it. Heart surgeons, popes, presidents, it makes no difference. Look around and you will see an existence replete with people who are betraying, in a most egregious manner, the powers and responsibilities that have been entrusted to them.

Which is to say that M would not have given a thimbleful for most of the eight men and women considered important enough to sit up at the round table. Abilene and Celise were there, of course, at opposite ends of the circle, and though he disliked the former and distrusted the latter, he had to admit that they were the only wizards on the podium whom he would not have preferred to see buried in a coffin and dropped into the sea. They had power and they weren't simpering fools, and if they had not already been the de facto rulers of New York, he'd have been happy to vote them into that miserable position.

Especially when compared with the other candidates. To the immediate left of Celise was Herald Sampson Fitzgerald Dupont VII, or maybe VIII. He seemed unable to sit still for more than a second or two, every pocket concealing a different electronic device competing for his attention, like a John Cage symphony of cacophonous beeping. Clockwise to Dupont sat Qashi Corlo, looking like he'd come straight from a board meeting and would be going back to one as soon as he was through with this business. Across the table sat a wizened East Asian in a perfectly tailored suit whose name M did not know. Next to him was Alatar, leaning back in his chair and straining his hand around his oak staff. And next to him was—oh, hell, M didn't even want to look at them anymore. It was enough to make a person want to go square, work a regular nine-to-five, grow old and fat, and crumble to dust—at least you'd be surrounded by other adults.

"Would you like to begin, Celise?" Abilene asked.

"I think you already have, Abilene," Celise answered coldly.

"A point of etiquette, nothing more. The floor is yours, unequivocally."

"Jesus Christ," M muttered, "I'm never getting out of here."

M felt a hand on his shoulder, which was a bit of physical intimacy that he found unattractive among his closest companions and in far less tense situations.

He turned around to discover the hand belonged to Talbot.

"You miss me?" Talbot asked.

"Daily," M said. "Several times a week, at least."

"How you been?"

"I get by. I think I sort of thought you were dead."

"What, New Year's? Not quite. Woke up three weeks into January, sitting in the corner of an empty warehouse with a Rip Van Winkle beard."

Back on the main stage, Abilene and Celise had managed to put aside the question of who would begin the meeting and moved on to actually beginning the meeting, though that was as far as they'd gotten. Of course, the issues at hand were all but infinite—how exactly was the ritual to be performed, what somatic and verbal and material components would be required, who would offer them, the endless and endlessly complex minutia required for a spell of this magnitude. It was like putting on an incredibly elaborate stage play without any rehearsal, arriving at the theater to have some overworked grip grab your shoulder and whisper, "You're Peter Bottom. Here's your mask. Hope you know your lines!" with a bad review meaning the destruction of all life on Manhattan. And behind all that, interfering with every other decision, however minor, was the question of how to balance the ritual such that all of the major parties were weakened equally, or approximately so, thus ensuring the perpetual stalemate continued as it had in years past.

"This isn't going to work," Talbot muttered too loudly, while Abilene and Herald Sampson Fitzgerald Dupont the whatever were quibbling animatedly over whether or not dried Cactacae flower could be used as suitable replacement for *Mors ontologica* and, if so, whether the ratio was seventy-four to nine or one hundred and forty-eight to seventeen.

"It worked last time," M said.

"Last time we knew it was coming; last time we had the muckety-mucks planning things, laying the groundwork in advance. And for that matter, last time it barely worked, if you remember; left me so drained I couldn't light a cigarette or read a palm for three months."

"What do you suggest?" M asked.

Talbot made a show of looking around, then leaned in close and whispered, "The heart of the city."

M scowled. "That's the worst idea I've heard so far today," he said. "And the morning has been chock-full of foolishness."

"What's the heart of the city?" Flemel asked. He had leaned in close to M when he had seen Talbot do so, and thus become a de facto participant in the conversation.

"What does it sound like? It's the middle, it's the navel, it's the axis mundi."

"Everything in the city goes into it," Talbot added, "and everything comes back out again."

"So the heart is inside the turtle?"

"The turtle is just the island of Manhattan," M explained tiredly, "and possibly also the entirety of existence. Forget about the turtle, OK? The turtle and the heart are two different things. You've gotta get rid of this notion that A always equals A. Sometimes it equals B. Sometimes it equals Ω. Sometimes it doesn't equal anything."

"I've never liked the Rosicrucian pentacle," Abilene said. "The Celtic broken cross offers superior stability without the normative monotheistic overtones."

"So what do you think?" Talbot asked.

"I think it's like opening a peanut with a sledgehammer."

"It would save everyone a lot of trouble, wouldn't it?"

"So would drinking cyanide."

"Your ancient Phoenician needs work, I'm afraid," Celise said witheringly. "That particular series of consonants evokes Yamm to ensure the good fortune of the cod yield, which is a worthy enough endeavor but rather unrelated to the situation at hand."

"At the moment it doesn't sound so bad," Talbot said.

"Have fun, then."

"With the cyanide?"

"With tapping the heart."

"Well, therein we run into a complication."

"Life abounds in them, I'm afraid."

"I don't know where the heart is."

"No?"

"Though I'm told you do."

"Who told you that?"

"You did."

"That doesn't sound like me."

"We were on acid."

"Which time?"

"At the Talking Heads show? Two tabs with a picture of the Golden Gates on them?"

M scowled. "You really don't think they'll be able to piece it together?"

Talbot waved his hand at the proceedings. "Are you feeling optimistic?"

"Of course you'd prefer that we used powdered mandrake root, you've got a controlling interest in the only mandrake farm within half a reality," Abilene told Celise angrily.

"Fortuitous for all of us, given its value as a binding agent. I'd think you'd be happy that someone had the foresight to lay away a stock substantial enough for our purposes."

"Yes, we're all so blessed that your instinct for monopoly has run off any competition."

"Well, I think it's about time I toddled off." Talbot tipped his hat. "There's a Murphy bed a few blocks from Washington Square Park that ends up in the city of Cleveland. You're welcome to come along, if you'd like."

"No, no," M said. "I like New York. I mean, I like it OK. Actually I often find myself sort of lukewarm on the place, but perhaps not to such a degree that I want it to go the way of Atlantis."

"If we're going to do it," Talbot said, "then we ought to do it now, and we ought to do it quiet. If the queens get wind of it, we'll be tramping down there with half the room."

"I'd just as soon the location remain between the two of us," M said.

"The three of us," Flemel altered, "or I make a scene." Flemel had long since realized that the only way he could learn anything of importance from M is if he tricked or bullied him into it. Normally this was a difficult task, but draped over a barrel M didn't bother to argue.

The trio found themselves making their way back through the crowd and asking one of the spectral bartenders where the exit was, the gloved hands pantomiming a series of directions that, when followed, took them up a sort of fire escape and onto a busy Midtown street.

"Well?" Talbot asked. "Where is the thing, exactly?"

"It takes a bit of getting to," M explained. "Just follow my lead."

M abruptly stopped in front of a Sbarro, opened the door, and waved them through. Flemel discovered himself standing not on polished floors surrounded by the smell of cooking grease, but on lush carpet, surrounded by oak bookshelves leading up to a ceiling mural of a centurion falling on his sword.

"No time to dally," M said, "there's a city to save." Striding forward with purpose to the nearest exit, a great oak monstrosity that he pulled open and stepped through.

The door to a broom closet in Penn Station led to the bathroom of a steak house in Queens, where they squeezed into a dumbwaiter and went up three flights to the top of the Empire State Building.

"You know, I've never actually been here before," Flemel said, stopping for a moment to enjoy the view.

"You look much longer," Talbot returned, brushing a bit of lettuce off his shoulder, "and you'll get to watch it disappear beneath the water."

Which was spur enough for M to brush past a security guard and through a door marked NO ENTRY and into an executive office overlooking the park, interrupting a grunting bout of lunchtime cunnilingus.

"Don't bother, don't bother," M said, waving the CFO of a Fortune 500 company back between the legs of his assistant. "We won't be but a moment."

And indeed they weren't: The ebony double doors exiting the CFO's office turned out to be the egress to the bonobo cage at the Bronx Zoo, where M narrowly avoided being struck with a handful of feces by disappearing through the warden's gate and into an abandoned warehouse.

Flemel was not so lucky, however, and they wasted a few minutes as he tried to find something in the vastness of the concrete bunker with which to scrape shit off his flannel shirt. "How do you know where this place is, exactly?"

"The Engineer showed it to him," Talbot answered.

"Who's the Engineer?" Flemel asked, ever curious.

"The Engineer was the man who built the heart," Talbot began.

"No one built the heart," M said definitively, trying to undo the rusted-shut latch on one of the doors. "When the first avaricious Dutchmen cheated the first innocent Iroquois, the heart was here. When Alexander Hamilton got caught by a cheap shot from Aaron Burr, the heart was here. When Monk Eastman fought Paul Kelly to a hundred-and-seventy–round draw over control of Five Points, the heart was here. The Engineer just knew the location."

"And how did he know that?" Flemel asked.

"Because he was the Engineer, obviously," Talbot explained. Sort of.

"The Engineer was . . . special."

"Like we're special?"

"You aren't that special. And no one was special like the Engineer was special."

"What happened to him?"

"No one knows," Talbot said.

"Someone might know," M explained. "But we don't know, and neither does anyone else we know."

"I don't understand," Flemel said.

"This insistence that questions have answers," M said. "It's one of your less attractive qualities."

M managed to unjam the lock, and Flemel managed to mostly wipe the shit off his shirt. Through the front and out into a crack house, the smell of waste and body odor and mildew and human misery and, of course, crack, so overpowering that M pinched his nose shut, pulled aside a door long rotted off its hinges, and headed into a craft-beer bar.

"What do you have by way of an IPA?" M asked the bartender, bearded and tattooed as appropriate.

"I thought we were in a hurry!" Flemel reminded him.

M scowled. "Three shots of Jameson," he said. They downed them, then walked into the doors of the women's bathroom and out of the changing room into a boutique lingerie store in the Village, customers shrieking and blushing.

They ended up finally in an apartment overlooking the park—a sunny day, a city that would not be around much longer if swift steps were not taken. The apartment was in the middle of renovations: The wood floors were unfinished and stacks of building materials took up most of the corner.

"And here we are," M said, pausing for a moment and pointing at a door that should have led into a bathroom. "That's the last one, right there."

"I'm afraid you won't be the one opening it, however," Talbot said. "Turn around slowly, and don't do anything to spook me."

"What an unexpected development," M said. "Is that a shrunken head you're pointing at me?"

"A bit much, I agree. But it's my employer's and it works. A quick hit of this and your mind will be as scrambled as bootleg cable."

"We wouldn't want that."

"I have to say, M, if I had known it was this easy to get you to give up the location of the heart, I'd have made a go at it years back."

"I guess I'm just too trusting. It's my most severe character flaw. It might be my sole character flaw, now that I think of it. What happens next?"

"I open the door and become God."

"Is that what's in there?"

"The heart of the city," Talbot said, all but salivating. "The pulsing soul of the urban center of the world, of any of the worlds, every thought and fear and passion and instinct and bit of energy all coursing through, mine for the taking."

"Don't burn yourself," M said. "Mind if I roll a cigarette?"

"You touch your pockets and I'm going to fry out your brain," Talbot said, dropping quickly out of his reverie and turning the shrunken head on M once again. "Friend or no friend."

"I think it's clear we're the latter," M said, but he kept his hands up. "Well, have fun becoming God. Try to remember us mortals fondly."

Talbot looked at M a long time, as if expecting further resistance. Then he shrugged and, with one hand still pointing the shrunken head firmly in M's direction, he crossed slowly over to the door, reached his hand around the knob, twisted, pulled the door open—

M kicked Flemel in the back of the leg, just below the knee, hard enough to send him sprawling. M took the opportunity to look at the wall a while, and thus the only person who can claim with any certainty what exactly it was that lay beyond the door Talbot had opened was Talbot, whose eyes went wide as beer mugs and whose mouth began to drool.

"I'm going to go ahead and roll that cigarette all the same," M said, though while doing it he sidled over to the door, careful not to look at it, and then slammed it shut.

Talbot gave no sign that he noticed. Whatever he had seen was working fast: His face began to droop like wax melting off a candle, and then his shoulders drifted downward as well. "How . . . did . . . you . . . ?" Talbot managed, each word coming with great and growing effort.

"Know you were going to betray me? A lot of reasons. First of all, your plan was terrible and didn't make any sense, and if there was anyone in this damn city with an ounce of self-possession, it wouldn't have worked. The World Turtle just happens to wake up thirty years ahead of schedule? You just happen to suggest tapping the heart? Absurd. But more importantly, Talbot, we were never friends; you were just a guy I bought drugs from." M turned away abruptly. "I have no idea why I'm still talking to you."

Indeed, it was clear that Talbot was not paying attention to anything M was saying. His eyes were open, his pupils were dilated, his body was frozen stiff.

"What is he looking at?" Flemel asked.

"I'm really not sure. The spirit that used to inhabit Lou Reed showed it to me. Well, the door to it at least. Whatever it is, he seems happy looking at it, doesn't he?"

"What happens to Talbot?"

M shrugged. "He might get over it. He might not. No idea, really."

"Then this isn't the heart of the city?"

"No."

"But you know where it is?"

"I didn't say that."

"But you do."

M didn't answer. He retreated back to the exit and opened it to reveal a normal-enough-looking hallway. Apparently whatever magic had allowed them to flicker across the city did not work in reverse. M held the door for Flemel, then followed him out.

• • •

By the time M and his starstruck apprentice returned, it was all over—the turtle coaxed or quieted back into its slumber. No small task, not even for every single individual with the slightest shred of talent in the city. For many of the weakest of them, it was the last endeavor they would ever attempt, their minds and souls and bodies burnt out as part of the collective effort. Even the stronger of the adepts would find themselves exhausted for weeks, the goodwill of the Management substantially exhausted.

"What happened?" M asked.

Boy was lying partway against one of the paneled back walls and partway against Andre, who was sound asleep. "It's done," she said. "Where the fuck were you?" But she was so tired that she couldn't even put much into it, sounded nearly concerned.

"Yeah, sorry." M called over a spectral bartender, the mobile hands pouring him a shot of gin. He threw it back and continued, "I kind of got caught up solving the mystery behind who made all this trouble for us, saving the day, ensuring that justice and truth prevail." M ordered and drank another shot of gin. "The American way, also," he added, before strutting off to the center of the room.

The central dais was half full with the crème de la crème of magical society. The queens, Alatar, and the East Asian man whose name M did not know remained at the table. The rest had found their way to some other corner of the room.

"The prodigal son," Abilene said. She looked tired but not exhausted, in contrast to the rest of the assemblage, and M didn't doubt that she had more than enough left to snuff him out.

"Your absence was noted," Celise said from the other end of the table, and with as much sweetness.

"I wasn't the only one missing for the finale," M said. "Talbot was with me."

"We'll make sure to have stern words with him as well," Celise said. It was a sign of how exhausting settling the turtle had been that her eye makeup was slightly smeared.

"I'm afraid that's going to be rather difficult. He's set to be spending a while staring into a porthole into the nothing that lies between the worlds."

"And why is he doing that?"

"There are a lot of ways to answer that question," M said thoughtfully. "Because he was weak-willed and venal and not very smart. Because he thought that power was a thing to be grasped at rather than avoided. Because he started trouble with me. Because he was a big dick. But mainly because Alatar here ordered him to." M took the shrunken head out and tossed it over at Alatar's feet. "Look familiar?"

M did not like Alatar, but Alatar had not become one of the most power-ful wizards in the city, and thus the planet, and thus all of existence and the many existences attached to it, by being entirely a fool. He did not shout or sneer or even blink. "I've never seen this before in my life."

"There's no one else here who could craft a fetish of such potency and would choose so tasteless a form. A shrunken head?" M shook his head back and forth. "Good God, Alatar, all that power and you're still a child."

"I have no idea what you're talking about," Alatar said, stroking at the curved oak of his staff.

"You knew that Talbot was my friend, or that Talbot thought he was my friend at least, and you supposed that in the confusion he might manage to worry something out of me. Except that I don't worry, and Talbot wasn't my friend, and your fingerprints are so clear on this that you might as well have dipped them in ink."

"To what end?" Alatar asked, his raptor eyes blinking. "What is it that you possibly possess that I might have interest in?"

"Don't play the fool," began the White Queen.

"You want to know where the heart of the city is," finished the Red.

"There's no proof," Alatar said, hands gripping the wood of his staff tightly. "It's his word against mine."

Abilene looked at him wonderingly for a moment. "This is not a court of law," she said. "This is the jungle."

"Red in tooth and claw," Celise confirmed. "And I believe him."

"And I believe him also," Abilene added, "and really that's all there is to the situation."

"I invoke the peace!" Alatar said, and now you could see a crack in his facade. "No harm to be done to another within the conclave. I've kept my end of it. None could say otherwise. Word was given! Oaths on the old things, the true things, the things of power!"

Abilene laughed. Celise laughed also. M thought it was the only time he had ever seen the two act in concert. He found it immensely unsettling.

"It's our peace, Alatar," Celise answered. "And we can break it any time we please."

M wondered if all of the rest of the members of the convention had pulled themselves together and thrown themselves at the two women—well, goddesses, if we're being accurate about it—would they have been able to overcome them? And he thought probably, maybe, but it would have been a shitty way to spend what for most would end up being the last afternoon of their lives.

Happily, this was not an eventuality that needed to be explored. M, for one, believed himself, and it seemed that most of the rest of the people in the hall agreed. Certainly, they did not disagree so much that they were going to ally themselves with Alatar.

"Shall I handle this, Abilene?" Celise asked. "Or would you like to do the honors?"

"It's your borough these days, Celise," Abilene said sweetly. "I wouldn't want to steal your thunder."

Celise smiled back. You wouldn't even have known that they hated each other, unless you had eyes in your head.

Alatar went for broke then, because whatever Celise was about to do to him wouldn't be any worse than what would happen if he violated the unwritten but harshly enforced rules of the Management, or at least not much worse, and also they were down in the subterranean caverns of existence and the Management generally didn't mind if you mucked about a bit. His display of offensive magic was as impressive as M had ever seen, or nearly so, but then again those sorts of fireworks were not really in M's line. Bright as hell though, energy streaking out from his staff and toward Celise, a swarm of parti-colored orbs flying off to engulf her, fire rising up from the ground, lightning coming down from the ceiling—the whole gamut. M realized watching it that he had allowed himself to be fooled by Alatar's Renaissance-faire getup and his crippling lack of hipness—but the man could spell, you had to give it to him. And all this after he had spent the afternoon calming down the World Turtle! Impressive stuff, it really was.

Of course, it wasn't anything close to Celise, not within a kilometer or a mile or a fucking light-year. After a moment, the fire died down, the pyrotechnics dimmed, Alatar struggled to breathe, and the target of his attention remained standing where she was, calm as the surface of a subterranean lake.

"All finished?" Celise asked, her garden-party affect unperturbed, no hair ruffled, no thread of clothing out of place. "I wouldn't want to spoil your last performance."

For once in his long years of carrying it, Alatar really needed the staff, would have collapsed without it to support him. He didn't respond to Celise's taunt, didn't even look at her, too exhausted to raise his eyes from the ground.

Celise smiled and whispered something and gestured with her open hand, as if calling for a maid. And then Alatar, who had up until that point been a six-foot-something man, with a white beard and a long nose, was a mouse sitting mournfully on the floor.

Isn't that cute, you think—well, think for another moment longer and you'll think otherwise, having your form folded and crushed and bent into that of another, a human brain and the body of a rodent, performing horrible little rodent tasks, eating trash and shit, ferreting between walls, dodging cats and rats and humans. It was like a lot of those things from the old fairy tales: You realize they aren't cute, they aren't cute at all, they're horrible, and why exactly do we keep telling them to children?

Not that Alatar didn't deserve it. Manhattan was a nice place, after all, and even if you didn't love it, you could hardly want its many million inhabitants to die miserably, drowning in the Hudson River. And as for what would have happened had he gotten his hands around the heart, if he had ever managed to tap that geyser of power—well, that did not do to bear thinking about.

"Thank you for the help, M," Celise said, after the rodent had scampered away.

"Yes, thank you, M," Abilene said.

M did not appreciate the two of them staring at him at the same time; it was like being drawn and quartered. "Don't mention it," he said, leaving the dais and stepping down into the sea of staring eyes and wan faces.

"Hero of the day, mate," Stockdale said, slapping him on the shoulder. "Your name just gets louder and louder."

If M was happy about this fact, he did a good job of hiding it.

21

Boy and the Forest Spirit

"What are you doing tonight?" Boy asked, arriving unexpectedly at The Lady late one July evening.

M nodded at his beer. "I'm doing it."

"Up for a walk?"

"Why?"

"Just thought I'd give you something to do."

"So this is a favor? How kind of you. But I'm just not sure I feel comfortable asking you to put yourself out any further than you already have."

Boy scowled, ordered two shots of rye, and drank one of them. "It's maybe not entirely a favor to you."

"No?"

"In fact, it might be the reverse."

"Mightn't it?"

"A while ago I convinced this guy to live in the park."

"All right."

"Not a guy, exactly."

"Which park?"

Boy gestured broadly. "All of them."

"I see. And?"

"Every so often, he needs to be given a good reason to stay there."

"What's a good reason?"

"It varies. Last time it was tickets to a World Series game. The time before that he wanted a vegetarian slice from Bucoli."

"Surely you can order a pizza without my assistance?"

"The time before he wanted me to climb to the top of the Empire State Building and kill the thing that was living there."

"Is there a thing living at the top of the Empire State Building?"

Boy drank the shot of rye she'd been saving. "Not anymore."

"So, in fact, the favor would be really more from my end?"

"I'll owe you one."

"Deal! And I'll trade that future assist for not having to go along with you on this one."

A step too far, and Boy, more comfortable with anger than weakness, got up from the chair that she was sitting on and pointed a skinny finger like the barrel of a revolver at M. Her face swelled up red.

There would be spleen all over him if he didn't act quickly, so he did, joining Boy on his feet and making tranquil gestures with his hand. "Just playing hard to get. You know I'd never let you out unescorted." He ordered two more shots of rye, even managed to hold on to one of them this time. Then he paid the bill and left.

M walked out of The Lady less sober than he liked to be when dealing with things beyond human ken. "Where we headed toward? Prospect? Don't tell me we're going all the way to Central."

Boy shook her head and pointed toward the small triangle of green across from The Lady, where Washington Avenue intersected St. Marks. "That'll do fine," she said.

They crossed against traffic, though there wasn't much of that so late in the evening. The area Boy had indicated was twenty square yards, perhaps half of which was grass, the other half being red dirt and condom wrappers and empty forties and dog shit.

"This isn't much of a park you've stuck him in," M said.

"I told you, he lives in all of them."

"Why do you want him to hang around so badly?"

"He's good for the plants."

"Sort of a supernatural fertilizer?"

"If that helps you." Boy shook out her pack of Gauloises and smoked two so rapidly that M barely had time to roll one of his own.

The nearest street lamp fizzled, then went out. There was an old homeless man sitting on one of the three benches that marked the outline of the small plot of untilled land that only a desperate real estate agent could pretend was a park. He got up and lumbered over, and M started to say that they didn't have any money, which was a lie, but it felt better than saying that he had money but wasn't going to give it to the man, because he suspected he would only spend it on drink, and also he looked smelly and generally distasteful, but Boy put a hand up to M's chest and whispered, "That's him."

The Park Manager—for this was the way M now thought of him—was old and gnarled, and walked along with the aid of a staff, or what looked like a staff, though as M got closer he realized it was actually an entire tree, a weeping willow or something, three or four times the size of the manager himself, with a full bough of summer leaves. And his skin wasn't just gnarled, it was actually knotted, like the wood of an oak, and his dreadlocks looked more like roots than hair, and his smile was moss green. He stopped a few feet from the two of them, and the butt of his staff knitted itself swiftly into the ground, roots branching out through the grass and into the asphalt itself, smaller shrubs growing off of the cutting with supernatural rapidity.

"We hope that the evening finds you well," Boy said, bowing deeply, "and that you drink deep of the moonlight."

Aren't you the charmer, M thought, but he kept his mouth shut. These things that were not people could be testy at times, and you never knew what times those would be, so you were better off just being polite, period.

The Park Manager didn't say anything, but a squirrel that M belatedly noticed standing on one of the lower branches of his tree-staff did. "The moonlight is bright on you tonight, Cinnamon Siddhartha Moonbeam."

It sounded particularly funny coming out of the mouth of a squirrel, but it would have been pretty funny regardless. Boy's pupils swelled wide in her head. M kept his face as blank as a washed chalkboard, but he did blink twice, very rapidly, and hoped Boy didn't notice.

"What boon do you wish of me, O Keeper of Fields," Boy asked finally.

"I have heard whispers and mutterings and tidings and rumors," the squirrel said.

"From Van Cortland Park to Governor's Island," squeaked an up-stretched caterpillar, "they speak of it."

"Yuppies and indigents, smiling children and bitter freaks and bleary-eyed hippies," croaked the bullfrog sitting in the roots of the staff.

"Wall Street execs and city workers, cops on the beat and pensioners, throwing me scattered bits of bread, all, they all speak of it," cried a pigeon resting on one of the branches.

"Cast of fucking *Bambi* out here," M said under his breath.

Boy ignored him. "And what do they whisper, Boon of the Green?"

"Dough-Cro," twittered the bird.

"Dough-Cro," croaked the toad.

"Dough-Cro," squeaked the squirrel.

"Why don't you just step on my balls in stiletto heels," Boy exclaimed. The pigeon returned to the boughs of the tree. The squirrel hid. The Park Manager himself continued smiling.

"She does not speak for me," M clarified. The squirrel peeked back out of the hole and made the sort of sounds that squirrels make.

"A Dough-Cro?" Boy less asked than cursed.

"What's a Dough-Cro?" M asked.

The caterpillar stretched down from the branches of the tree, took up residence on the Park Manager's head, and chirruped, "it's like a doughnut-croissant."

"You want a doughnut and a croissant?"

"No," Boy said, face redder than her dyed-red hair. "He wants a Dough-Cro."

"Before noon tomorrow," the Park Manager himself said, voice weak from disuse. "It's no fun without a timeline." The Park Manager smiled and went back to being silent. Boy swore loudly.

"Looks like we need to go find a Dough-Cro," M said unhelpfully.

"Fuck you, tourist," Boy said, happy to have someone to turn her anger on that wasn't an immortal spirit of the forest. "Bloomberg can't get a

Dough-Cro. Jesus Christ is seventh on the wait list. Fathers trade firstborns for a Dough-Cro, and maidens their virginity."

"I'm not a virgin."

"Not even your asshole?" Boy got vulgar when she was angry, which was most of the time. She took a pocket watch from her leather coat, looked at it, and cursed. "It's almost midnight," she said. "By now the line will be all the way to Prince Street."

"That's it, then," M said happy to wash his hand of this thing that was credibly threatening to ruin his evening. "No Dough-Cro."

"Do you like the parks?" Boy asked furiously. "Do you want them to continue growing, in defiance of the soot and the smoke and the trash and the endless fucking waves of people? Then we need to get this thing a Dough-Cro, and we need to get it for him before sunrise, or the deal is off."

"It's your show, doll. I'm just here for moral support."

"I know a guy," Boy said, turning south and starting rapidly toward the nearest subway station. "But it won't be easy."

Because it turned out that the guy Boy knew lived in Williamsburg, and they were in Prospect Heights, and since Boy refused to go anywhere in the city except via public transportation—which Boy insisted was a point of personal pride but which M suspected was a curse or some sort of bargain she had made with something—it took an hour and a half to get there. The moon was high and full when they walked out of Grand Street Station, the streets thronged with the hip and the desperate to seem so.

"This place becomes dreadful at night," M said. "It's like a haunted carnival."

"I had a nose ring before nose rings were cool," Boy said.

"Where is this place?"

"It's a warehouse."

"Williamsburg is entirely warehouses."

And indeed the block they were on seemed to consist of nothing but. Boy stopped at one with loud music and a bunch of people smoking out front.

"You on the list?" asked the not-quite human working security at the front, beer-bellied and seven feet tall not counting his horns.

"No," Boy said.

"You gotta be on the list if you want to come in. Or you gotta defeat me in a physical trial."

"Thumb wrestling," Boy said, pulling up the sleeves on her T-shirt.

Being the best thumb wrestler in the history of the world was not something that was going to get you so very far in life, sad to say, but wherever you could go with it, Boy had been. This now included the inside of a half-real party in Williamsburg, M taking the opportunity to slip past while the goon was busy trying to force his fingers back into place.

Boy's guy looked like most of the rest of the party—sallow skin taught in undersize jeans and a throwback Nets jersey. "I can get you a box of Dough-Cros," he admitted, "but I'm going to need something in return."

"Yeah?"

"I'd like tickets to the new Captain America musical."

"No one wants to see the new Captain America musical," M said, "come on."

"I do."

Boy sighed. "I don't know anyone who has those."

"One of my brothers has a pair," the guy said. "But he lives out in Carroll Gardens."

Which was where they went, though it took a while. The address they had led to an all-night pizza parlor, the kind that advertised one-dollar slices and occasionally got cockroaches mixed in with the dough. There was an old-fashioned rotary phone in the back, and if you dialed six three times a false door opened beside it. Up four flights of stairs a rooftop party was coming to an end, the remaining few guests pairing off desperately, terrified at the prospect of going back home to face the dawn alone with their own crippling horribleness.

The Second Brother, for this was how M now thought of him, looked nothing like his predecessor, being black and—well, maybe not morbidly obese, M wasn't a doctor, but fat enough that he'd have had trouble meeting women or walking upstairs or standing unaided. But there was something that he had in common with the first man they had met, or the first boy they had met—whatever—some shared facet of douchebaggery. He was wearing a hoodie with a symbol on it that M did not recognize but supposed was ironic.

"I've got tickets for the Captain America musical," he said. "But you'll have to get something for me."

M was not at all shocked to discover this was the case. "Which would be?"

"I want box seats at Yankee Stadium."

"Sure you do," M agreed. "And I bet you even have a brother who can get his hands on them."

"Yup."

"But you won't just give him a call yourself?"

The Second Brother gave them a look that suggested this was not just impossible, but utterly absurd—like finding the square root of a negative number.

By now, M had accepted that this was just going to be one of those nights, and there was no point in fighting it. A lot of nights were like that for people like Boy and M, nights that made sense the way things make sense to a small child or someone deep in the midst of a dream. It was part of the price they paid to the Management for being what they were, or at least that was the way that M thought of it.

Boy, predictably, dealt with the situation less gracefully and was still cursing while they were on the subway going toward Bed-Stuy, the scattering of late-night passengers eyeing her warily.

"Don't worry," M explained. "She's on cocaine."

The audience nodded and went back to thinking about themselves.

The Third Brother wanted reservations to a restaurant on the Lower East Side that hadn't opened yet but was already booked solid for six months, some sort of Taiwanese-Scandinavian fusion thing, reindeer-meat baos and whatnot. It sounded perfectly ghastly to M, but there was no accounting for taste.

By the time they walked out from meeting with the Fourth Brother, who lived on a sixth-floor walk-up in Windsor Terrace and wanted tickets to see a band M had never heard of but was certain he would not have liked, and who was, paradoxically, a slightly overweight woman with dyed-blue hair, the moon was growing dim, and Boy was getting nervous. "It's like a goddamned matryoshka doll," she said. "How many of these are there?"

"Seven."

"That was rhetorical."

"All the same."

"How can you be so sure?"

"It's always either three or seven," M explained.

Despite the deadline, they grabbed a late-night snack at a nearby diner on Park West. M had eggs with corned beef hash and wheat bread with two pads of grape jelly and two pads of strawberry and an orange juice and several cups of coffee and two pink pills that Boy said would "help keep the edge on." For dessert, he had more coffee and another one of Boy's pills and a slice of apple pie à la mode. Boy didn't eat anything, but she drank three chocolate milk shakes and chain-smoked cigarettes and guzzled down her supply like so much PEZ.

They left, shadowboxing their way through the borough, walking supersoldiers with Booker T and the MG's playing as their backup. M found himself stepping over telephone wires, and it was all he could do to keep Boy from starting a fistfight with a passing cop, just for the hell of it.

"We're on a mission!" he yelled, grabbing her by the shoulders and shaking her back and forth until her mohawk looked like the lure on a fly-fishing hook. "We don't have time for this!"

"I know," Boy yelled back at him. "I know!"

But M would not let go. "What was it? Can you remember?"

Boy reminded him and they were back on their way to Bay Ridge as fast as the choked silver snake wiggling through the city's rib cage could carry them, which was not all that fast, the R train only coming around once every thirty minutes—minutes that, with M and Boy's dilated sense of time, seemed to last far longer. They spent it grinding their teeth and scratching themselves. Passersby stared.

The Fifth Brother lived in a housing development, and his room was guarded by a crackhead with six arms, holding (in descending order, and going right to left) a dirty razor, a scale, a crumbled wad of five-dollar bills, a Saturday-night special, a human head, and nothing. Blood dripped from its mouth. "What is the secret to life?" it asked.

"Crack," M said.

"Correct!" the thing replied happily. "Do you have any?"

"No," M said, but the crackhead with six arms let them by anyway.

The Fifth Brother wanted the number of a twenty-four-hour, farm-to-table weed-delivery service that was known exculsively by major rap stars, ex-mayors, and, apparently, the Sixth Brother, who lived in Brooklyn Heights and wore a wifebeater ironically. He didn't have a beard, but his mustache had been waxed and twisted and waxed and twisted until it extended out a foot and a half in either direction, sharp-bristled as a wire-headed brush. Sleeping at the entrance to his room was what to M looked very much like a hellhound, big as a small horse with teeth the size of a large rat, exhaling little bursts of flame when he snored. The Sixth Brother wanted VIP passes to the Sleet Room, which Boy explained was a special exhibit in the Museum of Modern Art at which people did not quite get sleeted on.

"I could not sleet on you right now, if it's such a big deal," M said, holding his hands up in the air and making wavy motions with his fingers.

But for whatever reason that did not satisfy the Sixth Brother, and so they were off again. It was getting late and M was getting antsy, antsy on top of the speed, which had made him pretty antsy to begin with. "So, what happens if we don't get your friend this Dough-Cro? Is this trouble like the Botanical Gardens aren't going to be as nice as last year, or is this trouble like crop blight crippling the Eastern Seaboard?"

"How do you feel about the color green?"

"Strongly in favor."

"Then we'd best get the man his Dough-Cro."

The Seventh Brother lived in the basement of a brownstone off Atlantic Avenue. His room was dank and dirty and so was he. He was wearing the same wifebeater as the previous sibling, but he was wearing it unironically. Indeed, to judge by its rather used quality—the yellow underneath the armpits and the BBQ sauce stains on the front—it might well have been the only thing that he owned. His beard was white and wispy and ran down to his ankles. "I can get you into the Sleet Room," he said. "But I'll need something in return."

Boy was making hurry-up motions. M seemed to be concentrating very hard on his shoes.

"I require," he said, pausing until M looked up, "a Dough-Cro."

M actually thought that was funny and was going to say something about being "bitten by ouroboros," which was pretty clever given that he hadn't slept in a while and was high on speed, but Boy beat him to it, shrieking and popping the Seventh Brother in the face with a small, bony, savage, pointy fist.

"I think you killed him!" M said, kneeling down beside the now-supine Seventh Brother. But just then he came to with a pained breath, and it was clear that she had not.

Boy rifled through his clothes with a speed and coolness that suggested long practice. From his right hip pocket, she pulled out a laminated badge for the Sleet Room.

"If violence was an option," M asked, "why didn't we take it earlier?"

But it was too late to play coulda-woulda-shoulda, too late to do anything but go back through the whole process again, as rapidly as possible, crisscrossing the borough at a frantic-seeming pace. Again they complained about the gap between north and central Brooklyn. Again the R train was late. They took more speed.

With the sun moving swiftly through the sky, they arrived back at the little triangle of greenery that M now knew, beyond any possible doubt, was legitimately a park. The Park Manager waited on a bench. He looked more like an old man now than he had looked earlier, when he had looked mostly like what he was. But there was a rather too-intelligent-seeming squirrel seated near him, and the starling in the tree above him *caw-caw-cawed* their arrival.

Boy dropped the box of Dough-Cros onto his lap. "I hope you choke on it."

The man, or whatever, did not look at Boy, but he opened the box slowly. The squirrel skittered over, pulled off a bit of the pastry, and set to eating it with small, swift bites. The starling in the tree swooped down and began to peck at one as well. The man did not try any, but he smiled wider and wider.

"You had better grow like an adolescent hard-on," Boy said to him.

"Do you mind?" M asked.

It did not mind, offering the open box to M. He took one with strawberry frosting, nibbled at it, and shrugged. "It tastes a lot like a doughnut."

"You shut your fucking mouth," Boy commanded.

M went back to eating his Dough-Cro.

22

Rollo of the Laughing Eyes

M's cell phone awoke him one morning around nine, flashing the name of a girl whom he had gone out with several times but who had abruptly and without explanation stopped calling him some weeks earlier. He pitched his voice to characteristic nonchalance. "Hello?"

"M," Celise said from the other end, "how wonderful it is to speak to you."

"You're not Kristen."

"Is that what your phone was reporting? Technology these days. The world has been going downhill since the gramophone."

"Indisputably. Well, no harm done."

"While I have you," Celise continued smoothly, "perhaps you'd be a doll and look into something for me? It concerns an old friend of yours—"

"Friend? That doesn't sound like me at all. A renowned misanthrope, I rarely leave the house, have no close acquaintances, quite loathe unsolicited phone calls—"

"Rollo of the Laughing Eyes?"

The line went still.

"M? Have I lost you?"

"What about him?"

"He's been making rather a ruckus in a townhouse near South Ferry Station. Of course, if you aren't up to it, I'd be happy to pay him a visit myself, but it might end in a bit of a mess, and I couldn't make any promises about the collateral."

"I'll take care of it."

"Of course you will, you darling thing you. Just head to Wall Street and start smelling the air. You're sure to find him. Get it done today and I'll send something jingly as a sweetener. Just a gentle nudge off the island. Perhaps out Brooklyn way. I'm sure the bitch would be happy to have him."

M hung up the phone and thought about that last lie. Even Abilene, with her half-tender heart and her love of all things eccentric, would not want to have anything to do with Rollo of the Laughing Eyes. M showered quickly, pulled on a pair of jeans and a clean T-shirt, and went to grab the train.

He caught a whiff walking out of the subway, fresh-baked cookies and the color crimson and a Fela Kuti groove. North a bit and it gave way to day-old musk, like you'd smell on your sheets the morning after a hard night of lovemaking, and a sort of yellowish chartreuse and an early Edith Piaf song. He walked a few blocks in the wrong direction, started to lose his sudden synesthesia, realized he'd taken a wrong turn, and circled back.

Rollo of the Laughing Eyes now lived in a townhouse sandwiched between two very large apartment buildings near the corner of Beaver and Broad Streets. At first glance M was given the impression that what he was looking at was not a building, but a representation of one, and not a very good one either—a picture made by a toddler, pointing at the squiggly lines and saying, "That's a door, and those are windows, and can we put it up on the fridge?" After a moment it snapped back into coherence, sort of, in a manner of speaking. Each and every brick was a different color: crimson and sky blue and puke green. Out-of-season plants bloomed side-by-side with horticulture of a distinctly apocryphal nature—century-old Banyan trees flourished over mandrake, petioles like Jewfros.

The passersby couldn't bring themselves to notice yet, but you could see it infecting their reality. Finance bulls hurrying to working lunches slowed as they passed, dollar-sign eyes gone hazy. Packs of East Asians flitting north toward the tourist traps of central Manhattan stopped and looked aimlessly around for something to take a picture of, cognizant of the spectral emanations but not quite able to identify the source. Most of them kept walking, though M knew that the more sensitive or joyous or miserable—those who had just lost a parent or gained a lover—might get a stronger glimpse of it, might even find themselves inside. Celise was right, as she had an unpleasant habit of being: The chancre was growing, and it needed to be excised.

The door was open, as of course M had known it would be. The entry was unfurnished, as was the room beyond it and the room beyond that, empty except for tobacco ash and dead soldiers and the artwork that caked the walls and the floors and also the ceilings—a stunning and unstable panorama that M made a point of trying not to look at too closely. In the third room there was a foldout couch. On top of it were a banker type wearing a sport jacket and tie but no pants and a lithe, dark-haired youth of striking and effeminate beauty who scowled hard when M came in, possessive of the flesh with which he was intertwined. Above them was a reproduction of "The Birth of Man" with David Bowie standing in as God. M kept walking.

In the small kitchen a girl cooked breakfast half dressed. She was willowy and fair and stunning-looking and clearly not yet twenty. Pink nipples were clear against her white cotton undershirt. "Rollo's upstairs," she said, smiling. "Would you like some breakfast?"

"No."

"I'll make something anyway," she said, turning back to the stove.

The art inside Rollo's room was fresh, less than a day old, so young that it didn't quite know what it wanted to be yet, a mural extending across the walls that was either a beautiful woman or the noonday sun and either way, too bright to look at directly. Rollo was wrapped in a sheet below it, sleeping soundly on an eggshell pad. M crouched down and lit a cigarette and looked at Rollo for a moment without saying anything. He seemed younger than he had the last time M had seen him.

"Hello, Rollo."

Rollo's eyes were bright green when they opened, and his smile was authentic or seemed to be so. "If it ain't the boogeyman himself." He wasn't wearing a shirt, and his chest was sallow and fleshless. He had long leather gloves over both his hands, unusual sleeping attire in any bed M had ever shared.

"Were you maybe thinking of putting on pants today?"

"I guess if it'll make you more comfortable. Go grab yourself some coffee, I'll be down directly."

In the kitchen, the girl whom M was a little bit in love with was cooking up a storm. Eggshells gathered atop coffee grounds, potatoes bronzed and onions fried, severed orange halves awaited exsanguination. It was unhygienic but appetizing. The dark-haired boy and his playmate were sitting at the counter, the latter looking blank-eyed and lost, like he'd just come off the line at the Somme. When Rollo came down a few minutes later, he kissed each in turn, on the lips but not quite passionately, informed the girl that he would "take breakfast in the garden," then led M through a back door.

Outside a small jungle grew in the shadow of the neighboring apartment buildings. Lengths of ivy climbed up the glass and steel, thick roots the size of M's arms. A baobab tree offered abode to a chittering pack of golden-furred monkeys, diving and gamboling and almost laughing, though, of course, man alone was given the capacity for laughter, uneven recompense against his foreknowledge of death. If you stared straight up, you saw the normal Manhattan sky, but if you were looking at something else—at one of the tricolor parrots that chirped away in the tree, or at the foreign, pear-shaped fruit at which the birds gnawed, or at Rollo himself—then you would have sworn above you was the eternal blue sky of the Pampas, or the Garden Route down Africa way.

"Christ, Rollo," M said. "How much of that shit have you been doing?"

Rollo shrugged. "I don't really keep track anymore."

"The entire house is painted with it, you can smell it from five blocks away. You think that day trader has a family he should maybe go back to?"

"I'd always heard that day traders reproduce asexually. Cut off a finger and throw it in a pot of water and wait a week."

"I bet they're wondering what happened to him. I bet they've called the cops. I bet they've put up posters."

"Calm down. He's only been here a few days."

"How much has he seen in those few days? Enough to put a fissure right down into the center of his brain. And he isn't the only one, either. A few more weeks and we're going to have Burning Man taking place in Lower Manhattan."

"Would that be so bad?"

"It would be terrible," M said, as he did not at all like Burning Man, "although happily it's an impossibility, because if you don't shut down this little circus you're running, the next visit you're going to get is from the White Queen, and she won't be sitting down for breakfast."

This did not seem to interest Rollo very severely, at least not nearly as much as the soft weave of the dandelion he was holding. His Lower East Side Lolita came out carrying a tray with two plates of huevos rancheros, two cups of coffee, two cups of freshly squeezed juice, silverware, and a bottle of hot sauce. She set everything down and kissed Rollo on the forehead. "I'll be in the front room. Call if you need anything."

"She's very pretty," M said, after she had left.

"Hannah?" Rollo nodded happily. "She's a darling, just as sweet as God's grace."

"What did she look like before you found her?"

"So far as as I'm concerned, exactly the same."

"And when it runs out? When midnight comes and she goes back to being fat-assed and sad-eyed?"

"Who says it has to run out?"

"Everything runs out, Rollo. You can only keep the tinsel up so long."

"Then she'll have had her few shining moments—how many can say that even? You worry too much about the future."

"You're the only person who thinks that."

"How are the eggs?"

"Fucking incredible," M said, unhappy and unsurprised. In Rollo's state, beauty and pleasure accrued naturally around him; any creative gift would be enhanced. That very pretty black-haired boy would be on a top-twenty list within five years time, and a very pretty black-haired corpse five years after that. He had that look to him that they all got when they'd been around Rollo too long, beautiful and damned.

Rollo didn't eat any of the eggs or drink any of the coffee, but after M had done a fair bit of both, he started to talk: "Heck, M, you know me. I'm not trying to make any trouble."

"Just seems to find you?"

"I liked the look of the building," he protested halfheartedly. "If it's such a problem, I'm happy to blow town."

"I think that would be best for everyone."

"Or at least I would if I could."

"How much are you in for?"

"More than I can pay."

Which wasn't much of a surprise. Enough bliss to ink half the building, enough bliss to grow this garden cheek by jowl with reality, to push it out like a cuckoo does a rival's egg. M saw now that the things he had thought were monkeys shifted color against the tree, and were those little nubs going to be wings some day soon if Rollo didn't leave Lower Manhattan? Yes, M thought that they were. "I'm a bit light at the moment," M said. "And while I appreciate the personal bonds of loyalty between a dealer and his client, under the circumstances it might be best if we solved both of our problems by having you disappear."

For the first time in the conversation Rollo looked a bit chagrined. "I'm afraid I've given . . . guarantees."

"Guarantees?"

"Hair and fingernails."

M pushed his plate away in disgust. "What the hell is the matter with you, Rollo? Hair and fingernails? Did you sign away your firstborn as collateral? You didn't have a true name you could tell them?"

"There was a project I was working on," Rollo said. "I needed a few cans."

"A bathtub, more like. A child's fucking swimming pool." It is as wise to argue with an addict as it is a madman, or the sea. M chewed over his tongue a while and smoked a cigarette. When it was done, he ashed it into the verdant jungle grass and stood. "Let's go meet your man."

Rollo took him on a side route back through the house and onto the street. They stopped in one of the antechambers, where Rollo had crafted a *pietà* that took up most of the room and somehow space beyond that as well. "What do you think? I put it up yesterday."

"It's the most beautiful thing that I've ever seen," M admitted unhappily.

It was a long subway ride up to the Bronx. Rollo smiled at babies and flirted with old women. Between 66th and 110th Streets, a group of Latino

youths demonstrated a limited grasp of break dancing for the dubious pleasure of the passengers, dubious save for Rollo, who found the exhibition a
source of toddlerlike joy, got up from his seat, and took part enthusiastically
if not with any great skill.

M mostly just scowled.

They disembarked at one of those stops in the Bronx that might be anywhere in the city or anywhere in the Western world, for that matter, faceless
and indistinct. M followed Rollo down a few blocks of sidewalk overpasses
and blank asphalt, stopping at one of the anonymous hundred-unit apartment buildings. Rollo buzzed a number. A voice answered. Rollo spoke
briefly. The door opened.

The elevator wasn't working, so they were forced up the stairwell,
near-lightless and well-defaced. Some of the graffiti were tags, jerky and incompetent or sweetly curved. Some of the graffiti were slogans, coarse gibberish regarding the habits of the neighborhood girls, lyrics to rap songs.
Some of the graffiti were stick-finger cartoons of the pornographic variety.
And some of the graffiti were incantations written in a language that had not
been spoken aboveground since before the last ice age, strange symbols that
seemed to fade when you stared at them.

"What do you know about these guys?" M asked.

"They're good people. Nice folk all around."

"Then they would be the first friendly drug dealers I've met in a spare
century of using narcotics."

After what seemed to M, whose regard for physical activity was less than
overwhelming, a very long time, they came finally to the correct floor. Rollo
led M down a long, not particularly well lit hallway, stopped at one of the
doors, and knocked loudly.

The man who opened it was short and stout and sad-eyed, and M did not
find that he hated him right off, which was disappointing. It was always easier
when you could loathe a man, when you found his existence such an affront
as to want to move swiftly into violence. But this one looked like he could
have been a pen salesmen or a professional mourner. A child was crying in a
nearby room, another reason that M did not want to have to do anything too
permanent to him.

"Rollo," said the man, less than smiling.

"Arturo, sorry for the short notice."

"Not at all," Arturo said, but he gave M a long stare that did not seem overwhelmingly friendly, an impression reinforced by the thin, scarred Latino standing behind Arturo and carrying something that looked like a sawed-off shotgun except the hammer was a scorpion's tail and the barrel—at that moment, happily, pointed away from everyone—was a dried snake.

Another thing that M liked about Arturo was that he did not start fast and heavy with the pleasantries, which is something you normally get with drug dealers, sweet-mugging you like a letterman at junior prom.

"Who's your friend?" Arturo asked.

"I'm M."

"Just M?" asked the one holding the gun.

"You can call me Martha, if it'll give you something to do."

It was one of those typical, horrible New York apartments where the kitchen is a diagonal line drawn down the center of the living room, where tile meets carpet like ocean meets the sand. There were couches and chairs. M waited for Arturo to choose one, then sat down opposite him. Rollo did a lotus on a divan in the corner, gloved hands resting on his knees. The man with the gun stayed in the kitchen.

"You stop by to pick something up?" Arturo asked. "We got a special arrangement with Rollo, but I could see my way to decanting a few fingers of bliss for a friend of a friend."

"Is that what I am?" M asked.

"I'm hoping so."

"I'm hoping so too, Arturo. I'm hoping that very much. I'm hoping that we can part today having shook hands and traded phone numbers. I'm hoping to invite you to Christmas dinner and the bris of my firstborn son. But mainly I'm hoping that you're going to forgive Rollo his debt and hand over whatever assurances he's offered you."

"I'm afraid those desires are mutually contradictory." Arturo would have been a good inquisitor, back when that was a job that a person might have— bereft of sadism but lacking utterly in compassion, the sort who would pull out nine toenails but leave the tenth untouched.

"Who the fuck are you, man?" the one with the gun asked, not quite angry but moving in that direction. "Coming in here and playing king?"

"I told you," M said. "I'm M."

"I know who you are," Arturo said quietly, before settling his muscle with a look. "But I didn't know you were you so close with Rollo. Are you so close with Rollo?"

"I'm sitting here, aren't I?"

"Do you know what bliss is?"

"Yes," M said, "but I suppose you'll tell me anyway."

"You ever meet one of those things that seem a little bit like people but really aren't that at all? You ever meet a concept wearing human skin?"

"I've had some experience with them."

"Bliss is what they leave behind after they've visited their worshippers or their enemies, the little bit of residue that remains on their altars, in the ceremonial cups of wine and the bodies of their sacrificial victims. Spirit cum," Arturo explained, the vulgarity casual and unexpected. "Spirit blood, spirit breath."

"Such was my understanding."

"Not so easy to find one of those things these days," Arturo said. "Not so easy to summon it. Not so easy to placate it once you've got it in place. Not so easy to ask it to leave in a way that won't make it angry. Not so easy to harvest what it leaves behind. Not so easy to transport it."

"Sounds like a rough business. You ever think about maybe opening a salon?"

"Infrequently. Point being, it's a lot of trouble to get even a little bit of bliss—and we've been giving quite a lot of it to your friend these last months."

"So what does he owe you exactly?"

Something passed between Arturo and Rollo. "Rollo's an artist," Arturo explained, still looking at Rollo. "And an artist needs a manager."

"So that's fifteen percent of nothing, or have you not noticed that our dear Rollo is an indigent?"

"We have faith in our long-term yield. Regardless, we're convinced that it's in everyone's interest if Rollo continues as part of our stable for the foreseeable future."

"Not everyone. Where you live, Arturo?"

"Where does it look like to you?"

"To me it looks very much like the Bronx, but I must be mistaken. Because the White Queen owns this part of the Bronx, as everyone knows. And one thing about the White Queen—we're personal friends she and I, so I can tell you—she would not be happy to see a pocket existence take root in the Financial District. She wants Rollo gone, and she doesn't care about any deal you may have made with him. Another thing about the White Queen: She's not the White Duchess, or the White Lady, or the White Princess even; she's the motherfucking White Queen. You understand what I'm saying?"

"I think I might."

"She's the top dog, she's the stud bull, she's the one and only," M shrugged. "She's one of two, anyway. I'm not sure if I think you're a smart guy yet, Arturo, but you can't be dumb enough to suppose yourself in a position to take a shot at the title."

"I don't think that."

"I'm happy to hear it."

"But you aren't the White Queen."

"Not the adjective or the noun."

"And if the White Queen is so concerned about your boy in the corner, then why didn't she come and visit us herself?"

"Because she likes to see us peons dance. It's a preoccupation of royalty. I can assure you, however, if things don't get wrapped up to her satisfaction she'll make time for a visit."

"Wrap things up like maybe kill the two of you? Would that be wrapping things up so far as the White Queen would be concerned?"

"Death has a certain finality to it—though you'll find you won't get much for two corpses."

"You'd be surprised some of the people I know," Arturo corrected. "But most importantly I'd be getting the satisfaction of knowing that I didn't get fucked over by a cleft-assed faggot and his big-talking, empty-chested partner."

M waited a while for the threat to spread to the far corners of the room. Then he asked, "Got a pen?"

"What?"

"A pen. Or a pencil. A writing instrument of any sort."

"You planning on putting down a number? I told you, it's not about money. Rollo and I have an arrangement."

M stared at Arturo for a while, who sighed finally, looked over at his boy in the kitchen to make sure that someone was still paying attention, then went into a corner and got a ballpoint from a desk. He gave it to M, who, in the interim, had managed to find a cocktail napkin that had been hidden about his person. He doodled on it aimlessly, or seemingly so. "You ever kill a chicken, Arturo?"

"Only in the figurative sense."

"Thing about chickens is that they don't like being killed."

"Clever creatures."

"To a point. Anyway, if you're by yourself, and you need to kill a chicken, there's this little trick you can do: Hold their necks down and draw a line in the dirt."

"And?"

"That's all. The chicken goes numb when it sees it, insentient. That's when you make with the butcher knife."

"A fascinating digression into homesteading, but . . ."

"Nothing organic runs straight, you ever notice that?" M continued, attention focused on the picture he was drawing. "Crooked or curved or bent, but never straight. You show a chicken a straight line, you're exposing it to a conception of reality that its mind has not evolved to comprehend. The resultant comatose state is a kindness, a blessing, a defense to avoid pondering matters that would otherwise break its machinery. Follow?"

"I follow."

"People are no different. Do you understand how big the universe is, Arturo? Or that behind and inside and all around it is an infinite set of universes of the same scope? Or that there is something beyond that also, something that no human words could hope to express? What if there were a symbol that could transmit this understanding to you in one sudden and blinding flash, as the line does to the chicken? Which would flood your mind with revelations such as to blank the very canvas of your soul—not, like the chicken, for a few blissful seconds, but for the remainder of your life, a span that would surely seem an infinity to you, drifting endlessly between frag-ments of eternity?

"And what if," M said, capping his pen and putting it onto the table and holding the cocktail napkin up, faced away from Arturo, "I just finished drawing that sign? Do you think you would want to look at that, Arturo? Do you think that you could avoid looking at it before your man puts two in my back? Do you think that whatever Rollo's lost you is worth taking that sort of chance, with your kid crying in the next room?"

A girl, M could tell in the silence that took hold then, her wailing for a long moment the only sound that could be heard, apart from the hum of the refrigerator and the distant bleating of sirens.

"Is that what's on the napkin?" Arturo asked.

"Could be."

"Then how come you can look at it?" the gunhand asked.

"Maybe I'm lying," M said, "or maybe I'm the sort of person who remains unfazed by the face of God. If I was the latter, I bet I could get to you before you managed anything with that cannon."

Arturo's sad, hard, heavy eyes stared at the coming conflict unblinking. "This is where we're at with this?"

"It would seem to be the case."

"He worth that much to you?"

"That would also seem to be the case."

"Who's going to make me whole?"

"I don't know that anyone can do that for anyone," M said sadly. "But if you contact the White Queen, she might see her way to peeling off a few bills." Which would bring M's compensation for the afternoon back down to nothing, but he hadn't really supposed he would get through unscathed.

Arturo looked at his man in the kitchen. His man in the kitchen looked at M. Rollo looked at the wallpaper and smiled softly.

"Done," Arturo said.

On the windowsill was one of those garish votary candles that you can buy in the Latino section of most grocery stores, except this one had a picture of *Santa Muerte* floating over a pile of decapitated skulls. M held the napkin over the flame, then blew the ashes softly out into the late afternoon.

...

When they got back to Rollo's pad, what would become his going-away party was steadily building steam. The wispy blonde girl had called a dozen of her friends, brunettes and gingers and green-haired pixie-cut queens of hipsterdom. The smell of marijuana almost overpowered the synesthesic overflow of the bliss. Rollo gave greetings all around but bopped on past, up the stairs to his room, then out the fire escape. M followed in train. Out on the roof, the sun hadn't quite yet given up the ghost, the last dim rays illuminating the concrete. Rollo slipped on his sunglasses. M rolled a cigarette and started to smoke it.

"What was on that napkin?" Rollo asked.

"A smiley face," M said, which might have been the truth. "Where you going to go?"

Rollo shrugged. "San Francisco, maybe. Or Pondicherry. New York in the summer is the pits, anyway."

"And when did you hear I was back in town?"

"A month ago."

"She's predictable, the queen. Likes to have problems taken care of but doesn't like to dirty her hands. I guess you figured all you needed to do was get a little loud, make a little trouble, and she'd send me out to put things right."

Rollo took the cigarette out of M's mouth and shifted it into a smile. He spread his arms out to encompass the street below them and the horizon beyond that. "I missed you. Shit if I didn't miss you. Do you remember that time with Janice, when we all took peyote and wandered around Central Park, and we met that couple that was about to break up, and Janice convinced them to get engaged?"

"Yes."

"Do you think they went ahead with it?"

"No."

"What ever happened to Janice? I haven't seen her in forever."

"She died."

Rollo shrugged. This was not the first time someone told Rollo someone else was dead. Rollo was well practiced in surviving the misfortune of others. "Those were times, man. Those were times."

"Yeah."

Rollo took another puff off the smoke, then handed it back to M.

"You could have called me if you needed help," M said.

"You wouldn't have picked up."

"And why might that be, do you wonder?"

"You don't have as good a sense of humor as you used to?"

The thing about an addict, as anyone who has ever dealt with one knows, is that it becomes impossible to determine where exactly their instinct toward self-destruction becomes intertwined with a desperate need for attention, if they're running into walls because they want you to help them up or because they've come to love the taste of blood.

"I'm sorry," Rollo said. "You know I'm sorry. I shouldn't have done it like this. It's me, man, it's me. You got the whole thing backward. I didn't set you up to help me with Arturo. I set him up to help me with you. I knew you wouldn't come if I called you, not after last time. What can I say? I'm fucked up."

The addict's lament—the addict and everyone who knows him. M didn't seem angry, but then again M often didn't seem like much one way or the other.

"Just come back downstairs. The band will be getting hot by now. We'll sit out in the garden and get high and talk about the past. Hannah was staring at you earlier. I think you've got an admirer." He put one gloved hand on M's shoulder. "Life is too damn short for grudges. Even immortals don't have time for bitterness."

And the mad thing was that M found himself seriously considering it, in the moment before he flicked his cigarette off the roof and watched it fall onto Broad Street. It would be a good time, he was certain. It was always a good time with Rollo. And that little piece of blonde sunshine was probably wearing a tight skirt, and M didn't think very much convincing would be required to get her to take it off. And it would be like old times, and Rollo wasn't the only one who could remember those fondly. And one has no choice in who one loves, not in the last instance. One does not love because doing so is prudent; one loves because it is ultimately the only thing powerful enough to offer distraction from what we see and what we are. Rollo with his kind eyes and his love for everything, who lied all the time but who was honest when it counted. M had missed him these last years and hadn't realized how much until then.

But the difference between a man and a fool is that a man only makes a mistake once, or in any event not over and over again, ad infinitum. "Janice killed herself, you know."

"Yeah?"

"A straight razor."

"I'm sorry to hear that."

"Rollo of the Laughing Eyes," M said. "I gave you that nickname. Do you remember?"

"Yeah."

"But the joke's never on you, is it? It's on me or it's on Janice or it's on one of those poor dumb kids downstairs, thinking it's all a game until the bill comes due, discovering you aren't around to pay it. What do you care, anyway? Just things to break, and there are always more of those."

Rollo didn't say anything for a long time, though when he turned back to M his eyes were a different color, and then he fell into a belly laugh, rich and full—laughter that slipped neatly and without warning into weeping or perhaps remained laughing, it was impossible for M to tell. And then Rollo removed one of his elbow-length gloves and then M lost track of things for a while.

It was like looking into a very bright light or hearing an explosion of sound or slipping into a drug-induced coma, though it wasn't exactly like any of those, as M, who had experienced each, could attest. It was like having your brain wrapped up in heavy cotton. It was like losing seventy or eighty IQ points in the span between an instant. It was what happened when one got face-to-face with the raw mess of creation, when a physical thing was transitioning into the infinite, on the way but not there yet. The bliss was up to Rollo's wrists and had turned his flesh into some strange amalgam of color and thought and light. Like glorious gangrene it would spread up to his elbows and his shoulders and into his trunk, and once it reached his heart there would no longer be anything in existence recognizable as Rollo of the Laughing Eyes, just one more demigod dashing through the ether, spinning eternally between realities. "Put them back on," M was saying, on his knees, hands pressed fiercely against the side of his head, neither action providing much remedy. "Jesus Christ, put them back on."

And then Rollo did, and the sun went away, and M was able to stand again, though doing so made him violently nauseous, and it took no small effort to keep from booting onto his shoes.

"Arturo's been giving it to me free," Rollo said. "After a while I noticed I couldn't clean it off my fingertips, and then I realized I didn't really want to. I'm not an addict anymore, M, not like you'd understand it. I'm the thing itself. I sweat bliss and I've started to piss it. I can't eat anymore and I don't need to. I can taste the currents in the air and the sweet-swelling joy coming from the party downstairs. I can taste your despair right now, like sour plum sake. That was the deal that we made: They'd give me all I wanted, as much and more, and then once the turn rolls around I'd let them bleed me a while."

They were back again where they always were, with Rollo beyond reach of aid, with everything that M had wagered and sacrificed made pointless by the bottomless depths of his friend's misery. "So you understand," Rollo said, leaping up onto the low stone wall dividing the building from the empty air. "The joke is on me. The joke is always on me."

23

An Offering to Moloch

It was around two in the afternoon on a hot August Saturday when M realized the rest of the people at the beach house were planning on using him as a human sacrifice. The mansion was a hundred rooms, easy, and perched on a stretch of rocky coast that M had earlier found picturesque, but that he would now admit might reasonably be described as ominous. Getting lost coming out of an upstairs bathroom, he had stumbled upon a large library and immediately grown suspicious, not because there was anything suspicious about it so much as because he did not think that most of the other people at the beach house could read. In evidence of this, the many hundreds of leather-bound tomes on the shelves inside were thick with dust, except, rather dramatically, for one—a copy of Goethe's *Faust*. M might perhaps believe that one or the other of the guests could be literate, in the sense of occasionally flipping through a fashion magazine or a stereo manual, but he supposed the great German to be beyond them. And sure enough the book had been the trigger for a secret door: The stone fireplace at the other end of the room swung open to reveal a narrow spiraling staircase. The descent took him to the set of a Scandinavian death metal video—black stone facades and wall sconces and an altar with hand restraints stained with what was probably not ketchup. Above it, chiseled into the wall in Gothic script, was the name Moloch.

"Damn it," M said.

M went outside, an operation that, given the scale of the premises, took him about fifteen minutes. Sedentary on the front roundabout was a fleet of cars, each costing more than open-heart surgery. M was a competent car thief under normal circumstances, but they were all of the hypermodern variant, which relied upon keypads or magnetic wands or retina scans or some such, and were too far out of his bailiwick to warrant an attempt.

"Damn it all to hell," M said.

In retrospect, he had to admit, he should have seen it coming.

In matters of money, M had long felt one was best off having slightly less than one wanted, along with a solid supply of wealthy friends. This allowed one all the spiritual benefits of poverty while still occasionally offering the opportunity to visit Palm Beach or the Upper West Side. So M had made a point of being extra friendly when he met Spencer in a bar in the East Village a few nights earlier, even though M had not liked very much about him. Spencer was, for instance, wearing an ascot, which M did not think should be countenanced outside of an F. Scott Fitzgerald story, and also he had dowsed himself in enough cologne to asphyxiate a horse. Spencer had been impressed by M's vague patina of Brooklyn-hipster street cred, as well as the fact that M had a joint on him, in exchange for which Spencer insisted on buying the rest of the evening's drinks, a balance of favors to which M was willing to abide. Three hours later and with a half-dozen cocktails in him, M was almost willing to admit that Spencer was not a vacuous, half-witted frat boy or, at least, if he was a vacuous, half-witted frat boy, that he was good-natured. And when Spencer asked M what he was doing this weekend and suggested that M come out to an acquaintance's beach house, M thought that Spencer might even turn out to be one of those not-quite friends who nonetheless prove more useful than any number of people whose company he actually enjoyed.

That was Tuesday. Friday M climbed into a Bentley just south of the Holland Tunnel a few hours after noon. "Be careful getting in," Spencer said. "The stitches in the leather were done by hand."

It took them two hours to get out of Manhattan. Tourists shuffled past at ten or twenty times the pace they had managed, obliging Spencer in staring at his contraption with bug-eyed astonishment, like a rube touring a geek show. Spencer played techno music at a volume that cannot be generated from cars that cost less than a house. M slid down in his seat and hoped that no one he knew would walk past.

Interstate 495 was just as busy, bumper-to-bumper with six-figure husks of gleaming steel and tinted glass, an accumulated billion horses' worth of power all held in stable, a fleet of rocket ships in a parking lot. M got out, smoked a cigarette, and walked around a while, the drivers glowering at him and the passengers sneering.

Back in the Bentley, Spencer was fiddling with the digital console, trying to get the navigation to work. "Built-in GPS," he explained. "It can find a pimple on a porn star's ass," Spencer said.

"Good to know," though privately M thought the fact that they could not move made direction-finding something of a moot point. Still, it was better than listening to Spencer talk, which he did any time he wasn't playing with one of his gadgets, a steady flow of product placement and casual elitism that made M want to turn Menshevik, or at least throw a brick through the window of a Starbucks.

Eventually they started moving again, and with the top down, it was impossible to make out anything that Spencer was saying. To tell by his flapping mouth, like a figure on a muted plasma TV, Spencer didn't realize that, and certainly M saw no point in enlightening him, just nodded along and enjoyed the scenery, which, it had to be admitted, was quite spectacular. M had never been this far out into the Hamptons, but he could see why the upper crust of the Big Apple had decided to make it their playground. Winding roads, looming vistas. It was almost enough to forgive the company.

When they arrived at Spencer's friend's estate a few hours after sundown, M was feeling all right about things, a state of mind reached with the copious use of marijuana. The rest of the party were in the back gardens grilling up thick hunks of steak and drinking gin like mother's milk. They were the sort of people whom Spencer would be friends with. They had names like Brad and Britney and Ashleigh and Ashley. The men were in finance and the women were mostly married to or in the process of marrying a man in finance. Both sexes counted former All-American lacrosse stars among their number. They argued over whether this house was nicer than some of the other properties they or their families owned, but came to no conclusion. They seemed more banal than evil, but then again, the same was said of Eichmann.

Still, it was a beautiful night. The stars were as bright as you could ever want them to be, and the house was magnificent, the sort of manifestation of wealth that proved M's philosophy, because who in their right mind would want to be responsible for the upkeep of such an absurdly oversize edifice, and what person of equal sanity wouldn't have wanted to spend a few days in said environs? Of the fifteen or so other guests, three of them were attractive, single women whom M thought he could talk himself into not disliking by the end of the weekend. He had hoped to talk one of them into not disliking him by the end of the evening, but it was late and everyone seemed tired, and not long after dinner Spencer had led him up to his room, which was bigger than his apartment in Brooklyn and a good deal more opulent.

He had woken up late the next morning. A few floors below, a liquid brunch was being prepared: Grey Goose and freshly squeezed tomato juice. M knew this because they told him. Poorly compensated spokesmodels, every one of them. M drank three, then went to relieve himself. This is where we came in.

M sat and thunk. He thunk and sat. He smoked a cigarette. He smoked another.

What was particularly galling was that, so far as M's not insubstantial experience had revealed, there was no such god as Moloch, or at least there had not been for some millennia. Admittedly, absence of evidence is not evidence of absence, and even after all his time, M was still running into things that he had not previously thought were real. But just the same, the murder room, the name of the deity itself—which was probably what you got when you typed *dark god* into Google—these all carried with it a distinct whiff of bullshit.

For that matter, M did not think that any of the other guests were in tight with the Management. It was not that they were too stupid—though some of them, Buffy and Bryce in particular, seemed to possess cogitative limitations that he had supposed unknown among vertebrae. M had met plenty of people who could do all sorts of things that conventional physics did not allow but were, simultaneously, not bright enough to understand the rules they were violating. Still, M had been around long enough to have a pretty good idea when someone was mucking about with the firmament, and he did not think that there was any more to these people than what you saw immediately, and perhaps a good deal less. Which meant that, if things went as intended, his life would be ended by a dozen and a half yuppies who had watched *The Omen* too many times.

Well, M thought to himself after a few minutes. *Things do not always go as intended.* He stood up, brushed off his jeans, and went back inside.

Spencer and Bryce and Laurence were speaking quietly to one another around one of the tables in one of the kitchens. They shot M long, searching looks as he came in, the looks of predators, or people who thought they were predators.

"Everything all right there, sport?" Spencer asked. "You were gone a long time."

"Fucking office," M said. "Can't get away for twenty-four hours without the whole thing collapsing on top of itself."

"But today's Saturday," Bryce said.

M laughed and slapped the beefy bourgeoisie on the shoulder. "Not in Shanghai!" he poured himself a glass from the pitcher of Bloody Marys that sat on the counter.

"I . . . hadn't realized you were so up on the markets, old boy," Spencer said, skeptical or concerned.

"What did you think, Spencer? I'm some wastrel, wandering stoned around central Brooklyn all day? I push high-yield derivatives on third-world buyers. Long-term and low interest, am I right, boys?" M did not know what most of these words meant, but he had learned years earlier that no one in finance understands the arcane processes beneath which they labor. Sure enough, all the men laughed, anxious that anyone might think they missed the joke. The ladies were demure enough to admit ignorance, however, smiling with dimwitted loveliness.

"I'm just surprised: You work in finance, but the other night at the bar you said you'd never been to the Hamptons before," Spencer said.

"I said I'd never *driven* to the Hamptons before. Normally, I take my helicopter—not that I mind roughing it," M said graciously. "Besides, if I'm going to take a weekend off, I'd just as soon jet the red-eye to Cannes."

"Cannes?"

"I know, I know—you're going to say the south of France is dead—but it's been in the Hanover family for ages, just ages. Almost an obligation."

"House of Hanover?"

"The nouveau riche call us Windsor," M said with a strong note of disdain. "And, of course, Uncle Nathan always insisted we had a touch of the Hapsburg jaw, but personally I never saw it." M laughed like he was trying to catch a fly in his mouth, and after a moment everyone joined in. "So," he began, finishing his drink, "are we about ready to get down and do this, or what?"

The assembled looked around uncomfortably. "Do what?" Misty asked. Or maybe it was Muffy, M wasn't sure.

"The games, of course. When are we going to start the games?"

Everyone looked very confused. Not M, obviously. M looked certain as a mother's love.

"Sorry, sport?" Spencer ventured finally.

"The games in honor of the dark lord. To determine who gets sacrificed."

Bailey's drink shattered on the floor. M pretended he didn't notice.

"Excuse me?" Spencer asked, after a long, breathless interval.

"That's what we're all here for, right? I mean, it is the seventeenth of August."

"You . . ." Laurence looked concerned. "You know about Moloch?"

"Who works in derivatives and doesn't?" M asked, incredulous. "I ensure my bounty of good fortune the same way you do yours—by sacrificing the loser of the sacred games to the dark lord."

"The sacred games?" Bryce asked.

M looked at Bryce like he had just defecated on the lace. "Yeah, the sacred game. What do you guys do?"

Bryce looked at Spencer. Spencer looked chagrined. "We kind of . . . get a different person every year and then kill them at midnight."

M's jaw dropped. M's eyes bugged. M flushed and sputtered. "I just . . ." M shook his head back and forth, trying to pull himself together and only barely succeeding. "I just don't even know what to say to that. Amber, can you get me another drink—that's a dear thing, thank you so much. I mean, I had heard standards had gone to hell here in the colonies, but I had no idea, just no idea."

Spencer and Bryce and Laurence and Hunter hemmed and hawed a while. Amber brought M a drink, then sat down next to him, close enough that he could feel her leg against his and smell her hand lotion. "Look," M said, "I don't know how you do it down in the Hamptons, but my family has been sacrificing human souls to the Emperor of Dust and Shadow since the high middle ages, and there's no way in the lord's home that I'm going to break with tradition because you poor saps haven't done due diligence with the scripture."

Everyone looked down at their feet, justly shamed.

"Well . . ." Bryce began after a long few moments. "What does your coven do?"

"First of all," M said, "we don't call it a coven."

"What do you call it?"

"A hootenanny," M said. "And every year on the seventeenth of August, you get your hootenanny together and you play the sacred games, the loser getting . . ." M brought a finger sharply across his throat.

Everyone nodded at each other. This was a good idea, they all seemed to agree, this idea that M had made up a minute previous.

"How do we . . ." Amber began but didn't finish.

"How exactly does one play the games in honor of the dark lord?" Madison asked in her stead.

"One does not play the games in honor of the dark lord," M said rather testily. "One *undergoes* them."

"Of course, of course, so sorry," Madison apologized.

"It's not me you need forgiveness from—it's the Prince of Wasps and Scorpions."

"Forgive me, dark lord Moloch."

"The dark lord Moloch does not forgive!" M declared. "As far as the games go, first we need to determine who will be the officiant."

M, with the near-unanimous support of the group, consented to adopt this position—though he claimed to be greatly disappointed not to be able to participate directly, and insisted that, should he return next year, someone else would serve as referee. "With that settled then," M said, "I suppose the thing we need to do now is find a couple dozen eggs."

A few minutes later they were out at the beach, Bryce watching his yolk seep into the sand with undisguised horror. Spencer, still holding his own egg aloft on a sterling silver spoon—not the one he was born sucking on—put a hand on Bryce's shoulder. "Tough luck, old boy."

"I'm afraid that's a point against you, Bryce," M said. "But worry not! There's six more events to go!"

The three-legged race was next, followed by the rock-paper-scissors contest. Spencer proved oddly unbeatable in this game of random chance and was disturbed in the extreme to discover at the end of it that, in contrast to the previous two events, the winner of the rock-paper-scissors contest was the loser of the who-gets-sacrificed contest, at least in so far as Spencer picked up a point. "I don't have time to explain to you every single rule," M said, irritated. "Read your scriptures—everyone knows that Moloch hates rock-paper-scissors. Your victory is compelling evidence of the dark lord's disdain."

None of the rest of the participants argued this point.

Madison and Bryce tied for last in hokey pokey and picked up an extra point each. It looked for a while that Bryce was going to head into halftime so deep in the hole that it would be impossible to ever climb out, but Spencer failed dramatically at shaving whipped cream off of a balloon, and by the end of it, he and Bryce were both tied.

Dinner was held to be a pleasant affair by all involved, laughter expelled and liquor imbibed—although Allison got an extra point for calling the hootenanny a coven and Phillip for drinking rosé with the second course, an act which, M explained, the dark lord considered blasphemy most foul, and not in a good way. But still, there was an energy to the entire endeavor that had been missing the night before, that had been missing, M pretty much suspected, in the entirety of his newfound not-friends' lives up to that point.

Then it was back to the games, less steadily but more hastily, since the events had to be finished by midnight. Flashlight tag took rather longer than

M had anticipated, though Madison proved a rare hand at hunting down the other members of her party.

"All right, Amber," M was saying some time later, sitting in a heavy leather chair in the main drawing room, the great bay windows behind him offering a magnificent view of the beach and the sea and the night. "This one's for the win. What's your answer going to be?"

On the couch across from him, Amber considered the matter silently, brain straining beneath her lovely cream-colored forehead. Muscles long unused sloughed off their torpor, struggled to life. "Brittany Murphy?"

M looked long at the card from the Trivial Pursuit: Girls Only! game that he had found in one of the back closets, and turned it around slowly. "Correct!" he yelled.

It was the single greatest moment of Amber's life, the first time in almost thirty years of pointlessness that she had wagered anything of value and won. She felt so happy she wanted to weep. With this loss, however, Bryce was once again tied for last with Spencer, and thus also wanted to weep, though for different reasons.

"What happens now?" Amber asked, still flush with her victory. "We need a sacrifice, don't we?"

"Of course we need a sacrifice," M said, rather gruffly. "Imagine such a thing! Not having a human sacrifice on the seventeenth of August! We just need to turn to the tiebreaker."

"Which is?"

"It doesn't come up much," M admitted. "But in case of a tie, loser is the poorest."

Spencer and Bryce paced each other like bucks feuding for a mate. Or like the bucks feuding for a mate that M had seen on the National Geographic Channel, before the National Geographic Channel dedicated itself entirely to proving the existence of Bigfoot.

"Do inheritances count?" Spencer asked.

M laughed. "Liquid assets only, I'm afraid."

To judge by Spencer's sudden drop in color, this was not good news from his end. He put his hands up and began to back away from M, but before he could say anything, Amber had snatched up an empty bottle of merlot from the table and struck poor Spencer a telling blow across the back of his head. Popular wisdom to the contrary, this generally does not knock a man cleanly unconscious. It does, however, hurt terribly, and rendered Spencer capable of little more than rolling on the ground and moaning.

"That was excellent, Amber," M said. "The dark lord would be very proud."

Amber blushed with happiness. Simply glowed with it.

M was happy to let the other participants take the lead for the sacrifice itself, which was long, over-elaborate, and breathtakingly painful. It was not the worst thing that M had ever seen, but it would have been for most of the rest of us.

Breakfast, by contrast, could have been filmed for a spread in *Ladies' Home Journal.* Heaping platters of blueberry pancakes with maple syrup, thick slabs of bacon just the right side of burnt, and endless cups of rich, hot, dark coffee. The surviving members of the hootenanny carried with them the telltale signs of people who have woken up from a truly magical evening, a once-in-a-lifetime evening, quiet and smiling and content to enjoy the sunlight. The couples seemed honestly and authentically happy, losing themselves into each other's eyes. They had survived something spectacular together, had risked and won and come through shriven, purified.

There was something legitimately like heartbreak when M revealed that he would not be able to return next year. "My mother would never let me hear the end of it," he said. "She's become quite sentimental about family, after we lost little Adelweid two summers past." M took a quick aside with Bryce, "You never saw a worse egg carrier."

Bryce nodded sympathetically.

"But I tell you truthfully that I feel comfortable leaving the event in your capable hands. You've made real strides, all of you. In fact"—M found the tab of a beer can in his pocket and handed it to Bryce—"I want you to take this, Bryce, as a symbol of your new position. I hereby name you high officiant of next year's games."

Bryce's blue eyes swelled to the size of duck eggs. He closed his fist around it and bit back tears. "I won't let you down," he said.

M patted him on the shoulder. "I know you won't."

And all too soon, or much too late, it was time to make their good-byes. It went without saying that M would take Spencer's car, now that Spencer would have so little use for it. There were handshakes and bro hugs and air-kisses all around, and then M was adjusting his mirrors and about to take off.

"Remember! The dark lord's feast is a time for friends and family, so make sure to invite all of them that you can. And feel free to drop the bottom two next year, if you have enough people. The dark lord just lives for that kind of shit." And then he was off, burnt rubber and black exhaust.

M totaled the car about a week later, trying to re-create the chase scene from *The French Connection* with Boy, which, ultimately, was just as well—wealth might have proved corrupting to his rigid moral instincts.

24

A Night Out With Bucephalus

August is a time for standing on sand, M thought, or at the very least grass, not for slapping sandals against concrete, dodging between the shadows of skyscrapers and housing projects, sweating through your hair product.

This was a point of view widely shared by his fellow citizens, most of whom did their best to flee the metropolis if at all possible. Stockdale had returned to England for the month, using as his excuse that he wanted a pint of bitter at an appropriate temperature, and that it was cricket season, and that he secretly hated all Americans. He would be back in the fall, complaining of pea-soup fog and desperate for a decent tamale. Andre and Boy had recently split, broken dishes but no bones, which put this one at about par, though you wouldn't know it by how hard each was nursing the wound. "I am thinking about getting away from everything for a while," Andre had told him, with the wistful tone of melancholy that had dropped panties from Toulouse to Tehran. "Perhaps visit an ashram." Though ultimately he bought a ticket to Monaco, which is a fine country if you liked beautiful women and hated the income tax, but which would not have been at the top of M's list had he been searching for inner peace. Boy made less of a fuss; upon arriving to pick her up for a concert one evening, M had discovered a note pinned to the front door. GONE TO THE DESERT TO TAKE ACID, it read in neat blue ink, and below that, in block letters and crayon, DO NOT LOOK FOR ME. Even Flemel, whose presence M had grown used to the way one does a sty or a nut allergy, had headed back west to see his family. Another reminder, as if M needed one, of just how young his apprentice was. If M had ever had a family he could not remember them. Or he chose not to, at least.

M did not like being around when other people were not. It went against the way of things. He had spent the better part of his life happy to be exploring some third-world hellhole or distant, sun-baked wasteland, secure in the knowledge that in a trendy bar half a planet away, one attractive person was asking, "Where is M, exactly?" and another attractive person was answering, "Who can say, darling? That one's not for being tied down."

But not being around required money, and that summer, for some reason M could not quite put his finger on, he had none, or at least not much. His savings dried up and no one came by to offer him any of the odd jobs that were his bread and butter. He had a streak of bad luck with cards that left him breaking even three straight weeks in a row. By the time the dog days had really hit, he barely had enough left to pay for rent and weed. He spent most of that August reading in bars until the sun went down and then walking home very slowly, hoping the heat wouldn't ruin his hair.

M was getting high on his front stoop, waiting for late morning to become early afternoon to become sunset to become evening. It was a Saturday, which was not one of M's favorite days, because it meant that there were more people on the streets—hipster kids sweating through their graphic T-shirts and neighborhood folk walking past shirtless, too fat or too thin, and all of them smelling. And M smelling, though he had showered twice that day.

A car pulled up, but leaning the way he was M could not see much of it, and it wasn't worth the effort to move. An immense pair of Wallabees impacted the sidewalk and walked over to M, interrupting his view of the concrete.

"Let's go," Bucephalus said.

Straining to look up M saw his reflection in Bucephalus's sunglasses, or maybe just in Bucephalus's eyes. "OK," he said.

Bucephalus's car was something between a Cadillac and a steam engine. It was bright as a recent bruise. It had rims like Ben Hur's rival—razor-sharp and gleaming. It had enough legroom for an NBA center and air-conditioning amenable to an emperor penguin. They weren't using the air-conditioning, though. They were flying up Eastern Parkway with the top down, Hall and Oates blaring out of the speakers, which were, needless to say, terrifyingly loud.

Bucephalus drove eastward and eastward, farther out that way than M had ever been. There was a rumor that Brooklyn went on forever, that it just continued onward until you reached the end of the world, a flat drop into nothing. M did not believe this personally, but he could understand how it had gotten started. Finally, they stopped at one of the endless rows of projects—those strange, magnificent, cancerous contusions, monuments to naïveté long devolved into outright anarchy. Some boys loitering around the entrance hooted at Bucephalus's car, in admiration and threat. If a man is someone old enough to kill a person, then some men loitering around the entrance hooted at Bucephalus's car. They stopped hooting after Bucephalus got out, though, deflated at his very presence, made a hole for him to walk through, and stared sideways, at their shoes and the street and the sun itself.

M hadn't thought the elevator would work, but it did. The light inside didn't really, though, flickering back and forth between overbright neon and blank darkness.

"How come you never return my calls?" Bucephalus asked.

"I had a feeling I'd end up doing something like this."

"That was a good guess."

The elevator opened, and M followed Bucephalus down a corridor that did not smell like roses. Bucephalus stopped and banged on one of the doors, hard enough to bend the hinges.

"Who is it?"

"It's the man," Bucephalus said. "Now open up."

The door opened. The quarters were tiny, nasty, dilapidated. They had been furnished with things that you find out on the street, or that should have been put there.

Bucephalus brushed through quickly, M following with rather less enthusiasm.

"Who the fuck is this?" the caretaker asked. He was the sort of skinny one gets from living through a war or being addicted to narcotics.

Bucephalus pivoted the one-eighty in a flat quarter second, swelled up like a puffer fish. "He's the motherfucker just walked in with me, and that makes him the second most important motherfucker in the room. He's gonna chill for a minute. Now offer him some motherfucking Froot Loops."

The man shrunk his head into his shoulders. "You want some Froot Loops?"

M did not.

Bucephalus went into the bedroom and closed the door. The junkie sniffed and blinked. M looked at the couch and decided to remain standing.

Time passed uncomfortably. M began to realize that there was something very strange inside the bedroom, and living beside it was having an insalubrious effect on the man. The crack wasn't helping, but crack hadn't grown a line of gills up his neck.

"What number am I thinking of?" the caretaker asked.

"Twelve?"

"No."

"Thirty-seven?"

"No."

"I don't know."

"It was twelve."

M nodded.

"The name of the Lord is a hundred and twenty-seven syllables, and the sixty-eighth is *ba*."

And how the hell had he learned that? M wondered.

"I know what Cain did to Abel."

"I think we all do."

"But I *know*," the man said.

When Bucephalus opened the door, M got a glimpse of vast, pale flesh, pitted like old cheese, as well as the strong scent of a woman's perfume. "Let's go," he said.

M did not desire to dispute him.

"I can't do this much longer, man," the junkie said as M followed Bucephalus outside.

"A few more days," Bucephalus told him and slid a small roll of bills into his hand.

"You said that last time." But he took the money.

Bucephalus's car had not been touched. M got into the passenger side. They did sixty out of the parking lot, eighty down the road, and a flat hundred once they hit the freeway. Crossing the Williamsburg Bridge, Bucephalus reached over and opened the glove compartment. Inside were fifteen years in prison if you caught the wrong judge. He pulled out a plantain-size blunt, lit it against the tip of his finger, and puffed out fat worms of smoke like exhaust from a diesel engine. After a long time, he handed it to M.

Bucephalus barely slowed down once they hit the city, running all the yellows and most of the reds. M thought of being in the pocket like he was doing Fred Astaire to the universe's Ginger Rogers, seamlessly pirouetting past bad luck, a divinely assisted two-step. But for Bucephalus it was more like a mosh pit, with him being the biggest bull in the crowd—just plow straight into shit and make sure you ain't the one gets knocked over.

Bucephalus parked his car next to a fire hydrant in the West Village, opened his door, and exited without speaking, and what could M do but slip out as well. The next few hours were something of a blur. They drank a lot. M realized that whatever was in that blunt was not weed, or not exclusively weed, and he thought about asking what it was but decided he was probably better off not knowing. Bucephalus started and won a fight with a bouncer whom he claimed had made a crack about his indigo eye shadow, though M had not heard anything. In a small room in the back of a dive bar, Bucephalus played tic-tac-toe with what M thought was a kobold and won three times in a row despite having to go second. They bought illegal fireworks from a Mexican bodega, then ran up and down Houston Street throwing them at tourists. Later, M would have vivid memories of being bitten by a fluffy, white, two-headed dog, but checking his ankles he found neither mark nor scar. That did not mean it did not happen, of course, but it suggested there was little reason to worry about it.

Evening found M in a very fancy restaurant somewhere near Harlem, wearing a suit, which he had not previously owned and knew for certain he could not afford to purchase. Curiously, Bucephalus was dressed the same as he had been all day: baggy jeans and a white T-shirt and a chunky gold chain.

He was on his third highball—or at least there were three empty highball glasses in front of him, though he might have been far deeper into them than that.

"You ever eat dog?" Bucepehlus asked.

M discovered that his body was now lighter than air, desirous of rising up into the firmament. It could only be kept still through the sort of rigorous mental effort that left little energy for conversation. "What?"

"You ever eat dog?"

"Yeah."

"How about snake? You ever eat snake?"

"Once."

"Shark fin?"

"Back when it was still legal."

"What did it taste like?"

"I didn't love it."

"What about man?" Bucephalus asked, forking a long spur of carpaccio and chewing it over while smiling. "You ever eaten man?"

M didn't say anything. Bucephalus was just trying to frighten him. That it was working did not invalidate that fact.

When the waiter came by, Bucephalus demanded two orders of foie gras, a T-bone steak, and another highball. M ordered a cheeseburger.

"What kind of an ignorant motherfucker comes to a restaurant like this and orders a cheeseburger?" Bucephalus shook his head. "He doesn't want a cheeseburger, he wants the filet, medium rare. And he wants the brussels sprouts with bacon as a side. And he wants another beer." The waiter nodded. It seemed that M did not have so much of a say in the matter. And indeed the brussels sprouts were delicious.

By the time desert came—raspberry cheesecake for Bucephalus and Armagnac for the both of them—gravity had regained its implacable hold on M's torso. When the bill arrived, Bucephalus paid without looking, setting down a series of crisp hundred-dollar bills in even time. He gave the *maître d'* one of these as well, and the kid who brought them their car.

Blazing south, the city seemed at once vicious and fecund—things in the darkness howling and fucking and eating each other, creating life at a just slightly faster pace than they were destroying it. Street lamps broke the shadows playing across the face of his chauffeur, though not for long and never entirely. Stopped at a red light next to a police cruiser, Bucephalus pulled another blunt out from the dash, lit it, and blew smoke into the direction of the adjoining patrolman, who, worry-lined and on the back end of his twenty, studiously ignored the provocation. There were things out in New York that night that a man did not want to face on his own, not even with a siren and a loaded service weapon.

The bar they went to was at the top of a building a few blocks from the river, and it had a nice view so long as you pressed your face against the window. The women had bodies that looked like someone's idea of human, all tight skin and smooth curves, and M hated them and wanted them simultaneously. The men they were with he just hated, tall and broad-shouldered and vapid as the monologue of an Alzheimer's patient.

One of them, straight as a rod and dark as berry, caught Bucephalus's eye. "How you doing?" he asked, in a Spanish or perhaps Italian accent, the son of a leather-jacket magnate, held together with cocaine and hair product.

Bucephalus smiled at him and flexed his chest muscles. "Sweetness and light, gorgeous, sweetness and light."

Gorgeous laughed and moved a little closer. M moved a little farther away.

"You new to the city?" Bucephalus asked.

"Been here since the winter," the boy said.

"What do you think?"

"I love it," he said, his melted chocolate eyes heavy on Bucephalus.

What's not to love, M thought, barbarism and hypocrisy nestled cheek to cheek. M had lived too long among the impoverished to have any illusions about their nobility of spirit; they were loud and ignorant and generally unhygienic, every bit as amoral and prejudiced as their social superiors and far more likely to mug you. But even so, they weren't any worse than the parasites roaming across Midtown and the Financial District—men and women who would die without ever having created anything, without ever having accomplished anything, whose sole and exclusive goal was to consume and to consume and to consume until their shriveled black hearts gave out in one final belch of selfish ecstasy.

"It's the center of the universe," the boy continued, "a microcosm of the world."

And whose decision had this been, to cull together humanity in its vastness and narcissism, to distill the species to its essence, and to offer the spirit without a chaser? What ignorance, what inexperience, what idiocy was required to think that what one yearned for was more of humankind, rather than less!

M said something vulgar, which Bucephalus and his willing victim seemed to take as a suggestion, disappearing into the bathroom. M was left with nothing to do but drink heavily and think ill of the world.

Bucephalus came back a little while later, but the boy did not. Bucephalus ordered a shot and drank it, and then he slapped a C-note down on the bar. "This place is dead," he said. "Let's get the fuck out of here."

And M was too drunk or too bitter or too bitterly drunk to object.

They found themselves in a club, as M had feared they would. As a rule, M did not enter a club unless he was high, and he found a guy selling something that he could not prove was not Tylenol, and so he took two of them for his headache.

The music was awful, gibbering drum and beat, like the next-door neighbors fucking, the arrhythmic pounding of their four-poster against your TV wall. M bought a five-dollar bottle of water from the kid selling them, finished it, and bought another. His head began to spin. After a while he realized he was dancing. The music was incredible, the pulsing *thump-thump-thump* of existence, refined until it was as potent as ethanol, and M wallowed in a teeming crowd of flesh and sound.

A hand fell onto his shoulder, and M whirled around to embrace its owner, almost certain to be a member of that happy fraternity of bipeds to which M himself belonged, a brother or a sister beneath the moon. Best yet the hand belonged to Bucephalus, who actually *was* sort of M's friend already, M's friend in so far as he had brought M to this party, which by M's thinking was probably the greatest party in the history of human existence. "I'm on ecstasy!" M yelled happily.

"This place is dead," Bucephalus intoned. His bass came keenly through the club music, though he didn't seem to make any particular effort. "Let's move."

And move they did, nestling themselves into Bucephalus's waiting Cadillac and jamming across the bridge. Midway through the ride, the ecstasy seemed to start to wear off, or at least M no longer felt so ecstatic. Bucephalus pulled over on a quiet street in Park Slope, brownstones silent so late in the evening. Emerging from the shadow of an elm tree a uniformed valet opened the door, nodded with submissive familiarity to Bucephalus, took his keys, and drove around the block. His partner led them inside.

It was not the first orgy M had attended, but it was the most elegant. There were mirrors and black silk. In the corners and in the alcoves and in the coatroom and on the light fixtures, people were doing things that M had never thought to do to anyone before—enthralling and horrifying perversities etching away at the nonchalance all modern people are supposed to hold about the act of sex. He wondered which of these burrs would take root in the fertile filth of his mind. That was the way of things, wasn't it? Nauseating, then forbidden, then erotic, then banal.

Bucephalus, M felt, had long ago reached the last stage, overlooking the proceedings with something that bordered on contempt. "Why did you bring me here?" M asked.

"I like you, M," Bucephalus said. "But you're a faggot."

"Is that a proposition?"

"You dip your toes, but you don't plunge in."

"I like to test the waters."

"Faggot, like I said. You don't trust yourself to come back."

The party was like the bottom half of your mind sawed off and presented on a platter—every lust and vice and abomination that ever flavored your dreams and nightmares, just reach out and take it. He thought he saw a woman he once loved doing terrible things with a man he once hated. He thought he saw his mother writhing in ecstasy beneath the embrace of a half-dozen men. He thought he saw the devil.

"This is what it is, M," Bucephalus said. "Gold and shit, cum and blood, intermixed, layered over top one another. And it won't last forever." Bucephalus took off his sweat-stained beater and strutted into the tide. "It probably won't even last much longer,.

M was not sure if he felt that to be a good thing.

25

Infinite Grimoire

Magic is as old as the word, and the word is very old, passed down mouth by mouth during humanity's long adolescence, an eternal-seeming childhood, bereft of history or tragedy. And then someone—we won't name any names, there are statutes of limitations on this sort of thing—came up with the notion of putting some of these words, or runes, or characters, down on paper, or papyrus, or into the living rock, and everything pretty much started to go to hell. And the first of these tomes, the primogenitor of story, the platonic ideal of the book, was the Infinite Grimoire. There, in primordial script, in a testament that was ancient when Old was very young indeed, was written the knowledge of how things had once been, malleable and half-formed, inchoate, subject to the whims and desires of passersby. How things once had been and how to make them so again. In short: magic as thought, magic without ritual or chant, magic as practiced by the divine.

Supposedly, at least, for it had to be said that no one had actually seen the Infinite Grimoire since well before the fall of the Roman Empire. Of course, the fact that no one had ever seen the Infinite Grimoire did not prove that the Infinite Grimoire did not exist. Every day, or close to it, one woke up and found out that the universe was bigger and stranger and less coherent than you believed it before. But still, M hardly thought searching for it was a sound financial strategy. One drills for oil, not pixie dust.

It was good work though and strangely steady. M had been not finding the Infinite Grimoire for years, admittedly only some small fraction of the time during which humanity, and for that matter any number of things that were not humanity, had failed to find it. And yet he still kept getting contracts for it, running down a lead by some or other bibliophile, certain that this time—this time definitely—he had the hot tip on a line to divinity.

Tannery was one of these aspirants, a minor mage with a penchant for things rare and things lost, sallow-cheeked, loose-limbed, generally clad in black. On a warm evening in early September, M found himself in the basement of Tannery's house in Queens. Actually it was Tannery's mother's house, though Tannery had been living in it for as long as M had known him, which was far, far longer than a man ought to live with his mother. M had never seen the woman, though hearing her putter about upstairs, M had formed the impression of something vast and yet somehow dainty.

Tannery was spinning punk records, and M was doing some of Tannery's coke. Tannery wasn't doing any coke, which worried M, because Tannery loved cocaine, indulged in it from when he woke up in the later afternoon till he went to bed three days later. The only time Tannery didn't do cocaine was when he had some sort of caper planned, which was, coincidentally, more or less the only time that Tannery remembered he had M's number in his cell phone.

Well, you couldn't blame him. M was a lot of trouble. Tannery was a lot of trouble also, but there was no reason to double down on misfortune.

"I've always preferred Lou's later stuff, personally," Tannery said, which was absurd and insane, but M had a policy of not arguing aesthetics with anyone who was giving him drugs. "But I have this version of 'Sweet Jane' that was only ever issued in a limited run on mammal skin, and I think you'll enjoy it."

"What kind of mammal?"

But Tannery was too deep in the groove to answer. "Those licks still kill me," he said, tapping his hands along arrhythmically. Set out on a table behind him, a vast army of fully articulated G.I. Joes reenacted the Battle of the Bulge, dozens of superhero statues standing mute witness on a shelf above them, painted pewter statues of goddesses in red leather and black vinyl.

"Yup," M said, doing another bump.

"I got a line on the Infinite Grimoire."

"I think I heard this one before," M said.

"No one's heard this before," Tannery said, visibly angered. "I had to trade three empty djinn bottles to a traveling peddler for it."

"Not the record—that you've got a line on the book."

"Oh. But this one's a lock, this one's for dead certain."

"Where's it supposed to be?"

"You'll never believe it—it's been in the Library the whole time."

"How counterintuitive," M said. "And completely irrelevant. Finding a book in the Library, not to get all *Purloined Letter* on you, is an exercise of almost figurative futility."

"Not if you know where to look."

"What, like if you had a map? A map of the Library would be the size of the Library."

Tannery began to rattle off a stream of directions, a left at Gender Theory, your third right after the hall of High Fantasy, straight on till morning. "I bought directions from Sheelba at the Bizarre Bazaar. She hasn't steered me wrong yet."

"And what's your way inside?"

"There's a gate from the back of the main Brooklyn branch."

"Great! I live right by there. You can drop me off on your way."

"I was sort of thinking you'd come along."

"Why were you thinking that?"

"Infinity doesn't interest you?"

"Have you seen my apartment? I don't have enough space for a wardrobe." M had found a bit of used cellophane from a pack of Camels and was rolling it into a very tight tube. "Who gets to read it first?"

"It's infinite—we each get to read it as long as we want."

"But let's say we both had to go for a dump: Who would get to take it into the bathroom?"

"I would."

"So it's yours, then?"

"Yeah."

"In that case, I think you ought to toss me in a sweetener."

"You've already gone through half my stash of sugar."

"That was just basic hospitality, Tannery. Someone comes by, you offer them a glass of water, a cup of tea, fifty or sixty dollars' worth of cocaine. You want me on a ride along, I'm afraid it's going to set you back further than that."

"How much?"

"Who else is looking for it?"

Tannery scratched at his acne with a sudden burst of intensity. "Most of the world, I would think. We're a power-mad sort of species, M, present company excluded."

"Let me rephrase: Who is it that you're sufficiently afraid of that you've decided you want me riding along as shotgun?"

"Falcor Khat."

M hoovered up more of Tannery's blow and thought a while, and what he thought was that Tannery had been boondoggled, hogswalloped, was apt to discover that this Nigerian prince was not everything he had built himself up to be. If Sheelba, whom M had never met but who was not renowned for her trustworthiness, had some idea where the Infinite Grimoire was, why hadn't she gone to find it herself, rather than trade its location for something worth less than infinity? M set his teeth against each other and enjoyed the familiar absence of feeling. On the other hand, if Tannery had been able to pay Sheelba, he would be able to pay M as well. On the other, other hand, while the jury was yet out on the existence of the Infinite Grimoire, Falcor Khat absolutely did exist. He was a name known of old and not known, if it wasn't obvious, for being overwhelmingly friendly.

But then finally, on the last hand, and it had not escaped M that he was counting like Charybdis, was the fact that he had simply done too much cocaine at this point to feel fear, or really much in the way of anything but the desire to get moving, get going, make some trouble.

"Twenty," M said.

"Ten."

"Twenty."

"Twelve."

"Twenty."

"Fifteen."

"Fifteen and the record," M countered.

Tannery sucked his teeth miserably, then said, "All right," and went to get the money and his coat.

Tannery was that peculiar sort of person who preferred to concentrate the vastness of his wealth and resources on things that he and a select handful of associates—not friends—could look upon exclusively, which is to say that he owned a conversion van and drove it wearing sweatpants and beat-up tennis shoes. He also refused to bring along any of his cocaine, which M thought displayed a shameful lack of gallantry.

"How is it that Falcor Khat has the same information you do?" M asked.

"I'm not positive he does. But I know he's been looking for it. Why—you worried for your skull?"

"I am. I like my skull. It's got all my thoughts inside."

"But think of the rewards! Infinite power! Eternal life! The dream of man since time immemorial!"

M grunted. Infinite power would have been OK, at least he could see how it might come in handy on occasion. But M had found that the bigger you got, the more people tried to lean on you, for favors or just to see you fall, and who wanted to deal with that? As far as immortality went, that was obviously not any sort of good at all. Who had ever met death without some partial measure of joy?

Also, the book did not exist. That was the main point, M reminded himself. Foolish to feel tempted by a mirage. Pleased with his maturity, M weathered the rest of the drive in silence.

The main branch of the Brooklyn Public Library was closed at one in the morning, so any negligent elementary students hoping to finish their reports on the first Thanksgiving were going to need to spend the intervening hours coming up with a decent excuse. Or they could just use the internet. Tannery left his van next to a NO PARKING sign on Eastern Parkway, which was foolish, but then again M would be walking home, assuming he survived the evening, and thus figured it was Tannery's problem should the thing be towed.

It surprised M not at all to discover that though the library had technically been closed for hours, there was a small door in the back that was still open, and that it led to a long, hushed corridor, and then into a chamber, which was more like the nave of an immense cathedral than the checkout room in a library. Libraries—like train stations, crossroads, church belfries, and attics—are places where worlds leak together, where the Management, in its ineffable wisdom, tends not to look too closely on what goes on.

They were in an octagonal room, exits at each cardinal point leading farther into the labyrinth, and peeking down one of them, M got a strange sensation of vertigo, of endless antechambers of erudition reflected indefinitely beyond the visible horizon. The walls were partially stained oak and mostly colored leather and faded parchment and glossy newsprint, pulped paper leading up to a ceiling high above, the dust-covered rolling ladders mute testament to how rarely any of them were unshelved.

In the center of the chamber was a circular checkout desk, and at the desk, in the process of stamping a card—for the Library, like the federal government and our neanderthal ancestors, has not gone digital—was a librarian, or the Librarian, as the library was the Library. She might have been of any age between spinsterish and old maid. She was shrewish, or perhaps waspish. She resembled the sort of animal that one would not want to be enclosed with in a small area. She was not, for instance, Angora rabbit–ish, or pygmy hedgehog–ish.

M put a hand on the counter and hung his head over it. "That's a beautiful scrunchie."

The Librarian hissed, pushed M's arm off the desk with a ruler, then pointed at an embossed gold sign in front of her that read, in capital letters, SILENCE PLEASE.

"That's a beautiful scrunchie," M whispered.

Tannery finished running through the directions in his head, pulled at M's shirt, and directed him northward. "This has been a distinct pleasure," M assured the Librarian as he left. "With luck I'll see you on the way out."

Though as it turned out, he didn't even need to wait that long, because after a long jog through the celebrity memoir section, they found themselves back in the same room they had initially walked into. At least it seemed the same room to M, four doorways, an unpleasant woman stamping cards behind a circular desk.

"Reunited at last!" M said to the Librarian.

"*Shhhhhhhhh!*" she hissed.

"Doesn't she remember me? Or is that her twin?"

"No, it's her," Tannery explained. "Somehow this antechamber is mirrored across the Library, regardless of where you are in the stacks."

"Then why doesn't she recognize me?"

"She recognizes you. She just doesn't like you."

"Impossible!" M said, hurt and flabbergasted and coming down off the cocaine none too gently.

They crossed the threshold into the children's section of the Library—the children's wing, the children's labyrinth, the children's closet infinity. The walls were festooned with bright pictures and cheery slogans encouraging the viewer to GET LOST IN LITERATURE! and warning that FICTION'S MY ADDICTION! M paused for a moment in front of a large table covered with a dozen different embossed hardbacks below a sign saying THE COMPLETE WORKS OF HARPER LEE.

"That's far enough," came a voice hidden by a cardboard display of characters that A.A. Milne never got around to inventing—Cynthia the rottweiler and Hunter the androgynous girl-child.

The sound of a gun being cocked was followed by the sight of that selfsame gun. It was a custom model, not that M knew anything about guns really, but it was hard not to notice the filigreed silver, or that the end of the barrel was shaped like a pentagram. The man carrying it was just about average height if you included the varicolored Mohawk, which, comblike, stretched above an ochre head. He wore a red leather jacket with an eight ball on the back and a number of fetishes dangling from the zippers—harpy feathers and mandrake mandalas and fully stocked dream catchers. On one hip he had an empty holster for his gun, and on the other a curved skinning knife. He was dressed just oddly enough to warrant a double take at your average Brooklyn dive bar.

"Don't think about trying any gimmicks," Falcor Khat said. "The gun is ensorcelled."

"Ensorcelled," M repeated, enunciating each syllable. "I don't think I've ever heard that spoken aloud before. What's the deal? You here picking up the latest E.L. James?"

"Cute. No, I'm really only here looking for one book, the same one you're here for, I imagine."

"You're only interested in one book? That's absurd, Falcor. That's just indefensible. There are lots and lots of books worth reading. Proust is very good. Bolaño, Borges. Rebecca West is great, not sure why more people don't read her. Maybe we could hook you up with something simple—*The Phantom Tollbooth* might be a good start. You know, minds are like parachutes— they only function when open!" M had picked this last one up from a poster hanging above Tannery's shoulder, but he stood by it all the same.

Khat sighed. One might have got the sense that Khat did find M as amusing as M found M. "Are those going to be your last words?"

"Apparently not?"

"Good-bye, M," Khat said, about to simplify the situation with his index finger.

"You won't find the book without me," M informed him, quicker on the draw.

"Bullshit. The only reason you'd be here is because Tannery hired you as protection—why he thought you capable of that, I have no idea—ergo, Tannery has the location."

"Tannery is my silent partner. We went in halves on a spell of location," M pulled his phone out of his pocket, opened a map app, and waved it around in front of Khat. "See? It's been ensorcelled. Ensorcelled," M said again.

Khat scowled. "Good-bye, Tannery," he said, swiveling the aim of his cannon.

Tannery, white-faced, choking over an explanation, squeaked loudly. The Librarian, visible from the doorway but thus far showing no interest in their growing feud, looked up and cleared her throat unpleasantly.

"This is a library!" M said to Tannery in a stage whisper. "Keep your voice down!" Then, back at Khat, "But still, you can't shoot him; the spell doesn't work unless he's above the ground. You're going to have to give up on killing anybody for a little while. Think of it as a new challenge."

"I guess I can wait a bit," he said, gesturing at M, who headed deeper into the library, following, or so it seemed, the map on his phone.

The practice of magic is as diverse as any other art or craft, filled with endless specialties and subspecialties. Khat was one of those who had gone in for violence—war mages, battlefield sorcerers, sword saints, hex-wielding gunslingers, kung-fu masters, and priestesses of the goddess of death. It seemed a rather pointless way to spend the time they were given, at least to M's mind, hours at dojos and ranges when you could be drinking sidecars in bustling Brooklyn bars—though, admittedly, there were moments, like this one for instance, when M supposed it wouldn't be altogether useless if he had any serious idea of how to throw a punch.

"I'm surprised you'd be chasing after the grimoire, Falcor," M said, walking briskly from Children's Books to Books Intended for Adults but More Appropriate for Children. This was rather less well-cared-for than the zone they had come from, old copies of *The Fountainhead* and *On the Road* gathering dust in corners. "You know *grimoire* is another word for book, right? Really you'd need to be literate to get any use out of it."

"You're not nearly as funny as you think you are."

"But I think I'm really, really funny, and so even at half rate, I'd still be hysterical."

They found themselves back in the front room. "What are you going to do with your share of infinity?" M asked, then snapped his fingers excitedly. "Imagine the size of the gun you could carry! And all the weapons you'd have around to play with! Gun-blades, razored nunchuks, poison-needled cock rings . . ."

"I've never met anyone so contemptuous of the instruments by which he'd be murdered."

"Just the man who carries them."

"Sure, what issues have ever been resolved through physical force? I can draw faster than Doc Holiday, outwrestle a panda bear, and I learned *iaijutsu* from the ghost of Miyamoto Mushashi. What do you have, M? What do you have?"

"A healthy sense of the absurd," M said. "I assumed from your haircut that was a quality we shared."

"Keep talking," Khat said, raising his voice beyond the conversational. "It'll make killing you that much more fun."

"*Shhhhhhh!*" the Librarian commanded. The coke-bottle glasses she wore might have been the reason her eyes seemed bigger than her head was, though it failed to explain their strange darkness.

M checked his phone and took them left, into Popular Histories of World War II, 1967–1978, exiting about a half mile later into Monster Erotica. M wanted to take a detour into Aquatic Amarous Adventures, but Khat had that gun and was not slow to remind anyone of that fact.

"You talk absolutely endless reams of shit," Khat said, "for a man who could be broken in two by a JV lineman."

"Oh, I wouldn't think of competing with all that hardware. You look like one of Tannery's action figures."

"They're collectibles," Tannery interrupted.

"No doubt future generations will accord them a niche in the Louvre," M prophesied, before turning back to Khat. "We all have our specialties."

"And what's your specialty, M? Talking bullshit?"

"Don't knock talking. We aren't out here tonight looking for Excalibur or Terminus Est or storied Snaga. Words are the thing. What's the point of killing a man when you can run him round to your point of view or poison his memory for future generations?"

"I find most people don't look beyond the knife sticking out of their chest."

"You aren't really planning to murder us, are you? What would be the point? I'm cooperating. You get the book and whatever comes with it; we get to shuffle back to our day-to-day."

"I still owe you for that thing in Taipei."

"Who can even remember that thing in Taipei?"

"You tricked me into eating dumplings laced with arsenic."

"Right," M said, nodding. "That was the thing that happened in Taipei. And Tannery?"

"Tannery I just don't like."

"Sorry, Tannery. You don't think that there's any chance that upon merging with the godhead or whatever, you'll feel beyond such petty concerns as revenge or random murder?"

"Quite possibly, now that you mention it. Which is why I'll probably just go ahead and kill you before taking a look at the book."

"That makes sense," M admitted. They were back in the lobby. "I've been wondering: Does your hair do that naturally or does it require some sort of product?"

"Don't . . ." Khat said, smiling around the anger, shaking his head back and forth. "Don't annoy me, M. This could go worse for you than it has so far."

"You already told me you were going to kill me."

"But when I said that I was still planning on killing you quickly."

M gave an exaggerated shudder and turned south. They spent a while lost in the halls of fan fiction, thousands upon thousands of volumes exploring the burning questions of what exactly would happen if Spock met Skywalker, or if Neo from *The Matrix* found himself mysteriously transported aboard the *Serenity*. Turning left before they had even scratched the surface, they found themselves back in the lobby.

"If you've been feeding me a line," Khat began, "I'm going to kill Tannery and make you watch."

"That's less threat than you suppose," M said.

"It's not the only one I got," Khat said nastily. "How about I poke a little hole in your stomach and tie one end of your intestine to a bookshelf. You know, you've got miles and miles of that stuff inside you. It would make it easier to find my way back out."

"Sounds complicated. Do you dabble in rocketry or is this pretty much your only line?"

"You don't think much of me, do you, M?"

"I don't think about you much, but I guess if I did I wouldn't think much of you."

"I got this cannon, though," Khat said, smacking the butt.

"You've got me there. Who ever heard of an idiot with a gun?"

Khat smiled and reached forward, then M was doubled up trying to make sure that what was in his stomach remained there, rather than on the floor or his pants. The Librarian looked up from her cards.

"You better watch your mouth with me, you little fucking faggot," Khat grunted loudly, "or I'll see you gagging on the end of my pistol." This time, the Librarian shot them all a look of rancor.

"And I'm the one struggling with his sexuality," M coughed.

"Fuck you!" Khat yelled, drawing his weapon from its holster.

"That's it," said the Librarian, slamming shut a book.

All of the lights went out. Something vast and black and nearly silent came out of the darkness, so quiet in fact that you could only tell it was there by the beating of its stygian wings and the suddenly overpowering scent of wet paper. And of course by Khat's prolonged and horrific screaming.

Sure enough, when the lights came back on, M was still there, and Tannery, and the Librarian was back at her perch—assuming she had ever left—continuing with her endless busywork as if nothing at all had happened. Khat, however, was nowhere to be found. Nor his gun, nor his knife, nor his groovy leather jacket, nor any of the objects of power he had been carrying. Looking about carefully, however, M did notice a few streaks of blood on a pile of unshelved Hardy Boys paperbacks.

"Well, then," M said. "Shall we get started?"

Tannery was so shaken by having spent the better part of an hour thinking he was certain to be murdered, as well as by the rather savage nature of his reprieve, that he needed twenty minutes before he could remember the directions he had memorized. Then it took them another few hours trying to retrace their way back to that portion of the Library they had originally come in at. They thought briefly of asking the Librarian for help but decided against it.

Eventually they found themselves back where they had started, and from there Tannery was able to reconstruct their intended route, though walking it lasted until the wee hours, and they turned left into Fetishes: Mysophilia–Narratophilia when they should have gone right into Supernatural Romances: Twee Vampire–Nonconsensual Werewolf, and it took them a while to get on track, especially because M insisted on sticking around for a few moments and expanding his base of knowledge. But by the time dawn was rolling round—according to M's cell phone, the supreme fortress of knowledge is, of course, windowless—they came to a small alcove simply labeled "???".

Tannery scrambled around for a while, pulled a book off the shelves with an unmarked leather cover, and put it down on a nearby table.

"This is it?" M asked.

"It is," Tannery said.

M looked at Tannery. Tannery looked at M. M found himself wondering, perhaps rather belatedly, if he really thought that Tannery was the sort of person who ought to be given unlimited power—if there was anyone who could be trusted with it, really—and, if not, whether it might not be better to do something so that Tannery did not acquire it. But before M could turn thought into action, Tannery threw open the book, revealing its knowledge to an unresisting world.

The first page was a woodcut of a man being spanked by a zaftig woman. The following pages were essentially similar.

"I told you this was horseshit," M said, though you might have noted a touch of relief in his voice.

26

An Infernal Elliptic

M was at The Lady late in the afternoon, not doing very much of anything with the capable assistance of Flemel, when Stockdale entered in the sort of fervor that suggested their languor was at an end. He slapped a copy of the *Daily News* down on the counter. Most of the front was taken up with the nip slip of a modest celebrity. The part that was not read in large print TODDLER MISSING, and below that in smaller print LAURAINE THOMPSON UNSEEN SINCE THURSDAY.

"I don't really see the big deal," M said. "She was wearing pasties."

"There's a vacant building at the corner of Willow and Pierpoint," Stockdale said, ordering a few fingers of whiskey, "and I'm pretty sure it ate a kid."

"Sounds like a job for the Buildings Department."

"No. It doesn't sound like that at all."

"What makes you think it's this house?"

"I've had my eye on it for a while. Something's always been wrong with it, but lately it's been getting worse."

"The city always gets nasty this time of year. It'll ease up two weeks before Thanksgiving, once everyone stops watching *Saw II* and starts on *It's a Wonderful Life*."

"And next October? What then?"

"Have you called the Red Queen? Brooklyn Heights is her area."

"No, I didn't. I don't call her every time I take a piss either."

"I try to keep her informed of any particularly noteworthy bowel movements."

"Does it ever occur to you, M, that this is sort of what we're around for?"

"I can honestly tell you that nothing like that ever occurs to me."

"The body of a child doesn't mean much to you either?"

"I didn't kill her."

"We're just about straddling the line between curmudgeonly cute and outright prickish," Stockdale said. "But you can do whatever you want. I'm finishing this drink and going over to take a look." He downed what was left in one go, then stood and put on his hat.

"Fine, fine," M said, waving for the bill.

Up till then, no one had said anything to Flemel, but he drank his beer anyway, stood as if to accompany them.

M looked him up and down, then shrugged. "All right, junior," M said, "let's see if I've learned you anything useful."

Flemel bit down around his smile, swallowed the flutter of excitement rising up from his stomach, pulled on his coat, and followed the two of them to the subway.

Half an hour later they were standing at the intersection of Willow and Pierpoint, and M said, "I really think we ought to call Abilene."

In a row of million-dollar brownstones a few blocks from the Hudson, it stuck out like a rotted tooth in a friendly grin. The windows were boarded up, and grass overran the small front plot. The brick was crumbling and ivied, but apart from that it was unmarked, the neighborhood artists, what few remained in so gentrified a part of the city, unwilling to approach, even with a virgin canvas as lure. Looking at it, Flemel remembered the time his father had accidentally backed over the family dog—the miserable squeak, the pink that came out of the poor beast, how it suffered for long moments as his dad, guilt struck and useless, ran about frantically trying to find a way to salve or end its misery.

"We're not calling Abilene," Stockdale said.

"Something is very wrong here," M said. "You feeling that tightness in your fists right now? That little itch toward violence? I can't be the only one."

"You aren't."

"It's twisting our minds around it."

"Don't think you're up for it?" Stockdale said nastily.

"I prefer to keep the deck stacked in my favor whenever possible," M said, speaking in the slow way he did when trying not to get angry. "And Abilene is two aces up each sleeve."

Stockdale took a long breath and shook his head free. "This is my neighborhood, M," he said, calmer now, though not much. "If you can't look after your own, then what the hell good are you?"

"An admirable expression of civic pride, but in fairness, I only moved back to the city a year ago." But then his shoulders slumped and he said, "Flemel, go home."

"Fuck you, go home. I came all the way out here."

"I'll repay you the $2.75 if we ever see each other again. Skedaddle."

"You said I could come."

"That was before I saw the place. You aren't ready for this. For that matter, I'm not ready, either, but somebody's got to keep Stockdale out of trouble."

But Flemel had not gotten this far by listening to M. "I'm coming in, with you or after you."

"I get lucky a lot," M said, sticking a finger into his apprentice's chest. "Not everyone gets lucky like I do. And my luck doesn't always extend to the person standing next to me, do you understand?"

"I got my own luck."

M watched him a while, then shrugged. "Let's see what color it runs," he said, then started up the stoop. There was a CONDEMNED sticker plastered across the door. It was a busy neighborhood in early autumn, a fine time to be walking about near the water, but no one was. The block was empty. Stockdale put a boot against the rotted wood, and the door swung open.

"Now remember," M said, "nothing that you see in here is real."

"Except that some of it might be," Stockdale added.

"Yes, some of it might be. So be careful."

"Be careful."

Crossing the threshold, Flemel found himself fully erect, erect and recalling a particularly vile bit of internet pornography he had watched recently, something degrading and immoral and secretly exciting, something

that Flemel wished he hadn't seen but couldn't forget. Inside was a long hallway that smelled of rotting wood and dead flesh and something worse than
both of these. A tongue-colored plush carpet ran along the corridor into an
inky blackness beyond.

"Keep moving," Stockdale told Flemel. "Don't let yourself get focused
on anything too long. And for the love of Christ, don't lose sight of us." He
rubbed his hands together until they each glowed bright as a halogen bulb,
then stretched one into the darkness and followed it forward.

They came to a door and opened it. Inside a tall, naked woman was seated
at a vanity mirror, straightening her blonde hair with a bone comb. Turning
to greet them, she revealed an incision running between her navel and the
bottom of her throat, the skin peeled back and pinned against itself, like a
butterfly behind glass. Her organs had been removed, there was only the stiff
white of her spine. "It's better this way," she explained. "It's so nice not to feel
things. You'll see." She turned back to her mirror. "You'll see."

The door at the other end of the room opened easily enough, and beyond
it a circular staircase extended down beyond the boundaries of the vertical
horizon. Flemel was not sure how long the descent lasted. It seemed a while.
It seemed a long while.

At the bottom was a corridor, whitewashed and sterile, and then a room,
dark and mildewed, and inside an old man, gray and withered. He sat on a
three-legged stool and held the headless corpse of a child in his hands. His
teeth were stained red. "I'm one of the nice ones," he said sorrowfully.

Out the door and down another flight of stairs, step after step after step,
each one falling a moment slower than the one before.

"Enjoying yourself so far?" M asked Flemel with a sneer. "It's not all elves
and fairies."

"I'm still moving, ain't I?"

"For now," M said. "For now."

The next room was the size of a football field, unfinished wood and broken windows stretching far out into the distance. Below them sat row after
row of gurneys, a corpse or near corpse on every one. Sisters in white shifts
moved silently down the thoroughfares, ministering to men long dying.
Above starched collars were red-flecked canine muzzles and chattering

mandibles, mosquitoed proboscises, the maw of a shark, duplicated rows of razored teeth. The matron mother wore a black frock with a broken cross embroidered on it. "We've room for more," she said through a baboon's leer. Behind her, a novice with the face of a star-nosed mole shoved fleshy mouth tendrils into the wounded leg of one of her charges, the screaming and the slurping nearly drowning out her superior. "We've always, always room for more."

Flemel tried not to see anything, walking between the rows of the wounded, war-ravaged and poxed, shattered legs and spines, viscera everywhere, an endless choral interlude of screaming. One of them grabbed at his shirt as he passed, revealing himself as the brother Flemel had last seen five years earlier in a funeral suit that hid his wrist scars, and Flemel forgot himself and began to scream.

The hand on his shoulder was M's. Above M's left wrist Flemel saw a lit candle. "You have to keep going," he said, if not desperately then too close to desperate for Flemel's liking. "If we stop, we're dead, and worse than dead."

Flemel nodded and broke the grip of the thing that was not, that could not be, his dearest Frederick, and followed M and Stockdale forward, reaching the end of the room finally and passing into a stairwell. They descended farther and farther. The back of Flemel's throat felt like hot asphalt, though if he had to rank them, thirst would have been far down on his list of concerns.

The wallpaper in the next room was bright and cheery. A pile of toys lay in one corner—well-stuffed teddy bears and painted rocking horses, half-finished puzzles and alphabet blocks. Waiting patiently was a mad wall of tissue, an incomprehensible puddle of skin and eyes and hair and little sprinkles of outdated children's clothing that Flemel only belatedly managed to recognize as conjoined octoplets, or decoplets, or perhaps some higher sort of oplet. Trying to count Flemel grew dizzy. Two of them, attached to each other at the neck and to the rest of their brood from waist to ankle and shoulder to tailbone, respectively, held a sign scrawled awkwardly in crayon reading SACRED JUSTICE MOVED OUR ARCHITECT!

"Welcome!" one of the children said.

"Welcome!" said a twin on the other end of the line, and then they were all chittering salutations.

There was no visible means of egress, though after a moment Stockdale identified a part of the wall that had rotted through and began to worry at the weakened wood with his knife.

"What happened in this place?" Flemel had not realized that he had voiced the question aloud until it was answered by one of the smiling girls stuck in the middle of the meat.

"Nothing much, nothing in particular," she said. "A wife killed one of her children in the upstairs bathroom, back when it was a tenement slum, started squeezing and couldn't stop. Several rapes, dozens of assaults, endless thefts, infinite acts of petty cruelty."

A hand at the other end opened to reveal a baby's head grown into the palm. "No worse than any other house on the block. It's bones atop bones atop bones."

A towheaded boy from the very end of the line, one ankle plunging downward into the amoeba of flesh, informed them, "It's all like this. We could have manifested anywhere. It's all like this."

"How many floors are there?" Flemel asked.

"Hell is a circle," a girl in pigtails responded, holding a porcelain doll in one flipperlike appendage. "Once you're in, you never leave."

The blow brought Flemel back to his senses, or something near them, M pulling back his hand in readiness to deliver another. "Don't fucking talk to them. They're lying to you, they're just telling lies."

"No sirs, not lies," came a response from somewhere within the swelling flesh. "It would be easier if it was a lie, but you know in your heart it isn't!"

Stockdale had broken through the planking and moved swiftly into the darkness yawning beyond it, so quickly that M had to hurry Flemel onward, the plaintive cries of the children echoing against his back. "We'll see you again! And again and again and again . . ."

M yelled for Stockdale to slow down from the top of the staircase, and he turned back with a snarl but waited for them to catch up. The walk seemed as long as ever. Flemel's ears rang from the terrible clamor of the house's indigestion.

The door at the bottom led to a small, shabby-seeming office—that of a claim's adjustor, or a minor government functionary, or a less-than-successful seller of time-shares. "Come in, come in," said a fat man sitting behind a business desk. His head was the size of a basketball, sweat dribbling down past the tufts of his ear hair and over a thick neck. His lips were swelled pink, his eyes friendly little dots, like holes cut into a Venetian mask. "And how can I personalize your misery this afternoon? Any dietary restrictions you'd like us to be aware of? Religious traditions we might blaspheme? Survive a war, famine, plague, or earthquake? Let me ask you something," he said, licking a thick finger with a rose-colored tongue and opening a file. "Any familial trauma in your background? Daddy in the doorway, a bottle of gin in one hand and a strap in another? Uncle beneath the bed sheets, a special secret, just him and his special boy? Because I've got some fantastically disturbing scenes prepared for the survivor of child abuse. No? Don't worry, don't worry," he said, smiling teeth the size of dominoes, "we'll find something for you. We always do!"

"You only exist if we both agree on it," M said, though he was sweating. The room they had come in seemed to have only the one door, and M began searching for a hidden exit, fidgeting about with the bookcase and various paraphernalia.

"I'm afraid I'm extremely real," the man said. "It's all real. All of your nightmares, everything that your parents ever told you were pretend so that you'd sleep better. Vampires, werewolves, zombies, man-eating plants, and the creature from the black lagoon. Corpses that gnaw and babies that weep, lovers raped, friends mistreated, siblings tortured, things that crawl and scrape and claw. They're all down here, waiting to meet you."

"You talk a lot," Stockdale said, turning and presenting an index finger. There was a popping sound, and the man's skull exploded outward, a spray of red and white knocking him off his chair.

The house giggled.

"What the fuck good did that do?" M asked, still at his search.

Stockdale shrugged and cracked a knuckle. "I enjoyed it."

"Of course you did, sir, and why wouldn't you?" The fat man rose and reassumed his seat. The center of his face had been destroyed. Flemel could see the press of bone beneath the flesh and the pink folds of his brain and the wallpaper behind. "You can't pretend forever, can you? We all enjoy it. *Sadist* is just another word for human."

"Finally," M muttered, knocking over a bookshelf to reveal a door that had been wallpapered up. Stockdale pulled his butterfly knife out from his jacket and ran it along the seam, breaking the blade while wedging it open.

"Don't go down that way!" the man at the desk warned. "It only gets worse!"

They ignored him, though he turned out not to be wrong.

"How many rooms have we gone through?" Flemel asked, the descent taking long as ever, taking longer.

"I can't remember," M responded.

"Hell is a circle," Flemel reminded him.

But M didn't answer.

In one of the rooms, a woman fed herself into a meat grinder, one hand swiveling the crank, the other disappearing into the apparatus and coming out as strands of pink meat, the woman laughing all the while. More stairs. A pack of insects the size of dogs burst forth from the chest and belly and loins of a grotesquely obese man. Stockdale fought them off furiously with his switchblade. Stairs. An old man shoved a child into his gaping maw, weeping and muttering, his words unintelligible. More stairs. M took a tumble on one set and rolled for a long time before he managed to right himself. On his arm was a tattoo of a snake eating its own tail. Three policemen stopped their interrogation long enough to smile, then turned back to their suspect, his face destroyed from violence, his wooden leg broken on the ground before them. Stairs. A mother sat on a stool, one pendulous breast hung outside of her shirt as a thing somewhere between a rat and a piranha gnawed it bloody.

"Hush, baby, hush," she said, her voice sweet and soft. "Don't you know it was all like this? It was all always like this. It was never hidden. You couldn't look at it straight on because you're a coward, because you're all cowards, and the ones who aren't cowards you call mad. But they aren't mad and neither are you, dear things. You're just honest. Life is a rusty blade scraping whimpering flesh, a child weeping uncomforted, a chancre swelling into infinity. There isn't anything in here that you can't see out there, that you haven't already seen, that you'll go on seeing forever."

M and Stockdale continued past unanswering, thousand-yard stares. "You're not right," Flemel said simply, before following them.

The next room was small and dark and silent, and it was only now that it was gone that Flemel realized that for a long time, so long that he had almost (but not quite) grown used to it, he had been hearing the hideous rumbling of the house, the screams and cries, the moans of pleasure, the chittering laugh of madmen. But it was gone now, replaced by the mewling of the creature in the center of the room, the size of a newborn, pink and hideous as an open wound.

There was a sense of familiarity, as if what was coming next had come before, would always come.

Stockdale went first, and after a dozen steps, he shook his head back and forth frantically, as if denying an evident truth. When he turned back he was smiling, more than smiling—leering, beaming, the face of a man in the throes of a revelation or an orgasm. "I see it all now," he said. "I see the truth. I couldn't look at it before, but I can now. They've helped me, they've freed me. I have seen the light, and the light is darkness!"

"It's the house, man, it's the house," M said. The transformation had been going on so long that Flemel had stopped noticing it, shifting strangely, seamlessly, into madness; the difference between this Stockdale and the Stockdale they had known was one of degree rather than kind.

Stockdale shook his head, "But it isn't, M, it isn't! Best to look straight ahead at the matter and admit it!" He pulled up the sleeves of his shirt, his biceps thick even in the gloom. "I'll show you. Don't worry, I'll show you."

Stockdale dove at Flemel then, but M intercepted him with a shoulder, was repaid for his gallantry by a swift straight shot from Stockdale's left fist, and stumbled backward against the assault. Now the difference in size between them seemed plenty evident—M thin and lightly muscled, Stockdale as broad-shouldered as an action hero.

"It's the house," M said, his voice rendered jagged. "Remember who you are."

"It's clearer to me than ever!" Stockdale said, laughing. His hand was bright again, but bright like an acetylene torch, and it seemed to throb in the darkness. "I want to rend your flesh, M, my dearest friend. I want to dance amid your viscera. I want to break my teeth on your bone. I want to spill my seed into your chest cavity. I want to cut you and laugh and cut you and laugh and cut you and laugh and . . ." Stockdale came forward swiftly mid-monologue, hoping to catch M unaware.

But M made a motion as if scattering seed, and a flare of light lit up the room, and Stockdale was catapulted against the back wall, his shirt and flesh aflame.

"Kill it!" M shrieked, gesturing to the creature in the center of the room, then dove atop Stockdale, who was struggling to right himself and laughing once again, laughing against his burnt flesh and the smell of barbecue. They rolled about, struggling with each other, and though Stockdale's clothes were still bright with fire, he seemed not to be losing.

It lay on the floorboards, naked as if in spotlight. Shriveled and grotesque, pockmarked or perhaps only burnt, it looked up at Flemel with sharpened teeth and clever eyes. "Well?" it asked, as it had asked Flemel a hundred times before, or a thousand, or . . . "Well? Well?" Its fragile skull was placed perfectly for the heel of a boot, cruelty done to a cruel thing, the cycle continuing, a savage and irreconcilable tautology. "Well?"

Cresting above the déjà vu, as if coming up for air, Flemel squatted and lifted the thing cleanly in his arms and pulled the wounded creature against his breast.

A voice wept in the darkness.

Flemel opened the door and stepped back into the front hallway, still dilapidated but no longer quite so ominous. M was on the ground holding Stockdale, the skin of his neck and shoulders mottled red.

"I'm glad we brought you," Stockdale said.

"He's all right," M said. "He's all right."

27

Righting a Wrong

Of course, M did not drink exclusively at The Lady. It would have been unjust to distribute himself so unevenly among the watering holes of southern Brooklyn, many of them oak-lined things, with extremely credible beer selections and friendly bartenders. The Crown's Commons had all of these in spades, particularly the last.

Alice was the sort of homely that encouraged admirers. She had no breasts and dressed exclusively in flannel and surplus East German army gear. Her nose ring did no one any good, and her haircut was likewise unjustifiable. And yet, all of these things taken together, along with her bad skin and her earnest smile, somehow added up to something endearing and even just short of lovely. Alice gave one the impression of a young child or a small secret, something that needed to be kept safe against the world's savagery.

That was the impression that Alice gave to M, at least. But M had learned by his age, whatever that was, that for most of the species, a wounded bird is an invitation to cruelty rather than a demand for succor. Her boyfriend wore ladies' jeans, but he had the heart of a cad, eyes roving even when he spoke to her. He came into the bar often and bought drinks for girls and ran them on Alice's tab. He was the kind of guy who would do things like that, and Alice was the kind of girl who would let him, and the world is filled with both of those sorts of people, and there's nothing that anyone could do about that fact, or at least nothing M had ever learned.

M stopped into the Crown's Commons toward the start of October, just before that thing with the house—you remember—and he found Alice in a more than usually desperate state of disarray.

"Everything all right today, Alice?" M asked, because that was what one asked in these situations, as one grabs a paper towel when a drink is spilled.

She sighed and looked around and dripped down onto the counter. "You have a girlfriend, M?"

"Not such as I'd admit to."

"Keep it that way," she said, her heart so tender you could have spread it over white bread.

M thought about asking more, offering that proverbial shoulder, but it was getting late, and M had a date, and anyway he didn't want to be drawn too deeply into Alice's misfortunes, which were probably unresolvable, an essential part of what it was to be Alice, impossible to remove without killing the patient, like a tumor nestled tight against the brain stem.

Another customer came in then, and Alice went to deal with him. M finished off his beer and split, then gave her a little wave without slowing down.

M did not see Alice for a while, though he still stopped inside the Commons now and again. Things got busy; a black dog had been plaguing Prospect Park, bringing visions of death to stroller-pushing breeders and hot-bodied little runners alike, and Abilene had asked M to take care of it, agreeing in exchange to forget some things M preferred forgotten. Also, it started going well with this model who lived on the Upper East Side, and between the commute and the constant narcissism of the excessively good-looking, M was very busy indeed.

And anyway Alice could have been on a vacation; although M thought she would have mentioned that to him. She was always so thrilled at whatever modest kindnesses the world bestowed upon her, as if they indicated the first turning of the tide, rather than an aberration, a brief lapse in the ever swelling storm that life shits out on the weak and misbegotten. Or potentially she could have been fired, although that seemed even less likely. The rest of the bartenders at the Commons all seemed to feel the same sort of sympathetic sweetness toward Alice that M did, and he couldn't imagine her thrown out onto the street.

But in truth her presence one way or the other was not a source of great concern to M. The Commons was the other woman, after all. If he was occasionally unfaithful to The Lady, there was no doubt whose bed he would ultimately wind up in. And there were a lot of people like Alice. You couldn't get to looking at any one of them too long, you had to develop—as a requirement for the continuation of your day-to-day existence—a hard shell, a selective blindness, a bad memory.

If only for so long.

"What happened to Alice?" M finally asked one of her colleagues toward the end of October, after he had drank enough to pretend that the answer might be something good, nonsense he was quickly disabused of by the cast of the man's face.

"You two friends?"

"That might be stretching a point. Friendly."

"I'm not sure how to tell you this . . ."

"Briefly," M said, "and using small words."

"You know Alice has some problems?"

Of course he had known. Who wouldn't have known? She was a thirty-year-old woman with an MFA in Romantic poetry working at a bar, and not even one of the hip ones where you got to play with shakers, just a regular sort of neighborhood dive bar. She took her shift drink twice an hour. Her nails were always bit to the quick. She often smiled when it was clear she did not really want to.

The bartender shrugged. "They found her in her bathtub," he said. "I heard it was a razor."

M didn't say anything.

"Sorry," the bartender said, then found an excuse to busy himself at the other end of the counter.

M drank often but was rarely drunk. By natural constitution and long practice, he required a concerted effort to push himself into serious inebriation, one that he rarely found a point in making. Often he found himself almost at the point of making it, of coming within a stone's throw of making it, but M rarely, almost never, slurred his words, let alone hugged a toilet.

Almost never is not never. After a moment M told the bartender to bring him a bottle of whiskey, and it wasn't a request but a command, one backed by a little bit of force. And after he had brought it over to M, brought it over immediately and glassy-eyed, M had dismissed him and taken to making sure what was in there wasn't in there much longer.

Something needed to be done, was the conclusion that M came to about the time the upper half of the bottle had gone translucent. Someone needed to do something.

"That boyfriend of hers," M said, grabbing the bartender's cuff as he walked past. The bartender had forgotten M after he had ordered the whiskey, as M had intended him to. "You've got his number?"

"Why are you asking?"

M choked down most of what was left in the bottle and repeated the question with a little bit more force than it needed, enough that it left the bartender suffering from an extreme case of logorrhea, words spilling forth with diluvial force, a river overflowing its banks.

"I don't have it. I didn't know him very well. His name is Thom, but I didn't know him very well. I didn't know Alice very well, either, 'cause I was only working here for a few weeks when she killed herself, and also I didn't want to get to know her that well because you could see there was something a bit off. I mean, of course she was nice, and I was sad about what happened, but you can't be running all around town taking in strays, you know, at least I can't, I got enough troubles on my own. Also, I was worried that if I was too nice, she might start to think that I had a thing for her, and I didn't, but you know how girls like that can get, you're going to come in and save her from her boyfriend or her ex-boyfriend or her father. You gotta keep a wall up, man, you know how it is. But anyway I didn't want to see anything happen to her, of course I didn't. I mean, can you imagine what that would be like, sawing at your arm, *cut-cut-cut, cut-cut-cut*, and then watching it bleed out into the water? 'Cause I can't."

M found that he could.

"Anyway I don't know, but Christine might know. You know Christine?" he asked, but then continued without waiting for an answer. "Of course you do. She's that tall Ukrainian chick that works weekends, hot as hell. You know how those Slav girls are, least all the ones that come here. But she was close with Alice, I think they were roommates for a while, I never got the whole story."

"Where's Christine live?"

The bartender told him. Then he tried to give M the addresses of four other colleagues who Alice knew a bit, and also the address of his sister-in-law who he thought might be able to shed some light on the situation, and also the addresses of two ex-girlfriends, who M did not think would be of any great service, and also a guy who had once played bass in a band the bartender had been in, basically just because. M had leaned too hard on him. Too much drink and his mood and M had overshot his mark. M figured the condition would dissipate with a night's sleep, but he made sure to take down his address and schedule—the bartender was extremely keen to tell him—and to remind himself to check back next week and make sure nothing had come permanently unhinged.

M took the bottle of whiskey with him when he left, walking down Franklin Avenue, drunk and furious and daring the world to jump at him, just daring it. Christine lived about a dozen blocks south, and he swayed the whole way, weaving from sidewalk to median. His intangibles trailed out behind him like a diaphanous cloak of despair, everyone he passed got pulled, casually and without deliberation, into his story, into his funk, found their days getting that little bit worse, went home and drank too much and missed work the next morning, screamed raw throats at husbands, set cruel hands on children.

Christine would not have opened the door normally, not to a stranger standing on her stoop at eleven-thirty in the evening, not even a hipster dude with the name of a popular band imprinted on his T-shirt. But M was not to be denied that night, M was the Management's favorite customer, M was at that narrow point where desire and reality turn to meet each other, like lovers twisting in for a kiss.

"What do you want?"

"Retribution?" M realized that the bottle was empty, and he tossed it off the stoop. "A vengeance bloody and righteous? To unbind the eyes of justice and see her sword fall on a well-deserved target?"

He was leaning on her too hard, he realized then, like he had the bartender.

They were so fragile, minds like tissue paper or cobweb, you could crush them and not even notice. "Where does Thom live?"

"Thom?" Christine asked, dead-eyed and mind-fucked.

"Thom, Thom, Thom, Alice's boyfriend, Thom the cruel, Thom the dick-ish, Thom the damned. Where the fuck does Thom live?"

And of course she told him, and then she told him a number of other things, unable to stop herself, tongue lolling out like a character from a Tex Avery cartoon, traumas she'd suffered as a child, fears and dreams, but mostly fears, about her job and her boyfriend and what sort of mother she'd make, if she even wanted to be a mother given the state of the world—oh, the state of the world, the state of the world, the state of the world. But M hardly man-aged to listen past the first sentence. He had enough misery to take hold of; he didn't need more. He told Christine to get some sleep and to feel better in the morning, and she slammed shut her door and went to do just that.

No rest for the wicked, however, and at the bodega downstairs M bought two cans of Steel Reserve, butting in front of the big black youth waiting in line for a sandwich, snarling at the Arab behind his bulletproof glass, leaving twenty dollars on the counter, and pitching off into the nearest subway sta-tion. The train pulled in just as he got down there, the universe tilting in his direction like a round loading into a chamber.

There were a dozen-odd passengers in the car, but they emptied out as soon as they came to the next station, as if M was a particularly foul-smelling or unstable-seeming indigent. At the top of the stairs a drug addict was ask-ing people for change, but he didn't bother to ask M, indeed as M passed he decided to head right over to see his dealer even though he was a couple of bucks short and the man did not take credit, DID NOT TAKE CREDIT, discovered he needed his evening hit immediately, needed it as much as he'd ever needed anything in his life, which is to say as much as he needed every other hit he had taken.

M walked on, despair spreading in his wake. Everywhere else also, though you couldn't blame that on M.

A soft-souled sort like Alice, thin-skinned, far from steady, and a prick like that in his hipster jeans, quoting Pitchfork reviews and the one Bukowski poem he had ever learned. Easy prey, he must have figured, easy prey, maybe

not quite pretty enough for him normally, but there she was just standing behind the bar, why not throw out a few lines, snarl her with his charm. But you
get tired of that sort of thing eventually, after a few fucks, tired of her bony
hips and her too-kind eyes. And what else do average-looking girls exist for
but to catch a bit of cum and then get tossed away, like multiuse condoms?

M was very drunk by this point.

Well, Thom would find out otherwise, wouldn't he? The world was a
crooked place but M would see it run straight this time, even it right out,
Management be damned. Management be good and damned, because what
was the point of all this esoterica, ritual, meditation, study, all this chicanery
and brouhaha, what was the point of delving about in the darkest and most
obscure corners of reality, what was the point of jeopardizing the very existence of your soul if you could not occasionally right a wrong?

Approaching the building, M held up his hand, as if getting ready to wave
at someone, and his palm glowed a shade of red that no one has yet managed
to name. He skipped up the steps of Thom's stoop, and he pointed at the
door, and the lock snicked open. M stopped outside of 1C, and he banged on
the door three times, each blow like a sledgehammer against the wood, each
blow like a fall from on high, each blow like the retort of Gabriel's great horn.

The man who answered it was Thom, and Thom wasn't as pretty as M
remembered, not at all. He was skinny and not very tall and actually, now
that M looked at him, his jeans weren't even that tight; they were just jeans.
He had a stupid beard, but that was about the worst you could say of him.
Coming over, M had imagined he'd bust in on the man midcoitus maybe,
Thom's new Alice languishing on his twin-size bed, and M could save her
from the same fate as her predecessor. But he was alone, and behind him his
apartment was quiet and dark, and he wasn't wearing a shirt, and his eyes
were bloodshot, and he seemed to have been drinking.

"Yeah?" he asked.

"What did you do to Alice?" M asked, the words slurring into one another, coming like a pressure boxer, punches in bunches, and Thom flinching
from each one. And the funny thing is that M didn't even need to lean on
him, as he had the bartender and Christine, didn't need to use up any of
the Management's favor in breaking him down. Thom had somehow been

waiting for this, like a child awaits the strap, waiting for someone to show up at his door, maybe not M necessarily, maybe he didn't have the particulars in mind, but *someone*, some agent of order, to call him to account, to offer punishment, and after punishment, redemption.

"I killed her, man," Thom said, his head hanging as from the noose. "I killed her."

And how much did M want this to be true, how much did he want to believe it. What joy it would have been to stand among the righteous for a moment, just for a moment, to lay a fierce and terrible reckoning upon the head of this boy who so clearly deserved it. But what if he didn't deserve it, or what if he didn't deserve it any more than everyone else did?

After a while, the light from M's hand went out, and then M did the same, without another word, back down the steps and through the front door and four blocks north to the subway.

Some days, there seemed very little point in magic. Some days, there seemed very little point in anything, but M soldiered on just the same.

28

Brooklyn Murder Mystery

It was shaping into a pretty good party, until they stumbled over the corpse.

This would be the last outdoor gathering of the year. You could tell that without looking at a calendar or the mall decorations, turkeys grinning at their slaughter and Indians doing the same. Tell it by the kernel of real cold on the wind and the occasional scattered scent of wood smoke. But winter hadn't come quite yet, and you could still make do in a flannel shirt and a leather jacket. At least that was what M was wearing when he and Flemel had met Boy and Andre in a bar in Carroll Gardens, en route to Ibis and Anais's spacious two-bedroom condo in Park Slope, wooden floors and exposed brick and the last backyard garden left in central Brooklyn. Of course, in reality, there was barely enough space for a few rows of maize, but then what is reality after all? Ibis opened the door looking blue-eyed and handsome, Anais on one arm, almost smiling. Backs were slapped and goodwill was enunciated, and then they were led through a concrete corridor and out a wrought iron gate and into a miniature Versailles, bonfires illuminating a starlit sky, ancient elms bowed with autumn's parti-colored bouquet. On a decayed Roman ruin, beside a trickling spring clearer than any body of water New York had seen for a century, a handsome man did a credible cover of a Neil Young song. There was booze and music and girls and a hint of winter in the air, of mortality, and between all of that, M was starting to feel some of the last few months' nastiness slough off him. They found Stockdale at the bar, his burns healing better than the most optimistic dermatologist could have predicted, and he greeted M and Flemel enthusiastically. Boy passed some cocaine around to those who were interested. M had rolled a few joints before coming, because one never knows, of course, because one just can't say for certain. They were stepping out to find a quiet place to light up when Boy gasped and Flemel pointed and Stockdale said, "Shit."

M reached down and put two fingers on Ibis's still-warm neck, though he couldn't have held out much hope, simply by virtue of the yawning aperture that offered a clear view of his internal organs. There was a moment, kneeling over the corpse, when he looked old, our M, very old indeed, perhaps almost as old as he actually was.

Then he was standing and scowling and crossing swiftly to the exit.

"Shit," Stockdale said a second time.

"Those motherfuckers," Boy said, her face had gone from cream to rose to summer tomato. "This is the White Queen's doing, sure as stone."

"You don't know that." Stockdale said.

"Who the fuck else would it be?" Boy asked, standing furiously. "Celise has been trying to get her grubby little claws on this section of Brooklyn for years. This was the opening salvo, and I'll be damned if it passes without a response."

"Celise, like Celise the White Queen?" Flemel asked.

"Sweet Christ, boy," Boy said, face hard, "doesn't M tell you anything?"

"Not really."

A pair of partygoers, stumbling through the evening in hopes of finding a comfortable spot to copulate, saw the four of them, and then saw the thing they were looking at. The male squealed loudly.

The crowd was swift to gather. There was a brief and pointless period during which some of the more optimistic imagined they might render Ibis medical assistance, and then things turned quickly to recrimination.

"Son of a fucking bitch," Cavill said. Cavill was wearing jeans that would need to be removed with a razor, and would have been difficult to take seriously were he pointing a gun at the skull of your firstborn child. "In his own home!"

"Don't get to doing nothing foolish, junior," Salome answered, standing tall to meet him, a cocktail dress riding up her shapely thighs. "We were invited with full promise of safety."

"Did you notice the man who pledged it has his rib cage visible?"

"An unfortunate tragedy," Salome said, her tone flippant but her eyes very dark. "But that doesn't mean you get to scapegoat any of us into a tomb." Behind her you might have seen M performing a series of complicated passes beside the exit, though you probably wouldn't have, there being more compelling things to look at just then.

"Who the fuck else would have done it?" Cavill said. "Did the White Queen plan this outright, or did you just see an opportunity and take it?"

"Yes, it's been a long-standing plot of mine to kill an old friend at his party while surrounded by the enemy."

"Why don't we all just go back to using our indoor voices," M said, having finished his business by the door and returned to the main stage.

"The fuck are you?" Cavill asked.

M started to roll a cigarette. "You know who I am."

"Yeah? So?"

"So, me being who I am, and you being who you are, I just told you to lower your voice."

"Fuck this," Cavill said, though Flemel noticed he didn't yell it. "The Red Queen will hear of this atrocity. By God, she will."

"In good time," M said. "Though not quite yet." He struck a match and brought it to his cigarette, and the night went bright with a corresponding series of trailed explosions flickering from the exit, firecracker pops and swirls of illuminations, strange patterns of flame writhing across the length and breadth of the metal gate before disappearing as suddenly as they came.

Everyone stared. Except for M. M smoked his cigarette.

"What the hell was that?" Cavill asked.

"You're such a tough guy," M said. "Why don't you go find out?"

Cavill sneered and began walking toward the exit, purposefully and with swift steps—but somehow he ended his journey a dozen feet from the promised egress, looking round bewilderedly.

"Just can't pull yourself away from me, can you?" M asked.

"This is nonsense," Salome said, trying to outdo her rival. A second failure, though she managed to get her hand nearly within clutching distance of the door handle before finding herself, dazed and flustered, back where she had started, smoking a cigarette seriously.

"It's called the Rite of the Exterminating Angel," M explained. "And it means you won't find yourself able to leave. No one will. Of course, if you keep trying, maybe you'll force yourself through. Or maybe it'll shatter your mind like a mirror. Seven years bad luck, you know. Have fun either way. While you're dicking around, I'm going to go ahead and figure out who killed my friend."

That managed to turn the crowd's attention, for the moment at least, away from the gate and back toward the corpse growing cold on the lawn.

"Ibis?" Cavill asked.

"Whoever done him is still at the party. As of now, it's a simple process of elimination."

"How do we know it wasn't you?" asked a member of the crowd, one of the Red Queen's people, guessing by his white-boy dreadlocks.

"You don't, which is why it's in everyone's interest to stick around until we've got this thing wrapped up."

"And once we do," Cavill said, "once we've found whatever piece of shit did Ibis at his own party, what happens then?"

"I'm a cross-one-bridge-at-a-time kind of person," M said, turning to stare full bore at Cavill, "but nothing very good, I suppose. Now how about you go grab a drink and leave the adults to do some thinking."

"I'm not thirsty."

"You don't have to drink—you just need to stand where I can see you and keep your mouth shut."

One of Salome's people, a cynical sort or just a glutton for punishment, made a motion for the door. But then she found herself, as M had suggested, over at the counter, pouring a glass of champagne, and the rest of the party decided it was easier to skip the middleman and go straight to the booze. Unbidden, the two factions separated, the tight core of Celise's contingent, fashionable bordering up on severe, taking up one end of the counter, leaving Abilene's crunchy conglomerate to hold down the other.

Belatedly, very belatedly, it occurred to M to check on Anais, who stood a short way out in the greenery, silent and pale as a wraith. "Why don't you head inside, honey," he said.

But she remained where she was, seemed not even to have heard him speak.

M set one hand on her shoulder, "Go inside. I'll take care of whoever did this, I swear."

And though his words carried with them a weight of gravity which was unusual for a man as generally feckless as M, they did no good. Anais remained where she was, immobile from grief, and after another moment M sighed and went back to join Boy, Stockdale, Andre, and Flemel over the body of her murdered lover.

"What's your plan?" Flemel asked quietly.

"This was about as far as I'd gotten," M admitted. Below his left wrist was a tattoo of a magnifying glass.

"Shit."

"Somebody has to do something, or they'll be dating the start of the next war from tonight. At the moment we've still got a shot at heading off any more bloodshed."

"And why would we want that?" Boy asked nastily. "I think a little blood is what we need right now, balance the scales. Remind the White Queen's people who they fucking with."

"You'll forgive me if I take your judgment with a grain of blow."

"Ibis has been my friend for a generation, and Abilene my patron since long before that." Boy said. "Any attack on her is an attack on me."

"Don't you fall neatly into lockstep. I see that haircut is just for show."

"This is my borough, and I'd rather not see it become Tribeca. I've known Abilene for as long as you have, and I'm not so quick to forget the things she's done for me, or for the city."

"Ingratitude is one of my stronger qualities," M admitted. "Andre, you're a coward. Stick up for me."

"I am brave as the Maid of Orléans," Andre said. "And I live in Manhattan and work in high finance. I acknowledge the White Queen, as a fisherman does the tide."

"That extends to dying in her service?"

"I'm afraid that weekend I have a wedding in the provinces. But it extends at least to saluting the flag when my fellow comrades in arms are looking."

"Surely you're not buying any of this nonsense," M said, turning to Stockdale.

"What can I say? I'll take Abilene over her opposite. Didn't you ever want to be a crusader, fight for something bigger than yourself?"

"I more saw myself as one of those guys who follow behind the army, finishing off the wounded and stealing rings from corpses."

"That *is* how I think of you," Boy said, grinding a cigarette beneath a platform heel and stamping off to take her place among the ranks of Abilene's other willing killers. "That's always been exactly how I've thought of you."

Andre shrugged regretfully, then went to stand near Salome.

"And where are you standing, Stockdale?" M asked.

"Ibis was my friend."

"Mine too. That's why I'm trying to find who killed him."

"Is that what you're doing? Or are you just trying to head off trouble?"

"Yes, peacemaking, how ignoble an activity."

"Not every peace is an honorable one," Stockdale said. "Ask Neville Chamberlain."

"Zero to Hitler in ten sentences flat, very impressive. I'm shocked you aren't running Question Time with the Prime Minister." M picked a cigarette from a sneer. "I don't have time to argue. Are you with me, or are you going over to help Boy sharpen her claws?"

"What does being with you entail, exactly?"

"Dunno yet. But make sure to play along once I do."

"There can't be many people here strong enough to have put down Ibis," Stockdale said. "Fair enough he wasn't quite elite, but . . . he was close."

M thought about this for a moment, then he went to find Salome at the bar.

"Hello again, M."

"Salome," M said, thinking that she had gotten prettier since he had last kissed her, just before setting her into a cab on a wintery December morning some ten months earlier.

"It wasn't one of our people," she said. "I can say that for a fact."

"How could you possibly be certain of that? Were you all walking around together in a group? Does Celise implant tracking cameras? The only thing you can say with any confidence is that *you* didn't do it." M poured himself a few fingers from the nearest bottle, realized it was bourbon, looked unhappy about the discovery, but drank it anyway. "Well? Did you?"

"No."

"I'm not sure I believe you."

"It's the truth regardless. The White Queen doesn't give a fig about Ibis, didn't even know his name. If she wanted to start a war, I can assure you, she wouldn't have scrupled to something so small."

"Maybe it's got nothing to do with politics. Maybe someone did Ibis out of some . . . personal animus."

Salome smiled bitterly. "I'd think you know me better than that, and if you don't know me, you knew Ibis. He had his . . . side interests. I was far from the only one."

"Yeah," M said, voice gravelly. "He did."

"And even if I'd lost my mind with jealousy," she said in a tone of voice that suggested this was more impossible than implausible, "do you really suppose I'd be foolish enough to kill Abilene's favorite in Abilene's territory?"

"I never give anyone the benefit of the doubt when it comes to stupidity. People do very, very stupid things, and smart people more than most." M pointed suddenly at one of the group, an inoffensive man wearing a splotch-colored hoodie. "Is that blood?"

"It's paint," the man said quickly. "I'm a graffiti artist."

"Make sure it stays that way," M countered quickly, then moved to the other end of the bar before his mystery had time to fade.

"If it's one of them," Cavill said, "they go in the ground. Tonight. No appellate judges, no calling up to the booth. A life for a life," he said, and among the dozen or so people standing round him four were stupid enough to repeat it—though not Boy at least, M was happy to see.

"And if it's one of yours?"

"Why would we do it?"

"People kill each other for all sorts of reasons," M said, picking a bit of lint off of Cavill's shirt. "Greed, envy, lust. A theological dispute, a fantasy-football rivalry, unresolved homoerotic tension."

"Don't let him fuck with you," Boy said. "He's just trying to stir up trouble so he can see what rises to the top."

"I know it's been whole weeks since you've gotten blood on your knuckles, but perhaps you could put aside playing the savage for another twenty minutes or so, just in the interests of justice?"

"Justice? That's a strong word for a hypocrite. Let me ask you, M, is there anything you believe in standing up for?"

"I believe in trying to avoid murder if it's at all possible," M said, though he shot Boy a look that seemed to refute the statement. "Perhaps that seems quaint."

"You'd best get to being the hero," Boy answered, "because I'm about ready to play the villain. Or do you think that little trick with the exit will work on me as well?"

M retreated from the scrum and smoked one of Flemel's cigarettes. Stockdale did the same.

"Well?" his apprentice asked expectantly. "Who did it?"

"Do I look like Phillip fucking Marlowe to you? I have no idea. That was a complete waste of time, I'm afraid, and the natives are getting restless." He stamped out his smoke. "We'll have to do this the old-fashioned way—with black magic. Stockdale," M began, speaking loud enough to grab the attention of the half mob, "if you'd hand me your switchblade, please. Flemel, head over to the bar and grab a pint glass and a bottle of the highest-proof liquor available. If the rest of you would be so kind as to join me round the body."

Stockdale pulled his knife from a pocket of his leather jacket and threw it over to M. M knelt down beside Ibis and flipped open the blade.

"Are you," Cavill asked, somewhere between furious and horrified, "you aren't really—"

"Going to decant Ibis's blood into this glass that Flemel just handed me? Yes, indeed I am. And then I'm going to have a sip of it—we all are," M said, a quick spray of red spitting out as he made the first cut, the flow turning to a trickle, which he directed into the goblet. "And then we're going to ask Ibis if he'd like to tell us who it was that killed him." M swirled the blood around in the glass, making an unappetizing rose tint with the corn liquor. "And anyone who refuses to take part, we're going to assume is the culprit, and we'll act against him in a manner most savage." M stood, gracefully so as not to spill anything from the glass. "This was what you wanted, wasn't it? Revenge?"

"Justice," Cavill said, taking the glass from M.

"Form a circle around the body," M said, "and concentrate on your memories of Ibis."

These were people well used to ritual. These were people accustomed to ceremony, to chanting in unison, to esoteric liturgy. It did not take long for them to follow M's directions. The goblet went clockwise, till it came back around to Cavill, at which point M, still standing, grabbed it and began to chant.

"By dusk, by ether, by circle squared," M said, drinking what was left in the glass, wincing and continuing on. "By monkfish's eye, by doe's horn, by blood shared," his voice echoing loudly back from the night. "By inviolate mother, by the last prophet, by the diamond sutra." Ibis's body took on a pale blue nimbus. "By Ilúvatar who lives alone, by the New Sun, by the Self-Created." That nimbus stretched and expanded into a shadow of a man, and then the details took form—the bright green eyes, the towhead, the slow smile. "By the Lord of Cups, by the Yellow King, by the Walker in the Darkness." Ibis stood fully formed beside M, unwounded, arms open, sad but not angry. "By the first seed, by the final frost, by the big bang and *Götterdämmerung . . .*"

Anais sobbed terribly, broke ranks from the circle, and threw herself at the feet of her former lover. As her hands passed through him, she let out a wail that was as much as a confession.

"Oh, God, no," Boy said, all trace of anger leaked out of her. "No."

"I didn't mean to," Anais screamed, the words all but indistinct amid her howls of despair. "I swear I didn't! It just happened!"

Easy to see how it might: Ibis too clever and not clever enough by half, a charming smile and wandering eyes; Anais long-suffering but long is not eternal, is it? An incautious text, or eyes held too long on Salome, one indiscretion more than Anais could overlook. A spark of rage in someone for whom the difference between a wish and a spell was thin as a razor.

Easy to see how it could happen, and not even so hard to forgive—but M had sworn an oath, and justice is an impartial bitch, after all. He clapped and Ibis dissipated. Anais screamed louder. The nimbus faded and coalesced around M's hands. He brought them to his mouth and breathed into them, blowing a bubble of light from what had been Ibis's shade. He held it up to the moon, then let it burst above Anais's head. Anais screamed once more and fell silent.

"His memory will dilute every happy moment, every drag on every cigarette, every sip of liquor, every embrace, every orgasm, every sunny day and smile. You will carry him on your shoulder until the day you die, a day that I think might not be so long in coming. And should any man think this insufficient punishment," M said, raising his voice suddenly and aiming it at the crowd, "any witch or wizard present who supposes my judgment less than just, you make good on your complaint now, immediately, or you forswear vengeance, in perpetuity, until the final unspooling of the cosmos."

Silence, apart from Anais's shuddered sobs.

"It's done, then," M said, waving his hands. "I've removed the spell on the door. You're all free to go."

And go they did, shuffling off with some speed, half ashamed of their bellicosity, half happy to be freed of the threat of violence. That left our heroes, or at least our protagonists, alone with Ibis's corpse, and Anais, and her memories.

"His eyes were blue," Stockdale said after a while.

"What?" M asked.

"His eyes were blue, not green."

"Of course they were. I'm not sure how I forgot."

"It was a good likeness apart from that."

"Thanks."

"That wasn't him?" Flemel asked.

"Dead is dead," M said. "If there's a way to contact those lost, I don't know what it is. That was just smoke and mirrors, a light show."

"Then what the hell did I drink his blood for?"

"For effect. Because it seemed scary. Because if you have to bluff, you'd best bluff big."

"What if she hadn't confessed?"

"Then we'd have been pretty fucked, I suppose," M said. Then, to Boy: "Call Abilene. Tell her she needs to come by and clean up the mess."

Boy nodded silently. It was hard to detect any trace of the bloody-minded vigilante she had been only moments earlier.

"What happens to Anais?" Flemel asked.

"Every moment poisoned, like I said." M threw a last glance over his shoulder at Ibis's lover and killer, still seated beside his body, though her sobbing had trailed off to a trickle. "She'll do it to herself. We all do it to ourselves." He leaned on Stockdale's shoulder as they headed down the stoop and out into the street. "Now somebody find me a cab."

. . .

29

Royal Audience(s)

"It's not like it used to be," Celise said, just after her watercress salad had arrived.

"Isn't ever," M said. There was nothing on the menu that M wanted, but he had ordered the lobster anyway, because it was expensive and Celise was paying.

"What I mean to say is, the privileged position that you've held on to all these years might well not be one that you can hold on to forever."

"Privileged?"

"How long do you wish to remain Switzerland?"

"It's done right enough by the Swiss."

. . .

"You must have noticed it by now," Abilene said, forking a slice of tofu.

Maybe M had and maybe M hadn't, but either way he saw no point in saying.

"Things have been going faster these last few years," she continued. "There's more to draw on, and you can do bigger things with what you take."

"With my life of strict monastic rectitude," M asked, "how would I have noticed?"

. . .

"And the menagerie of oddities that the city has been sending out this last year?" Celise asked. "Surely you can't pretend to be unaware that the five boroughs are shaking like an epileptic."

"It's a weird city," M said, "in a weird world."

"Yesterday I had to stop a cockatrice rampaging through Central Park."

"Can a cockatrice really rampage? I thought they were mostly chickens."

"The part that isn't a chicken more than makes up for it, I assure you. Walk down to Strawberry Field tomorrow. You'll notice a line of extraordinarily lifelike statues that weren't there last week. 'Guerrilla sculptures,' the press is calling it." She shook her head. "It's a wonder people haven't started to notice."

• • •

"Maybe I agree things are getting crazier," M said, "what's your point?"

"It's the heart," Abilene said simply. "It needs to be tapped."

"Great," M said. "Good luck with that."

• • •

"You were friends with the Engineer, back in the day, yes?" Celise asked.

"To stretch a point."

"But it's true that he gave you the location?"

"You know it is."

• • •

"Why do you think he gave you the location?" Abilene asked.

M was not certain. He had not known the Engineer very well, really. No one had. The Engineer was not someone whom you could get friendly with, any more than you might get friendly with the changing tide or a drop in air pressure. M assumed that it was part of the thing that made the Engineer so much more than human, so much more than what M was, or, for that matter, Celise and Abilene. "I suppose because he knew I'd never use it."

• • •

"Circumstances change," Celise said. "Nothing stays constant forever."

"I try to remain constant in my inconstancy," M said.

"It's not a question of ambition. You know that's never been a motivation of mine."

"You'd be the first saint I ever met with a Versace handbag."

• • •

"It's not about power," Abilene said. "It's about survival. Things can't keep going on like this."

"It's always about power," M said quietly, picking at his fakin' bacon.

• • •

"It needs to be tapped," Celise said. "And there's only one person capable of doing that."

"Only one person?"

Celise had been trying to be friendly to M. Just then she started trying a little less hard. "Dear as we are to each other, M, I'm sure you wouldn't do anything so foolish as to insult me by mentioning my rival in my presence."

"Convenient that this solution of yours would end up making you into something like a god."

"A benevolent one," Celise said, smiling. "One in a position to do any number of kindnesses for her favored servants."

"It's been my experience that gods make promises better than they keep them."

• • •

"It's only me or her who could do it," Abilene said. "Surely you don't think you're strong enough to hold onto all the draw?"

"I'm never one to underestimate myself."

"It's a narrow line between confidence and hubris."

"Part of my charm that I can straddle it so neatly."

• • •

"Can you imagine what it would be like if she got it? One big commune from Queens to Staten Island," Celise said, as if a mouse had just run across the table. "The hoi polloi squatting in the MOMA."

• • •

"Just think what the city would look like if she was in charge," Abilene said. "Like what they've done to the East Village, except *everywhere*."

• • •

"How awful," M said, and sipped his cocktail.

• • •

"Revolting," M said, and drank the rest of his beer.

• • •

"Then you'll do it?" Celise asked, shaking a thin black cigarette out of the pack.

• • •

"Then it's agreed?" Abeline asked, licking shut the seam on her hand-rolled.

• • •

"You can count on me," M said, leaning over with his lighter.

30

The Heart of the City

M spent the next few weeks walking around building up a charge. Grinding himself against reality, like scratching wool in the winter. He woke up early and went to bed late, and in the interim he strutted around the city, across the five boroughs and back again. He went to bars for hours and spoke to no one, just nursed a beer and watched the people. He sat in parks and on benches and in malls and did the same thing. He showed no preference in his wanderings for wealth over poverty, for beauty over ugliness. He would spend half a day in Central Park and the next half walking through Willets Point. He did not discriminate.

Fortune accrued thick around him. Everywhere he went, the radio or stereo or house DJ would play the exact right song to complement his mood. One day he was comped every single thing that he had bought to eat or drink, managers sprinting out from the back to say they liked the look of him, and he could come back anytime. Three times in a week he ended up going home with a model, sure evidence of someone slipping a finger onto the scales of fate.

Most days he would stop off at Union Square and play a couple of games of chess against the men there. One afternoon he won thirty-seven straight, trounced everyone who sat down against him, including a ringer who only played against the other professionals and three men from a nearby club who came over to try their hand.

The next day M called everyone and told them to show up at his house around six in the evening.

Flemel showed up at five-forty-five, as M had known for certain that he would, carrying a magnum bottle of Belgian beer. "There's something different about you today."

"Don't worry about it," M said, opening it. "Go take a seat in the den. There's this bauble I just got my hands on. It's in the box on the coffee table. Take a look, let me know what you think."

Flemel toddled off to do just that.

"Blood of Christ on my forehead," Stockdale said, "what the hell are you getting ready to do?"

"Better wait for everyone to arrive. I'd rather not explain the whole thing twice."

"Been sticking your finger into electric sockets lately?" Boy asked when she arrived.

"I prefer to use a fork," M said. "Stockdale is in the other room. I'm sure he'll make you a highball."

"Already started!" Stockdale said.

"What have you been taking, my friend?" Andre asked M once he had taken off his coat. "And can I get a taste of it?"

"Boy is here," M told Andre. It had occurred to him just before Andre's arrival that he couldn't remember if they were still together.

"I know. She told me to buy beer."

"Bring her one. I'll join you both in a moment."

"So we going to do this?" Bucephalus asked, the last to make his appearance.

M nodded and handed him a drink and followed him into the living room.

M explained the plan. Some of it, at least. Some of it he wasn't sure about himself yet, and some of it he figured would go better with only him knowing.

"You could not exactly call that a Swiss clock," Stockdale said.

"That has holes big enough to drive a truck through," Boy informed him.

"The blood of Roland, Bonaparte, and de Gaulle runs in my veins," Andre informed him. "And I must say this seems to be rather rash." He turned to Flemel. "What do you think?"

M's apprentice had been uncharacteristically silent during the discussion, his attention taken up entirely with the jewel M had given him—a polyhedron with so many faces that it was almost, but not quite, a sphere, and each one of them movable. The entirety of Flemel's focus seemed to be taken up with shifting them into different positions, and he gave no sign of having heard Andre's question.

"He's not coming," M said. "He's not going to get out of that chair for another twenty-four hours. Maybe eighteen. He's a bright kid."

"It's all right for us to risk our lives, though."

"I don't think we're quite at the arming-children stage," M said. "It's done regardless. Flemel is out. The question is, which of you are in?"

Bucephalus smiled and lit a joint. He enjoyed a good fight, and it sounded like this would be one. The rest took a little more convincing, but not so much. Stockdale and Boy did it because they were M's friends, true-blue, scout's honor. Andre did it because he did not want to shame himself in front of Boy.

M ushered them all out and turned off the lights. Then he turned them back on, found a sticky note, and wrote, "Apartment paid up until the end of the month. If you hold on to the records, I will teach you something next time I am in town. Assuming I am still alive." Then he put the note onto Flemel's head, turned the lights back off, and left for the final time.

At Nostrand Station, they dropped into the last car of an uptown 3 train, busy with Manhattan-bound scenesters planning a night out in the city.

"Any idea what to expect?" Stockdale asked.

"Not really. The Engineer had a set of keys. We're going to be picking the lock."

Midway through the Clark Street tunnel and without giving any warning, M reached over suddenly and pulled the safety cord. The train stopped abruptly, everyone tumbling against one another. A commotion erupted among the passengers, who would now be stuck for two hours easy, dinner dates upended, movie tickets wasted, and let's hope the person next to you doesn't suffer from crippling claustrophobia.

"Everybody calm down," M said, spilling a smidgen of his collected energy into the ether, enough to buzz the assemblage into an eager submission. "I'll make it up to you by saving the city in heroic fashion. Bucephalus, if you'd do the honors . . ."

Bucephalus slid painted nails into the seam of the door and flexed his biceps like pistons. M went first and led them single file toward the back of the train. A few steps past the last car and the darkness grew ubiquitous. M took a thin flashlight from his jacket pocket and ejected a flickering beam from its eye.

"Really?" Stockdale asked.

"You couldn't . . ." Boy waved her hands like a stage magician.

"I'm pacing myself," M informed them, banging his hand against the plastic frame.

"Could you at least have checked the batteries?" Andre asked.

It was a fair point, though as they kicked in just then there seemed no point in discussing it further. They turned down a side passage, following a train tread that hadn't been used in what seemed a very long time.

"Are you sure you know where you're going?" Boy asked.

"Confident."

"Confident isn't sure."

"That's true, they're different words entirely."

A tunnel, of course, is not simply a tunnel, any more than a beach is a beach or a mountain a mountain. One cavern is as different from another as an old-growth forest is a mile of badlands. The abandoned subway line our troupe had come through was old, worn-down, damp, graffitied, fetid, and unhygienic. But the side passage that they took then was another level of foulness altogether, like sliding down an esophageal track. Stared at straight on, the walls looked like walls, but seen out of the corner of your eye—and, really, how much time does one spend staring dead-on at a wall—they seemed to pulse, to reverberate like an oversize amp at a backyard summer barbecue, though the only sound that could be heard was the occasional nasal drip. Andre slipped at one point, coating his pants with some mucouslike substance, and he cursed vigorously, though to no great effect.

Around that point, it had started to smell, really smell, individual and distinct strands of rot, the F train at rush hour, clouds of body odor all but viable in the air, maggoty sliders left outside of a White Castle in late August, the sour plastic odor of cooked cocaine.

"Is that something we should worry about?" Stockdale asked M.

"Do I look worried?"

"You do."

"Best follow my example."

It got darker. The outline of M's torchlight died a few yards in front of him, and thus it was only from the change in the air that they realized the chamber they had come to was wider than the passage they had left. And it was only M's instinct—the dim sixth sense of a species long hunted—that led him to exhaust some of his draw just then, in a sudden burst of radiance that drew a scream from something inhuman and that hovered afterward in the air, illuminating the room and the monster living inside it.

Andre shrieked. Stockdale had his switchblade out in an eye blink. Boy tensed her fists. M said, "Bucephalus, this was sort of where I thought you would come in."

But Bucephalus was already walking forward, his grin as wide as a slit throat. He cracked one knuckle after another, each twisted finger echoing like a rifle shot in the dark. The beast was eight feet at the shoulder and seemed to consist mostly of large teeth and thick, odoriferous, matted fur. At first glance, M would have said it was mostly rat, but there was a lot of crocodile in there also, as well as platypus, and perhaps some squid. It smelled like you had shoved one dead thing into another dead thing and let them stew in the sun for a long while. When it roared, which it did just then, M felt a tremble of some distant ancestral fear, a time before walls or fire or sharpened sticks, when mankind was at the mercy of anything that ran or crawled or flew.

M would have given two-to-one against the creature if there had been anyone around to take the bet.

But there wasn't, nor was there time to linger and watch the fireworks, especially because two-to-one still gave a thirty-three-and-something percentage chance against Bucephalus, which wasn't at all low, and M knew that he would not stand a two-to-one chance against the creature or anything like that. So he hurried on, Stockdale and Boy and Andre in tow, skirting the fracas and slipping through the exit.

The last M saw of Bucephalus, he was strutting up to the thing, his proportions all wrong, his hands the size of cinder blocks and a skull the circumference of a basketball, and when he struck, a line of the beast's teeth shattered back into the depths of its maw, blood streaming out of the stumps, and the thing roared again, and Bucephalus roared as well, but louder.

The next cavern was the length of a football field and the height of a cricket pitch. The walls were covered with some faintly luminous strand of lichen, and it was shaped like an onion, the roof tapering into an open point. It seemed empty at first, the companions walking forward tentatively, knowing that they were not yet through with their trials, and by convention, the second round of a thing is never easier than the first.

There was a sound like rushing water, and a spectral smoke, bustling and burbling, flooded through the hole in the ceiling. M's eyes went wide and the lights went out and then there was only the screaming.

"—the fucking *schvartzes* taking over the entire damn city—"

"—I'm your mother, goddamn it, you'll show me some respect or so help me—"

"—Nurse? Nurse? Jesus Christ, nurse, it hurts, nurse? Nurse—"

"—I told you twice already I don't give credit, bother me again about it and I'll—"

M made a swift series of movements with his hands and then held them forward as if he were propping up a wall, and some of what he had been building up over the course of the past few weeks concentrated itself onto his open palms, and the voices went from deafeningly painful to extremely unpleasant.

Boy and Andre and Stockdale stood within M's aegis, taking shelter in the wind tunnel, clawing themselves back from the edge of madness. "Fuck, God, what was that?" Boy asked.

"It's the city, it's the city," Andre said, seated Indian style, taking it worse than the rest of them, though the rest of them had not taken it so easy. "It's the fucking city."

"The second guardian," M announced.

The voices got louder, and the nimbus of soft blue light that M had settled in front of him got fainter, the frantic dark eating through it like time wearing away an epitaph on a tombstone.

"—make sure you drop the gun in the canal afterward—"

"—give you a raise if I could, Eduardo, but with the margins these days—"

"—but you said you loved me, baby, I only ever did it because you said you loved me—"

"—that's enough to pay back the interest, but it won't affect the principal—"

"Someone do something," M screamed, and in the scant second that his head was turned, the darkness surged forward. Now the sound was like putting your head against an amplifier, and the light around M's hands was dim, very dim indeed. He gestured frantically, and the dark and the voices retreated for a moment, but only for a moment. Andre was on the ground with his hands against his ears, Boy helpless beside him, M looking pale and ghastly.

"—pretty little girl, Daddy's pretty little thing—"

"—not my problem, one way or the other—"

"—says she was too busy, but she'll get to it tomorrow—"

"—Spare a dollar so I can get something to eat? Anybody spare a dollar so I can—"

"—Do I look like I give a shit?—"

Stockdale thus far had not done much, though there was something in his motionlessness that might have suggested a coiled spring, had anyone been looking at him. Of course no one was, M's attention concentrated exclusively on keeping them alive a few desperate seconds longer, Boy trying to hold her mind together, and Andre all but lost. Stockdale hunched his head down into his shoulders and bruised his way out of M's shell, the darkness setting upon him instantly, swirling like a flock of ravenous birds, like a swarm of hate-sharpened hornets, battering him, cutting his clothes as neatly as a switchblade, streaks of blood beginning to appear on his hands and his neck and his face. But his eyes were closed and he didn't seem to notice, at least he wasn't screaming, indeed he seemed to be chanting a monotone, gaining volume against the gloom, stilling and silencing the chaos. Long strains of multisyllabic speech, speech that in a past indistinct from legend had chained the raksashas to their hell, had brought the pre-existential anarchy to book, had given form and purpose to the primordial stew. Continuing like the *thump-thump-thump* of a good bass line groove, ordering the shadows, which bent around Stockdale now, like a dog brought to heel or a student called to attention, a solid syncopation, the pulse of the divine. And even the cruelest spirits, those fragments of memory or thought or dream that had gotten lost down in the bowels beneath the city, festering like a wound, those splinters of souls razored through with misery, mouth-foamed and foul, pulled back into the corners of the cavern.

And then Stockdale went silent as well, and there was nothing left to hear but arrhythmic heartbeats, slowing gradually.

By the time M managed to turn on his flashlight, there was nothing left to see, the little beam dipping back and forth in his unsteady hands. "I thought you were high church?"

"Only aesthetically," Stockdale said. Boy helped Andre up from the ground, and as they moved into the next room, M could see blood running from the unfortunate Frenchman's ears, wondered again at how close they had come, and decided with firm effort to put it out of his mind. They were not through yet, M supposed, and he had already burned through most of his charge.

They entered the next cavern keyed up despite their wounds, ready to be leapt upon by some or other chimerical malefactor, by rotting zombies leaching up from the ground, by the tattered ghosts of adventurers long dead, by demons noxious and spirits most foul.

Nothing. The ground was smooth white stone. Brass braziers hung down from the ceiling, yellow light flung itself happily against the walls, smelling of camphor and rose oil. A door stood open and inviting across the room, though no one made any effort to pass through it.

"I could use a breather," Stockdale said.

"After what you just did?" Boy answered with uncustomary friendliness. "Take all the time you need."

"I wouldn't mind a moment myself," Andre said.

M found himself thinking about the first dog he had ever had, bringing it home as a puppy and resting next to it by a roaring fire, long walks in the sunlit fields as it bounded by his side. What a handsome thing it had been and how it had always loved him! "There's something in here with us," he said.

"Of course there is," Boy added. "Did you just realize that?"

"We need to get out of here," M responded sharply, though he made no move to follow his own direction.

"Have any of you ever had a really good croissant?" Andre asked. "I mean a really, really good one. My grandmother used to make them special for us when we would come to visit. She had a little villa near Carcassonne, and in the mornings we would sit out on the patio and she would serve croissants with apple jam and fresh milk."

"That sounds beautiful," Boy said, wrapping Andre's arms around her. "That sounds so, so beautiful."

"I will take you there sometime," Andre said, and seemed to mean it. He leaned down to kiss her, and she responded passionately. "You will love it," he said, tearing up with happiness. "You will love it."

Stockdale was walking back and forth with his hands held stiffly behind his back, singing "God Save the Queen" at the top of his voice. M slapped him hard across the face, but it didn't dent the grin. "You've always been a true friend to me," Stockdale said.

I probably got you murdered, M was thinking, but it was just about the last nasty thought he had left in him. Because he had been a pretty good friend to Stockdale, and Stockdale had been a pretty good friend to him. M started thinking about this one time when they'd both taken an impromptu trip up to Luxembourg, just the two of them, trying to figure out how to ride the pair of motorcycles they had just bought, drinking Trappist ale and eating mussels Portuguese. M shook his head back and forth as fiercely as he could, as if to give himself whiplash, and started chanting to himself, "Molotov cocktails and weeping children and the Department of Motor Vehicles and Dachau and Superfund sites and date rape and famine and the goddamned Eagles Reunion Tour . . ."

"T-shirts fresh out of the dryer," the last guardian said happily. "A crackling fire on a snowy day. Walking along the Seine in September, the little book dealers with their stands. The smell of a naked woman. Sleeping beneath the Southern Cross. Brazilian beaches. Belgian beer. Dutch weed."

"I love Dutch weed!" M said, catching himself by the fingernails then, and only barely. "I am a self-obsessed pothead, sliding through the day on liquor and self-delusion. My carbon footprint is the size of a monster truck, and if I die tonight I'll be ghosting three separate women. I'm jealous of everyone all of the time, I just hide it better. I'd take what you have if I thought I could get away with it."

"Hey now," Stockdale said, turning toward M and looking momentarily put out. "I won't listen to any of that nonsense." He put his hand on M's shoulder, brimming over with kindness, and M started thinking about what a good father Stockdale would have been, if any of them had ever gotten around to having children, and if Stockdale wasn't going to die soon. "It's not such an easy thing, being a man. You did all right for yourself. Better than all right." Stockdale handed M a flask of gin that he had secreted somewhere about his person. M took a drink to his dear friend's good health, and then another one because why not? There was so much good in the world, so much to smile at, blessings uncountable.

The thing was closing in, M could feel it spackling in at his peripheries, wrapping itself around them like fudge on a gingerbread cookie, leading them, head bowed and smiling, into the coffin it had prepared. A happy sort of coffin, a coffin with silk for a lining and a down comforter to lay atop you, but a coffin all the same. Stockdale was taking long swigs from his flask and reminiscing fondly about his family, of whom M had only heard him speak once or twice, in the most terrible and frightening situations, and even then only to damn them. Andre and Boy were waltzing very slowly, a quarter turn every half minute, gazing into each other's eyes, and is there anything to compare to love? Is there anything at all, anything that has ever been built, grown or coalesced that can compare to love? Love as deep as the Mariana Trench and wild as a summer storm?

"Boy," M said, all of a sudden. "Last week Andre called you a lipstick feminist, principles forgotten as soon as it's time to pay a check."

Boy blinked once. Boy blinked twice. On the third blink, her eyes were back to their usual furrowed fury. "You said what?" she asked, pushing Andre away.

"Andre, I can tell you with certainty that Boy has cheated on you twice since you've been together, though I suspect the actual number is considerably higher."

"Was it with Thomas?" Andre shook his head. "It is unreal what a slut you are."

The sweet-natured spirit surrounding them, the kindhearted strangler, that rolly-polly murderer, flinched back a bit. "Why can't everyone be friends?" he asked, "and laugh together, and play Yahtzee maybe, and sleep quietly deep beneath the earth?"

"You think I fake my commitment to feminism?"

"Would Elisabeth Cady Stanton let a man pay for everything?"

"Not all of us are comfortable taking a job shilling for a great corporate parasite that is destroying the planet!"

"But you're comfortable taking money from a man shilling for a great corporate parasite that is destroying the planet?"

"Then you admit your job is immoral?"

Andre threw his hands up. "I never denied it!"

"I fucked a stranger on your birthday!"

"I fucked two!" Andre yelled. "And one of them was Brazilian!"

Boy clutched her tiny fists together hard enough that M thought one might burst. "You are an insensitive lover!"

"I know you are trying to hurt me, but that's a lie, and a cruel one."

Boy looked down at her feet. "I apologize."

The guardian inched back toward them, a gaggle of happy puppies looking to be petted, multiracial toddlers giggling, emperor penguins bowing to each other. "You see," he seemed to say, "there is nothing really bad, not anywhere in the world, just misunderstandings between friends. If the lion and the lamb would come to visit me, I could convince that old kitten to rub his head against the downy softness of his prey, lick away the wounds he made."

"Andre, Boy has told me that she suspects Serge Gainsbourg to be an elaborate practical joke perpetrated by a nation too lazy to create their own form of popular music," M said. "Boy, Andre never served in *La Resistance*, though if you were dumb enough to believe otherwise, you can hardly blame him for the lie."

In fact, it seemed that Boy very much felt that she could, launching herself at Andre and screaming vigorously. Boy was about as dangerous a person as one might fear to find, but in the throes of passion, she regressed to a young girl's preferred means of combat, fingernails scratching at Andre's face. "All those stories about you and Camus!"

"I would have fought beside him!" Andre said, retreating from Boy's onslaught. "Had I been alive at the time!"

"You'd have been walking lockstep with Pétain!"

"I am mostly Jewish!"

"An excuse! An excuse from a Frenchman, what a change of pace! I bet you didn't even march in '68!"

"Everyone marched in '68! It was all that anyone ever did! I marched so much I got the clap from a Spanish girl! And when we marched, do you know what we listened to?" The thing inside the cave with them flinched. "Serge Gainsbourg!"

"Alsace-Lorraine is German! Croissants are pretentious rolls! You have a small dick!"

And now the spirit was retreating in full, burrowing back into the ends of his cave with a few metaphysical grumblings about the cruelty of the race, and what could you expect of people anyway, and this is why humanity can't have nice things.

With him went the better part of Boy's anger, though as a precautionary measure, and no longer weighed down by the spirit's falsified sweetness, Stockdale wrapped up the diminutive femme fatale in a bear hug and carried her to the other end of the cavern. Andre looked morose and bled a little, but not for long, because M wasn't entirely certain how long the spirit would remain subdued, so he hustled them swiftly into the chamber beyond.

It was smaller than the one they had come through, the ground and walls formed of sandstone, lit by a pyre that occupied the center of the room and much besides. It was like an atomic clock, or the infinite complexity of a circulatory system, or a gaggle of geese whirling in synchronous midair union. It was everything right and natural and ordered, water smoothed by the titanic forces surging below, anarchy shaved to equilibrium.

"Holy shit," Boy said.

"Yup," M said.

No one else said anything for a while. They just watched it swirl.

And then Celise, who had not been there before, or at least no one had seen her, said, "Marvelous. Absolutely magnificent. You've done splendidly, M, just splendidly."

"As is so often the case, my dear Celise, you speak rather sooner than you ought." Abeline said this, and she had also not been there before.

The two queens of Greater New York, these potentates, these modern-day Merlins, stared at each other with a hatred nursed through long ages until it seemed as much figurative as real, as if of the dog's hatred for the cat. And then, almost simultaneously, they turned their gazes on M, and M got the sense that whatever enmity they held for the other was, in this moment at least, dwarfed by their rage at him.

"If I didn't know any better," Celise said, fury eating through her makeup, "I would think that you had gotten it into your head to betray me."

"I know you entirely too well to think that you've done anything but," Abilene said. "You sneaky, ungrateful, reactionary bit of hipster trash."

"Let's not get personal," M said. "I didn't promise either of you anything."

"Yes, you did," Celise said.

"Yes, you did," Abeline said.

"Well, then, I guess I lied," M admitted, and without further ado leapt onto the platform and into the heart of the city. On his left arm, just above the wrist, one could see a question mark.

31

A Subjective Appraisal

If at any point M had imagined he might hold this vast torrent of force, this eternal pulse of light and heat, then as soon as he entered into it—as soon as his first jut of hair penetrated the periphery, the instant their quantum fields entangled—he knew that hope for madness. It was like riding a bronco hopped up on bath salts; it was like tapping an active volcano; it was an orgasm that crescendoed eternally. He could not wield it, he had not a fraction of the control required, but he could release it, act as a conduit, jettisoning it in a vast bloom, spilling out the overflow into the air and the night above them.

Well and good, but what was *it*, exactly? It was the city, of course. It was everything the city had ever been or ever could be, which is to say that it was everything, period. It was an old woman dying in an uptown apartment, unnoticed till the smell seeped through the walls. It was a toddler in a five-thousand-dollar stroller pushed past brownstones by an immigrant woman who didn't make that in three months. It was Slavic flesh burnt scarlet on Coney Island sand. It was dark-skinned men without a hundred words of English on the 5 train at six in the morning, a long commute to work a long day to make little money. It was Park Avenue adolescents ruined by too much too young. It was fat German tourists getting their pictures taken with the costumes in Times Square, off-brand Spider-Men and Disney characters played by potential pedophiles. It was the young and the cool and the tragically hip, burning brightly. It was cops on the take and indifferent politicians and a callous media. It was a garden blooming amid the concrete. It was people trying to be something that they were not. It was beautiful and hideous. It was a rose and a tumor. It was like a foreign taste, or the first hint that there is something in another person that could make you fall in love with them— you have to say either yes or no, you have to run forward at a dead sprint or shut yourself off entirely. You have to make a choice. It is required of all of us, in the end, even of M.

From the flickering still-beating heart of New York City a light swept upward into the troposphere, expanding out like a colored parachute, falling slowly and with kindness.

· · ·

Tommy had been staring over the side of the George Washington Bridge for a long half hour, the water dark and inviting, but just then he took out his cell phone and called Beverly, and lo and behold she picked up and said something kind to him (which was rare enough to be noteworthy), and even though it was late, she put Tommy Jr. on the phone, and Tommy told him he loved him, and Tommy Jr. acknowledged the same, and they talked a while longer, and when Tommy hung up the phone, he found he had walked all the way to Harlem, and he couldn't remember what had brought him to the river.

Bill was working late that night, like he worked late every night, but he stopped for a moment and looked out the window of his office, where far below people laughed and drank and danced. He couldn't see them, of course—he was too high up—but somehow he knew it. And he got to think-ing about a promise he had made himself to see Zanzibar before he died, and he was forty and in good health, but still, a promise is a promise is a promise. So Bill buzzed Anne, his assistant, a pleasantly plump divorcée with teeth of which she was unnecessarily ashamed who didn't mind working late but minded that she had nothing it was keeping her from doing. Bill said that he needed a plane ticket to Zanzibar, and Anne laughed and asked when, and then Bill said tonight of course, and Anne was quiet for a second, and then Bill asked if she wanted to come, and Anne thought, *My God, he's finally lost it*, but what she said was yes. And it is my understanding that Bill still lives in Zanzibar, and though Anne left after a few weeks, she remembers the place with great fondness.

Eddie was in the sort of Brooklyn bar that doesn't serve artisanal cocktails or microbrewed beer, and he was thinking about going out and making
a mistake, figured on calling for one more shot to steady him before he went
out and made it. There was a jukebox in the corner that had never worked
before, but it started working just then, pumped out one of those classic soul
tracks, Stax maybe or Twinight, a little burst of joy and rhythm. Eddie pulled
his hand out of his pocket and set it on the bar and snapped along, and then
sang along as well. The bartender, an elderly Latino man who had never
shown Eddie the slightest kindness in all the time he had drank there, started
laughing and clapping. And why had he stopped singing, Eddie wondered.
And why couldn't he start again? Maybe try to get a band together, a solid
four-piece in matching suits—classy, old-school, the way it had been done
once, the way it could be done again. The gun sat forgotten in his pocket.

Girls in Lower Manhattan, girls with dreams in their heads and inno-
cence in their eyes, girls working long hours as cocktail servers and hostesses,
girls kind enough to forgive their indecent beauty, came unexpectedly to the
attention of talent scouts and managers and agents, found the avenue of their
ambitions suddenly unclogged, and were quick to sprint down it. Bearded
boys all along the coast of Brooklyn put finger to keyboard or brush to canvas or pick to untuned guitar, and those few of talent produced things of
genius, and those without any—a far greater number, needless to say—still
when they woke up the next day and looked at what they'd done, said, "Hell,
this isn't so bad. This isn't so bad at all. At least, I like it, and who cares what
anyone else thinks?" Old couples locked in loveless marriages up and down
Queens looked over at each other and saw something they hadn't seen in a
long time, maybe had never seen, and fucked like whores and laughed like
children. Old friends who had not talked for years, who had fallen out of
touch for no good reason, no very good reason at all, ran into each other in
bars and clubs and subway stations, and they laughed and hugged each other
fiercely and asked, "How the hell have you been?" and conceded that they
had been "Not so bad, not so bad at all." Children were allowed up past their
bedtimes. Shy boys found themselves slipping off barstools and going across
rooms and even, God be kind, standing on dance floors, and homely girls
felt as pretty as they had always known themselves to be and got up to join

them. A thousand secret admirers took their courage in hand and spoke to someone to whom they had always wanted to speak, friends of friends and pretty bartenders, and if maybe only a hundred found their hoped-for results, still, better to have loved and lost, right? And anyway, even magic can only do so much.

In future years statisticians and sociologists would go mad trying to explain the extraordinary uptick in births that would take place nine months later—not the ones who had been in the city that night, though. They'd just smile at their colleagues' flights of fancy and contorted hypotheses, laugh a bit, look out the window, and remember that night, that one single, shining evening when the city was theirs, and the game seemed worth the candle.

• • •

M found himself on the ground, the cluster of faces in his field of vision looking concerned, then ecstatic at his revival. Even Boy was crying, though she'd have denied it afterward if you'd asked her. M remembered, though.

No point to it, he was fine, as soon as Stockdale pulled him up to his feet he felt just gorgeous, right as rain. And that little disagreement they had been having a moment earlier, about M's integrity, and which of the queens was going to become a god, that was small potatoes given the feel of the evening. Not even Celise felt like killing M anymore, though she would later, her future self cursing her present self's softheartedness. Abilene forgot the conflict entirely, never brought any of it up again. And soon they were all walking back the way they'd come, stopping to pick up Bucephalus, who looked tired and bruised and triumphant. They were still miles from the surface, but then Celise made a little snarl with her fingers and they came across an emergency exit door set into the rock face of the chamber, and walking through that, they found themselves just outside of the trestles in Prince Street Station, and then up on the street. Boy knew a bar nearby that she said she hadn't been to in a while but remembered fondly, and though the place was packed and loud and cheerful, they managed to find themselves a booth in the back.

Outside and all along the Hudson River Valley, from Yonkers down to the Statue of Liberty herself (a handsome woman, looking only a bare quarter of her hundred and twenty five years), lights shone, and people smiled.

Epilogue

Around nine the next morning, while most of the city slept off the gift M had given them, he stepped onto a plane bound for somewhere that was not America. He had a compass rose tattooed on his left forearm. I can't tell you where he is now, but I'll drop you a line when he decides to come back.

Acknowledgments

Thanks go out to—Mom and Dad, David, Alissa, Mike and Marisa. Julian. My grandmother Elaine. Chris Kepner, Oliver Johnson, Anne Perry, Judith Regan, Ron Hogan, Stacy Creamer, Lucas Wittmann, Gregory Henry, Pamela Kawi, Mia Abrahams, Jared Shurin and Justin Landon. Mike Rubin, Peter Backof, Robert Ricketts (apologies for a previous misspelling), Sam Feldman, Elliot Smith, Rusty Mason. John Lingan (and co), Alex Cameron, Will Crain. Will Pank, and Super-fan and frequent Nile Special drinker Rob Newton. The Boston kin and their new additions, the Mottolas one and all. Kiki. All the haters and most of the fans.